Where There Is Smoke

Elisabeth Rose

16pt

Copyright Page from the Original Book

Title: Where There Is Smoke

Copyright © 2019 by Elisabeth Rose

Published by
Escape
An imprint of Harlequin Enterprises (Australia) Pty Limited (ABN 47 001 180 918), a subsidiary c HarperCollins Publishers Australia Pty Limited (ABN 36 009 913 517)
Level 13, 201 Elizabeth St
SYDNEY NSW 2000
AUSTRALIA

romance.com.au/escapepublishing/

TABLE OF CONTENTS

i

Where There Is Smoke
Elisabeth Rose

In the small town of Taylor's Bend, some secrets are about to ignite...

When Taylor's Bend vet Oliver Johnson attends a car accident involving a horse float from a nearby stud farm he's not prepared for an encounter with Krista Laatonen, the billionaire owner's stepdaughter. Beautiful, prickly, and entitled, she is everything he despises about the world he left behind all those years ago. But he can't neglect an injured animal, and there is something about Krista he can't ignore.

Oliver soon discovers that first impressions can be misleading-the accident was not as it seemed, and there might just be more to Krista than he expected.

When two thugs arrive on Oliver's doorstep claiming the horse from the accident belongs to their boss, Oliver and Krista are thrown into the middle of a dangerous game of deception and greed. As the threats around them escalate into blood spilled, choking fire, and a violent abduction, Oliver must decide if Krista's ice-queen mask hides a woman worth risking his life—and his heart—for.

About the author

Multi-published romance writer **ELISABETH ROSE** lives very happily in Canberra with her musician husband. Travel is a big part of their lives now the family has left home. Elisabeth's original training was in clarinet performance, but she was also a tai chi instructor for twenty-five years. An avid reader, her preference is for a happy ending regardless of genre and is most annoyed if a main character dies or leaves—unless, of course, it's the villain.

If you'd like to know more about me, my books, or to connect with me online, you can visit my webpage elisabethrose.com.au, or like my Facebook page https://www.facebook.com/Elisabethroseauthor/

Acknowledgements

For this story I had to draw on knowledge from my childhood and teen years as a horse owner and rider. I sought specific information on panicky horses from my friend Beth and running a stud farm information from Arabian stud owner, Ally Hudson. Ally's next-door neighbour, a race horse trainer, put the mockers on my original idea by saying all race horses are microchipped so substitution is impossible nowadays. Facts and good ideas aren't always compatible.

To Colin, Carla, Nick and Paige

Chapter 1

The white four-wheel drive towing one of The Grange Stud horse floats roared down the main street of Taylor's Bend as though the road was empty of pedestrians, traffic and a tractor trundling along with hay baler attached.

Local veterinarian, Oliver Johnson, waiting to cross the road, stared after it in disbelief. 'Who drives like that with a horse in the back?' he said to the farmer standing beside him.

'Littlejohns,' came the reply. 'Mad bloody bunch. Too much money and half a brain cell between the lot of them to go with it. The stable manager knows what he's doing but that young idiot who's supposed to be in charge. Boss's son...' He spat into the gutter. 'Couldn't manage his way out of a haystack. They only have a couple of nags there anyway so God knows why they call it a stud.'

'Yep. Still, the horses aren't to blame. I'd better get going. Sick cow to see.' Oliver hurried across to his car and headed out of town for the next appointment, but he'd only just reached the farm gate when his mobile shrilled. Margie, his receptionist.

'The police called. There's been an accident involving one of The Grange horse floats. It's gone into the ditch just round the bend after Victoria Road. One horse trapped on board and panicking.'

'Okay, I'm on way. I'm not going to get to that cow today and you'd better cancel surgery, I've no idea how long I'll be.' And hadn't that driver and horse float been an accident waiting to happen?

Margie lowered her voice. 'Beryl's just arrived with her dog.'

He stifled the groan. 'She'll have to come back tomorrow.'

According to Margie, Beryl had a crush on him the size of a house and he believed her now, after Beryl's fifth visit dragging a hale and hearty poodle along for unnecessary check-ups and a total disregard for surgery hours. Margie thought it was funny, he thought it was excruciatingly embarrassing, not to mention a waste of time.

'Okey-dokey.'

'Thanks.' Oliver turned onto the road leading back to town. The Grange never called him out, being closer to the Jindalee practice, but this was a no-brainer because he'd be there in five minutes and the other vet was thirty-five minutes away. He wasn't about to let a horse suffer.

Witches hats marked the accident site and both police cruisers had lights flashing.

The Range Rover had come to rest nose down and canted to the side. Miraculously, the horse float stayed attached, teetering but upright. One occupant by the sound of it, who wasn't happy and vented its fear and fury by kicking and banging against the walls. The float would be on its side in the ditch along with the driver if they couldn't get the horse out. As Oliver got out of the car, the thrashing of hooves and panicky, distressed snorting coming from the float made him quicken his pace.

A young, dark-haired man sat in the rear of one of the cruisers, head back against the seat, eyes closed. He didn't stir when Oliver strode by. The young idiot in charge of The Grange?

The small door at the front of the float was open. Police Constable Shannon's voice came from inside, trying to calm the horse. The Senior Constable, Rupe, was examining the connection between the vehicle and the float. The towbar was bent where they joined and the angle of the four-wheel drive meant it wouldn't be easy to disengage. There was just enough room to open the ramp for the horse to back out safely onto the road. Each time the animal shifted the float tilted and wobbled, perilously close to the ditch.

'G'day, Ollie.' Rupe heaved a deep sigh. 'This is a bugger of a thing. Can you sedate that horse? I'm worried he'll have the whole thing over.'

'G'day. Can we open the ramp?'

'Yeah, I reckon we can try now you're here. I didn't fancy it with just two of us. The horse is pretty big.'

'What about him?' Oliver jerked a thumb in the direction of Rupe's car.

'Useless. He's in shock and he's done something to his wrist, sprained it I reckon.'

Oliver climbed in beside Shannon, who squeezed out through the narrow door. The horse was a big chestnut thoroughbred, built for speed; but now the body quivered, eyes wide with fear, nostrils flaring, and the glossy coat had a sheen of sweat. When Oliver straightened in front of him he backed away, snorting, pulling hard on the tether rope. The float shifted alarmingly. He squealed and plunged forward, crashing into the divider and rearing up. One hoof struck the padded metal front of the stall close to the top, making Oliver duck away in case he got a foreleg over.

'Sshh, shhh, shhh. Calm down boy. Calm down.' Oliver murmured a string of soothing words as he did a quick assessment. A mare. The shaking horse had scrapes on her shoulder, a cut over the right eye dripping blood and some torn skin on both back legs, probably from the initial crash, but otherwise seemed okay thanks to the thick padding lining the lower part of the walls. The big mare's main problem was blind panic and every time she moved, the float moved, which frightened her more.

Outside, he joined Shannon and Rupe at the back of the float.

'I reckon we can open it,' Shannon said. 'We can't leave him in there.'

'She's a mare. It's touch-and-go with just three of us,' said Oliver. 'Have you called The Grange?'

'Yeah. Someone's on their way but they'll be thirty minutes at least.'

A ute pulled up. The driver stuck his head out. 'Need a hand?' Rupe's neighbour and vineyard owner.

'G'day, Tim. How are you with horses?'

'Won't know till I try.' He moved the ute off the road and walked back.

'Okay, if you get in with the horse, Shannon, and untie her, we'll get the back open and steady her as she comes out,' said Oliver. 'Let's go.'

The horse snorted and fidgeted as the ramp came down and she sensed freedom, but when Shannon untied the rope and eased her backwards she came docilely down, stepping delicately until she reached the ground. She tossed her head up and down and snorted loudly, looking about with ears pricked although her body still shook with nervous energy.

'Good girl, good girl.' Oliver ran a hand down the sleek neck. He continued his examination. The cut over the eye was superficial and he could clean and patch it up here.

'She's beautiful,' Shannon said.

'Walk her over on to the grass.' Oliver watched critically as the horse crossed the road. She walked normally, no sign of injury to her legs beyond the superficial abrasions but a bang could lead to swelling later. When Shannon stopped, she bent her head and began plucking mouthfuls of the long, dry grass on the wide verge.

'I'll leave you to it,' said Tim. 'See you two tomorrow.'

'Yep, should do unless someone's goat gets sick.' The weekly tennis mixed doubles—hard fought matches they all enjoyed. He really didn't want to have to call in a sub again. He'd missed two sessions since they started after Christmas.

'I'll be there,' said Shannon.

Thanks, mate,' Rupe said, and Oliver lifted a hand in farewell.

Oliver opened his bag, unpacked what he needed and began attending to the cut. 'Bring her head up, Shannon, please, and hold her steady.'

The ambulance passed Tim's ute as he eased onto the road heading out of town, and pulled up next to the police cruiser. The paramedic jumped out and chatted to Rupe for a minute before leaning into the car to talk to the injured driver.

Moments later a white BMW convertible with the top up pulled over and came to a halt. The horse jerked her head away and sidled sideways, causing Shannon to take a few hasty steps. Oliver grasped the lead rope as well in case the horse broke free. She'd have no trouble pulling Shannon off her feet if she bolted.

'Another bloody genius from that place,' she muttered. 'That's the daughter. She's hardly ever here, most likely too busy jetsetting around the world.'

A tall woman with hair the colour of bleached straw slammed the car door and marched towards them.

'What's happened? What are you doing with my horse?' Her accent was slight but evident in the rounded vowels and precise enunciation. Sunglasses obscured most of her face and she had an asymmetrical hair style where one side was longer than the other, even though the whole effect was short.

Leaving the horse in Oliver's care, Shannon, stocky and dark-haired, walked to meet the fair woman. They came from different worlds, hard-nosed Shannon in the blue police uniform, and the elegant blonde in her rural version of designer faded blue jeans with those stupid ripped knees and sleeveless shirt, which never suffered from a speck of dirt or a crease and would have cost ten times what any of the Taylor's Bend women paid for theirs.

'Constable Shannon Chu.' Her voice would cut steel. 'Could I have your name please, ma'am?'

'Krista Laatonen. I own this horse.' She pushed the sunglasses up and took a couple of steps towards the horse, hand outstretched, but it tossed its head and snorted, backing away.

'Do you have proof of that?'

Oliver calmed the horse, hiding a smile at Shannon's deliberately blank expression, guaranteed to infuriate this blonde fury even more. Laatonen? Sounded Finnish. Explained the fineness of the white hair and the smooth, pale skin, not to mention the Arctic blue eyes.

'I'm from The Grange. Hugh Littlejohn is my stepfather and this is my horse. Ask him if you don't believe me.'

'We may do that. Your brother Angus, over there, was speeding and drove into the ditch. We've just freed your horse from the float. It was panicking and in danger of injuring itself. This is Oliver Johnson, the vet.'

'Angus is my stepbrother.' The icy pair of eyes coated Oliver with disdain. 'We have our own vet. Thank you.' Her tone altered to unexpected concern as she peered at the bloody cut over the horse's eye.

'Is she badly injured? What about her eye? Isn't that a lot of blood?'

'Minor skin abrasions on the head can bleed a lot, same as people. Her eye isn't damaged but I'll need to examine her more thoroughly.' Wonder if that bloke liked being thought of as 'their' vet. Oliver wouldn't.

Rupe strolled over.

'Senior Constable Perry,' he said.

'This is Krista Laatonen from The Grange,' said Shannon. 'Says she owns the horse.'

'I do own the horse. Her name is Calypso Secret.' She bit the words off and spat them towards Shannon. 'I was just informing your constable that we have our own vet and you should have called us first.'

'We are aware of that. We called The Grange but the Jindalee vet is at least half an hour away and your horse might have needed a sedative before we could safely get her out,' Rupe said.

'You sedated my horse? Without permission? How dare you?' She swung the icepicks back to Oliver. His jaw tightened. How dare she talk to him as though he were some unqualified upstart? 'Who did you speak to at The Grange?'

'Mrs Littlejohn,' said Rupe. 'She told us to do what was necessary and she'd send someone. Didn't she inform you?'

'Clearly not.'

'Your horse didn't need sedation. She calmed down quickly when she knew we were getting her out,' Oliver said. 'I was called by Senior Constable Perry for assistance. If she had needed it I would have made a professional decision in the best interest of the animal.' He couldn't resist adding, 'Something you might take up with your stepbrother over there.'

For the first time she glanced across to where the paramedic was assisting the driver to climb into the back of the ambulance.

'Is he all right?' It had a grudging sound to it. Not a loving relationship then. Not surprising given the lack of communication between them. She'd been more worried about the horse. So had he.

'He has mild shock, a possible cracked rib and a sprained wrist. Might be broken,' said Rupe.

'Was he drunk?' As though she expected he would be in the middle of a weekday afternoon.

'Not over the limit but he did register positive for alcohol.'

She breathed in hard, lips tight, but said nothing. One manicured hand gracefully swatted a fly from her face. Pink-tipped fingernails and perfect make-up straight out of a cosmetics ad.

'We have to get this car and float off the road. As it's your property, do you want to take care of it, Ms Laatonen?' asked Rupe briskly.

Oliver bit his lip to stop the laugh escaping.

'Or should I call the tow truck?' Rupe finished after the silence indicated she wasn't replying yes.

'One moment, please.' Mobile phone in hand, she turned away and spoke rapidly, furiously, to someone.

'Mad as a frog in a sock,' murmured Shannon.

The imperious voice cut in. 'Call the tow truck, please. Have them take both vehicles to the local garage.'

'The Range Rover might be drivable,' said Shannon.

'Not by me.' Her perfectly sculpted lip curled. 'Angus can handle it.'

'What about Calypso Secret?' asked Oliver while Shannon called the local garage.

'There's no float available to pick her up right now. Do you have a stable or a yard at your practice where I can leave her?'

'She needs more attention. I need to check for other injuries.'

'Can you do that?'

'Are you asking me if I'm qualified to treat your animal?'

'I'm asking will you. I can pay you whatever you want.'

Not quite what he'd asked her. Oliver met Rupe's eye briefly. He'd be thinking exactly the same thing. She figured money would buy her anything and it probably did. Except manners.

'If it wasn't for the fact your horse needs treatment I'd say no, given your assessment of my professional ability.'

A slight rose-pink flush tinged her cheeks. 'I'm sorry,' she said. 'I didn't mean to doubt your ability. I'm worried about Calypso. I'd hate her to be in pain.'

He let that one pass. If that was worry, insulting the vet was an odd way of expressing it. He'd hate to see unconcern. Come to think of it he had—towards her stepbrother. To be fair, underneath the spikes she did seem genuinely to care for the horse's wellbeing. 'My practice is about two kilometres from here. You'll have to walk her rather than ride. Head into town, turn right at the first intersection and follow Victoria Road. You'll see the sign. Shouldn't take too long. Try to keep her on the soft verge and take her quietly.'

After a moment of stunned silence, she said, 'What about my car?'

'Isn't someone coming from The Grange?'

'No, not now I'm here.'

'You can walk back.'

She looked around as though a minion might appear and offer to take the horse for her. When none did, she looked at her feet clad in red strappy high-heeled sandals. 'I can't walk that far in these.'

'I've got gumboots in the boot,' said Oliver. 'You can borrow those.'

The cool ice eyes held his gaze for a long, stunning moment. Something choked the breath in his throat, blood roared in his veins, a force crackled between them. Desperate lungs dragged in air.

Rupe and Shannon had drifted away to study the crash site and move along the trickle of cars dawdling by and stopping to chat or ask questions. Everyone would know the news by now and everyone's opinion of the goings-on at The Grange would be reconfirmed.

She repositioned the sunglasses on her nose.

'No thanks,' she said. 'I'll manage.'

'Up to you,' said Oliver. 'Take my phone number and give me yours in case you have trouble.'

She handed him her phone and he sent himself a text. 'Turn this off so it doesn't frighten her. She'll be a bit jumpy. A sudden noise might upset her.'

She stalked over to her car, leaned inside and pulled out a red leather bag, which she slung over a shoulder. She touched something and the roof came up, then she locked the doors with a touch on the door handle.

Fun car but impractical for a vet even if he could spare a year's pay to buy one. Stuey wouldn't have the electronic equipment to service something European and upmarket like that anyway. The simpler the better when you were out in the country.

Oliver returned his attention to his patient, ignoring Ms Laatonen when she walked back to join him, although every nerve ending tingled and the hand holding the lead rope turned clammy. Stuey arrived in his tow truck. Calypso had calmed down enough now that she wasn't startled by the engine or the screech of the brakes.

'Is she usually good in traffic?'

'I think so.'

'Then you should be okay. It's about six-hundred metres to the turn-off and my road's quiet. Watch she doesn't tread on your foot. Don't want a broken toe.'

She didn't seem to know much about the horse she was so adamant was hers but she should be fine and he'd jog back to meet her once he'd driven home, just in case. Might chuck in a pair of thongs for her because her feet would be crippling her after a few minutes on that terrain. Not telling her that, though. She deserved to suffer a little. Might make her think.

'All the roads around here are quiet. Damn these flies!' She flapped ineffectually at one crawling over her cheek. 'I'd better talk to that tow truck man.'

'His name's Stuey and he owns the local garage.'

'Right.' She strode away.

Oliver stroked Calypso's neck and the horse stopped grazing and rubbed her head against his chest. 'Good girl. You walk along quietly and I'll see you later, okay? I'll get you all fixed up and feeling better.'

'She likes you.' Her voice surprised him. Must have been a quick chat. Most likely one-sided. Her side. Orders didn't take long to give.

'I like her. How old is she?'

'Six.' She took the rope Oliver handed her and patted the silky nose. Calypso resumed eating. 'Come on.' She pulled at the rope and started walking, the horse following obediently behind and her high heels tangling in the dry grass and weeds.

Oliver grinned as Shannon joined him.

'She's in for a nice walk,' she said with an answering smile.

'I'll take the car home then go back and meet her. Don't want another disaster.'

'Softie. See ya, Ollie.'

'It's the horse I care about,' he called at her retreating back.

'Ha, ha, ha, sure,' floated over her shoulder. 'And I'm Cleopatra.'

***

Krista took her sandals off when that vet had passed her on his way home. She wasn't giving him the satisfaction of seeing her struggle in the rough grass on the roadside. Luckily, the thickness made the ground soft underfoot so walking barefoot was marginally better as long as she avoided the prickly looking weeds, and the stones and other hidden sharp objects like sticks.

So much for the pedicure she'd had yesterday.

Something squished under her toes but she didn't dare look.

Damn Angus. If he hadn't been carted off in that ambulance she'd have punched him. She'd almost told that cop to arrest him for horse stealing. He knew Calypso was her horse, a twenty-fifth birthday gift from her stepfather, given to her in typical lavish fashion just after he bought The Grange. Angus could ride any of the other horses he wanted so why did he insist on taking hers? And where was he going? Why was he racing along at breakneck speed? Was it because he knew she was arriving this afternoon and thought he'd get away with something? Unlucky for him she'd left Melbourne earlier than she'd planned. Lucky for her she'd taken this route on the way to The Grange and caught him in the act, instead of taking the other turn-off. The underhanded sneaky bastard.

Pity she hadn't packed better walking shoes but she hadn't intended to go hiking along the roadside. She'd packed for the weekend celebration which, apart from lazing by the pool, involved talking, drinking and eating. Plenty of drinking given the company she'd be forced to keep and the state her mother would be in, in the lead up.

Lucky the vet hadn't suggested she ride Calypso, that would have added another layer of humiliation. The cheek of that man offering her his gumboots. Laughing at her. They all were. Country yokels. Good looking, though. Especially that cop, Senior Constable someone. Shame he wore a wedding ring.

The vet ... well ... good body, strong ... sandy hair wasn't really her thing but he had a look about him ... clear blue eyes, like hers, but his were ... calm, kind. Her apology for snapping had been genuine even though he didn't think so by his expression. She'd offended him and for some reason that upset her. Not a lot. Upset was too strong. Unsettled her was more like it. She wanted him to like her but he didn't, he liked Calypso more. Why did she care?

Too bad. She'd pay whatever was owing for looking after Calypso tonight and bandaging her cuts, and she'd bill Angus herself. Hugh would be livid.

Crashing a Grange car, damaging a float, involving the cops, injuring the horse, all in time for the fifteenth wedding anniversary extravaganza.

She smiled. That was something to look forward to, Angus being told off by his father. The anniversary, well ... that was something to be endured. The best that could be said for Hugh was he was a generous host and provided top-notch booze and food. She'd be ready for a stiff drink after this experience.

It was hotter than she thought, should've taken her hat out of the car and brought her water bottle. She hadn't been thinking straight. Not with that man watching her with dislike in his eyes. She was parched already. Two kilometres was nothing, a short stroll, but in these conditions? Sweat trickled down between her breasts and her armpits were uncomfortably sticky. Her deodorant would be getting a work-out. The pool at The Grange beckoned. A swim, and after that a cool drink involving gin and ice.

Nearly ten minutes later she reached the turn into Victoria Road. Slow going with sore feet, hordes of annoying flies and a horse who wanted to dawdle and yank at mouthfuls of grass. Twice she'd stopped to remove prickles from her soles and she'd stubbed her toe hard against a hidden chunk of broken concrete skirting around a culvert. One car had passed coming from the town, the old boy behind the wheel slowing to ask if she was okay, love. Which she was. No doubt he'd stop around the corner and get the full story from those two cops.

Ahead on the right a couple of weatherboard houses in various stages of disrepair faced open paddocks across the side road. This was the edge of town. The house on the corner had a bizarre collection of garden gnomes, a yellow mini windmill and car-tyre swans painted peculiar, non-birdlike colours like turquoise and fuchsia. Two nature strips were mown and smooth to walk on but had nasty little bindi-eyes hiding in the lawn, which felt like walking on pins so she had to switch to the road, but the tarred surface ran out after twenty metres and turned to rough, potholed gravel.

The blocks of land were bigger after the first five homes, with houses set well back and a few cows and horses grazing in the paddocks. Calypso plodded along quietly now there was no available grass to tackle and every so often gave her a rough nudge with her head, which made Krista stumble.

'Cut that out,' she said sternly when she did it a third time. Was the horse laughing at her too? But she patted the silky neck. 'Poor girl, are you feeling better?'

How much farther was this damned place? The road was gently but definitely rising and curved to the left up ahead with tall gumtrees providing shade. A figure came into view, striding comfortably along with a carry bag in his hand, a wide-brimmed Akubra hat low on his head. The vet. Coming to check on her, no doubt. She slipped her sandals on, straightened her back and lifted her head. Calypso pricked her ears.

The man slowed. What was his name? They'd told her but she'd forgotten already.

'How's it going? You've taken a while to get this far. I thought you might've had some trouble.'

'No. How much further is it?' She swiped at another fly.

'Not far. I brought these.' He pulled a pair of black rubber thongs out of the bag. 'Thought your feet might be sore.' He glanced down. 'They're a bit big but ... your toe's bleeding.'

'I stubbed it on something.'

Krista looked at the offering. Thongs. Soft rubber, flat. Much better than either of the alternatives. But...

'I brought this too.' He produced a water bottle, the refillable type sportspeople use. He didn't wear sunglasses, causing the tanned skin around his eyes to wrinkle. Gave him a rugged, weather-beaten look. Very attractive. She looked away quickly.

'Thanks. I left mine in the car. And my hat.' She took some deep swallows. Cool and refreshing with a slight taste unlike city water.

He patted Calypso while she drank, and took the lead rope from her. 'I'll take her now.'

He began walking, leaving her to stumble after him. Her shoes were hopeless on the rough surface, twisting and turning at each step and the thin soles were hardly any better than bare feet. She'd do her ankle in at this rate.

'Could I try the thongs, please?'

'Sure.' He stopped and handed them over, refraining from comment. 'Want my hat too?'

'No thanks.' That hat was well worn and old, no doubt imbedded with sweat and dust. She dropped the sandals into the carry bag and set off again.

'Better?' he asked.

'Yes.' Who was he? She scoured her memory but came up blank. 'I've forgotten your name.'

'Oliver Johnson.'

'Right. Of course.'

'I'm the local vet.'

She nodded. 'I know.' Something about his tone made her whip her head around to look at him. He returned her gaze with a blank expression.

'Just checking,' he said.

'Checking what?'

'That you're not suffering from short-term memory loss. Heatstroke. From the heat.'

***

Oliver walked on, quietly pleased with the furious expression on Krista Laatonen's face. He'd been right about her feet. They were scratched and dirty, with the pink-polished nail on the big toe broken and bloody where she'd whacked it on something. Sweat ran down into the vee of her sleeveless blouse and along her hairline, although he'd been careful not to do more than glance in the general direction of her chest. In the mood she was in, he'd be in all sorts of trouble if he was caught ogling her breasts. Her cheeks and nose had a touch of sun too. Didn't take long to burn in this weather, especially for someone with such fair skin.

Calypso was in good shape. The easy walk would have calmed her down.

When they reached the house, Oliver walked straight across the wide parking area and put the horse in the stables in one of the three stalls he used when large animals needed to stay. Billy, his bay gelding, whickered, and trotted across the paddock to meet the newcomer but he closed the yard gate to keep him at a distance. He hung his head over the fence to watch.

'Is that your horse?' Krista broke the silence she'd maintained since his remark. Suited him.

'Yes.'

He filled a bucket with water and stood it inside the stable door. Calypso stuck her nose in and snuffled experimentally before drinking.

'Would you like a bandaid for that toe?'

She looked down at her foot. 'Thanks.' She took off the sunglasses and put them in the bag.

With the five o'clock surgery cancelled, Margie had hung the notice on the gate and given herself an early mark. Fair enough, she had three sons to wrangle at home, more or less on her own, because her husband was a long-haul truckie. She was also a very reliable, efficient person to have in charge of the office and one he didn't want to lose, but it was just as well she wasn't here to see his decorative but unwelcome visitor. He'd never live it down. Shannon was bad enough.

With the coast clear he took Krista along the path through his vegetable garden behind the surgery, and into the house. He showed her to the bathroom, found bandaids and antiseptic cream, handed her a clean towel and said, 'I'll be out with the horse.'

'Thanks.'

'Can you call someone to pick you up?'

'Yes.'

Krista waited until the back door banged shut, then tugged off her jeans and sat on the edge of the big old tub to wash her feet. He'd only taken her through a covered back verandah, the kitchen and a cool, dim corridor on the way to the bathroom, but his house was surprisingly neat and clean for a man who lived alone. A quick appraisal had established that fact—one toothbrush, one towel on the rack, no female necessities like make-up or moisturisers. Definitely a single male. The tub gleamed with no scum lines, the kitchen was orderly with no dirty dishes lying on the bench or in the sink. He must have a cleaner. She had one for her two-bedroom apartment and he had a rambling old house in the country—which in her experience, was full of flies, manure, dust and or mud. He'd need someone to do the housework.

When she reappeared in the stable doorway, cleaner if not refreshed, Oliver was swabbing antiseptic onto the scrape on a rear leg where the skin was broken. Calypso fidgeted at the sting.

'She's very well-behaved all things considered, used to being mucked around with,' Oliver said without looking up. He moved to the other leg and ran his hand down the horse's flank. 'She's a nice-looking horse.'

'She came with The Grange. Her dam was a champion racer. Jamaican Lady. You might have heard of her.'

'Sorry. Not into horse racing. Do you race her?'

'She's had a couple of starts but not since Hugh bought The Grange. He doesn't want to race the horses. He gave her to me.'

'Nice gift. Will you breed from her?'

'Maybe. She's had one foal already, which is doing well, I think.' She hadn't thought about it. Owning a horse wasn't an imposition on her daily life. Calypso lived at The Grange and was cared for by Rod along with the other horses. Hugh and her mother wanted her to learn to ride but it never appealed as an activity and she avoided coming out here as much as she could. It had seemed a very odd gift at the time. She liked animals but she'd never expressed any desire to own a horse, even at the age many girls went through a pony phase.

Oliver picked up a front foot to check the underside of the hoof.

'No problem there.' He straightened then frowned. His palm had reddish brown marks on it. He rubbed at it with the thumb of his other hand. He squatted and studied the hair on Calypso's fetlock and above the hoof. A few whitish patches were visible.

'Hand me that towel,' he said. 'Dip the corner in the water bucket first.'

Krista did as he asked. 'What's wrong?'

'There's something odd...'

He scrubbed at the hair. The towel changed colour and so did the hair for about ten centimetres up the horse's ankle.

'So what's going on here?' he asked, looking up at her. Accusing her!

Chapter 2

'What do you mean?' Krista moved forward. 'I have no idea what's going on. Ask my stepbrother.'

'I'm asking you. Is this your horse, Calypso Secret, or not?' Oliver stood and waited, hands on hips. What sort of scam were she and her brother playing? Whatever it was smacked of illegality.

She faltered then. Looked down at the white sock, back to Oliver, confusion mixed with anger. 'I don't think so. Calypso doesn't have any white on her.'

'So you're not sure now. You seemed pretty certain when you got out of the car.'

'It looked like my horse.' All the angry defiance had drained away.

'How often do you see her?'

'Who?'

'The horse.'

'Once or twice a year.' She sounded doubtful about that, too.

Oliver sighed. That added up to a grand total of four times max. 'So you really couldn't say when we saw you at the accident whether it was your horse or not.'

'No, but I know it isn't now.'

She pulled her phone from her bag and walked outside.

Oliver wiped down the other ankles but no more white socks appeared. He patted the sleek neck.

'Who are you, girl?' The horse turned her head to look at him with innocent big brown eyes. 'What are they up to?'

Should he call Rupe? This was odd but it could be nothing. See what Krista said after her phone call. She'd been genuinely surprised, he'd swear to it, and the icy facade had cracked momentarily. Maybe she wasn't involved and the stepbrother was doing something dodgy. She had an attitude problem, that was for sure, but it didn't mean she was up to anything. What sort of work did she do? If she did have a job at all. With stepdaddy's billions she might not need to.

The activity at The Grange was often the topic of discussion at the pub but no-one had ever suggested anything illegal going on there and she'd never been mentioned. It was more about the disdain the local farmers had for the millionaire who'd bought the place and installed his son, Angus, as general manager. Tax dodge for the bloke, they reckoned and some people suggested money laundering, but as a joke. Hardly ever there, used it to entertain and impress other rich businessmen. A place to show off and pretend he was a man of the land. The son, being in general a no-hoper, was given the job to keep him out of trouble. They had a stable of mares and a stallion. Five mares if this one was counted, and other mares came temporarily for servicing by the stallion. According to local knowledge, four of the horses including the real Calypso Secret and the stallion had come with the sale. Blow-ins from the city was the general consensus and most people hoped they'd blow out again.

Eighteen-year-old Sandy Lyall worked there as a stablehand when needed and helped Oliver out with the animals he had staying over in the surgery. She didn't say much about The Grange, other than that she liked the stable manager and his wife. He didn't remember the man's name and he wasn't interested enough to ask questions. He was now.

To compound their sins in the eyes of the locals, the owners of The Grange hardly ever came into Taylor's Bend, and apart from visits to the supermarket by the stable manager's wife, didn't shop locally or drink at the pub. If she'd visited Dot and Laurie's grocery store, everyone would know everything about The Grange, but she never did so real information was scarce.

Worst of all, the new owner had fired Curly who'd been head of the stables for fifteen years for the previous owners, who, in their eighties with no interested children to take over, had had no choice but to sell and move to Brisbane, near their daughter.

None of the few remaining staff had stayed on at The Grange. It was the end of an era, and one the older residents mourned. The newcomers had done nothing to foster good relations in the area, but if they were all like Krista

Laatonen it was just as well they kept to themselves.

Krista came back in with a face like an iceberg.

'Could you give me a ride back to my car, please?'

'What about the horse?'

'You agreed I could leave her here.'

'What's her name?'

'Arch Rival.'

'Who does she belong to?'

'She's from The Grange.'

'Are you sure?'

Her mouth tightened. 'Yes, Rod said Angus must have loaded her this afternoon. She's new. Calypso Secret is still there.'

'Right. So where does that leave me?' Rod was the name Sandy had mentioned, he remembered now—nice, ran the stables with his wife, she said. The one who shopped in the supermarket sometimes.

'This is Angus's responsibility.'

'I don't think so. I think this is your responsibility. Your brother is at the hospital and you brought the horse here.'

If she thought she could walk away from this she had another think coming. And he wasn't giving her a lift anywhere. She could walk.

The full lips compressed into a thin line. Shards of ice flew from her eyes.

'I suggest you get this sorted,' Oliver said. 'If you'll excuse me, I have work to do.'

He gestured she should leave the building. She stalked out onto the gravel parking area between the yard and the surgery. He latched the stable door and started walking.

'Aren't you going to lock that door?' Her voice made him grind his teeth. 'She's a valuable animal.'

'Is she? The way she's been treated today you wouldn't think so.'

'She wasn't mistreated by me.'

Oliver drew a breath and swallowed the rising anger. She was right. 'Okay. I lock up securely at night. She'll be safe here.'

She gave a sharp nod. Oliver left her standing there and went into the surgery to dispose of the used swabs and bandages. If he spent another minute in the company of that woman he'd regret it. She was the most obnoxious, arrogant piece of work he'd ever come across and he'd met a few. Forget the perfectly moulded body and the beautiful face with flawless skin straight out of a fashion magazine, this one had privilege and a sense of entitlement written all over her before she opened her mouth, from the stylish hair down passed the ripped jeans, to those stupid, useless, high-heeled shoes. When she did open her mouth, it got worse. That moment of debilitating attraction earlier must have been a brain fart caused by the heat.

He let the screen door slam in his wake. He'd look after Arch Rival until one of those Grange people came to collect her and he'd bill them for all the time he'd wasted on their behalf. Not to mention having to cancel surgery and postpone his visit to Harrop's.

He went to the office to look at the list of messages Margie had left.

Krista heard the door bang as she turned away to ring her mother. As usual, Mama didn't waste time with preliminaries.

'Krista, where are you?'

'I'm at the vet's. I need someone to come and pick me up.'

'I can't spare the time.' Of course she couldn't, she had people to order around organising the anniversary do.

'I'm not asking you to. Send one of the staff.'

'They're busy. Where's your car?'

'It's where the accident was. I told you I had to leave it there and walk the horse here.'

'Can't someone from the vet's drive you back?'

'He's here on his own and he has work to do.'

'Pay him for his time.'

'I can't do that, he's not a taxi driver.'

'Well, I'm sorry, I can't do anything about it.'

'Surely there's someone. Put me through to the stables. What about Rod or Amy?'

'They're all busy too. Everyone's busy. Rod left to collect Angus from hospital a few minutes ago. I have to go. Don't be late.'

The line went dead. Krista thrust the phone into her bag. She had two choices. Walk or beg. She looked across at the low, white building, silent, with a closed sign on the door next to a list of opening hours. Begging held no appeal but she could ask to borrow the thongs again. She'd left them in the bathroom. On second thought she needn't disturb him at all, the house was unlocked. She followed the path through the garden but stopped by the tomatoes. He'd accuse her of theft and trespassing if she didn't ask and he'd be right.

She stood for a moment, mentally debating the point. She wasn't a thief and she wouldn't give him any more reason to doubt her integrity. She retraced her steps.

Oliver wasn't happy to see her, that was apparent by the resigned expression.

'Yes?'

'I'm sorry to bother you again but could I please borrow your thongs?'

He closed his eyes briefly, opened them, said, 'Wait there,' and disappeared into the surgery. The door swung behind him but she wasn't game to follow him in. He said wait, she'd wait rather than risk losing the thongs. After today she need never see him again, remember that. Her humiliation in his presence, his disdain, would remain private.

Who was she kidding? The story would be all over town by this evening. Plenty of people knew he'd told her to walk her horse to his practice, knowing she wasn't prepared, she had the wrong shoes, showing her up as an idiot from the city. Those two cops would be having a laugh, as would that ambulance woman and the old man who'd stopped to see if she needed help. Half the damn town.

Oliver stepped outside and pulled the door to with a click of the latch. 'I'll drop you back at your car,' he said and strode towards his own car parked by the house under a carport.

'I can walk,' she called. 'If I can borrow the thongs.'

He stopped. 'Do you really want to walk or are you just being stubborn?'

'I don't want to put you out if you're busy.'

'I offered you a lift. Take it or leave it.' He folded his arms, head tilted to one side, face expressionless.

Krista took several deep, calming breaths as instructed by her yoga teacher for use in trying situations.

'I could have dropped you and been back by now,' he said.

'I would like a lift. Thank you.'

He strode across and opened the passenger door for her, a surprisingly gentlemanly gesture, waited for her to get in then banged the door shut. Was he making sure she was safely inside so he could get her off his property? Or was this an attempt to improve relations?

The drive was silent. Krista stared out the side window through the covering of dust and a large messy bird dropping. His car had a distinctive smell—animals, something vaguely medicinal and an underlying hint of manure. She wanted to say something but had no idea what it could be. She wanted to make amends and leave him with a better impression of her than the one he had at the moment. She didn't know how to do any of that.

Why? Men were usually falling over themselves to get to know her. Until they did get to know her and discovered she wasn't interested. Or interesting. Something.

He stopped opposite her car. The float and Range Rover had gone and the only sign of the accident was flattened grass and two deep grooves where the tyres had ripped into the dry earth of the ditch.

'Thanks for the ride,' she said stiffly, her hand on the door handle.

'No worries.'

She turned to face him. 'I'm sorry...' The words that weren't there dried in her throat.

'Okay.' He waited, one hand resting on the steering wheel, the other on the gear lever.

'Goodbye.'

Nothing happened when she tried to open the door.

'Push against the door at the same time,' he said. 'A roo ran into it and bent it.'

She lifted the handle and shoved with her other hand. The door flew open. She scrambled to get out but couldn't, restrained by the seatbelt.

He pressed the release button. She made as dignified an exit as was possible and closed the door. It didn't latch.

'Slam it,' he called. That's why he'd opened and closed the door for her earlier, nothing to do with a belated attempt to charm her.

She banged the door shut and stepped back as he drove off without a glance her way. She walked across to her car and got in, trembling with a mixture of relief, humiliation, frustration and anger, to sit with eyes closed for a few moments. What was she doing here? Taylor's Bend was the last place she wanted to be. If it wasn't for this bloody anniversary party she'd be curled up at home binge-watching Nordic noir crime, drinking red and eating chocolate. Unwanted. Unemployed.

The roar of an engine popped her eyes open. His car was on its way back. He must have turned a little way along. The dirty white four-wheel drive went by, giving her a glimpse of his face in profile, eyes fixed on the road ahead,

Krista Laatonen, the annoying, possibly criminal, nuisance from The Grange, already forgotten.

She pressed Start and pulled onto the road in the same direction with hollowness in her stomach, which might be hunger but might equally be disappointment.

***

Oliver finished his chores by six-thirty and headed into town for a meal at the pub before the Taylor's Bend Music and Drama Society's first orchestral rehearsal for Gilbert and Sullivan's *Patience*. This whole venture was a first. Newcomers to the area, Bill and Gina Locke, were enthusiastic amateur theatrical types, having spent most of their lives acting and singing.

They'd run an arts cafe in Queanbeyan and Bill directed many a local show there with Gina singing lead roles.

They'd followed a son, Barnaby, and his family to Taylor's Bend last November when Barnaby bought a block of land on the edge of town and started an organic vegetable business. It hadn't taken long before flyers appeared about the place calling for local talent to come to a meeting to discuss the formation of what became the Taylor's Bend Music and Drama Society—the 'MaDS' as the group quickly became known.

Oliver had gone along, as had most people, to see what the Lockes had in mind, and come away with a promise to drag out his long-neglected cello and join the orchestra. Gina was a very persuasive musical director and the Lockes were a highly organised force to be reckoned with. Taylor's Bend residents found themselves auditioning for parts in a work they knew nothing about but with the general attitude of 'What the heck? It should be a laugh if nothing else'.

The debut performance was in June. It was now mid-February. Oliver had snatched every spare minute to reacquaint himself with the cello he'd played through high school and university, and chip the rust off his technique. His fingers were frustratingly stiff and clumsy, hardened by the work he'd been doing, but the love of music was always there and as he persevered with the scales and studies he once used to fly through, the rich tone he'd produced so effortlessly in the past began to reappear. Tonight everyone would be sightreading through the music, which was nerve-racking in the extreme given the bouncy speed of most Gilbert and Sullivan pieces. Gina's confidence in his ability was doomed to crash and burn.

The pub was quiet with only a few people at the bar having a drink after work. He exchanged a few words, gave his order and took a bottle of water and a glass to his table.

'Keeping a clear head for tonight, Oliver?' Wally, rotund and red-faced manager of the feed and livestock store, paused on his way to the bar.

'Yeah, are you coming?' He had no idea who else's arm was twisted into joining the orchestra but he knew Wally played trumpet in the Willoughby Concert Band.

'Yeah, Gina got in touch with Les.' Their octogenarian conductor.

'Are they all coming along?' He'd heard them at the church fete last year and at the local gymkhanas. They numbered about twenty-five drawn from surrounding areas, and weren't bad.

'A couple of brass, some wind players and a percussionist.'

'That's good. I thought I might be the only one there. Me and Gina.' He grimaced. 'I'm having dinner. Care to join me?'

'Thanks. The wife and kids are out tonight so I'm on my own.'

Over the grilled steak and a beer, which Wally reckoned would get his brain in gear for the trumpet but Oliver wasn't risking, Wally said, 'I heard about the accident. Horse okay?'

'Yeah. She had a fright but calmed down when we got her out. Nice animal.'

'Shannon reckons the daughter was as friendly as a shark.'

'She wasn't too bad when she calmed down. Like her horse.' The other piece of information he'd keep to himself.

'Bit of a looker, she reckoned.' Wally sawed off a hunk of steak.

'Yeah, if you like icebergs.' He wasn't rising to any baits Wally threw his way. Since the most eligible bachelor in town, Rupe, had married Abbie a year or so back, attention had shifted to him. Until then he'd flown under the matchmaker's radar.

'Hah. That whole family is crazy.'

'Do you know the stepbrother Angus? The one who was driving the car?'

'Seen him a couple of times.'

'What's he like?'

Wally chewed and considered. 'He gambles.'

'Really?'

'According to the bloke who delivers feed to them.'

'Do they buy from you?' Surprising if they did.

'Nah, one of my customers told me. His brother knows the truck driver.'

'What does he gamble on?'

Wally shrugged. 'Dunno. But whatever he's into, it's for big money.'

'How does the bloke know that?'

'Dunno. Word gets round though, doesn't it? People talk.'

'Yeah. But that place is pretty tight lipped.'

And whether the word was accurate or not was another thing. Did Krista know that about her stepbrother? Hard to say. He didn't know how close they were. She disapproved of him, that was for sure, but that could be a general dislike rather than specific. Gambling in itself wasn't something to make you dislike someone. What constituted big money?

'So, what's your instrument?' asked Wally.

'What?' Lost as he was in speculation he floundered to pinpoint the question.

'What do you play?'

'Oh, cello. As soon as Gina heard that she wouldn't take no for an answer.'

'How long since you played?'

'At least ten years. Sounded like a dog when I started practising.'

Wally laughed. 'Should be an interesting rehearsal. Old Nils has a violin he hasn't played for twenty years.'

'He has arthritis in his hands.' And he'd thought his own fingers were stiff. Compared to Nils he'd be like Yo Yo Ma.

'I know but he reckons he'll be okay. Young Frankie Harris and her twin sister Bella both play violin quite well.'

'I don't know them.'

'They're from Bindubi, go to high school in Willoughby with my boy.'

'Right.'

'Reckon we'll have a few youngsters along tonight.'

'I hope some of them can play cello better than I can.'

'Doubt it, mate. Gina was saying how pleased she was you signed up because there's a cello solo in it that can't be done on anything else.'

'Why?' Oliver's hand froze on its way to the water glass.

'Someone on stage mimes playing a cello.'

'What? She never told me that.' A solo? This was a disaster waiting to happen. Maybe he could pretend he had an emergency call out. The way Doc Jensen did at community meetings when everyone knew he wanted to go home, have a few shots of whisky and add some words to the sci-fi saga he'd been working on for twelve years.

'She didn't want to scare you off.' Wally scraped up juices with a chunk of baked potato. 'Don't worry, you'll be fine. You've got months to practise.'

***

Krista drove straight down the long, tree-lined driveway to the stables when she arrived at The Grange. The usual mild sense of dread she experienced when exposed to the undiluted company of her mother was this time overridden by the fury and humiliation caused by Angus.

Why they'd chosen to celebrate the anniversary out here in the heat of summer, God only knew. These parched, gasping paddocks were as foreign and unfamiliar to her as the deserts of Namibia or the plains of Outer Mongolia, and almost seemed to return the sentiment to a European bred interloper from the city. Mama hated it too.

On either side white post-and-rail fences divided the fields, mostly empty and dried brown under the relentless sun. Only a couple of horses stood nose to tail in the shade, flicking their tails lazily at flies. Loose boxes and stalls were in the long shed with a peaked roofline, which stood a hundred or so metres past the house in the cluster of studwork buildings. Hugh had spent a lot of money on the place when he bought it, but his interest in being a country squire had waned quickly and now he and her mother only used it occasionally.

A silver sedan was parked by the large building housing the unused indoor ring. and Hugh, along with a man she didn't recognise, was standing outside the open door of the office discussing something. Both wore riding boots, jeans and short-sleeved blue shirts and new Akubras. Hugh looked as country as a politician on the campaign trail shaking hands with farmers for their votes.

He walked forward and kissed her on both cheeks, doing his public display of stepfatherly affection. 'Hello there, lovely girl. You're looking beautiful as ever.'

'Thanks.'

Hugh turned to the other man and said, 'This is my stepdaughter, Krista.

Krista this is Mark. He's brought a mare here for servicing. Lovely creature.'

The man offered his hand. 'Pleased to meet you.'

The words were polite but the grip was a little too firm and held a fraction too long, like the appraisal from two dark brown, small eyes. The man's features were all drawn together in the middle of his face like some weird puppet. His accent had a hint of Irish.

A client? A business associate of some sort, no doubt, but Hugh wouldn't bother explaining and she didn't want to know.

Krista nodded in return then said to Hugh. 'I need to talk to you.'

'Yes. Excuse us a moment please, Mark. Perhaps you would wait in the office there? Help yourself to a cold drink from the fridge.'

Mark nodded and strolled through the open door.

'What the hell is going on with Angus and that horse he was towing?' she asked as soon as he was out of earshot. 'He was passing a horse called Arch Rival off as Calypso.'

Hugh's jovial expression vanished and the familiar scowl appeared. 'What are you saying?'

'You tell me. I don't know what he's up to but he can damn well leave me and my horse out of it.'

'I've no idea what you're talking about. Calypso is right there in a stall. Rod brought her in because we knew you were coming.'

'I know Calypso's here, it's the other one that isn't. The one called Arch Rival whose white foot he painted over.'

'How do you know?' He had that condescending tone in his voice, the one where he dismissed anything she said as the ranting of a hysterical, probably premenstrual woman.

'I was there when the vet found out. How stupid did that make me look? I'd told him that it was my horse.'

'Where is Arch Rival now?'

'At the vet.'

'Which vet?'

'Oliver Johnson at Taylor's Bend. I had to walk her there after the crash because there was no-one here to come and get her. You were out and Angus had wrecked the float.'

'I know nothing about any of this.' Of course he didn't. He'd make it his business not to.

'Did you know Angus is in hospital in Wagga?'

'Yes. Rod told me as he was leaving to see him. He has a cracked rib. He'll be all right. Rod will probably bring him home. Rod said he'd had a car accident. I assumed in his own car.'

'The Range Rover and the float are at the local garage. The police called the tow truck.'

Hugh's lips tightened in anger as she knew they would when he discovered the local police were involved.

'What's Angus been doing, Hugh?'

'Nothing you need to bother about. I'll take care of it.' Another dismissal. Silly woman. Did he know or was he pretending? It wouldn't be the first time he covered up one of his son's indiscretions.

'But he was passing that horse off as mine.'

'Calypso is fine. Don't worry about it, I said. Go in and see your mother. Help her with the party.'

'I want to see my horse first.' Krista stepped around his solid bulk and into the wide doorway leading to the rows of stalls and loose boxes. Only three heads looked over the half doors as she walked, flicking their ears and watching her progress. Two would be just back from the ride Hugh and Mark had taken.

Calypso was in the third box on the right. Now she saw her with a more knowledgeable and critical eye, her coat was a slightly different colour to the impostor's—a shade lighter, more coppery. They were very similar in other respects and to someone who didn't know either horse well, or at least only from a distance, they'd be indistinguishable. Someone like her.

She rubbed the smooth nose but the horse tossed her head up and down, making Krista withdraw her hand and step back as she whirled away and circled the small enclosure, clearly annoyed at being locked up. Arch Rival was much quieter and enjoyed being patted and talked to.

A young female stablehand walking by with a bucket full of horse brushes looked at her curiously and paused.

'Hello. Isn't she beautiful? Her name's Calypso Secret.' About seventeen or eighteen, enthusiastic, wide toothy smile, with dark blonde hair pulled back in a messy ponytail.

'I know. I own her.'

'Sorry, you must be the boss's daughter.'

'Stepdaughter but yes.' Something about this girl's friendliness made her say. 'I'm Krista Laatonen. Are you local?'

'Yes, my dad has an orchard on the Bindubi Road. I grew up there but I really wanted to work with horses.'

'What's your name?'

'Sandy.'

'Do you think Calypso would be happier outside? She doesn't seem to like being locked up.'

'They all come in at night but the boss had her brought in early because you were coming. Will you want to go for a ride this evening?'

'No, I don't ride.'

'Oh.' A slight frown crossed the smooth brow as if to say *Why own a horse you don't ride?*

Krista didn't have to explain herself to a teenage employee.

'Do you know anything about Arch Rival?' she asked.

'Archie? She's a gorgeous girl. She's only been here a month. Mr Littlejohn Jr took her somewhere but he had an accident. I guess you already know that. I hope Archie is okay. No-one has said.'

Krista nodded. 'I walked her to the vet. She's fine, just a few scrapes. Do you know why she was taken out, or where?'

'No. I only come here once a week or when Rod calls me in.'

'Do you know the local vet?'

'Sure, everyone knows Ollie. I work there at weekends and three weekdays. He's the most eligible bachelor in town now since Rupe got married. Rupe's the cop,' she added.

'I met him. Both of them.'

'So you know what I mean.' She grinned, expecting some sort of acknowledgement of Oliver's attractions, then added, 'He's too old for me, unfortunately. Not that he's interested in anyone as far as we can tell.'

Krista gave a vague smile. How old was he? Mid-thirties at a guess. Way too old for a teenager. Who was 'we'? The women of Taylor's Bend? Why wasn't he interested in any of them?

'I really like your hairstyle.'

'Thanks.'

'I'd love to have something like that but I'd have to go to Wagga to get it done.'

'Isn't there a hairdresser in Taylor's Bend?'

'Yes, but Edie's not exactly up with the latest fashions. She's been here forever and does blue rinses and short back and sides mainly.'

'If you take in a photo she could probably have a go.'

'Of you?' The eyes widened with excitement.

'No, from a magazine.' Had she sounded too shocked at being asked to be a model? It was hardly surprising that a tiny place like this wouldn't have a decent salon and hairdresser. They were lucky to have one at all. That vet cut his own hair by the look of it.

'You must be here for the party.'

'I am and I'd better go up to the house and see my mother. Thanks, Sandy.'

The silver car had gone when she emerged from the stables, which meant Mark wasn't staying, thank goodness.

When Krista opened the front door of the large two-storey house with the wide porch and pillars Hugh had added that always made her think of *Gone with the Wind*, she was greeted by yapping and the clatter of nails on marble. Her mother's brown and white King Charles Spaniel, Lola, dashed across the foyer and proceeded to try to climb up her legs.

She bent to pat the silky head and was licked profusely in welcome. 'Where's Mama, Lola?'

Lola scurried away with Krista following, dress bag in one hand, dragging her suitcase behind her, and revelling in the cool air on her overheated skin. Where were the staff?

Her mother's strident voice with the accent that grew stronger the more annoyed she was, emanated from the living room, alternating with the deeper tones of Hugh. Judging by the strength of the Finnish component she was very cross. Lola yapped along with the argument.

Krista stopped in the doorway waiting for a gap in the row, but her mother turned and immediately strode across for a perfunctory kiss. 'Hello Krista, where have you been? I thought you were on your way here an hour ago. You smell dreadful. Like a horse yard.'

'I had to deal with Angus's horse and the vet, you know that.'

One elegantly manicured hand waved dismissively. 'That's not your problem, as I've been telling Hugh. You are here to help me with this monstrous event that your stepfather insists on having, not me. I'd be just as happy with scrambled eggs on toast and a glass of champagne at home in Sydney. Lola, shush!'

'You agreed to it,' said Hugh. 'Don't be so hysterical.' He turned away to the drinks cabinet and poured himself a whisky. Lola, chastened, curled up on the couch.

'That's right, have a drink and leave all the work to me.'

'What work? You don't have to do anything except issue instructions to the staff.'

'You don't have one idea how much planning goes into your extravaganzas. Especially trying to organise everything in this back-of-the-sticks town.'

'*Our* extravaganzas,' he corrected. 'Gustav is doing the catering and everything is flying in with him early on Saturday morning, I told you that.'

Krista backed out and escaped. Lola scampered after her. The bickering didn't miss a beat.

Brenda, her mother's PA and all-round organiser, came along the corridor from the kitchen as she reached the foot of the stairs.

'Hello, Krista. How nice to see you again.' Tall and gaunt with a thin angular face under a square-cut bob, Brenda was efficiency personified. Nothing ruffled her, which was saying something because she'd been in her mother's employ for the eight years since her husband died unexpectedly and she decided to fill the gaping hole in her life with a live-in job. Her mother didn't realise, but she wouldn't cope without Brenda.

'Hi, Brenda. Am I in the usual room?'

'Yes. Let me help with your luggage.'

'Thanks.' Krista handed her the dress bag, hoisted the suitcase and started up the stairs.

'You look as though you need a nice long bath.' Brenda and Lola came up behind her, the dog panting and resting on the landing between flights.

'Mama told me I smell like a horse yard.'

'You do have an agricultural whiff to you. *L'Air des Stables?*' Brenda smiled. 'I hear you had some excitement on the way.'

Krista reached the first floor and put her suitcase down, flexing her fingers. 'Angus had an accident.'

'Yes, but he's all right.' Brenda strode along the landing to the end bedroom. She flung the door open and went in.

'How many people are coming to this party?'

'It's not big. Only about fifty but Viivi's getting into her usual tizz.'

Fifty people to smile at and make small talk with. Fifty people, most of whom she didn't know and the remainder, wished she didn't know. Powerful men and their wives, some equally powerful; most, glamorous extensions of their husbands.

'Where are they all staying?'

'Hugh's brothers and sister and their spouses are here and the rest are at the Mountain Retreat Resort.'

'Where's that?'

'Up in the mountains. Not far, really. Very exclusive. They'll helicopter in and out or drive.'

Krista kicked her sandals off, dumped her jacket and slumped into one of the leather easy chairs by the window. Lola sat by her feet looking up hopefully until Krista stroked her head. 'Ugh. I don't know why I bothered coming.'

'Viivi wants you here.'

'Not a good look if the doting daughter doesn't turn up, you mean?'

Brenda unzipped the dress bag and extracted the silver evening dress. 'This is lovely.' She hung it carefully in the wardrobe and took out the pale blue silk dress. 'What's the matter, Krista? Something's wrong, isn't it? And it's not about that horse.'

How much did Brenda already know? Her networking skills were second-to-none so there was no use trying to hide the truth from her. Charles Petrovic and Irene, his wife, were on the guest list so the situation would be obvious soon enough anyway.

'I got the sack.'

'When?' She sat opposite, all her attention focused on Krista, drawing out the information as she always did.

'When Charles found someone younger and prettier and more ... amenable, to be his personal assistant. Friday was my last day.'

'The man's a slug.'

'I know but I thought he was happy with my work. I thought I was doing a good job.'

'I'm sure you were but that would have nothing to do with it. What did he say?'

'He said he was sorry but it wasn't working out and that he'd pay me three month's severance but I should leave immediately. I've only been there a few months.'

'Are you sure it was...' Brenda stood up. 'Never mind. You're better off out of it. You'll find something else.'

'I'm not sure ... I don't think I want to do PA work anymore but that's all I've ever done and they weren't jobs I earned. I was hired for my looks and my connections. Anyone could do what I did. The other staff knew it and I always felt like an impostor, as though I shouldn't be there.'

That's how that vet made her feel, too. Like an impostor who was out of her depth.

Brenda sat down again. 'Krista, you could do anything you want.'

'That's the trouble, I don't know what I want. Mama got my first job for me with Ernest Wise for exactly that reason. She thought it would keep me occupied and out of trouble until someone married me. He was a real gentleman and I loved working for him but he was doing Mama a favour. He gave me the easy things to do like booking hotels and restaurants for him and buying gifts for his wife.'

'I remember. He truly was an old-school gentleman. His wife was lovely too.'

'I haven't met anyone like him since and I've had three positions in three years. Men are creeps.'

'Not all of them.'

'I must be moving in the wrong circles.'

'I'll run the bath for you.' Brenda disappeared into the ensuite. When she came out, she said, 'You need to think about what it is you really want to do, what interests you most, and go for it. Nothing says you can't study, do something at university.'

Krista lay in the scented water turning Brenda's words over in her head. Not all men are creeps. She knew Brenda was right and her own statement wasn't really true. But where were the good ones? What is it you really want to do? Find it and go for it. Study for a degree. In what? What university would accept her? She'd barely scraped through high school.

What did she want to do and what was she actually capable of doing?

Nothing. Her mind came up blank.

But she didn't need to work. She had money. She didn't need to do anything. Maybe Mama was right. She should be looking for someone to marry instead of being serially groped in an office by the boss.

She extended her leg and studied the damage to her toe. He'd been kind, the vet. He had nice eyes, an appealing, calm manner and despite his obvious dislike of her, he was polite and he had given her a ride back to her car.

He wasn't a creep. He just didn't like her.

Chapter 3

Dinner was a study in politeness of a completely different kind to Oliver the vet's. This politeness was of the quality only a married couple deeply at odds could generate. The simmering tension between Hugh and Viivi had become familiar over the years but now held a new element of real dislike. If Brenda hadn't been at the table to keep up a flow of innocuous conversation, Krista would have made a run for her car and headed for Melbourne.

As dessert was being cleared away, Angus and Rod appeared in the dining room doorway, Angus sporting a sling and a pained expression, crying out for sympathy he was not going to get from anyone in the room. He really was a spoiled brat.

Brenda rose. 'I'll get them to bring dinner for you. Sit down.'

'Sorry we're late,' said Rod to the room in general while Angus made a show of manoeuvring himself onto a chair with winces and grunts of agony.

Hugh glared at him. 'So?'

'So what?' Angus poured himself a glass of wine.

'Can we not do this at the dinner table?' asked Viivi in her long-suffering voice.

Hugh shot her a black look but didn't pursue the attack.

'You have to pay the vet, Angus,' said Krista.

'I can't deal with that right now,' he snapped.

'And the tow truck driver and the garage where your car and the float are.' Krista drank some water to avoid looking at the odious man. How could she possibly call this person a brother of any description?

'I'll deal with it, for Christ's sake. As usual, you have no idea about anything.'

The viciousness in his voice so shocked her, the jerk of her hand made water splash down the side of her glass. Despite their cordial dislike of each other Angus usually didn't bother rising above casual disdain for anything she did or said.

'Don't worry, Krista,' Rod said into the ensuing black hole of silence. 'I'll take care of everything tomorrow.'

That's what Rod's main job was so far as she could judge. Cleaning up after Angus. Pathetic. Did he know that when he accepted the position as stable manager? Why he and his wife Amy stuck around she had no idea. He came from a horse racing family, he knew about horses and had been a good choice by Hugh to ensure the place had a chance at succeeding, but why put up with an idiot like Angus as his boss?

That he and Angus and been at school together wasn't reason enough, surely? Neither man was gay, Amy being proof if any was needed, so there was no emotional attachment beyond an inexplicable friendship. A big pay packet probably helped.

The maid came in with two entrees, served them and made a hasty escape.

'Rod and I are going riding early tomorrow. You should join us on Calypso,' Hugh said. 'You might enjoy it, Krista. It's about time you climbed aboard.'

In other words, get your arse out of bed at dawn, not that that would be a problem. She never slept well, always rose early and often swam before work. Out here in the country the quiet and the heat made sleeping even more difficult and early morning was the best part of the day.

'I'd rather not, thanks,' she said. 'I haven't brought the right clothes and I'd prefer to swim. Rod can ride her.'

Hugh glowered but said nothing.

'I'll need Krista's help tomorrow.' Viivi spoke as though she had to clean the house single-handedly and cook for an approaching army. In reality it would entail fussing over the floral arrangements and annoying the florist by changing her order, then ringing the chef and the caterer and doing the same. That would fill the morning, and in the afternoon, she'd start in on the music and the people bringing the marquee and the extra seating.

Brenda caught Krista's eye and winked. Thank God for Brenda.

'No problem, Mama, that's why I came early.'

***

Oliver arrived home at ten-thirty with Gilbert and Sullivan setting up an ear worm. Much to his surprise, Taylor's Bend and surrounds housed a number of reasonably competent musicians, some of whom, mainly the teenagers, played with style and finesse. Another cellist had been dragged along, a very shy, blonde teenager named Emma whose mother played flute and when she wasn't doing that, talked for Australia and also on behalf of Emma.

Emma's mother introduced her daughter to Oliver and said she'd only been playing for two years but was very talented and would benefit greatly from the experience. When she finally went away to unpack her flute, Oliver said, 'I'm really glad you're here, Emma. I thought I'd be all on my own.'

That remark elicited a tiny smile and bright red cheeks. 'I'm not very good,' she murmured.

'I haven't played for ten or twelve years so that makes us about even. We can muddle along together.'

Except she had been telling the truth. She wasn't very good and spent most of the rehearsal either getting lost, not playing or playing wrong notes in the right place and the other way round. Luckily she was a sweet kid and took his suggestions well.

Gina certainly knew her stuff and conducted with enthusiasm and buckets of patience and tact. She raised an eyebrow during the tea and biscuit break when he commented that his playing was very rusty and said, 'You're a dark horse, aren't you, Oliver? Why didn't you do a music degree and play professionally? You certainly would have been good enough. Your tone is beautiful.'

'I wanted to be a vet.'

'Fair enough. And the MaDS benefit as well as the animals.' She laughed and saved him from painful explanations about why he hadn't gone down that path and how this was the first time he'd been able to touch his cello in many years. And why, as his father put it, he'd run away to hide in the back of beyond and spend his life surrounded by horse manure and flyblown sheep with both hands up a cow's arse.

As usual, before going to bed Oliver checked the animals and made sure all the gates and doors were locked. The surgery had extra security and sensor lighting because of the drugs he kept on the premises. So far he'd had no trouble but times were changing and he wasn't about to take any risks.

Billy was across the far side of the field, a dark outline in the faint light of the half-moon. Arch Rival whickered when he opened the stable and said 'hello'. She seemed fine so he rubbed her nose and left her to it, locking the door as he went.

The surgery was secure and he crunched his way across the parking area to the front door of the house. The strong scent of the old honeysuckle vine covering the far side fence hung in the warm night air. Lovely night. He breathed deeply then let himself in. He had to fit in the visit to Jess Harrop early tomorrow morning and had day surgery at ten, which would be busy because of yesterday's cancellation. Bed beckoned.

Heavy pounding on the front door woke him. He raised his head groggily from the pillow and focused on the bedside clock. Five-eleven. Daylight filtered in around the edges of the blind. He tossed the sheet off, pulled on shorts and a T-shirt and went to open the door. Must be an emergency although people usually phoned.

Yawning, he swung the door wide. Two men stood on the step. One, in a black shirt and jeans, with tattoos like sleeves on his arms, was either on steroids or spent far too much time pumping iron and looked like an inflated barrel with a beard. The other, taller by a head, wore beige slacks and a white long-sleeved shirt and resembled a sleazy accountant.

A souped-up red Holden ute with a rental company horse float attached was parked outside the gate on the road. He'd be very surprised if either of these two had ever handled a horse.

'Morning,' Oliver said. 'Got a problem?'

'No, mate,' said Shorty. 'We're looking for a horse and word is it's here.'

'A horse?'

'Yeah. Mind if we have a look? Your stable's locked.' The tall one smiled, revealing a space where an upper canine tooth should have resided. An accountant would have had that fixed and claimed it as a business expense.

'What's your horse look like?' Oliver forced a casual tone into his voice as a sudden awareness of danger flooded his body. These two thugs wouldn't think twice about belting information out of him.

'Brown. Big.'

Not a lot to go on. 'Mare or gelding?'

'Mare.'

'Brown and big? There are two horses here. One is mine and he's a bay gelding, the other is a chestnut ... you can have a look but the owner brought it here yesterday. Why are you looking for it?'

'It's our boss's horse.'

'I doubt it's the horse you're looking for. What makes you think it is?' Was it? He only had Krista's word for any of the information he had about Arch Rival. What if Angus had nicked the horse from a Mr Big? Was he that much of an idiot?

'Listen, mate, we've got no beef with you. Just open the stable and let us take the horse.'

'I'm sorry, but I can't let someone walk in and take an injured animal that's been left in my care. Wait a moment, please, I need to get dressed.'

Before either man could react, Oliver closed the door.

What the hell was this? Who was their boss? Some Mafia-type character? And what did they want with a horse? Krista Laatonen and her stepbrother had some questions to answer.

Should he phone Rupe or Shannon? Not yet.

He washed and dressed quickly then phoned Krista. He didn't think she was going to answer but too bad if she was asleep, she'd just have to wake up. After a lengthy wait, she said, 'Hello.' Slightly breathless. An image of pink flushed cheeks and partly opened lips flashed into his mind.

'Oliver Johnson, the vet, here. Sorry for waking you but there's a problem with your horse. Not medical, something else.' He added that on the off chance she was concerned.

'I wasn't in bed, I was swimming laps,' she replied tartly. 'And it's not my horse, remember?'

'I don't have a number for anyone else so you're it. There are two blokes here wanting to take Arch Rival. They reckon she's their boss's horse.'

'Who's their boss?'

'Probably the Godfather by the look of them.'

She cursed softly.

'What do you want me to do?' he asked.

'I don't know ... I ... It's bloody Angus.'

'That's as may be but these two aren't going to wait quietly out there for much longer. If they get rough I'm calling the police.'

'No. Don't do that.'

'Okay, so do I have your permission to let them take the horse?'

'No. I'll get Angus to come. Ask them to wait.'

'I can try. Don't know if they'll agree.' But he was talking to himself.

When he opened the front door, the dodgy-looking pair were having a smoke by the stable yard. Billy was stickybeaking again but if they thought they were going to lay hands on him they had another think coming.

'The owner's sorting this out. Someone's on their way'

They dropped their cigarette butts on the gravel and ground them out with their feet. Perhaps their attire was a uniform of some sort. Thug wear. The 'smarmy-one' line and the 'enforcer' line. Would they thump him if he asked them to pick up the butts?

'How long?'

'Fifteen, twenty minutes. Like a cup of tea?'

They exchanged a look.

The tall one said, 'Listen. mate, all you need to do is give us a look at the horse and if it's not the one we want we're gone.'

'How will you know if it's the one you want?' These two looked like they'd be hard pressed to sort a horse from a cow.

'Photo.' Smarmy pulled a phone from his pocket and scrolled for a minute. 'Here.'

Oliver looked. The horse was in a yard. A bright coppery chestnut mare, tall and elegant with no white socks. Arch Rival pre-accident and pre-wash.

'That's chestnut, not brown, and it's not the horse I have here,' he said. 'The one in my stable has a white hind fetlock.'

'Prove it.'

'Why should I?' hovered on his tongue but after a second's calculation he shrugged. 'Okay.' The sooner this pair left the better.

He took the key from his pocket and led them to the stable. As she'd done last night, Arch Rival snickered her welcome. He opened the half door so the thugs could have a look.

Smarmy studied the horse then the photo and handed the phone to his mate who did the same.

'What's your horse's name?' asked Oliver, although he knew before the reply came.

'Calypso Secret.'

'Meet Arch Rival,' he said.

'He's right. It's got a white foot,' said Shorty.

'Where's Calypso Secret?' asked the other one.

'No idea. I've never seen it, or this one, before yesterday. It's not local or I'd know it. Why don't you try The Grange? They have horses.'

'We will, but we'll wait here for the owner to show up first.'

'Okay, suit yourselves but I have work to do, if you'll excuse me.' Work, as in making breakfast. If he didn't have something now before the morning began in earnest, he'd be starving by ten.

'How about that tea?' Smarmy displayed his missing tooth in what passed as a smile.

'Take a seat.' Oliver pointed towards the old wooden bench along the wall of the office. No way was he letting them into his house.

'Got any coffee?' Shorty tried his own style of smile. He looked like a bulldog with its mouth open.

'Yeah.'

Oliver locked the stable and yard gate and strode back to the house.

***

Krista wrapped her towel around her waist and headed for the house. Damn

Angus and his idiocy. He could bloody well get out of bed and deal with this himself, injury or not. She charged inside and up the stairs to his room at the far end of the corridor to hers. The door was open. She marched in ready to deliver her ultimatum, but the bed was empty. Unslept in empty. The ensuite was cleared of personal paraphernalia, and when she looked into the walk-in robe most of his clothes had gone.

Angus had done a midnight flit. Krista ran back downstairs to the kitchen where Brandon, Hugh's private chef, was pottering about.

'Good morning, Brandon. Have you seen Angus this morning?'

'Morning, Krista. No, sorry. There's fresh coffee.'

'I'd love a cup, thanks. I'm on my way out so I'll have it while I change.'

Coffee and a warm croissant in hand, Krista ran upstairs.

Ten minutes later she was running back down again, and fifteen minutes after leaving The Grange, having planted her foot on the accelerator, she slowed to a law-abiding speed for the right turn into the main street of Taylor's Bend and then the left into Victoria Road.

A car and float blocked the vet's driveway so she pulled in to the side of the road. The gate was locked with chain and padlock. How was she supposed to get in? Climb over? Climb through the fence? She beeped the horn.

Two men appeared from the side of the stable, cigarettes in hand. The door to the house opened and Oliver came out. Krista waited by the gate as he walked across the yard.

'Hi,' he said. 'I thought your brother was coming.' He spoke quietly with none of the previous disdain and the frown on his face indicated concern. For her?

'He's gone.'

'Where?'

'I've no idea. He came home last night but when I went to wake him just now he'd gone. With most of his clothes.' She glanced over his shoulder at the two men. Oliver was right with his Godfather remark.

'Bastard.' He unlocked the gate and swung it wide enough for her to enter, then relocked it. 'How did he leave? His car's at Stuey's.'

'That's a work car, he took his Porsche. Who are those men?'

'A couple of thugs. I don't know what your brother was up to but he was tangling with some nasty types if these are a sample.'

'Why do they want the horse?' Thugs? What did that mean? They'd beat information out of her? She wasn't about to protect Angus but neither was she handing Calypso over to this pair.

'I don't know but they know Arch Rival isn't the right one.'

'And Calypso is?'

He nodded. 'I haven't told them anything. Just said I don't know either horse.' He started walking back towards the two men who were watching, smoking. A pair of guard dogs on alert.

'So they don't know where she is?'

'No.'

'What should I say?'

'Tell them you own this one and don't know anything else.'

'Thanks.' She meant it.

He flicked her a tight smile. 'Then you can tell me what the hell is going on.'

Before she could reply, he strode ahead. 'This is Miss Laatonen. She owns Arch Rival.'

Would they know her name and associate it with Angus? Too late.

The man in brown slacks held out his hand. 'Tony Griante, Miss Laatonen. Sorry to get you up so early but we hoped you could sort out this little problem for us.'

Krista grasped his hand firmly, staring down the familiar appraisal of her looks and body from the rodent-like eyes, pleased she'd grabbed a cotton skirt and T-shirt in her haste to dress, and not shorts and tank top. Another creep but this one looked nasty with it. And there was no recognition of her name, thank God.

'Good morning. I was up already. What seems to be the problem?'

'We understood a horse belonging to our boss was brought here yesterday. Calypso Secret.'

'So? My horse is Arch Rival.'

'That's what the vet said. We want to know where Calypso Secret is.'

'Why are you asking me?'

'We just wanted to verify that this is your horse.'

'Why? What right do you have to ask that? Besides, I thought the vet told you.'

'He did.'

'And why don't you believe him? I'm sorry, but this is ridiculous. I don't know who you are or what you're doing but it has nothing to do with me.'

She gave him her best glacial stare and he glanced at his sidekick, who'd stood impassive as a brick wall during the exchange, then back to her.

'If we find out you're lying, you'll be very sorry,' he said.

Krista turned her back on them and said to Oliver. 'Seeing as I'm here, how's Archie doing?'

He met her eyes and smiled, a little conspiratorial smile that warmed her heart.

'Come and have a look. I haven't had time to give her a thorough check yet what with ... one thing and another ... but she's got a bit of swelling on her upper hind leg. Must have hurt it somehow.'

She nodded. 'Okay. Thanks.'

'If you'll excuse us, please...' Oliver said to the silent pair. 'You can climb over the gate, can't you? The way you got in?'

Without a word, they turned and clumped towards their vehicle.

Oliver led her to the stables but he waited just inside the door to watch the men clamber over the gate and get into the ute. The engine started up and they were gone.

Krista exhaled loudly and sagged against the wall. 'My God! Who *were* they?'

'I'm sure your brother knows. Have you any idea where he is?'

'He's not my brother. I'm not related to him, not really. He's my stepbrother. I was hoping they wouldn't know my name in connection with him.'

'They didn't. Can't you call him?'

He eyed her, doubt clear in the raised eyebrow.

'I have, of course I have. He's not answering. Did you tell them Angus was involved?'

'They never mentioned him so I didn't. They must know he comes from The Grange so chances are they'll go there next.'

'Hugh will send them packing.'

'But if they start insisting Calypso belongs to their boss he'll say she belongs to you.'

'Oh!'

'You'd better warn him.' He stepped around her.

'I can't. He and Rod are out riding. Hugh never takes a phone with him. He'll be out for another hour. I think Rod was riding Calypso so she won't be there. None of the house staff or my mother know a thing about the horses and Mama won't be up yet. She wouldn't talk to them even if she was and the staff know not to talk to anyone about anything. They sign a nondisclosure agreement when they're employed.'

While she was speaking, Oliver walked along to Arch Rival's stall and began checking her injuries. 'Let's hope they give up,' he said over his shoulder.

Krista called Brenda, who wouldn't ask awkward questions, and gave her a brief rundown of the situation, finishing with, 'If they turn up, don't tell them anything. Say you don't know anything about the horses and don't let on Calypso is mine.'

'I don't know anything about the horses and Viivi will give them short shrift. You'd better get back here soon too.'

Krista joined Oliver. 'Is she all right?'

He straightened and ran his hand over the horse's back. 'Yes, she'll be fine. It's all minor injuries. She wants her breakfast.'

He didn't give any indication she should leave so after a moment's indecision, Krista followed him to a small room at the end of the shed, which housed feed bins, two saddles, bridles and a collection of halters and ropes. Oliver picked up two large buckets and ladled measures of chaff and grain into them. Four bales of hay were stacked against one wall. The smell of horse mingled with leather and dried grass. Not unpleasant. Krista stood watching from the doorway.

'I don't know why I'm covering up for Angus,' she said. 'Or why you are, for that matter.'

'I don't like being bullied and I'm not covering for the guy. I don't have the horse they want.'

'But you know who does. Me.'

Oliver hefted the buckets and walked back to Arch Rival's stall. She whickered in anticipation as he poured the mix into her feed bin.

'Yeah, well,' he said. 'I wasn't going to set those two onto you.'

'Why not? You think I'm involved in whatever it is, don't you?'

He continued outside to where his horse was waiting impatiently, straining over the fence then stamping its foot and turning in a small circle.

'Calm down, Billy boy,' he said. It stuck its head into the bin before he'd finished pouring the feed and he pushed it away. 'Wait a minute, greedy.'

The horse wheeled away in impatience.

He quickly emptied the bucket. Job done, he turned.

'Look. Yesterday I didn't know what to think. Today ... well, it's pretty clear you know as much as I do, which is next to nothing, and your bro ... stepbrother,' he amended, 'has cleared out and left you holding the baby. I reckon you should call the police.'

'I can't do that. Hugh would be furious. Anyway, what would I say? No-one's done anything illegal as far as I know.'

Oliver shrugged. 'Are you going to tell your stepfather?' He started towards the storeroom. Krista followed. She was like a dog trailing after him. Annoying him? Hard to tell.

'I asked him what Angus was up to yesterday and he brushed me off. Said he'd take care of it.'

'So he knows what's happening?'

'I don't think so, but he wouldn't tell me even if he did. To him I'm a brainless bimbo and Angus can do no wrong.' Try as she might she couldn't keep the wobble from her voice. It shouldn't hurt but it did.

Oliver stacked the empty buckets and closed the door. His eyes flicked her way, lingered for a moment. 'Come and help me feed the patients,' he said.

'What patients?'

Lines crinkled the tanned skin around his eyes and mouth as he smiled. 'Come on.'

He took her into the surgery building, through the waiting room. Posters about dental care for pets, flea and tick treatment, grooming, snake identification and a large poster of dog breeds adorned the walls. The receptionist's counter held more flyers with information about pet care and also upcoming community events. She'd never been part of a community. Never belonged anywhere.

Oliver disappeared through one of the side doors and down a corridor to the rear of the building. It was larger than it appeared from the front. The room she stood in had cages along one wall, mostly empty but for two sad-looking dogs and a sleepy cat.

'That's Joey, he's feeling a bit sorry for himself. He's been desexed,' he said indicating a Dalmatian. 'He's going home today.'

'Poor boy.' The sorrowful brown eyes gazed at her reproachfully but his tail gave a tiny thump when she stroked his head through the bars.

'And this is Tiger, he had a tooth out.' A kelpie with a swollen jaw wagged his tail at the sound of his name.

The ginger cat barely lifted its head. 'Poor old Ginger Megs has a brain tumour. I'm going to tell the owners today. She's paralysed down one side of her body and she'll have to be euthanised.'

'How sad.'

'Yes, it's the worst part of the job. But she's nineteen and wouldn't survive an operation so major.'

Oliver washed his hands then prepared two bowls with food. 'Could you give these to the dogs, please? Red one is Joey, blue is Tiger. He's on mush. I'll take care of Ginger Megs.'

Krista did as she was told, carefully depositing the bowls inside the cages without letting the occupants escape. Not that they tried. Their breakfast was more interesting.

'Do you have many animals staying over, usually?'

'It varies. I never know what's going to come through the door.'

'It must be really interesting.'

'I love it.' He led her back to the reception area.

'Have you been here long?'

'Nearly five years.'

'How do you manage by yourself?'

'I could do with an assistant, actually. It's getting to the point where I need another pair of hands. Margie is on reception from eight till one, and till five some days. A local girl, Sandy, comes in to help, mainly in the afternoons. If I'm doing a difficult surgery I call on Rob Blackwell from Willoughby to help out. We share a vet nurse. She comes over on surgery days. You can wash your hands in the sink,' he added.

Krista turned on the tap. 'I met Sandy yesterday at The Grange. She's nice.'

Sandy's comment about Oliver's number one eligible bachelor status made her stifle a laugh.

'She is.' Oliver handed her a towel. 'What's funny?'

'Nothing.' She glanced at the clock hanging over the door. Six-fifty. 'I'd better go.' Oddly, she'd much rather stay, but Oliver would be busy. He was probably waiting for her to leave.

'Yes, I have to go out on a call.'

'This early?'

'It's one I had to put off because of yesterday's accident.'

'Oh right. I'm sorry.' He didn't sound cross but she felt guilty, which was silly.

'It's not your fault.'

'No but...'

'Krista, don't take the blame for something your stepbrother has done.'

'I...'

'I'll open the gate for you.'

'Thanks.' Defeated, she followed him outside.

He unlocked the padlock and swung the gate wide.

'See you later,' he said but it was the usual casual goodbye, not a promise, not an expectation or a desire for more contact.

'Goodbye.'

'Arch Rival can go home today if you can organise it.'

'Oh. Yes, of course. I'll let you know.'

'Leave a message with Margie at reception.' He smiled blandly.

'Right, thanks.' She stood for a moment. Was there more to say? She felt there was, but what? She had to leave. Right now. He was waiting. He was in a hurry. But he wasn't moving either.

'See you,' he said and turned away.

Chapter 4

Krista drove back to The Grange more slowly than she'd left. She approached the house half-expecting to see the red ute with the float parked by the stables, but it wasn't and all was quiet.

She left the car in the shade and went into the house where Lola ran to meet her with the usual burst of yapping.

'Shut up.'

In no mood for such a shrill greeting, Krista ignored her and headed for the morning room and more coffee. Dappled sunlight streamed through floor-to-ceiling windows onto the slate floor, masked by the leafy trees in the garden outside. Deceptively simple but wildly expensive Scandinavian blond wood chairs with red and white cushions and a round table, along with potted flowering plants and sketches of horses on the wall, gave the room a casual, comfortable air. Brenda sat alone, eating toast.

'Hello, what's been going on?'

'I've no idea.' Krista took a seat and poured herself coffee.

'Would you like eggs? Toast?'

'I had a croissant earlier.'

'That's not enough.' Brenda frowned. 'Gemma,' she called.

The maid appeared.

'Scrambled eggs, please, for Krista.'

'Of course, anything else?'

'More coffee, I think. Thank you.'

'It's like being in a hotel, staying here,' Krista said.

'I know. Hugh likes his familiar routine wherever he goes. What happened this morning?'

'Angus has gone, did you know?'

'Gone where?'

'I don't know, but he's packed up and disappeared. His bed was empty when I went to wake him.'

Brenda drew in a deep breath, released it slowly. 'That'll go down well.'

'I know. Is Hugh back yet?'

'No. I wonder if Rod knows.'

'Probably not. Angus would have snuck out after they left and I was in the pool. His car's gone. I had a quick look when I left this morning.'

'Those men haven't turned up. Who were they?'

'One was called Tony Griante. The other one looked like the enforcer—all muscles and tattoos but no brain. They were scary.'

'I doubt they'll confront Hugh.'

'Maybe not. I've no idea who their boss is but he'd be something to do with gambling, for sure. Angus must owe him a lot of money.'

'Hugh will be furious.'

'So will Mama. It'll spoil her party if the Mafia turns up.'

'Are they Mafia?'

'I don't know. I'm not up on who's who in the world of crime. Angus goes to casinos, though, so who runs them?'

'Biker gangs have a lot of control.'

'They didn't look like bikers.'

'Why would they want a horse?' asked Brenda.

Krista waited while Gemma slid a plate of eggs in front of her and topped up her coffee from a fresh pot.

'Thank you.'

Gemma cleared away the used toast plate and knife and withdrew.

'I've no idea,' Krista said. 'But Angus clearly tried to palm off Arch Rival as Calypso. Maybe he promised them a horse instead of money he doesn't have.'

'And when he crashed he didn't turn up for the exchange,' Brenda said.

Krista nodded. 'So they came to get her and didn't find her. But they know where she comes from. Here.'

'Is that horse worth very much? I mean it wouldn't be anywhere near a million, would it?'

'Don't know but I doubt it. Hugh wouldn't have given her to me if she was.'

'You'll have to tell Hugh.'

'I tried to but he brushed me off. I should leave too. Leave him to deal with it. He said he would.'

'I doubt he knows exactly what Angus has been doing but doesn't like to admit it. He thinks putting him out here running The Grange is keeping him out of trouble.'

'Big fail. He has a massive blind spot where Angus is concerned.'

The eggs were done perfectly with a creamy texture she could never manage. Krista ate a few mouthfuls, debating the wisdom of bringing up the next subject.

'Mama and Hugh don't seem very happy together. Are they, do you think?'

'Krista, I can't discuss that sort of thing.'

'No, I know but they seem to fight all the time.'

'This party is a strain. Viivi is always tense when she's organising something, you know that. She didn't want to have it out here and she hates the heat. Always has.'

'I know. Why did they choose to have it here?'

'It was Hugh's decision.'

And what Hugh said went. Like son, like father. The women in their lives were to be seen and not heard; decorative, smiling, obedient but silent. Why did Viivi gravitate to men like that? Was her first husband, Krista's father, the same? She'd never know. He died in a fiery crash on the Formula One circuit when Krista was three. The newspaper clipping she'd read years later said 'An up-and-coming Finnish racing driver, Ilke Laatonen left a *beautiful young widow and small daughter'*, but didn't say the widow was accustomed to mixing with the wealthy aficionados of the European circuit and determined to stay there. He left most of his money to his little daughter in a trust fund. Perhaps he knew his young wife had expensive tastes and her daughter would always come second.

It took Viivi just one year to find a replacement in husband number two, Italian fashion entrepreneur, Marco Van Zetti. Five years later she was on husband number three, American billionaire, Jason Hodges. He had the effrontery to leave her for a younger woman, one of many he had on tap, but a woman who wanted children. Viivi always made it clear one child was plenty and she'd already done that.

For a few years she decided three husbands was enough, she'd remain single. Then along came Hugh Littlejohn, big and boisterous with an attractive Australian accent and most importantly, lots of money. For teenage Krista it seemed, for a while, he could possibly be the father she'd never had. But he wasn't. He was generous and kind but his son Angus was his priority. She sometimes wondered what it would have been like had she been a boy.

This marriage had lasted longer than any of the others but it was creaky.

Brenda said, 'Don't worry, Krista. Viivi won't walk out on him. They're flying to Tokyo on Monday. She loves Tokyo.'

'Tokyo? I didn't know that.'

'Oh yes, it's been in the calendar for weeks. Hugh has meetings there and then they're skiing in the Japanese ski fields for two weeks.'

'Are you going with them?'

'Yes. Excuse me. I have to get to work.'

Krista finished her breakfast slowly, enjoying the quiet. Lola came in and sat by her chair. What were they doing with Lola while they were away? She couldn't go with them or she'd be quarantined for ages when they came home. Perhaps she'd be staying in the Sydney house. Or here.

'You could become a farm dog,' she said, looking down. 'Running about outside.'

Lola panted and stood up, wagging her tail.

'Do you want to go outside?'

The wagging increased. Krista pushed her chair back. 'I need to go upstairs first.'

Five minutes later, she and her excited little follower stepped out onto the lush, manicured green of the back garden where a man in a battered straw hat and khaki shorts was moving slowly along a row of rosebushes in full magnificent bloom, clipping and tidying and dropping the refuse into a wheelbarrow.

Lola raced across the grass and back again then stopped and rolled over, to jump to her feet and start running again.

'Good morning,' Krista said.

The man gave her a cursory glance. 'Morning.'

'The roses look beautiful.'

'Helps if you've got water,' he said. It sounded vaguely like an accusation.

'Where does the water come from? Is it town water out here?'

'Hardly. Wouldn't be allowed to water the garden if it was. Water rationing,' he said when he saw she didn't understand. 'Only house use and hand watering the garden. You probably don't have to bother in the city.'

'Yes we do,' she replied, stung by the implication city people guzzled more than their share of the water. 'We had very strict rationing a few years ago.'

'It's bore water here and tank water for the house.'

'Do you live in Taylor's Creek?'

'Yeah. I come out here every two weeks but there's some big do on so the boss wanted extra done.' He spat into the grass.

'The garden looks lovely.'

He scanned the area. 'It'll do, I reckon.'

'Do you know Oliver Johnson, the vet?'

'Why?'

'No reason, I met him yesterday, that's all.'

He squinted at her from under the hat. 'He's a good bloke.'

'Yes.'

Gemma, the maid, appeared on the wide, slate-covered terrace. 'There's a truck out the front with the marquee and chairs,' she said. 'I can't find Brenda.'

'I guess they go out here,' said Krista. She smiled at the gardener but he'd already returned to his job.

She called, 'Come on, Lola. Fun's over.'

***

Krista didn't see Hugh until lunchtime so busy was she with the disposition of multitudes of white chairs and tables. Fortunately Brenda appeared with a table arrangement plan and instructions as to the position of the marquee, so it all had to be done only once by the taciturn pair from the hire company. According to them their job was delivery. not erection of the marquee and tables, which Krista had assumed was the case. A phone call to the boss and the offer of extra cash changed their minds but not their attitudes.

Viivi wandered through the garden in time to see the final chairs put in place and to exclaim how pleased she was that at least the guests wouldn't be left standing for hours, but that some of the tables need to be moved.

'Could you take care of it, please?' she asked the nearest of the two delivery men.

'Sorry, love, you'll have to do it yourself, we're late for the next job as it is.' He turned his sweat-stained, green T-shirted back and the pair headed for the truck muttering to each other that, 'the whole bloody schedule was off now.'

'Well! What a very rude man.' Viivi turned to Brenda. 'I want a discount from that company for not completing the job.'

'Their job was to deliver the things, not spend hours setting it all up,' said Krista. 'I had to give them extra in cash to do what they did.'

Viivi waved her arms, silver bracelets jangling. 'I told Hugh we should have this party in Sydney, not out here where everything is difficult or not available.'

'It's done now,' said Brenda. 'And the garden looks lovely.'

'Hmmm.' Viivi grudgingly cast her eye around the area. 'Not bad, I suppose.'

'The guests will be entering through the gate, rather than going into the house when they arrive, so you should be out here to greet them.'

'Very well,' said Viivi.

'Did you know Angus has gone?' asked Krista as she walked with her mother back into the house.

'Has he?'

'He's in some sort of trouble.'

'Just as well he's gone then, isn't it? I don't want any of his messes spoiling the party.'

'No.'

Would Tony Griante and his mate have the balls to turn up in the middle of the big event and start causing trouble? They'd be more likely to wait. They were probably discussing what to do next with whoever the big boss is. Or they'd give up on Calypso and go after Angus. Whatever happened, it was nothing to do with her. Hugh could do as he said yesterday—handle it himself.

At lunch Hugh was taciturn, and told Krista in no uncertain terms to mind her own business when Angus was mentioned.

'I told you I'd handle it.'

'Do you know where he is?'

He breathed in heavily and shoved a forkful of potato salad into his mouth.

'Just leave it, Krista,' her mother said.

'It's hard to leave it when I get threatened by a couple of thugs,' she retorted.

Hugh's eyes narrowed. 'Who? When was this and what did they say?'

'That if I was lying to them I'd be very sorry.'

'You weren't so there's nothing to worry about.' He resumed eating.

'They'll come here next,' she said.

'And I'll deal with them.'

'Fine.'

'After lunch I want you to look over the lunch menu with me, Krista,' her mother said. 'I'm not happy with the entrees.'

Krista caught Brenda's eye and looked away quickly before she laughed.

***

Oliver checked on Arch Rival when he finished morning surgery. She was pleased to see him and rubbed her head on his chest when he patted her neck. Margie had reported no phone calls from The Grange in regard to collecting her, which didn't surprise him.

He let the horse into the yard and Billy immediately trotted across the paddock to say hello. He left them getting to know each other over the wooden railing. Margie was closing up for her lunchbreak when he went back into the surgery.

'Karen Boyd is coming in this afternoon at two to be with Ginger Megs when you put her down.'

Oliver nodded. 'She took the news well.'

'Life and death is part of country life.'

'It's still sad.'

'Yes, but you can't let the poor old thing suffer.'

'No. So we'll have no animals staying over now the dogs have gone home. I might get tennis in this evening.'

'Apart from that horse,' Margie said. 'Nothing like free board and lodging.'

'If no-one has called by the end of the day I'll phone the woman again.'

'Surely they've more than one horse float at that place, or someone could ride it home. Typical rich people. Sponge off the rest of us who work to make ends meet when they can perfectly well afford to pay their bills but choose not to. That's how they get rich.' Margie shook her head in disgust. 'See you later.'

Oliver went to the house to make his own lunch, after which he'd get the cello out for some practice before Karen arrived.

***

Krista powered up and down the pool early on Friday morning, churning through the water in an attempt to put the embarrassing phone call from Oliver out of her mind. He rang while Hugh and her mother were having a pre-dinner drink last night, wanting to know when someone would collect Arch Rival.

'I'm sorry, I forgot,' she said to him. 'We've been busy here organising a party.'

Silence greeted that remark.

'I'll put Hugh on,' she said when it became obvious he wasn't going to say anything. 'Angus isn't back yet.'

'Fine.'

She took the phone to Hugh, sitting out on the terrace with a whisky in his hand.

'The vet wants a word about your horse,' she said.

He took the phone. 'Hugh Littlejohn. What can I do for you?'

A frown appeared as he listened. 'It's not convenient at the moment. We'll be up to our ears out here with guests all weekend. Keep her till Monday and someone will pick her up then.'

Oliver must have objected because he growled, 'If it's money you're worried about, don't. Send me your account and I'll see it gets paid.'

Krista remembered the notice she'd seen at the reception desk. *Payment due at time of appointment.* Small businesses like Oliver's couldn't operate on credit, even she knew that.

Hugh handed her the phone. He hadn't disconnected Oliver.

'Hello?' Krista went inside.

'He made himself pretty clear.'

'I'm so sorry. I'll talk to Rod about it.'

'What is it with you people? All you do is pass the problem off onto someone else. Doesn't anyone take responsibility for anything in your family? Meanwhile I'm treating, feeding and housing your horse and I'd like to be paid.'

'I'm sorry. I'll come in tomorrow and fix the account.'

And she'd rung off quickly before he could hit her with any more home truths. His question and the disgust in his voice kept her awake most of the night. He was right—her family didn't face up to their responsibilities. Viivi never did, Krista being one of them. Viivi had preferred to find a rich husband and employ someone to deal with the inconvenient truth of her small daughter.

Angus either ran away from his responsibilities or called on Hugh. Hugh dealt with his problems at arm's length through money and influence. She herself? She had no responsibilities except to herself and she hadn't faced up to that either. With no clear goal or ambition, she'd allowed her mother to dictate her actions and shape her life and in this current situation, knowing how Angus and Hugh would react, she'd fobbed the responsibility for the horse off onto Oliver.

She came to rest at the deep end of the pool, breathing hard. The sun was just breaking over the roof of the house but its rays hadn't reached the side where the pool was. Another scorcher today. Not a cloud to break the relentless heat. No sign of rain. It hadn't occurred to her the area might be in drought conditions, not until the gardener mentioned it. No wonder the locals had a poor impression of the new owners of The Grange. Viivi would barely know what a drought was and would regard it as an inconvenience someone should fix, if she did.

Krista hauled herself out and padded across the already warm tiles towards the house. Lola came to greet her and she bent to scratch the silky head. The little dog seemed to have formed an attachment to her yesterday after spending the morning running about outside while all the chairs and tables were set up. Viivi didn't like Lola to go out because it made her dirty, and if there was one thing Viivi hated it was dirt. Lola, of course, loved nothing better than to sniff about in the flowerbeds and roll on the grass.

Lola wasn't so bad, in fact she was good company. Maybe she should offer to mind her while Hugh and her mother were away. She'd help to fill her suddenly empty days.

'Want to stay with me next week, Lola?'

A little yip came in response which she took as a yes. 'Okay. You're on.'

***

At nine-thirty, Krista pulled up in the vet's parking lot. His car was in the carport and a little yellow hatchback was parked under a tree. That would belong to his receptionist.

Arch Rival was in the yard attached to the stables. She hung her head over the railing, ears pricked, watching Krista approach. She really was a beautiful animal, elegance personified. Her coat gleamed coppery red in the bright sunshine but the one white sock stood out in stark contrast. Angus had taken a terrific risk with his paint job.

Krista rubbed tentative fingers down the smooth neck. 'Hello,' she said softly. Arch Rival nuzzled her arm. 'Want to go home?'

A warm horsey smell wafted into her nostrils—not unpleasant, more wholesome than anything. She turned away and walked across to the surgery.

The woman behind the counter was on the phone but she smiled and beckoned when Krista opened the door and peered in. Dark curly hair formed a riotous frame for a round, friendly face.

'Yeah, okay Phil,' she said into the phone. 'Oliver can get out there about eleven. I'll let him know. See you later.'

She hung up and immediately redialled. 'Hi. Phil Macklin just called about a goat with a stomach-ache. I said you'd be there about eleven.' She listened for a moment. 'No idea. Bye.'

She tapped furiously at her computer then looked up with another broad grin which belied the shrewd assessment from a pair of deep brown eyes.

'Krista Laatonen, I take it.'

'Yes.' Oliver wasn't here. Disappointment flooded through her, along with the realisation he wouldn't put off his calls just to be here when she came. This woman could take her money, it was her job and Krista was just another client. A nuisance client at that. Any link she might have thought had formed between them over the horse debacle was all in her head.

'Come to pay the account?'

'Yes. Can I use a card?'

'Sure.' She leafed through some accounts and handed the page to Krista then pulled out the credit card machine.

Krista ran her eye down the neat list of charges. Not an exorbitant total by any means. She'd spend more than that on clothes and shoes in a couple of weeks.

'Everything okay?' the woman asked with a touch of acid in her tone.

'Of course. It's very reasonable.'

'Yeah, well, Oliver's a very fair man. He doesn't overcharge.'

'No, I'm sure he doesn't.' She swiped the card hurriedly.

The woman handed her the receipt and stamped Paid on the account. 'Thanks for that. When can you collect the horse?'

'Oh. I thought Hugh Littlejohn arranged to pick her up on Monday. It's covered in the bill I just paid.'

'Did he? Okay. That's all done then.'

'Thank you.' Krista tucked the papers and credit card into her bag.

'Got a big party on this weekend, I hear.'

'Yes, Hugh and my mother's wedding anniversary.'

'Nice. Have fun.'

'It's not really my scene ... the guests are friends of theirs. I don't know them, most of them. I'd rather not have come.' She stopped in confusion. Why was she telling the woman any of this? Explaining herself, distancing herself from The Grange, knowing how unpopular it was with the locals.

'Family things can be like that. You go because she's your mum and she wants you to be there.'

'Yes, that's exactly right.' Krista smiled, although it wasn't really. Viivi wanted her to be there as a duty, not out of any great desire for her company as a daughter. 'We're all the family we've got. It's always been just the two of us.' And various stepfathers sailing in and out of her life.

'It's important then and you've done the right thing being here.'

'Thank you.'

'No worries.'

The phone rang and she picked it up, said, 'Sorry,' before answering.

Krista nodded goodbye and left.

Back at The Grange, she went straight to the stables to find Rod and give him the account and receipt for reimbursement. She found him in the office staring at the computer screen, a frown creasing his tanned face. He looked up. His mouth had a curiously attractive crooked twist when he smiled.

'Hi Krista, you've been out early.'

'Hi. I've just been in to Taylor's Bend to pay the vet's bill.' She handed over the papers and he glanced at the figures before putting the pages on his desk.

'Fair enough. I'll see you get the money back.'

'Thanks.' She dragged up a spare chair and sat down. 'Where's Amy? Mama said she was away.'

'She's in Sydney. Her sister has just had baby number three so Amy went to help out with the other two.'

Krista nodded. With no siblings and no close friends with children, the world of kids was a mystery to her. 'What's going on here, Rod? Where's Angus?'

'I really don't know.' He must have read the disbelief on her face that she thought was only in her head. 'I honestly have no idea where he is.'

'But you must know what he was doing with Arch Rival.'

'I knew he'd taken her out but I didn't know he was trying to pass her off as Calypso.' She snorted at that and he said, 'He doesn't tell me everything, you know. In fact he's been very secretive lately—bad-tempered, and if I asked him what was wrong he'd bite my head off and tell me to mind my own business.'

'Does Hugh know what he's up to?'

Rod grimaced and shrugged. 'No idea. I'm just the hired hand around here.'

Krista pursed her lips. Was he telling the truth? Hard to tell. She hadn't seen Angus for months.

'More importantly,' Rod indicated the computer screen. 'I was just looking at the weather map. There's a fire in the mountains that I'm keeping an eye on.'

'A bushfire?'

'Yeah. It's a fair way away but it's in inaccessible country so anything could happen.'

'But it wouldn't come here, would it?'

'It's always a possibility. It's been so dry and hot the whole area's ready to go up if the wind picks up and blows the wrong way.'

'Can't they water bomb it with those helicopters?'

'If it gets to be a problem, sure, but there's that big fire in Victoria taking priority.'

Was a distant bushfire more important than a threat from a couple of thugs or her mother's imminent party? Not at the moment.

Krista stood. 'I'd better go. Hugh's brothers are arriving today.' She pulled a face. 'Angus should be here to help entertain them. You might have to take his place and tell them about the horses.'

Rod sucked in air between tight lips. 'Such a pity. I've got lots to do out here. Can't spare the time to entertain guests.'

Krista laughed. 'Lucky you.'

'My job is with the horses.' He smiled but it faded quickly. 'Speaking of horses, I might have to call that vet in. Our stallion had a bit of nasal discharge and a cough this morning. I'll see how he is by lunchtime but I think he should be checked out.'

'Don't you use a different vet?'

'Yes, Angus's choice, but this bloke is closer and he seems good from what I hear from Sandy.'

'He is.'

Krista strolled back to the house. How would Oliver react to that phone call? He'd come for sure, because he cared about the animals, but The Grange wasn't top of his favourites list.

Chapter 5

Oliver had a quiet start to the weekend, devoid of animal disasters. Saturday morning surgery produced the usual queue of cats and dogs needing shots or minor attention and with no patients staying overnight, he and Margie were able to close up by midday.

He let Arch Rival out into the paddock with Billy. If she was staying till Monday she could stretch her legs and both horses would have some company. He watched the pair eye each other, sniff noses, then saunter off across the dry grass together, flicking their tails against the hovering flies.

Fine. Lunch first and then he'd start the weekly vacuuming and clean up. After that, with any luck, he'd fit in some cello practice. Pottering in the kitchen it occurred to him that The Grange mob would be entertaining today. How would that be going? According to Margie, Krista wasn't keen on it at all, which surprised him. She'd given the impression she was here to help her mother and get right into the whole upmarket party thing.

Margie amazed him, although he didn't show it, by saying, 'She's a bit of a lost soul, that girl.'

Lost soul? How on earth did she come to that conclusion after two minutes of interaction? Secret women's business, no doubt. A black hole to him. His mother kept her thoughts to herself and he had no sisters to initiate him.

Come to think of it, when the attractive and very beautiful Krista calmed down, she was a different person to the one he'd met at the accident site. A bit vulnerable underneath the brittle facade—but dangerous nonetheless.

He mustn't be distracted from the stark truth she was from another world entirely. Money, to her, came from a bottomless pit, as did people who did her bidding. She expected to be obeyed and her words to be treated as pearls. In that respect she was very like his father.

She was uncomfortable in the wilds of rural New South Wales and no doubt she'd be out of here as soon as the party was over. She'd already absolved herself of responsibility for the horse and one of the minions would be over on Monday to collect it.

He'd seen the last of the rather disturbing Krista Laatonen, which was a good thing. She was like an exotic and unattainable fantasy that if allowed full rein could become completely debilitating.

He'd done the bathroom but the phone rang while he was assembling the vacuum cleaner.

'Knew it was too good to be true,' he muttered as he went to pick up. Didn't even get the cleaning finished before someone needed him.

The voice was unfamiliar but the location wasn't. Rod Smythe, stable manager from The Grange.

Oliver listened to the man's precise description of the symptoms. Sounded like a cold or an allergy, but could be flu. Also sounded like someone who knew and cared for his horses.

'I'll be right out,' he said.

When he swung the car into The Grange driveway, a man in a dark blue security company uniform stepped forward from under a shade umbrella and flagged him down.

'Good afternoon, sir. This is a private function. Could I see your invitation and photo ID, please?'

'G'day, mate. I'm the vet. Rod Smythe called me in to see a horse.'

'Wait one moment, sir.'

He turned away, pulled out a walkie-talkie and spoke rapidly into it. Oliver waited. The man walked back to the car.

'We don't have any notification of your visit, sir.'

'That's because Rod only just called me twenty minutes ago. You can't predict when animals will get sick.'

'We only have your word for that, sir,'

'Call him and ask him.' Christ. He didn't have the time or the inclination to wait around in the heat while these bozos messed around. 'I'll be at the stables.'

Fortunately the ornate metal gate was open. He put the car in gear and continued on down the long driveway. In the rear-view mirror the failed security bloke was staring after him in the rising plume of dust, gesticulating with his radio pressed to his ear. Lucky he didn't have a gun. Or maybe he did. Ridiculous. Who was he protecting the place from? None of the locals gave a damn about The Grange and its inhabitants or guests.

Four luxury cars were parked neatly in the large open area in front of the stables. A man with the uniform shirt straining over his belly strode to meet him when he reached the house, alerted by the gatekeeper, no doubt. Oliver continued on to the stables.

The guard arrived panting and with sweat running in rivulets down his face. 'Sir, you'll have to step out of the car.'

'Okay.' He turned off the engine and got out. The sun belted down on his bare head. He'd left his hat on the passenger seat. 'Would you tell Rod, the stable manager, I'm here to see the stallion?'

'I'm waiting on confirmation of that. Mr and Mrs Littlejohn are the only people who can authorise guests who aren't on the list.'

'Right. I'm not a guest and I'm sure Rod didn't want to bother them with this. He said he'd be in the stables so you can come with me and ask him yourself.' Oliver opened the rear door and retrieved his bag.

'What's in the bag, sir?'

'Drugs.' He straightened and looked the man in the eye. 'I need to see the horse. Equine flu can be lethal. Do you want to be the one to tell the owner his horse died while you were asking the vet for ID and phoning people?'

The man hesitated but while his brain cell began working overtime on that problem, a voice said, 'Oliver Johnson? Thanks for coming straight out.'

Rod Smythe had the workworn hands and sun-battered skin of a man who worked outdoors. Tall and gangly, he had sinewy strength under the cotton shirt and jeans, evidenced by the grip in his handshake.

'G'day. Tell this guy who I am, will you?' Oliver jerked his head slightly.

'I'm just doing my job,' said the guard stiffly.

'Thanks. It's fine. I called the vet,' said Rod. He began walking to the stables. 'It might be nothing but I can't take any chances.'

'Of course not.'

'I've got him on his own at the far end.'

The cool dimness of the large high-ceilinged shed was welcome after the unrelenting glare of the yard. Two heads poked over the stall doors watching with interest as they approached.

'Is Calypso Secret here?' Oliver asked with a smile.

Rod shook his head. 'She's out in the paddock. How's Archie? I'm sorry about all that.'

'She's fine. Only minor abrasions and one cut over her eye. I put a couple of stiches in. Shouldn't leave a scar. It wasn't your fault. Was it?'

'I had no idea what Angus was up to. Still don't.' He sounded angry.

'His stepsister said the same thing.'

'There's no love lost there.'

'So I gathered.'

'Here's your patient. He's called Firebrand but we call him Fred.'

The big black stallion stood with his head drooping slightly but he flicked his ears and shuffled nervously when Oliver and Rod entered his stall.

'Is he quiet?' Stallions could be unpredictable.

'Yes, pretty good. Nips sometimes but he's not up to much at the moment.'

Oliver studied the horse. He was wheezing but not heavily, moisture around his nostrils indicated a clear discharge. Rod said he'd been sneezing and coughing occasionally.

'He's a beautiful animal.'

'Yeah, he's booked up solid for breeding.'

Oliver began his examination. After completing all his checks, he said, 'It's a cold. Is he outside much?'

'Yes, he's usually out but I bring them all in at night.'

'Keep him in for a few days and see how he goes. Keep him away from the others. Damp his feed a bit just before he eats to settle any dust and make it easy for him to eat. Call me straight away if you think he's any worse.'

'Okay, I've handled colds before. So you're sure it's not flu?'

'His temperature's almost normal. Any other horses affected?'

'Not that I've noticed.'

'Any new horses come in recently?'

'Two new mares. I guess one of them could have passed it on.'

'It's not too bad at the moment but we don't want it to get worse. At least it's warm weather for him.' Oliver patted Fred's neck. 'You'll be fine.'

'Come to the office,' said Rod, 'and I'll fix up the account.'

'Thanks. Would you like me to check these two horses before I go?'

'Would you? I don't want to take up your afternoon.'

'I'm here now. Won't take long.'

'Thanks.'

'Is there somewhere I can have a wash?'

'Sure. The washroom is just by the entrance. When you've finished, come through to the office.' He pointed to a door marked Office.

Oliver rejoined Rod with the news that the two mares showed no signs of illness. 'I don't need to tell you, I guess, but make sure you keep Fred quarantined and wash your hands after handling him and his feed.'

'Yep. Know the drill. Thanks, though. Like a beer before you go?'

'Thanks.'

'Take a seat.' Rod opened a small fridge and pulled out two chilled bottles. He handed one to Oliver and sank onto the chair behind the desk.

'Stinking weather we've been having,' he said after a long drink. 'Did you know there's a fire to the north?'

'No, I haven't seen any weather reports. Been busy.'

'It doesn't seem to be a problem for us but you never know.'

'Fire's always a worry.'

'Yeah. Specially if the wind picks up. You been in Taylor's Bend long?'

'About five years.'

'You like it?'

'Yeah. It's a nice place. Good community.'

'We go to Jindalee for the mail. Closer,' Rod said. 'Not much going on there though.'

'You should check out the Bend.'

'Yeah. You have a wife? Family?'

'No. You?'

'Wife, no kids yet. Amy's away at her sister's at the moment. She shops at the Taylor's Bend supermarket but she's not good at meeting people. Neither am I. We're flat chat out here, to tell you the truth. Hardly have time to scratch ourselves, and we're so tired at the end of the day we just want to crawl into bed.'

'I thought Angus lived here.'

'He shows up occasionally.' His expression gave no hint as to his opinion of Angus.

'Isn't he the manager of the place?'

'Yes, but Amy and I do all the work. Most of it,' he amended. 'A local girl comes in about once a week, and a gardener.'

'Sandy. She helps out at my surgery. Nice kid. Good with animals.' So the gossip wasn't entirely accurate. Two Bend residents did have work here and the stable manager was a good bloke and knew his job. He wasn't avoiding the Bend, he and his wife were just too knackered to socialise. He knew what that felt like. Oliver looked at the clock on the wall above the fridge.

Close to four. 'I'd better get going. Thanks for the beer.'

'You're welcome. Thanks for coming.'

***

Krista was enjoying the family lunch as much as she'd expected to. Hugh's brothers and their wives were friendly enough but talked of things she either knew nothing about or wasn't interested in. Her mother's closest friend, Gwen, and her husband, Felix, had been invited but Gwen and Krista had never been on more than cordial terms, and the few occasions when she'd met Felix he'd made it clear he'd be up for a cosier relationship, something Brenda said he was well-known for. That also went for Hugh's brother Edgar but he knew better than to try anything under Hugh's roof.

None of the five offspring of Hugh's siblings had accepted the invitation. Three lived overseas and the other two were estranged from their father. Angus hadn't reappeared and, as far as Krista knew, hadn't been heard from either.

If Hugh was concerned about his son, he gave no indication and deflected enquiries as to his whereabouts with the statement that Angus, unfortunately, was away on business. 'Couldn't be helped,' he said with a shrug. 'You know how it is.'

Not that any of them gave a damn whether Angus was there or not.

Krista smiled and spoke when she was spoken to, ate and drank and was politeness itself. Brenda had made sure she wasn't seated next to either Felix or Edgar so, because of Angus's absence, she had her other step uncle, Robert, on one side and Edgar's wife Shirley on the other, neither of whom took much notice of her.

After dessert was served and coffee was brought in, Krista excused herself and escaped. She heaved a vast sigh of relief outside the dining room and wandered out to the rear terrace for some fresh air. It was scorchingly hot with hardly a breath of wind when she stepped from the air-conditioned house. She shaded her eyes and scanned the cloudless sky for signs of smoke from the fire Rod had mentioned. Nothing.

Lola appeared and pattered to the open door but didn't venture out.

'Too hot for you.' Krista went inside and pulled the sliding door closed. With the little dog following at her heels, she headed for the stairs and her room. The main party was kicking off at four, which gave time for a rest before having to change and the guests began to arrive.

She wasn't sure what woke her. A sudden noise of some sort. A car engine accelerating away. Lola barking downstairs. Krista sat up, head heavy, clammy-skinned and disoriented. It was late. Twenty to four. Yawning, she went to the bathroom. She'd have to be quick but her make-up was minimal in this heat, and she never wore much anyway because her skin was so fine and unblemished thanks to her Finnish heritage. Fifteen minutes later she emerged, awake, refreshed and ready to slip on the plain Arctic blue silk dress with the modest neck and hemline. She'd brought the silver evening dress as well but it had a low-cut neck and bare shoulders as well as a figure-hugging long skirt. Hotter to wear despite the spaghetti straps.

She'd given quite a bit of thought to the two choices. Mama would say the blue silk was plain, but with a two-thousand-dollar price tag she wasn't wearing a sack and no way was she giving the rich old men with a sense of entitlement, roving hands and lecherous eyes any encouragement.

Some sort of confrontation was going on outside. The front door stood wide open and Hugh's imperious voice echoed through the foyer.

'Why do you want to speak to my stepdaughter?'

Frowning, Krista ventured forward. A black limousine was parked outside, only partially visible from where she stood. Who was it? Where were Viivi and the other guests? Where was Brenda?

Another voice sounded, low and insistent. Familiar?

'You can speak to me,' said Hugh.

'Mr Moran would like to speak to your stepdaughter.'

The two men were out of her line of sight but now she could hear more clearly as the visitor spoke. It was the man who claimed Calypso belonged to his boss, the thin one with the Italian name. A chill scampered over her body, raising goosebumps on her bare arms. He knew she'd lied, he'd said she'd be sorry. Very sorry. For the first time she could remember, she was glad of Hugh's authoritative manner. He didn't take kindly to demands at the best of times and this was not one of those.

A car door opened and closed with a low click.

'Good afternoon, Hugh,' said a new voice.

'Stefan. What's this about? Why are you here?'

'You know why I'm here.'

'Do I? I don't think so.' But he'd lost some of the arrogance. Who was Stefan?

'Would it be possible to talk inside out of this heat?' The visitor spoke mildly, with the confidence of someone who is always obeyed.

'I'm expecting guests any minute.'

'I won't take up much of your time.'

Footsteps sounded on the tiles, shadows eclipsed the glare from outside. Krista had no time to hide. She had to brazen it out.

The man who preceded Hugh was slim, a head shorter and several years younger than her stepfather, but with a presence that radiated control like a stalking tiger. Calm, relaxed but focused, constantly alert. Intent on the result he expected, whatever that was. To punish her?

His eyes landed on Krista.

'Miss Laatonen. What a pleasure to meet you.' He held out a pale hand in greeting. She shook the cool fingers briefly.

'How do you do.' Her eyes flicked to Hugh and back to the man who had so easily and quietly inserted himself into the house.

He said, 'Thank you, I am very well. I'm a business associate of both your brother and your father. My name is Stefan Moran.'

Forcing a sociable smile, Krista took a step back. 'We're serving drinks on the terrace. It's still terribly hot, but there are shade umbrellas and those who can't take the heat can stay indoors.'

'Thank you,' He inclined his head.

'Stefan isn't a guest,' said Hugh.

'Oh. I'm so sorry. I didn't realise.'

Moran smiled. 'A cool drink would be most welcome.' He turned to Hugh. 'While we discuss the matter I came for.' Back to Krista. 'Perhaps you will join us?'

'I can give you a few minutes, Stefan.' Hugh led the way into the small drawing room to the side of the foyer. 'What can I offer you to drink?'

'Sparkling mineral water with a slice of lemon. Thank you.'

'Krista, please?'

When she returned a few minutes later with the chilled drink, the two men were engaged in an awkward chat about the weather, although Hugh seemed just as at ease as the visitor.

She handed Moran the glass. 'Thank you.' He took a small sip. 'I shall come straight to the point. Miss Laatonen, you lied to my men about the horse. Why was that?'

His tone was the same but his eyes had turned to stone.

'I had no idea who they were and why they would claim my horse. Any of The Grange horses for that matter.'

She returned his gaze with her own, ice-filled. 'They were quite aggressive.'

'The vet also lied.'

'He knew nothing about the horses.'

'We use a different vet. The man has never been here,' interjected Hugh.

'But you see, you are both still lying to me. The same man was here this afternoon seeing to one of your horses. I saw him myself come from the stables and my men confirmed he was the person they spoke to.'

'If that's true, it's the first time he's been here and I didn't know. Perhaps our regular man was unavailable. I'm not told every small detail that happens in the stables.' Hugh's voice had a tinge of anger now. 'What the hell is this about, Stefan? What are my horses to do with you? All the horses you're talking about belong to The Grange and therefore indirectly to Krista. She told me what happened. How dare you or your men threaten her.'

Moran placed the glass precisely on the small table by his chair. 'Your son Angus has somewhat of a gambling problem. He owes me a large sum of money, which he seems unwilling to repay. He promised me he would but he has failed to make any of the deadlines we agreed. He offered a horse, Calypso Secret, as part payment. I understand her bloodline is very good and one of her foals fetched nearly half a million recently.'

Krista stifled the urge to gasp. Did Hugh know that when he gave her Calypso? Did he know anything about his investment in The Grange? Surely Rod knew, and Angus must.

'Calypso Secret is not my son's horse to give away.'

'That's not my concern.' Moran stood up. 'I want my money, Hugh, and in the absence of your son, I will expect his family to honour the debt.'

'I will not pay my son's debts and he knows it. You will have to pursue him if you want your money.'

'Where is he?'

'I don't know. He left here the day after the accident.'

Moran's eyes narrowed. He studied Hugh and then swung his attention to Krista. 'I am sorry you and your vet friend have become involved in this but you have insulted my intelligence by lying to me. If this debt is not repaid by five pm Monday there will be consequences you will not like. For you and your friend. I will see myself out. Enjoy your party.'

Hugh strode forward and flung the door open, making sure Moran left the house. Krista followed on shaky legs. The black limousine slid from view.

'Who *is* that man, Hugh?' she asked.

'He owns a string of casinos and nightclubs, amongst other less legitimate business dealings.' His jaw tightened.

'He's a gangster, you mean? A criminal?' Oliver was right when he made that remark about the Godfather.

'Yes. God knows why Angus got himself mixed up with him, the bloody idiot.'

'Will he hurt me, or the vet? Oliver was just trying to protect me.'

'He's a ruthless man, Krista.'

'Will you pay him?'

'I'll find Angus first.'

'But he doesn't have the money or he wouldn't have promised him Calypso.'

Viivi's voice cut off his response. 'Hugh, our guests are arriving, what are you doing in here? And Krista, you should be out there mingling. I can't do everything myself.'

'Coming, my love.'

Hugh squeezed Krista's arm gently but it wasn't affectionate. 'Invite your friend the vet. I'd like to meet him,' he said in a low voice.

'To warn him? He should know, don't you think?'

'If he saw Moran's men as he left, he'll already know.'

'He won't come.'

'Make him. I want to thank him.'

Hugh strode away to where Viivi was fidgeting and fuming in the doorway.

'It's always business with you, isn't it?' she said. 'Even when we're celebrating our anniversary. Couldn't you put me first for once? Krista, come. You're needed.'

'Krista has to make a phone call first. Another guest.'

'Who?'

'A friend of hers. I asked her to invite him.' He took her arm. 'Now, my darling, let's greet our guests.'

'Is that what you're wearing, Krista?' Viivi asked. 'Surely you have something better than a housedress. You could make a bit of effort for my sake.'

Krista went upstairs to change and make the call she really didn't want to make. Why on earth did Hugh want to meet Oliver? Even as she asked herself the question, she knew the answer. Hugh liked control. He wanted all the pieces in place so he could evaluate their usefulness or otherwise. Oliver was a pawn in this affair thanks to her and she had no doubt he wouldn't be thanking her for it.

Chapter 6

After phoning Oliver, Krista took her time changing. To her surprise he was coming. She needed to look her best and the blue dress wasn't up to the task. No rush now. She took off the offending silk number and showered again, standing under the cascade of warm water while her body recovered from the shock of Moran and his threats. She changed her underwear to suit the slim fitting long dress and slipped on the right shoes. Her phone rang as she was smoothing the silver fabric over her hips and checking her reflection in the full-length mirror on the wardrobe door.

A little twinge of disappointment made her shoulders sag as she picked up the mobile. Oliver? Cancelling and using a sick cow as an excuse?

That was mean, he wouldn't lie to her. If he hadn't wanted to come he would have refused and if a cow was sick of course he'd go.

'Hello.'

'It's Angus.'

'Where the hell are you?' Why did he sound so calm? What was he up to? And where?

'At the airport.'

'Which airport?'

'Melbourne. I'm flying out in a few minutes. I just rang to tell you I took your apartment keys.'

'Is that where you've been? At my place?'

Took her keys? She hadn't noticed because her car had keyless entry and she'd zipped the bulky key into a separate part of her bag to reduce the keys on the key ring. The conniving...

'Yes, listen, will you? I've posted them to The Grange.'

'Well, thank you very much. Have you any idea what's been happening here thanks to you? Your friend Stefan Moran sent his thugs to threaten me and take Calypso, then when I refused, with the help of the vet who discovered your stupid plan to paint Arch Rival's foot, Moran turned up just now and threatened all of us, including Hugh, if we don't pay your debt by Monday at five.'

'What did Dad say?'

'No. What did you expect him to say? How much do you owe this man?'

'A fair bit.'

'Meaning?'

'Nine hundred thousand.'

'What? You complete idiot. How dare you run away and leave us to deal with this?'

'I'm getting the money, I promise.'

'How? More gambling? We have till Monday and Hugh and my mother are leaving for Tokyo on Monday. That leaves me and the vet, who by the way has nothing to do with this at all but you've dragged him into it, to be punished by Moran in your place.'

'He won't do anything to you.' He didn't sound convinced and she certainly wasn't. 'I'll get the money, Krista. You can tell Moran that.'

'And he'll believe me, of course. Just before one of his heavies breaks my fingers. Where are you going?'

A voice sounded in the background, coming over a PA system. She caught the word Auckland, or thought she did. He was leaving the country.

'Better you don't know. I have to go.'

He disconnected. The total bastard! Not even a goodbye or a sorry.

She stomped into the bathroom to redo her make-up.

***

Oliver drove back out to The Grange wondering why he'd accepted Krista's invitation. He couldn't deny curiosity was the main reason. Curiosity about The Grange and its owners. He wanted to meet Hugh Littlejohn and he wanted to ask him a few pertinent questions about the men who'd threatened Krista and who had turned up this afternoon, presumably as guests, as he was leaving. He wanted Littlejohn to make it clear to these people he was in no way connected with anything his family might be involved in, and he wanted the man's assurance of that.

If treating Firebrand was going to implicate him in some way, he would refuse to come out again and they could call in their regular man.

Whether any of that would wash with a billionaire he had no idea. Probably not, in which case why was he showered, shaved and in his best shirt and pants with a nervous flutter in his belly? The other reason and one he also couldn't deny, was Krista.

When he heard her voice on the line, the rush of pleasure it brought was unstoppable. She'd sounded hesitant and awkward, unusually so for her. It sounded as though she assumed he'd refuse and she even said as much, finishing the invitation with, 'Hugh wants to meet you and thank you for treating his horses.'

So if that were true, it was Hugh's idea, not hers, which was a whole different scenario. The hole in that scenario, however, was that when he'd phoned about the account Hugh was hardly grateful enough to invite him anywhere.

'Do you want me to come?' Oliver asked her.

'I owe you,' she said.

'You've paid my account.'

'Not that, I mean you helped me and...'

He waited.

'I would like you to come.'

He hesitated just long enough to make her uncomfortable. 'Okay. What time?'

'Whenever you're ready. Guests are here now. Dinner is at eight.' The relief washed through the connection.

'Do I need a tie?'

'Have you got one?' He visualised her smile.

'Of course. Just the one.'

'No need. It's too hot. Be comfortable.'

'Right. And thank you.'

'You're welcome.'

The same bozo was at the gate, checking names. He scowled when Oliver wound down the window. Beads of sweat ran down his face and the white shirt had dark stains under the arms.

'G'day. Remember me?'

'Name?'

'Johnson, Oliver. Vet.'

'ID?'

Oliver pulled out his driver's licence. The man glared at it, grunted and made a show of running his pen down the list of names.

'I'll be right at the bottom,' Oliver said, hoping like hell someone had added his name. 'Late invitation.'

'Go ahead.'

Grinning, Oliver continued on to the next checkpoint but this time the man opened the driver's door with a flourish and said he'd park sir's vehicle. Sir got out and walked across to a decorated gateway leading to the gardens. Music from a jazz guitar trio wafted on the warm evening air. They must have been flown in, no-one local played that well. A woman in a stylish pink dress, with silvery grey hair in an equally stylish bob, smiled her welcome. Had she been waiting for him?

'Hello, you must be Oliver, Krista's friend. So nice to meet you. I'm Brenda. If there's anything you need, just ask. I know everything.'

How had he gained the status of Krista's friend in this house? Acquaintance was more like it, and technically, she was a client.

She directed him down the path to the lawn where a white marquee was set up housing the band and tables and chairs. The sides had been rolled up for ventilation but the guests wandered about on the lawn seeking shade either from the large umbrellas dotted about or the leafy deciduous trees lining the boundary. No shortage of water here by the looks of the lawn and the heavily scented roses lining the area. Must have a bore.

'Come and meet your hosts, Hugh and Viivi, then get yourself a drink and find Krista.' She made it sound as though he'd need a drink. Either that or get the duty out of the way and then enjoy himself. Maybe she meant both. He'd assumed Krista would be on hand to greet him.

She led the way to a small group on the terrace. Krista's mother was easily identified by the willowy, blonde good looks, although on her the natural slimness had taken on a gauntness absent in her daughter. The two men in the group were similarly tall, with the paunchy softness acquired by sitting at a desk, long boozy lunches and no exercise. Brothers, at a guess, and he had no way of telling which one was his host.

Brenda said, 'Excuse me, Hugh, this is Oliver Johnson. Oliver, this is Hugh and his wife Viivi. Hugh's brother Edgar and his wife Shirley.'

Oliver shook hands all around, conscious of two pairs of assessing eyes on him and two pairs openly curious. Shirley's were obscured by big round dark glasses but the lenses were turned on him like laser guns.

'Glad you could make it,' boomed Hugh. He was the larger of the brothers, both in height and girth. Neither could be accused of good looks with the greying hair retreating across the broad expanse of skull, a wide fleshy mouth and bulbous nose unfortunate family acquisitions.

'Thank you for the invitation.'

'Oliver is a friend of Krista's,' said Brenda. 'Excuse me.' She darted away, leaving Oliver captive.

'How do you know my daughter?' asked Viivi. That was a surprise. Surely Krista had mentioned the incident, but if she hadn't known about the last-minute invitation she hid it well.

'I treated her horse after the accident.'

No reaction. She could do iceberg far better than her daughter.

Shirley couldn't. 'Krista never mentioned an accident with a horse,' she said. 'I didn't know she rode.'

'She doesn't. She wasn't in the accident, the horse was,' said Viivi shortly. She glared at Oliver. 'You must be the vet.' The Medusa-like gaze was turned on her husband, the message clear. How dare he invite a common as muck vet to her party?

'I am,' he said. 'Congratulations on your anniversary. It's a lovely setting you have here.'

'Thank you. Get yourself a drink, bar's in the terrace room,' said Hugh. 'Krista's about somewhere. She'll be pleased to see you. Someone her own age.'

Viivi proffered a tiny brittle smile while the other two chuckled at his witticism.

Thus dismissed, Oliver said, 'Thank you, I will. Excuse me.'

He walked cross the terrace and into the coolness of the house. His confrontation with Hugh would have to wait. The room he entered was a large, open sitting room with a permanent bar at one end rather than a temporary set up for the function. Waiters circulated outside with drinks but he approached the barman and asked for a beer.

'Nice party,' he said.

'Yes, sir.'

'You're not local, are you?'

'No, sir. The client always uses the same catering company and they always use the same staff.'

'So you were flown in specially?'

'Yes sir, from Sydney this morning.'

'Are you staying overnight?'

'In a motel at Taylor's Bend.'

'Wow.'

The barman smiled. 'All the entertainment has been flown in. The Littlejohns don't do things by halves.'

'So I see. Bit out of my league.'

The man smiled. 'Enjoy the evening, sir,' he said. 'Excuse me.' He moved away to refill glasses for a waitress.

Oliver took up a place by the doors to the terrace where he could look out over the lawn. Krista wasn't in the room behind him and he couldn't see her from his raised vantage point. It would help if he knew what colour dress she was wearing. There were a lot of blonde-haired women, although the vast majority were a generation older. His parents would fit in well here.

The random thought made his mouth tighten. His father and Hugh had quite a bit in common. They both wielded their authority with a sense of divine right. No-one else's opinion mattered because no-one else was ever right, unless it was on a subject or in a profession they took little or no interest in. Then they didn't care, they just expected it to be done correctly and to their satisfaction. And why was that worthy of praise or thanks?

He sipped the beer, the tall glass imparting a welcome chill to his hand. Getting his nose inside The Grange was a first for a peasant from the Bend. He hid a smile. Margie would be all over him for gossip. She'd expect a rundown of the celebrity guest list but this crowd would be a sad disappointment for her. He didn't recognise anyone and there certainly weren't any actors or entertainers here beyond the jazz trio. The faces out there more likely belonged to politicians and people in the upper echelons of the business world. No-one he knew, or wanted to, particularly.

An elderly woman in pale purple paused in the doorway, empty wine glass in hand, her expression slightly glazed. 'My goodness it's hot out there,' she said. 'I have to sit down in the air conditioning.'

'Let me take your glass.'

'Thank you.'

Oliver led her to a cane chair away from the small crowd near the bar. 'Stay right there and I'll bring you some water.'

'You're very kind.'

A quick trip to the bar and he was back with a glass of iced water. He sat next to her. She drank a few mouthfuls and rested her head back. Her face under the make-up was pale, skin clammy.

'That's much better.'

'Drink it all. It's easy to become dehydrated in the hot weather,' he said. 'You must be sure to keep up your fluid levels. Are you here alone? Can I find someone for you?' Her fingers on the glass were clogged with precious stones set in silver and gold.

'No thank you. Are you a doctor?'

'No, a vet.'

To his surprise she burst out laughing. 'I'm sorry, she said. 'I'm not laughing at you. I just didn't expect you to say that.' She drank more water. 'I didn't know Hugh knew any vets. Although he does own a stud farm, I suppose.'

'Don't worry. I'm as surprised as you are. I've only just met him and I'm not the regular Grange vet. I've known Krista a bit longer.'

'Krista's the stepdaughter?'

'Yes.'

'I don't know her. I don't know Viivi well either, although we have met socially on occasion.'

'They look very alike. So why are you here, if I may ask?'

'I'm on the same board of directors as Hugh. A charity.'

'I see.'

She raised a pencilled eyebrow at his expression. 'It's the way the game is played when you're rich and powerful and want to stay that way.' She straightened and leaned forward. 'It's not something I'd do, invite a whole bunch of business associates and so on to a personal celebration, but Hugh is adept at greasing the wheels.'

'And you're one of them? The wheels.'

'I can be a particularly squeaky one.'

'Why accept the invitation?'

'I just told you.' She swallowed the remains of the water. 'I do feel better now, but I must go and powder my nose. Excuse me.'

She rose to her feet and held out her hand as he rose too. 'Eleanor De Vere.'

'Oliver Johnson.'

'So nice to meet you, Oliver, and thank you.'

'Remember, stick to the shade and drink enough water.'

Oliver resumed his seat, sipped his beer and watched the guests on the lawn outside. How many were actually the type of friend a regular person would invite to a party like this? One brother and sister-in-law were in attendance with the possibility of more. The son wasn't here. Krista was, somewhere, but although he understood now why she wasn't keen on attending, it didn't explain why she hadn't appeared, knowing he was coming.

He glanced at his watch. He'd been here nearly half an hour. If she didn't show up within the next fifteen minutes, he'd plead an animal medical emergency and leave.

A very overweight man with a completely bald head wheezed across to the chair vacated by Eleanor and collapsed into it. He raised a pudgy hand and clicked his fingers at a waitress heading for the door with a laden tray. 'Service,' he called. She changed tack.

'Champagne,' he said. She handed him a full glass. 'Leave another.' She placed a second on the coffee table between the two chairs.

'Would you like a refill, sir?' she asked Oliver.

'Yes, please.' He swapped his empty beer glass for a full. 'Thank you very much.'

'My pleasure.' She favoured him with a tiny smile.

'Bloody hot,' grunted the man. 'Don't know how they stand it out here.'

'It gets hot in the city, too.' Grime, fumes, baking concrete and tall enclosing buildings increasing the heat factor.

'Too many flies and dust. Bloody horrible.' He squinted at Oliver. 'What's your game?'

'I don't have a game. I'm a vet.'

'A vet? You mean animal, not military, I take it, if you're a local.' He contemplated that unlikely profession for a few moments. 'What's your name?'

'Oliver Johnson.' Why a returned serviceman wouldn't live in the Bend remained a mystery.

'Are you local?'

'Yes. Taylor's Bend.'

'Never heard of it.'

'It's the nearest town.'

'Johnson. Any relation to Francis? The doctor?' He regarded Oliver briefly. 'I guess that's unlikely.'

For a fleeting moment Oliver considered saying no but the disdain on the man's face sparked a little fire. 'He's my father.'

'Is he? He's my cardiologist. Good man.' He looked at Oliver with renewed interest. 'A vet. What are you doing in this godforsaken neck of the woods?'

'I like it here.' Oliver stood abruptly. 'Excuse me, please.' Why the hell did he admit to the connection? This bloke would undoubtedly mention the meeting next time he had his check-up which, judging by his appearance would be fairly soon, and they'd both get stuck into the disappointing, inexplicable folly of the son for choosing such a life, town and profession.

Seething, he headed for the terrace. One circuit of the garden for a last attempt at finding Krista and he was off. He'd rather spend his evening in the pub than here with these people. Why on earth had they invited him? Neither Hugh nor Krista had shown any interest in talking to him.

Glass in hand, he scanned the group seated under the nearest shade umbrellas then went down the steps on to the grass. A King Charles Spaniel wandered between the guests, looking up hopefully as it passed each group but being completely ignored. Brenda caught his eye and winked as he strolled by. He paused and she edged away from the people she was chatting with.

'Excuse me, is Krista about somewhere?' he asked.

She frowned. 'Haven't you seen her yet?'

'No. I'm about to leave but didn't want to without saying hello.'

'Hugh wants to talk to you so make sure you see him before you go. I'll nip up and see if Krista's in her room.'

'Thanks. Who owns the dog?'

'Lola belongs to Viivi but she's taken a liking to Krista this visit. Probably because she brings her outside whereas Viivi has a thing about dirt. Krista is minding her when Hugh and Viivi go overseas on Monday.'

'Where are they going?'

'Starting off with business in Tokyo and then skiing, also in Japan. I'm going too.'

'Nice.'

'Yes, but it's work for me.' She placed a light hand on his arm. 'I'll be back in a minute. Don't go anywhere. Promise.'

'Promise.'

Oliver hovered in the shade of a tree listening to the music. The waitress from indoors went by with a smile his way, which he returned, but no-one else gave him a second glance. Lola trotted up and sniffed at his shoes. He bent and patted her head.

'Hello, Lola.'

She looked up and wagged her tail then resumed the exploration of the interesting smells on his shoes and trouser legs.

A few moment later Hugh strode by, looked his way and changed course. 'How are you enjoying yourself? Got a drink? Good.'

Lola retreated behind Oliver's legs, which was interesting given the dog belonged to his wife.

'I'm fine, thanks.' Still buoyed by annoyance, Oliver snatched his opportunity. 'This afternoon I came out to see to Firebrand at the request of your stable manager. Two men were here when I was leaving, the ones who came to my practice and wanted to take Calypso Secret. They threatened Krista and me. I want you to make it quite clear to them I have nothing to do with this family or anything your son might be into.'

Hugh's jaw tightened and he edged Oliver around to face away from the other guests. Lola scampered away, sensing the anger. 'That is my son's affair, not mine. You need to speak to him.'

'I would but I don't know him and no-one seems to know where he is. The first and last I saw of him he was being helped into an ambulance. Why were they here today?' Oliver took a punt as it dawned on him that the car was a luxury model and the two men he recognised were waiting outside like the lackeys they were. 'Did they bring their boss to speak to you?'

From the working of his jaw Hugh was grinding his teeth as he prepared his next disclaimer. He must have decided on truth, or part of it. 'My son owes Stefan Moran money. Moran is a business acquaintance of mine so he came to discuss the matter with me.'

'Right. All the way to Taylor's Bend in a heatwave. Doesn't he have a phone? I'm no genius but even I know that's extremely unlikely unless it's a very large amount of money and he wants you to know it's personal.'

'Tell him the truth, Hugh.'

Krista's voice startled him, so intent had he been on trying to read her stepfather's face. She'd come to stand beside him, elegant and beautiful in a long silver dress that shimmered in the late afternoon light. He caught her eyes and for a moment nothing else registered except the nearness of her, her scent and her cool composure. His brain emptied as though a plug had been pulled.

When Hugh said nothing she continued, speaking to Oliver. 'Angus has a gambling problem and Hugh has finally stopped bailing him out. He was sent out here to keep him away from the Melbourne casinos and give him something to do.'

'And it didn't work?' So she did know about the gambling but had kept that detail to herself.

'No. He's not here much according to Rod.'

'How do you know?' demanded Hugh.

She gave him a withering look. 'Rod told me.'

'He told me the same thing,' said Oliver. 'But it's common knowledge in the Bend.' Gossip but still, it wouldn't hurt to ram the point home.

'I think Angus owed so much money he couldn't pay it back and tried to palm off Calypso as part payment.'

'But it wasn't the right horse.' Oliver frowned. 'You mean he tried to disguise Arch Rival and fool them? How stupid does he think they are?'

Krista said, 'Moran told us Calypso was very valuable as a brood mare. I had no idea. And neither did you, did you, Hugh?'

'She came as part of the deal when I bought The Grange. Rod said she was of very good bloodstock but we were more interested in the stallion.'

How nice to have so much money that a valuable horse was lumped in as 'part of the deal'.

'Why don't you just give the man the horse?' asked Oliver. Neither of them seemed to want her very much.

'She's mine,' said Krista. 'I'm not paying Angus's debts.'

'I don't react to threats,' stated Hugh.

'You haven't been threatened,' said Oliver. 'Krista has.'

'And you too,' said Krista. 'He said today he doesn't like to be lied to and we both lied to his men so we're both accountable.'

'This whole thing has nothing to do with me.' Indignant rage roared through Oliver's body. 'This is your family we're talking about.' He glared at Hugh. 'So fix it or I'm going to the police.'

'And tell them what?' snarled Hugh.

'Everything.'

He gave a mirthless laugh. 'Meaning nothing. Moran is smarter than you and he's entirely ruthless where his money and his honour are concerned. He hasn't done anything yet.'

'So what happens? Are you going to ignore those threats against us?'

'Moran won't touch me.'

'He included you, Hugh, in case you've forgotten,' said Krista. 'He made it clear that with Angus missing, he holds the family responsible for the debt, that's why he came to see you.'

'Where the hell is he, your son?' asked Oliver. 'You must have some idea.'

But Hugh shook his head. 'I don't. If I did I'd wring his useless neck.'

'I do,' said Krista. 'He was in my apartment in Melbourne. He stole my key.'

Chapter 7

'How do you know that?' demanded Hugh. 'You could have lost the key yourself.'

'He called me.' She looked at Oliver. 'That's why I wasn't down here to meet you. Sorry.'

'What else did he say?' Oliver asked, relief that she hadn't deliberately avoided him moving through his body like sweet honey.

'He's flying out of the country, I think. He'd be in the air now. He called from the airport and I heard an announcement in the background about Auckland so it must have been the international terminal.'

'Where's he going? It wouldn't be Auckland.' Hugh's voice grated with fury.

'He wouldn't tell me. He said he's posting my keys to me.' She bit at her lower lip. 'You have to pay Moran off, Hugh.'

'I do not. I'll tell him Angus has left the country.'

'Why aren't you worried about what he'll do?' Oliver asked slowly. The man was angry but it was directed at Angus and it wasn't fear driven, as far as he could tell.

'He wouldn't dare do anything.'

'Why?'

'That's none of your business. If you'll excuse me, I have guests to attend to, and your mother is giving me the evil eye, Krista. As usual.'

He strode away.

'Christ! Where does that leave us?' Oliver exhaled in exasperation. 'What a total crock.'

Krista touched his arm. 'I'm so sorry. It's all my fault you got involved.' Her voice wobbled.

He moderated his tone. 'Hey, it's not your fault at all. The police called me to the accident, not you, and your brother started the whole thing and wouldn't lift a finger to sort it out.'

'You're being very kind but you know that's not strictly true. You stuck up for me when those men came.'

He gave a little snort of derision. 'And look how that worked out. Fat help I was. It made things way worse.'

'Not really. You were in the right, and I still have my horse.'

Oliver smiled. 'Thanks. You should leave here, you know.'

'I have to stay until my keys turn up.'

'No, you don't. You have your car, you can go anywhere. Hide out in Cairns or somewhere. Rod can send the keys on or keep them here until this thing is sorted.'

'And leave you to face them?'

'They're not interested in me, not really. They'd know Hugh wouldn't give a damn what happens to the local vet so I'm not much of a lever for them. Not like you are. If they come around again I can always tell Rupe what's going on.'

She sighed. A waiter wandered by with drinks and she flagged him down and took champagne. Oliver replaced his beer.

'I wonder what your stepfather meant when he said Moran wouldn't dare touch him.'

'He said earlier when I met him that Moran was a business associate.'

'What sort of business?'

'No idea but Hugh's involved in lots of things. All sorts.'

'Illegal things?'

She hesitated. 'I'm not sure. He probably has some close calls but straight-out illegal? I think it'd be too risky.'

'But he's an associate of Moran and he's clearly a crook—or has a very weird way of doing business.'

'He has legitimate businesses as well. His casinos, for example.'

'And what else, I wonder? Do you think he imports drugs or something?' How much did she know?

'Maybe. Indirectly. It'd be at arm's length if he did.'

'So Hugh might know some choice details.'

'Possibly, but Moran didn't sound to me as though he was treading carefully around Hugh.'

'Could have been a front. And he is owed money.' Oliver glanced at the assembled guests. 'I wonder if any of these people are involved as well.'

'I wouldn't trust Felix Schwartz as far I could kick him.' She almost snarled.

He looked at her, surprised by the vehemence. 'Who's he?'

'My mother's best friend Gwen's husband. He's a total sleaze.' She surveyed the garden. 'He's over there. Cream pants, green shirt. Bald, big nose. Can't keep his hands to himself.'

Oliver looked where she indicated. The man appeared harmless enough, but then he himself wasn't an attractive young woman and highly unlikely to be a target. He changed the subject.

'I've met your friend Lola. She likes my shoes. Interesting smells.'

Krista smiled, as he'd hoped. 'I'm looking after her while they're away.'

'Will you stay here?'

'Yes, I think so. I don't fancy being on the run and I don't see why I should be. It might be the safest thing.'

'So you trust Hugh's word?'

'He must have some sort of business arrangement that Moran relies on. Hugh has a lot of influence both financially and politically.'

'You mean he could organise a boycott, or get a government investigation or something into Moran's affairs?'

Krista shrugged. 'He's done it before with business rivals. He has a controlling share in one of the main media outlets and plenty of friends in radio and TV, not to mention politician mates.'

Oliver shook his head. 'Way beyond me.'

'Me too, but like him or not, Hugh does know what he's doing and he's as ruthless as Moran. You have to be to survive at that level.'

Oliver studied the woman standing beside him. She came from that same world but she spoke as if she were an outsider, even though she was a beneficiary of the ruthless pursuit of money and power, of her mother's single-mindedness as much as Hugh's.

'What do you do, Krista? Do you work?' He almost added, 'Do you need to?' but that would be a jibe too far, considering she was already upset.

'Not at the moment. I'm between jobs.' Something about her tone and the way her gaze slipped away as she answered made him doubt her. Was she embarrassed about saying she didn't have to lift a finger to support herself?

'What did you do before?'

'I was a PA but I...' She drained her glass, ran her tongue over her lips. Nervous, not seductive.

'Didn't like it? Quit?'

'Got fired.'

'Really? Why?' Why would anyone fire her? She was intelligent, articulate, probably spoke a few languages and he imagined would do her best in whatever work she did. 'I thought it was quite difficult to fire people these days. Without a very good reason, I mean, like doing something criminal.'

'Not if you've only been hired as a favour to your mother.' She glared at him. 'I wouldn't sleep with the guy I worked for. He's here tonight with his wife. Shall I introduce you?'

'No thank you. Unless you want me to cause a scene.'

She held a breath for a moment then exhaled slowly. 'It's not the first job I've lost, although I quit the one before.'

'Same reason?'

She nodded, then smiled. 'Would you cause a scene?'

'No. I wouldn't want to embarrass his poor wife. How can these blokes still do that? Haven't they heard of Me Too?'

'They're rich and they're the boss. Rules don't apply to them.' She pushed a strand of hair from her brow. 'They think because I look the way I do I'm fair game, and I'm also expendable. My jobs are always a favour to my mother.' Her lip curled. 'Why are men like that?'

Oliver quailed under her bitter focus. 'I'm not and I know plenty of other men who aren't.' Was his father the type of man she despised? He had no idea. Their paths rarely crossed now he was an adult.

'That's what Brenda said.' The set of her mouth indicated she was doubtful about the judgement.

'She's right.'

In the silence that followed, Oliver digested the other piece of information she'd let loose. A favour to her mother? Didn't Krista have any ambitions of her own?

'Maybe you need to look for a different type of job,' he said.

'I can't do anything else.' She gave a little snuffle of laughter which sounded perilously close to a sob. 'I'm apparently not even very good at what I do. That was the official reason I was sacked. I wasn't efficient and made too many mistakes.'

'What did you have to do? I mean, what does a PA do?'

'I arranged travel—flights, hotels and things like that. Booked restaurants. Made appointments, organised his diary. Collected dry-cleaning. Made coffee. Sent flowers to his girlfriends. Bought gifts. Looked decorative for clients at social functions. Other people did more important things.'

'I'm sure you'd be very good at all of that.'

'I thought I was until he added in the extracurricular activities.'

'Did you report any of this?'

'Who to? His wife?'

'Surely there was someone or some department in the business...'

'Maybe, but it was easier to leave. I'm never the most popular person in the office. It would have been very ... messy.' She glanced over to where her mother had begun chatting to the slimeball in question. 'I didn't want to work there anymore.'

'You should tell your mother.'

'She thinks that's what women have to do if they want any sort of security.'

Oliver had no response to that. He'd thought his family was bad but he had no sisters for comparison and his older brother, Julian, although very charming and popular, remained unmarried by choice after a disastrous affair. Unencumbered by a permanent woman—as he put it—he was a fast-rising star in the criminal law courts.

'Why were you here earlier?' she asked when the silence had stretched almost to discomfort. 'When Moran saw you.'

'Rod called me. Firebrand has a cold.'

She nodded. 'He and Amy do all the work around here. They love the place.'

'And no-one else does?'

'It was a whim for Hugh. He'll sell it soon, I think. Angus hates it. Mama hates it.'

'And you?'

'This is my third visit and the longest.'

'You've only been here three days.'

She smiled. 'I might stay longer this time.' Her mouth drooped. 'Actually, I have to. I can't go home until my keys turn up. If they ever do.'

'Won't Angus have sent them?'

'Who knows? He said he had but that would involve thinking, and acting on behalf of someone else.'

'You can always call a locksmith.'

'I suppose so. I haven't ever had to do anything like that,' she said.

No doubt Mama or Hugh took care of life's little inconveniences such as finding a job, buying an apartment and a car, replacing lost keys ... How could she stand it? She wasn't a child but sometimes she acted like one.

'Krista, you're an intelligent adult. Have you ever thought of running your own life?' His exasperation made the words sound sharper than he intended.

'I do.' She didn't miss the edge.

'Do you?' He looked over to where her mother had moved on to another group of guests, laughing and smiling, intent on being the gracious hostess and perfect wife. At what cost?

'You don't know anything about me,' she said tartly. 'Not really.'

'You've just told me your mother got you your last job and presumably the others, you don't know how to get into your apartment and you have no direction in life. I assume you don't actually have to work to survive but I think you want to be independent. Trouble is you're too scared of breaking away from your mother even though you resent her interference and control.'

She stared at him, her breath coming heavily, lips jammed together and cheeks a deep pink unrelated to the stifling heat of the evening.

'Thank you for coming. I hope you enjoy yourself,' she said in a tight voice and turned away.

Lola appeared from the rosebed and trotted after her. Oliver finished his beer. He might as well leave now. There was nothing left for him here, having insulted the only person he was remotely interested in talking to. He hadn't meant to do that but her acceptance of the situation and seeming lack of will to do anything constructive about it was infuriating. If she had to work for a living she'd see the world differently. If she had to struggle to pursue her goal—if she ever had one—she'd appreciate what she'd been handed on a platter and do her best to forge her own way. As it was, her helpless 'poor me' attitude made him grind his teeth.

He handed his empty glass to a waiter and began working his way through the crowd to the gate. Was it his imagination or was that a hint of smoke in the heavy air? A few cigarettes smouldered between fingers in the crowd but this was a different smell, one with the tang of eucalyptus. No breeze stirred the surrounding trees so the fire was a considerable distance away and probably not a threat, but the locals would be listening intently to the radio for updates and checking the online Fire Service site for news. Grassfires were common at this time of year but so far the Bend had escaped a major onslaught. Oliver looked up at the evening sky. Still clear and the sunset was golden without the telltale reddish tinge of a smoke-filled filter.

A microphone crackled and someone announced that guests should take their seats at the tables. Oliver hesitated. He should leave but he was hungry and the food was sure to be good—better than the leftover cold chicken in his fridge. Guests were moving about looking at place tags. He had no idea if there was one for him. The cold chicken might be the safer option, to avoid embarrassment.

He threaded through the guests, heading for the gate, but Brenda bustled up and said, 'I forgot to tell you, Oliver, I'm sorry. I've made a place for you on Table 2. Next to Krista.'

'Thank you.'

'I'm at the same table.' She smiled happily and hurried away. Oliver followed the chattering women in front of him and kept an eye out for Table 2 and a cranky blonde in a silver dress.

Krista took her place at the empty table after quickly scanning the other names. Gwen and Felix were seated two along, then a couple she hardly knew from one of her mother's charity committees, someone called Bunny Bancroft was next, Jack, an old golfing friend of Hugh's, Brenda, and next to her, unsurprisingly, Oliver.

He hadn't reappeared and she wasn't craning her neck to find him. He'd probably gone home. She eyed the hastily prepared name tag next to her and considered swapping it with Jack the golfer, but before she could act, Jack pulled out his chair and boomed, 'Krista, how beautiful you are. A silver goddess.'

'Hello, Jack. Thank you very much. Where's Wendy? Is she well?'

'Couldn't come. She's on a cultural cruise on the Mediterranean. Climbing about Greek and Roman ruins.'

'Sounds fun.'

'She enjoys it. How have you been?' He leaned his elbows on the table and studied her from under bushy grey eyebrows, like a benevolent koala.

'I'm fine. You're looking well.' He was. Unlike Hugh's usual friends Jack kept himself fit, loved his wife and children and was unfailingly polite and decent. No wonder Brenda had placed herself between him and Oliver.

A waiter appeared and poured iced water into their glasses, distracting Jack from replying.

Krista had her mother's charity friends on her other side. Calvin and Vanessa True. At least Gwen and the despicable Felix were safely across the table. He'd have to have octopus tentacles to grope her knee from there. Would Oliver make a scene if Felix did? Jack would, if he knew. He had three daughters not much older than she was. Brenda was right. There were some good men around.

The Trues appeared next. Vanessa was all sharp angles, in contrast to her husband whose shirt buttons were in serious danger of being propelled across the table like bullets when the stitching gave way under the strain. She flagged down the waiter and demanded red wine in a voice like gravel.

'I only drink red,' she announced.

'She does,' said Calvin. 'Whereas I drink anything.'

Krista nodded and smiled.

'You're Viivi's daughter, aren't you?' Vanessa asked, full glass in hand. 'You're exactly alike. Isn't she, Cal? She's the spitting image of her mother.'

'She is. The spitting image.'

'How long have they been married? Hugh and Viivi?' she asked next.

'Fifteen years.'

'Fifteen?' Pencilled eyebrows rose dramatically.

'Yes.'

'What do you do, Krista?' asked Cal. 'Are you involved in the charity thing?'

'No. I don't have a job at the moment.'

'I thought you were with Charles Petrovic,' said Vanessa. 'Viivi said you were.'

'I was until last week.'

'You weren't there very long, were you?'

'No. We had a disagreement.'

'Young people change jobs at the drop of a hat nowadays,' said Cal. 'No sense of loyalty at all.'

'It's all about themselves,' said Vanessa. 'As soon as something doesn't go how they want, they quit. It's so hard to keep staff these days. We've had three housekeepers in eighteen months. Nothing but complaints. You'd think they'd be glad of a job but no, they just don't want to work at all.'

'Brenda has been with my mother for years,' said Krista. 'They get on very well.'

'But Viivi is a delight, so undemanding,' said Vanessa. 'Who wouldn't want to work for her? I'm much fussier.'

'She is, she's very fussy,' said Cal.

Fortunately the other guests arrived at the table all at the same time, including Oliver. He slid onto the chair beside her while she was greeting Brenda and being introduced to Bunny, an attractive, auburn-haired woman in peacock blue whose connection to Viivi and Hugh wasn't made clear. No-one else at the table apart from Gwen seemed to know her either.

'I wasn't sure you'd stay,' Krista said to Oliver when the others were busy meeting each other. Her heart beat just a little bit faster as he turned to reply. Was he angry with her? He had every right to be—but here he was and he didn't look upset. He had the same calm expression he usually wore.

'Neither was I but Brenda caught me as I was making up my mind.'

Did that mean he was coerced?

'Is there a fire nearby?' boomed Jack. 'I'm sure I smell smoke.'

'There is but it's a fair distance away. No danger so far,' said Oliver.

'Rod said he was monitoring it,' added Krista.

'My goodness. A bushfire? How close is it?' shrilled Gwen. 'Are we safe?'

'Rod said if the wind picks up and blows our way we might be in trouble.'

'Who'd want to live out here?' said Cal.

'I do,' said Oliver.

'Why?' asked Gwen.

'Oliver is the local vet,' said Brenda.

'But you must have chosen to come here. Nobody forced you, did they?' Gwen said.

'I did choose Taylor's Bend and I love it. Five years ago now.'

He didn't sound the least bit defensive. If anything, he sounded amused by their horror. The way he and the two police officers had quietly laughed at her that first day. Hearing these remarks, she had an inkling as to why. And squirmed.

'Do you have a family?' was Gwen's next query.

'I'm not married if that's what you're asking.'

'Oliver is Krista's friend,' said Brenda helpfully.

'Oh, I see.' Gwen smirked at Krista. 'You kept that quiet.'

'That's because I met Oliver three days ago when he looked after one of our horses.' And she certainly wouldn't be telling Gwen the details of a budding relationship if there was one.

'Hugh invited me today, not Krista,' said Oliver. 'I've been treating the stallion here as well.'

'Firebrand is very valuable,' said Krista. 'So Hugh was pleased Oliver could come out quickly to see him.'

'What happened to that young man we met you with at the Christmas lunch?' Felix asked, eyeing her through partly closed eyes, which he would assume gave him a sexy, cool look but didn't. It made him look as though he needed glasses. 'Johann, was it? You seemed very cosy together.'

'Nothing happened to him as far as I know. I haven't seen him since.' One of her mother's set-ups. Johann from Germany, son of some friend of hers holidaying in Australia.

'That's a shame. He was very good looking and so cultured,' said Gwen. 'Viivi had high hopes for you two. She's very keen you should find someone and settle down, Krista.'

Luckily, Jack and Bunny had struck up a conversation so Gwen's remarks weren't broadcast to the whole table. Oliver, however, was well within earshot and the Trues' faces were alight with interest.

'Why should Krista settle down?' Oliver asked. The urge to kick him under the table was almost irresistible. He should ignore Gwen, the way she'd learned to do, not give her space to air her views on Krista's life.

'A girl needs a husband.'

'Why?' A spark of irritation was in his voice now.

Krista sucked in a breath and firmed her lips. This was heading for disaster.

Oliver was already annoyed by her behaviour and Gwen was always annoying.

Now Vanessa True shoved her oar in. 'Security. She needs a man to look after her. The world's a tough place for a single woman.'

'That's right.' Gwen nodded vigorously. 'Security and protection.'

'Excuse me, seeing as this is me you're all discussing,' said Krista loudly before Oliver could start. 'Can I say, I would like to marry one day, but I'm not settling for some man because Mama wants me to.'

'I should hope not.' Oliver swigged a mouthful of wine.

'Viivi only has your best interests at heart. She wants you to marry well.'

'What does that mean?' asked Oliver. 'Marry well?'

'It means she would be happiest with someone from her own social circle who is financially secure and can provide her with the lifestyle she's used to.'

'Ah, I see.' He nodded. 'You mean not someone like a country vet who should know his place and not have any ideas above his station.' He laughed and shook his head and murmured what sounded like, 'Unbelievable.'

'Oliver...' Krista began, but he said, 'Don't worry, Gwen. Krista and I are barely acquaintances. We have nothing in common and probably won't meet again after this evening.' He chuckled again. 'But I can assure you that when and if I do meet the right woman, I will take my vows seriously. I will love her, respect her and I will always be faithful, which is more than can be said for some married men.' He raised his eyebrows and his glass at Felix. 'I'm sure you, as a married man, will agree.'

On his other side Brenda caught Krista's eye and barely smothered a laugh.

Krista smiled but his words hurt on a level she hadn't expected in spite of what he'd said earlier. He thought they had nothing in common and that was true, apart from the Moran problem, but it didn't mean...

A waitress placed the melon and avocado entree in front of her. She stared at the artful arrangement as though it was plastic. She could no more swallow food than ride Calypso in the Melbourne Cup.

What didn't it mean? Just because she found him attractive and he was kind ... He'd made his opinion clear to her earlier, to Gwen and everyone within earshot with that statement a moment ago. Why did it matter so much? Why did it feel as though her future had become as bleak as the dry, dusty paddocks surrounding them?

Chapter 8

Oliver speared a melon cube. Delicious. Cool and refreshing. Krista sat unmoving and silent beside him and he couldn't blame her. That woman, Gwen, was a real shocker. What a nasty snobbish bitch to launch into a discussion of Krista's personal life like that, in front of strangers. If that was her idea of social superiority she was in a class all her own.

'Are you okay?' He spoke softly.

She picked up her fork. 'Fine. It's the weather.' Put the fork down.

'Drink plenty of water.' Ice tinkled as he pushed her glass closer.

'Thank you,' she murmured. 'For ... you know.' She glanced at Felix who was guzzling food like a starving man.

'Are they always like that?'

She nodded. 'I'm used to it.'

'My father's a bit the same.'

'Really?' She looked at him, eyes widening in surprise at the first personal piece of information he'd let slip.

'That's one of the reasons I came here.'

'To escape?'

'More or less, but I love my work and I love the town. It's home now.'

'I can see that. You're lucky it worked out so well.' She took a sip of water, then another.

'Yes, I am, but Krista, I made the decision to follow my own path.'

She took up her fork and jabbed it into a chunk of avocado. 'You knew what you wanted to do. And you're a man. It makes a difference.'

'Maybe.' Time to change the subject, that one had been done and he didn't want to break the delicate truce they'd achieved. She'd been picked on enough. 'This entree is really good,' he said.

'Yes, Mama changed her mind about five times before she and the chef agreed.' But she only nibbled at the avocado slice on her fork.

When the entrees were finished, Hugh stood and took the microphone for a welcoming speech. It was the usual thing except totally devoid of witticisms or jokes—or attempts at either. Very strange for a man who must be used to being the centre of attention and was presiding over what should be a happy occasion.

The bloke could be addressing a board meeting. Oliver's attention wandered as Hugh thanked a swathe of people for coming. He'd been to a few such celebrations in the Bend—Rupe and Abbie's wedding, two twenty-first birthdays, Connie Benson's fortieth birthday, and most memorable of the anniversaries, Laurie and Dot's sixtieth, which filled the town hall to overflowing, started at noon on a Saturday and finished at about four on Sunday morning. Minus the happy octogenarian couple, of course, who'd retired to bed at nine pm. At all of those events the jokes and anecdotes had flown thick and fast, with the guests more than happy to throw in their own comments if they thought the speaker needed help, was getting boring or waffling.

Hugh ended by thanking Viivi for fifteen happy years. She smiled and nodded graciously to the assembly but to Oliver she didn't look overjoyed by any stretch of the imagination. In fact, when after toasting his wife, amidst applause, Hugh took his seat beside her, she leaned in close and said something which wiped the smile from his face as effectively as if she'd smacked him.

He glanced at Krista. Her eyes were downcast, hands in her lap with the fingers tightly entwined. Without thinking, he reached across and placed his hand over hers. She looked up swiftly. For the longest of moments her eyes locked with his and the table, the guests, the garden, the chatter, the heat all faded to nothing, replaced by the warmth of her skin on his palm and the depths of blue swallowing him whole.

'How dare you!'

The shrieking voice cut through the languid evening air like machine-gun fire. Krista's hands jerked free as she turned her head, body tense. Oliver followed her gaze to the main table where Viivi was on her feet, face contorted by fury. She swung her arm back and struck Hugh's face a stinging blow with the flat of her hand. A collective gasp filled the stunned silence that followed her cry.

'Oh my God.' Brenda leapt to her feet and followed Viivi who, in a stumbling run, threaded her way clumsily between the tables towards the house.

Without a word, Krista pushed her chair back and followed them both.

Gwen began shoving her chair back as well but Felix wisely held her arm.

'I wouldn't, darling,' he said in the type of voice that really meant, 'Stay right where you are and don't interfere.'

'My goodness,' said Vanessa. 'What just happened?'

Gwen snatched her arm free but stayed put. 'It's obvious, isn't it?' she snarled. 'This has been brewing for some time. Everyone knows.'

Oliver and Jack exchanged bewildered glances.

'Do they?' asked Jack of the table at large.

Oliver shrugged with a grimace. Across the table the auburn-haired woman, whose name he'd forgotten, casually sipped her wine. More used to such dramas than he was, apparently. He wanted to leave but the other guests were enthralled.

'I have no idea what that was about,' she said. 'And I'm not sure I want to.'

'Me neither,' Oliver said.

'You should know.' Gwen glared at the woman.

'Should I?'

'It was you who started it by sleeping with Hugh.'

'I beg your pardon? Where on earth did you get that idea?' She laughed but it was brittle.

'I have my sources.'

'Well, I would change my sources if I were you or you could get yourself into some serious trouble.' Her tone changed to steel. 'Legal trouble.'

Gwen glowered but kept her mouth closed. Felix shifted in his chair uncomfortably.

Cal said, 'If that were true, I imagine Hugh would be a willing participant. By all accounts he usually is.'

'For God's sake!' Gwen said. She turned back to the woman. 'Why are you here, anyway, Bunny?'

'I was invited,' she said. 'By Viivi.'

Did Krista know about Hugh's activities? He really should get up and walk out. What was he doing getting himself involved with this festering madhouse? No-one apart from Krista would care if he left and she was busy with her mother. He could phone her later.

Hugh's voice cut through the rumble of voices. 'Please, everyone. I must apologise for Viivi's behaviour. She's been under a lot of stress organising tonight's party and she never does well in the heat. She's Finnish, as you know, so she's much happier in the snow, hence our skiing trip next week.' A little titter of laughter greeted this remark. 'Please enjoy the rest of the dinner and I'm sure Viivi will join us a little later when she's feeling better.'

Applause rippled around the garden.

Waiters appeared bearing the main course. Wine glasses were refilled, the music restarted, the dinner resumed. Oliver sliced into the chunk of barbecued steak on his plate. Apologising for Viivi's behaviour? That was a neat sidestep and deflection of blame if what Gwen announced as common knowledge was actually fact and not gossip.

A few minutes later, Krista sat down.

Gwen leaned forward. 'How is she? Should I go in?' Desperate to get in there and claw at the wounds.

'Brenda's with her and she doesn't want to see anyone else.'

'What an awful thing to do to her, on this day of all days.' Her gaze swung around the table hoping for a glimmer of interest in dissecting the situation but met with people studiously concentrating on eating.

'They'll sort it out,' said Jack. 'After fifteen years they know the best and the worst of each other.' He sent a kindly smile Krista's way then turned to Oliver. 'Are you a cricketing man?'

'I am. I play for the local team. Bat rather than bowl but I'm a reserve this season. Too unreliable because of work.'

'What do you think of the Test team this year?'

'Oh God. Not sport.' Gwen glowered and picked at her dinner.

Oliver gave his opinion and continued the discussion he would otherwise have enjoyed very much if most of his attention wasn't on Krista, silent beside him with the silver dress shining in the lamplight but the sparkle gone from her eyes.

When Cal and Felix weighed in on the state of the Australian team, Oliver said softly, 'Eat something.'

She obediently cut a small piece of steak and ate it. 'Mama's furious,' she murmured. 'She's packing.'

'Will she leave tonight?' And here he was thinking she'd be in floods of tears at whatever sin Hugh had committed.

'I think so.'

'Will you go with her?'

'Why would I?' Surprise sharpened her voice.

'Support?'

'She has Brenda. She doesn't need me.' She ate a bite of potato salad.

Oliver continued eating. He knew how that felt. Being abandoned by a parent. Not so much physically as emotionally. In his case it was both parents, because his mother did what his father said and had done their whole married life. She had no life of her own outside his sphere. She was Mrs Emily Johnson, devoted wife of eminent cardiologist Francis Johnson.

'I'm glad you're here,' she murmured. 'That you stayed.'

'One thing I've learnt over the years,' he said, and paused to swallow a forkful of lettuce while she waited, blank faced. 'Never knock back a free feed.'

The beautiful smile appeared like sunshine.

'And this is a very good feed,' he added.

'It ought to be, the chef is world class.'

'What's he got up his sleeve for dessert?'

'Wait and see.' Her voice had a touch of pleading.

'I will.'

She turned to her neglected plate and began eating with a touch more enthusiasm than previously.

'So will this shindig continue without the hostess?' he asked softly.

She nodded. 'Hugh can't send everyone away after making them come so far. He'll make up some excuse when she doesn't reappear.'

'Do they have often have fights like this?'

'No,' she murmured. 'This is different.'

He couldn't ask more, not with Gwen straining her ears to listen over the raised voices of the cricket tragics.

'Do you like cricket?' he asked in a normal voice.

'I do. I prefer tennis but I do watch the tests.'

'Do you play tennis?'

'Yes. I'm pretty good although I haven't played for a while.' She eyed him as she said it, raised one delicate eyebrow. 'Do you play?'

'Yes. We have a regular four on Thursday evenings. Mixed doubles.'

'Oh.'

'Yes, you've met two of them. Shannon the cop and Tim who helped unload Arch Rival from the float.'

'I missed him. Was he leaving when I arrived?'

'Right, he was. He owns a vineyard on the other side of town. He's Rupe's neighbour.'

'Who's the other person?'

'Shannon's wife, Vicki. She's an accountant. They live at the police station.'

'Sounds fun. Not living at the police station,' she said quickly. 'The tennis.'

'It is. The tennis club is pretty active.'

'What else goes on here?'

'Plenty of sport. There's a book group, a youth group at the church, school functions, a couple of fetes, fundraisers, music and trivia nights and karaoke at the pub. A fun run. The Show. And there's a new music and drama group just started up to put on a show.'

'What sort of show?'

'Gilbert and Sullivan. *Patience.*'

She laughed. 'Are you singing in it?'

'I'm in the orchestra. Cello.'

'My goodness.' She looked at him in astonishment.

He placed his knife and fork neatly together on his empty plate.

'Sorry,' she said. 'That came out wrong. I meant, I'm impressed. I'm totally unmusical although I love music. That sounds like heaps of fun.'

'Should be. We've never done anything like this before in town but the couple organising it are very experienced and seem to know what they're doing.'

'Maybe I could do something to help.' She sounded wistful.

He wiped his mouth with the napkin. 'It's not until June.'

She nodded and drank some water.

'You won't be here then, will you?'

'Probably not. Specially if Hugh sells the place,' she added in a low voice. 'Quite likely now.' She sighed and placed her own cutlery side by side on the plate.

A waitress whisked both empty plates away. Oliver took a sip of wine. Had he been too harsh? Handing out another dismissal when she was still smarting from the last?

'No reason why you couldn't lend a hand while you are here,' he said. 'What can you do?'

She frowned. 'Nothing special. I can paint sets or help with wardrobe. Help with publicity. Whatever's needed.'

Eager as a puppy given a pat on the head.

'I'll let them know. Rupe's wife, Abbie, is an artist. She's doing the set design.'

'Rupe the other policeman?'

'Yes.'

'Will you tell him—about, you know...'

'Not unless something happens.'

She grimaced. 'Maybe it was just words.'

But she didn't sound convinced and remembering that pair who banged on his door, he wasn't either.

***

If it hadn't been for Oliver, a calming, solid presence beside her, Krista would have excused herself and holed up in her room. As it was, the evening ground on. Hugh remained at his table, drinking and talking loudly to his companions as if his wife's spectacular exit was nothing special. Dessert came and went, as did coffee, then the guitar trio was enhanced by extra players and a singer to provide dance music. The evening was running like clockwork, an ironic tribute to her mother's organisational skill. She didn't reappear although Brenda did briefly, to draw Hugh aside for an intense exchange. He shook his head, face thundery. Brenda waited a moment but nothing was forthcoming so whatever he'd said was his final offer.

She glanced across at Krista as she headed for the house and gave an imperceptible shake of the head. No-one was giving an inch. Typical of that pair.

By the looks Gwen kept throwing at Hugh and Brenda, Krista knew she was itching to go in and see Viivi but wasn't game to disobey the earlier command and risk some of the fury being directed at her. The whole crowd would be speculating as to the enormity and nature of Hugh's crime. Infidelity would be the top runner but Viivi had turned a blind eye to his flirtations before, saying they were nothing more than an ageing man's attempts to recapture his fading youth. The implication was he was to be pitied.

This time might be different. This time Mama was deeply hurt and angry. Whether she would follow through with her decision to leave tonight she had no idea. Perhaps Brenda was trying to persuade Hugh to talk to her but he was unlikely to forgive such a publicly humiliating display and for once, she almost sympathised with him. He must have done something bad, something unforgivable. Who with?

She slid a sideways glance at Oliver. She couldn't expect him to stay much longer although he sat, legs stretched out, watching the couples dancing, showing no signs of wanting to go home. He was uninvolved, a spectator. He wasn't sitting there envisaging what might ensue after tonight's debacle. Another divorce, another hysterical meltdown from her mother. Anger, bitterness, blame. She sighed heavily. She'd just turned thirteen when the last one occurred, watching wide-eyed and fearful, ignored and all but forgotten.

Forget escaping to her bedroom, if she could go home she would. If Angus hadn't taken her keys...

Cal and Vanessa went to join the dancers on the artificial floor in the marquee.

'Dance with me, Krista,' said Jack, but she shook her head. A smile was hard to raise.

'Sorry, I don't feel much like dancing.'

'It'll cheer you up, lovey. Come on.' He pushed his chair back and stood, holding out his hand.

She looked up into his face and saw nothing but care and kindness. Was this what a father looked like?

'All right. Thanks.'

He held her in a waltz embrace and steered her expertly between the other couples in some old-fashioned dance style. After a few fumbling missteps, she picked up what he was doing with his surprisingly nimble feet and began to enjoy herself. He was right, concentrating on the movement and the music took her mind off the disaster.

When she returned to the table, Oliver had gone. She scanned the crowd. Most people were dancing, some chatted at their tables, others had wandered off across the grass. A few people had asked about Viivi as she passed but she smiled, was noncommittal and kept moving.

Hugh was talking to Felix and Gwen, her hand on his arm, a consoling expression on her face, her whole body inclined towards him. Something about the body language brought a frown...

Felix was fondling a tumbler of whisky, avidly assessing the rear view of a red-haired woman dancing close by. Bunny. Krista turned away. What a complicated, disgusting mess. At least she'd managed to avoid her despicable ex-boss Charles and his wife.

She headed indoors for the bathroom and found Oliver returning from the same mission.

'Wait here. I'll be a minute,' she said and ran upstairs to her own ensuite. A quick repair job on her make-up, a spritz of perfume, and she rejoined him in the terrace room. He was chatting to the barman, laughing and comfortable. Far more so than he'd been with the guests or Hugh.

He nodded to the man and drew her across to the other side of the room by the open door.

'Are you okay?' he asked.

'Yes, it was a surprise, that's all. I knew they'd been arguing lately but not...' She gestured helplessly. 'It's not the first time.'

'You mean they've done this before? I thought you said this was worse.'

'Yes, it is. I meant Mama has had husbands before. Hugh is number four.'

'Is she still here?'

'I think so. I should go and see her.'

'You should. I'll go home.'

'Okay. Thank you for coming, Oliver. I'm sorry you had to see this.'

'No worries. You're not responsible for your parents' behaviour.' Kind blue eyes studied her and then suddenly his lips brushed her cheek, leaving a tingling trail. 'Look after yourself, Krista.'

His fingers caressed her bare arm and then he was striding away, down the steps and across the grass for the gate. If only she could leave too.

But she couldn't. She asked the barman for a glass of water and downed it before going to face Mama.

She tapped on the bedroom door. Brenda opened it, saw who it was and let her in without a word. Her face said it all. Resignation, weariness, worry.

Three suitcases lay on the bed, half-full. A couple of bulging dress bags hung from the wardrobe door and a large carry bag held shoes. Mama had her back turned, emptying out a drawer.

'I said don't let anyone in,' she snapped. She'd changed her evening dress for white linen slacks and a sleeveless print blouse.

'It's me.'

'Oh, Krista.' She dumped an armful of lingerie into one of the suitcases and closed the lid. 'Make yourself useful and clear out the ensuite will you?'

'Where are you going?'

'Sydney.'

'Tonight?'

'Yes.'

'Why don't you wait until morning and talk to Hugh first?'

She didn't answer, just slammed the drawer closed and opened the next.

'We've been over that,' said Brenda. 'Viivi wants to leave.'

Krista picked up a capacious bathroom bag and went to the ensuite. She filled it with everything she thought must be her mother's and not Hugh's. Brenda came in and did a quick check of the vanity and shower recess, collecting a few bottles of shampoo and shower gel.

'She's adamant that we go now,' she said softly.

'Is she talking divorce?'

Brenda nodded. 'I've never seen her like this.'

'What happened between them?'

'Hugh had an affair with Gwen that lasted until about a month ago.'

'My God.'

'He tried it on with Bunny. Apparently, after he ditched Gwen but she told him where to go.'

'Good for her.' No doubt the seating had been deliberate. Whose evil idea was that? Brenda or her mother's. Felix's interest in Bunny would be the cream on top.

'She was the one who told Viivi what had been going on.'

'Who is she? She said Mama invited her but I've never met her before.'

'Viivi hired her and invited her to things so she could watch Hugh. She's a lawyer and her brother is a private investigator. They work together and sometimes both go to functions as a couple.'

'So she knew.'

'Suspected. She always played down his flirtations because they were with girls she knew weren't a threat, but this one was much more personal. Gwen was supposed to be her best friend.'

'Why didn't she expose them both? Why invite Gwen here?'

'I think because it would be more humiliating for her for everyone to know. She doesn't want to be an object of pity. At least not tonight. It'll come out, of course.'

'Hurry up.' Her mother's voice dripped irritation.

Brenda and Krista took the bag of cosmetics to the bedroom.

'In there,' Viivi said, pointing to the remaining open suitcase. 'I'm ready.'

'Who's driving you?'

'We're taking the Mercedes and sharing,' said Brenda. 'We'll stay in Wagga tonight. I've booked rooms.'

There was nothing more to say beyond goodbye. Mama hugged her but her arms were empty, her mind elsewhere. Brenda gave her a quick kiss.

'Take care, Krista.'

'Safe trip.'

She helped them carry the bags to the front door where someone had already parked the car. The security guard loaded the pile of luggage into the boot, the two women got into the front seat with Brenda driving and they were gone.

Krista watched the red tail-lights disappear down the driveway. She may as well have farewelled an acquaintance who'd stayed a few days before moving on.

***

Krista slept deeply and to her surprise, having expected a sleepless night, woke later than usual. The house was quiet. She hadn't heard the guests leave last night and had no idea how long the party had gone on but the band was booked until one. Her mother and Brenda had left around eleven-thirty and she'd been in bed asleep not long after midnight in a shutdown of mind and body.

She sat up and stretched. Eight forty-five. Amazing. Brassy sunlight streamed through the blinds she'd only partially closed the previous night. It had a reddish tinge and the branches of the gum trees visible through the gap waved in a brisk wind.

Ten minutes later, she padded downstairs in her bikini, barefoot with a towel over her shoulder, to do her morning laps. The terrace room was clean and tidy, as was the kitchen when she poked her head in to see what was on offer for breakfast. Nothing. Not a soul around, the benches clear and spotless.

The breakfast room was similarly bare, with no sign of Gemma waiting to provide coffee or eggs.

Had everyone gone? Had Hugh left late last night as well? It seemed he had. The large master bedroom where Mama had packed last night was empty. Voices outside took her to the terrace when she headed back to the kitchen for food. Two delivery men moved about folding and stacking the tables and chairs onto trolleys. The marquee was already gone as was the portable dance floor. They must have arrived early.

She ran into her own bedroom to throw on shorts and T-shirt over her bikini and shove her feet into scuffs before going down to greet them.

'G'day,' one said as she appeared. 'Good party?'

'Yes, thanks. What time did you arrive?'

'About seven. Orders were to get cleared here by ten.'

That sounded like Hugh. He and Mama were planning to leave The Grange by eleven at the latest. Those plans had changed drastically last night.

'Did you see anyone this morning?'

'That girl who was here when we set up—the blonde?'

'Gemma. What did she say?'

'Nuthin' much. Just asked if we were right because everyone was leaving.'

'What time was that?'

'When we got here.'

'Did you see them go?'

'Heard cars leaving around seven-thirty.'

He grinned. 'Didja get left behind?'

'No. Thanks.'

She walked out the gate to the yard and checked the garage on the way to the stables where Rod would be up doing the morning chores. Her car stood in solitary state.

'Gone without so much as a goodbye,' she muttered. Wind whipped dust up in little eddies and tugged at her hair as she walked. The sky had a coppery sheen, the scent of smoke stronger than yesterday.

The bushfire. Rod's words crashed into her head, driving out all other thoughts. 'If the wind picks up we could be in trouble.' Were they in trouble? Which way was it blowing?

She hurried over the remaining distance, heart pounding with a whole other primal fear.

'Rod,' she called as she entered the big open doorway, blinking as her eyes adjusted to the relative gloom inside. 'Are you there?'

'Down the end.' His voice came from the last stall on the left.

Two horses watched curiously as she passed them. Neither was Calypso. If a fire was coming what would they do?

She reached the stall. Rod was with the big black stallion.

'Hi,' she said.

'Morning,' he said. 'I'll have to call Oliver. This boy's not feeling too good.'

'Fine. Rod, did you know everyone's gone?'

He patted the horse's neck and joined her, closing the door carefully. 'I heard the cars this morning.'

'Did Hugh speak to you?'

He shook his head. 'Weren't they supposed to leave today?'

He didn't know. How could he?

'What's wrong?' He frowned, studying her face.

'They had a massive bust-up in the middle of dinner. Viivi slapped him and walked out.'

'Wow. That sounds...

'Serious,' she said. 'She's furious and she's talking divorce. She and Brenda left last night. Took the Mercedes.'

'And now everyone else has gone, too. Leaving you here alone. Are you staying?'

'Angus took my keys so I can't get into my apartment.'

He shook his head. 'Christ. I'm sorry, Krista.'

'He rang me last night just as he was about to fly out of the country.'

'He never said a word to me about doing that.' He cursed under his breath. 'Where does that leave you? What about the Calypso thing?'

'It's now my problem. Hugh isn't getting involved. He reckons nothing will happen.'

'Right. Okay. Well, something is about to happen. You can smell the smoke, can't you?'

'Yes. Is it dangerous?'

'Not right now, but I was going to bring the horses in and be ready to leave if we have to. I've had the owners of the two mares on the phone asking about it but they seemed happy enough that we were well prepared.'

'Where would you go?'

'I got a text from the local fire service saying the Taylor's Bend showground is the centre for evacuated horses and other livestock. They have some stables and yards. I'd like to get them out of here early to be on the safe side but they aren't expecting anyone until later today.'

'What can I do?'

'Call Oliver about the stallion. He might be able to house him there. I can't take him near other people's horses. Does he have a float?'

'I didn't see one but he has a horse so maybe.'

'We can't take all the horses in one trip thanks to Angus smashing up the double float. The other one takes four and we have six to move. Good thing Archie is already gone.'

'I'll ask him. What else?'

'Pack up anything you don't want to lose and load it into the car. I'll bring in the other mares so we're ready to go when we have to.'

Krista ran back to the house. The two men were loading tables into the truck, moving much faster than before.

'Not looking good,' one of them said as she hurried by.

'Are you nearly finished?'

'Just about.'

She sprang up the stairs, taking them two at a time, and pounded into her bedroom to snatch her phone from the bedside table.

Oliver answered almost immediately.

'Hi, it's Krista,' she said and had to pause, swallow and regain her breath.

'Morning. How are things?'

'Everyone's gone. It's just me and Rod and the fire is coming. He says we should get ready to evacuate the horses and he wants to know if you have a float because we can only move four and we have six.'

'Slow down. How close is the fire?'

'I don't know but he said we should be safe and take the horses into the showground soon, just in case.'

'Okay. I do have a float.'

'He wondered if you could take the stallion to your place because he was going to call you anyway about him. He's sick.'

'I guess so. Calm down, Krista. I checked the fire report a little while ago and it's moving slowly.'

'But the wind's much stronger.'

'It's taking it away from you at the moment.'

'But it can change.'

'Yes, it can. I'll be out there in about forty-five minutes.'

'All right. Thanks, Oliver. Thank you.'

'Are there any other animals out there? Chooks or whatever?'

'I don't know. Rod will take care of them. He's really good.'

'You're lucky he's there.'

'I know. See you soon.'

She disconnected, trembling, and for a moment stood frozen in place, undecided about what to do next. Pack. She sprang into action. Luckily she hadn't brought much but what she did have was totally unsuitable for what was happening. Idiot. Fancy not bringing socks and sneakers. She dragged on jeans and the T-shirt. Maybe Mama had left something behind. They wore the same size shoe. She dragged her bags downstairs to the front door then raced along the corridor to the master bedroom. Mama would have taken anything important with her and there was nothing personal here she needed to rescue for her.

She charged into the walk-in closet. Two pairs of shoes lay on the floor along with a hideous pair of yellow fluoro joggers. Her phone rang.

'Mama?'

'Krista, look after Lola will you, please? I couldn't find her quickly last night. I don't know where she was.'

'Sure.'

'Is Hugh there?'

'No, everyone's gone.'

'Did he say anything?

'I didn't see him. I was asleep when he left.'

'Typical. Bye-bye.'

'Mama there's...' Too late, the line was dead.

Typical of Hugh or of herself?

And Lola? Where was Lola?

Chapter 9

Krista shoved her bare feet into the joggers and yelled, 'Lola, where are you? Here girl,' as she ran along the corridor flinging doors open in case the dog was shut in somewhere. No answering yap came from anywhere downstairs.

'Lola.' She charged back upstairs

The dog hadn't been in the house this morning. Usually she was pottering about getting in the way of the kitchen staff and wanting food. Maybe Hugh took her with him. Doubtful but worth a try. Surprisingly, he answered.

'Krista.'

'Hugh, do you have Lola with you?'

'No, ask your mother.'

'She wanted me to look after her but I can't find her and there's a bushfire coming.'

Silence.

'I'm sorry to leave you in a mess,' he said and he sounded genuinely remorseful. 'How close is it?'

'Rod said it's not dangerous yet but that can change. We're moving the horses into Taylor's Bend later today.'

'Good man. Do what he says, Krista, and get out of there. It's not worth risking your life.'

'I won't.'

'I have to go. Look after yourself.'

Another line clicked dead in her ear. No mention of the other threat. Look after herself? She'd give it her best shot because no-one else in her family gave a damn.

'Lola.'

No response upstairs.

In the garden?

One of the men was closing the back of the truck when she ran out the gate. The other one, already in the cabin, started the engine.

'Have you seen our little dog this morning? Brown and white?'

'No, sorry.'

'Okay, thanks.'

He waved and climbed aboard.

Where the hell was she?

'Lola,' she yelled. Still calling, she went back into the garden and peered into the beds that had so fascinated

Lola yesterday. No sign of her. She stood, hands on hips, staring around the deserted area. There was no more she could do other than hope Lola decided to reappear.

Krista went to the garage to bring her car to the front door ready to scramble if necessary. The wind hadn't increased but swirled in unpleasant gusts. She scanned the sky anxiously as she brought her suitcase out and loaded it into the boot along with her dress bag. Still the same strange colour as earlier, and the same tangy smell of smoke.

Rod was in the yard adjoining the stables, putting a halter on the last horse.

'Oliver's coming with a float,' she said. 'He'll be about forty-five minutes and he said the stallion can go to his place.'

'Good. Is it a double float?'

'I didn't ask, sorry.'

'It's okay. We can do a second run if we have to.'

'Rod, I can't find Lola.'

'Damn. Have you looked all over the house? Opened doors?'

'Yes but she'd bark if she was shut in somewhere. Those two guys packing up the tables and chairs hadn't seen her this morning. They've just left.'

'Have another look around outside.'

'Oliver wondered if there were other animals here?'

'No. Amy and I are going to get chooks we but haven't yet. Too busy.'

'Okay. I'll look for Lola.'

She turned to go but he said, 'Love the shoes, by the way.'

He had a massive grin and she had to laugh.

'Mama left them behind.'

'I'm not surprised. Hope they don't frighten the horses.'

'Ha-de-ha.'

This time she did a more thorough search of the garden, kneeling to peer under bushes, opening the door to the changing room by the pool and peering in even though that was a highly unlikely place to find her, and standing on the tiled edge searching intently for any sign of a little brown and white body sunk to the depths of the water.

'Lola,' she yelled, louder each time.

She walked right around the outside of the large house. Where could she possibly be? Had someone taken her last night? Why would they? Everyone in attendance could buy their own pedigreed dog without a moment's thought. Everyone knew Mama loved Lola and everyone liked Mama enough to attend her party. No-one would want to take her pet and anyway, why would someone bother with Lola? She was yappy, getting on in years so past breeding, shed hairs everywhere and got in the way most of the time.

Krista walked across to the paddock fence behind the house and stared across the hostile, brown expanse. A few gum trees offered patchy shade from the relentless sun but now their upper branches thrashed about in the increasing wind. When she shouted, her words were snatched from her mouth and sucked away to disappear into the turbulent air. She turned and followed the fence line to its junction with the white-painted wooden rail fence running beside the driveway.

She crossed the dusty track and climbed onto the fence to scan the other field, deserted now Rod had brought in all the horses. Nothing. No small white and brown figure broke the dismal stretch of dried grass. It was as if this land had swallowed her whole.

The sound of an engine made her jump down and walk towards the stables. Rod had used his ute to bring the big horse float closer to the stable doors and opened the back, ready to load the first evacuees.

'Find her?' he asked.

She chased the mad imaginings of a cannibalistic countryside from her mind. The unrelenting heat and the wind, bearing with it gritty dust and dead leaves, was enough to drive anyone insane.

'No. Not a sign. Do you think someone might have taken her last night?'

'It's possible, I suppose. Why, though?'

'I don't know, I'm just guessing. Could she be hurt somewhere?' She pushed hair from her eyes. Short though the style was, the longer front bits were annoying in these conditions. Normally it sat neatly. Normally she wasn't outside being sandblasted by the wind.

'That's more likely, I'd say. There are a lot of snakes around.'

'Oh no.' She hadn't even thought of snakes, snakebite.

'Take a look around the stables. I haven't seen her in the yards or anywhere obvious, but she could be in one of the empty stalls or even over near my house. Check there too. Go round the back and look under the steps. She could have got under the house. There's a torch in the laundry.'

'Okay. Do you need help here?'

'No, thanks. I won't get the horses on board until Oliver gets here and we're ready to go, so I'll check the stables properly after I've loaded some feed into the truck. Do you have spare room in your car?'

'Yes. I'll bring it down here.'

Having reparked the BMW, Krista strode to the small, neat weatherboard cottage tucked away to the side, behind the stables. Amy had managed to keep roses alive in the drought and a flourishing herb garden grew in pots along the verandah. The front of the house was only two steps up, with no access underneath for even a little Lola-sized animal, but the land sloped down to the rear.

'Lola,' she yelled as she walked down the path. A Hills hoist washing line with a towel, underwear, shirts and socks pegged up spun in the wind. Krista ran across and caught the wildly flapping towel, bundling it and the other garments under her arm. She snatched the peg bucket up and ran to the house. The torch lay on a shelf in the laundry.

Back outside, she got down on hands and knees next to the steps leading to the verandah. 'Lola.'

The beam was strong and illuminated, through a wire-netting barrier, bare earth and the brick pile foundations under the house. 'Lola. Are you there?'

The only sound was the wind rustling busily in the trees nearby and the rattle of a loose board somewhere. Krista straightened and gazed around the yard. Lola could be anywhere and she had no way of knowing how long she'd been missing. If she'd been bitten by a snake she could have died immediately. She could be lying in a paddock, hidden by a fallen branch or a dip in the ground.

Krista walked slowly back to the stables. Rod had moved her gear to the front seat and was stacking sacks of something and a pile of empty buckets in the boot of her car. Her stomach growled, suddenly complaining about the lack of breakfast.

'No luck?'

'No. I've no idea where to look now.'

'Oliver phoned and said he'll be a bit late. Emergency with a pregnant pig.'

'Do we have time?'

'I haven't had any notice of immediate evacuation but we're on standby. Last update said the wind had shifted and the fire had swung around to the west a bit more, which is good news for us. Things can change very quickly though.'

'Shall I make tea? I haven't had anything to eat yet.'

'Sounds good. I could do with some food too. We might not get a chance later.'

'Sure. Come in when you're ready.'

In the kitchen, Krista discovered plenty of leftovers from last night's dinner in the form of avocados, sliced and unsliced melons, salads, bread rolls, cold meat and chocolate mousse. She prepared a pot of tea and set about making a couple of meat and salad rolls for Rod. Then she ate some of the fruit while eggs boiled on the stove for her breakfast.

What would she do if Rod said they had to leave before she found Lola? If Mama and Hugh didn't know where she was, no-one else would have any idea. She hadn't seen Lola since pre-dinner drinks in the garden when she was talking to Oliver. She wasn't in Mama's room when she was packing and Mama had been far too furious and preoccupied to think of her dog if she wasn't actually in sight. She was leaving Lola behind, in Krista's care, when she and Hugh went skiing, so in her mind Lola was taken care of whether plans changed or not.

After Rod had devoured the rolls and slurped down two cups of tea, he checked the fire status report.

'No change,' he said.

'What does that mean? Shall we leave?'

'Not yet. We might not have to at all if the fire keeps on the way it's going now.'

'Will you tell Oliver not to come?'

'I want him to check Fred and if he has the float he could take him anyway. Then, if we have to leave fast, we can.'

'Okay. I still need to find Lola but I don't know what to do.'

'I guess I could take a ride around the paddocks and have a look.'

'Would you?'

'It'll have to be a quick one.'

'Take Calypso.'

Rod stood up. 'You should learn to ride. She's a lovely mare.'

'Arch Rival is friendlier.'

'Yeah, she's a favourite here. She'd be good to start on.'

When he'd gone, Krista cleared away. Nearly twelve-thirty. The morning had blown by on the wind. She should check the house one more time. In the living area, she peered behind the cane chairs and looked behind the bar. Outside the wind had died down a little but the sky still had the sinister coppery look and the smell had seeped in to contaminate the house.

Krista walked through the whole downstairs and then up to the first floor, kneeling to look under all the beds and opening cupboard doors Lola couldn't possibly manage to slide open. Half an hour later she had to admit Lola wasn't indoors. She walked around the outside of the house again, looking under bushes and behind trees. Her only hope now lay with Rod.

How long would he spend out there? It was a horrible day for riding and very kind of him to offer. He'd been gone just over an hour. She walked down to the stables, averting her face from the full onslaught of the wind, which had picked up again and bullied and pulled at her clothes and body, forcing her to fight to reach shelter.

The horses were restless in their stalls, snorting and stamping their feet, watching with ears pricked as she entered the wide corridor. The stallion still looked miserable tucked away in his stall at the end. Rod had closed the double doors, and the building creaked and groaned, but it was well-built and in no danger of collapse. Hugh had spared no expense.

She continued on to the far end, opened the smaller door and stepped out into the light, steeling herself against the wind again. No sign of Rod. She climbed onto the post-and-rail fence of the yard to scan the paddock, but he must have gone around to the side out of sight. Nothing to do but wait for his return.

She retreated to the office. There, she sat at his desk and checked the fire report. Not good. Smaller fires had sprung up, causing their own problems and diluting the firefighting forces on the main blaze which was still raging out of control. A shudder of fear rippled through her body as she stared at the screen with its red warning markers. They seemed horrifyingly close to The Grange although no evacuation notices had been given yet. Taylor's Bend wasn't listed as under threat but Jindalee was. This danger was real.

She shoved the chair back with no clear idea of what to do next. Where was Rod? He should be back by now.

They had to get the horses loaded and flee to safety. She couldn't do that by herself. She called his number but the phone went to voicemail.

Oliver. He answered almost immediately.

'Krista.'

'Where are you? Are you coming? I'm here by myself and I don't know what to do.'

'Sorry, I'm on an emergency call. I can't get to you for a couple of hours. Where's Rod?' His lack of awareness of how dire her situation was sent a pulse of frustrated anger through her body.

'He took Calypso out to look for Lola in the paddocks over an hour ago but he hasn't come back yet. He said he'd be quick.'

'Why would Lola be out in a paddock?'

For God's sake! Was he being deliberately dense?

'I don't know. We can't find her. Mama left her behind and asked me to look after her but she's lost and...' A sob rose in her throat, drowning the anger, and she had to stop talking while the urge to wail subsided. Why didn't he get it?

'Okay, okay. Calm down. I'll be there as soon as I can.'

'I don't know who else to call. You're the only person...' The words stopped abruptly. How could she finish that sentence?

'I have to go now. See you soon.'

'Thanks.'

She slipped the phone into her pocket and went into the stables to wait with the horses. An hour and a half now he'd been out there. No-one would say that was a quick look. She patted the silky noses and murmured soothing words completely at odds with the turmoil in her head, but the horses seemed to like the company and a couple of them nuzzled her cheek and neck.

Then Firebrand neighed and the horse in the stall closest to the end doors did the same. Rod on Calypso? Were the horses greeting their friend? Krista ran to the door and flung it open.

Calypso stood outside the yard fence, reins trailing from her neck, with no rider.

'Rod?' yelled Krista.

Calypso flung her head up and moved away in a nervous jog, but spun around when Krista opened the yard gate and trotted inside. Krista grabbed the reins and led her into the stables to an empty stall.

A cursory check showed no injuries and Calypso wasn't limping so Rod must have either been thrown, or he dismounted and she bolted.

He could be anywhere. He could be walking back. He could be hurt.

'Where's Rod?' she demanded. 'What happened?'

Calypso bent her head and sniffed at the straw on the floor of the stall. Krista set about trying to get the saddle and bridle off with only the haziest idea of where to start.

***

Oliver turned into The Grange driveway much later than he'd told Krista but what else could he do? Col's sow was in big trouble giving birth when she called and he wasn't walking out on it to deal with Krista's histrionics. She had to take responsibility and not substitute him for her mother when it came to dealing with things.

Grabbing some very late lunch and hitching up the float had taken more time, then his mother had phoned to say Julian had had a bad fall and broken an ankle.

She was her usual self and delivered the news with a typically apologetic, 'Your father and Julian didn't want to bother you with the news but I thought you should know. He *is* your brother.'

'I know, Mum, thanks. I'll give him a call.'

The line crackled in his ear.

'Are you still there?' she asked.

'Yes. How are you?'

'I've been a bit tired lately but I'm all right.'

'Take care of yourself. Make Dad take you on holiday.' As if that would happen. If they ever went away it was to a medical conference where he was a guest speaker and Mum trailed about after him.

She laughed softly. 'Can you imagine? Your father can't sit still long enough to have a holiday. He's says they're a waste of time.'

'I know, but you don't think that so why can't he do what you want for a change?'

'Oliver, don't be like that. You know I don't mind.'

'Do I?' he muttered. 'Don't you?'

'Are you getting on all right out there?'

'I love it. You should visit. On your own,' he added quickly. 'I've joined the local theatre group and we're doing *Patience* in June. I'm playing cello in the orchestra. You could come to see the show.'

She didn't reply immediately then she said, 'I would enjoy that.' After another pause, 'We'll see.'

'Mum, I have to go, I'm sorry. Think about it. You're always welcome here and you've never visited.'

We'll see. As every child knows, that means 'we won't'.

As he drove between the rows of trees lining the driveway he wondered what had made him blurt out that he was playing cello again. A childish need to please or impress a parent? Did that never go away? His father wouldn't care. His father would think it a waste of his time, if he thought at all. But his mother ... she'd sounded pleased and she also sounded as though she would really like to come for a visit.

Families! He and Krista both.

He turned and parked next to the stables so the car was facing out ready to leave. Krista ran out to greet him, the wind whipping her hair into a messy tangle, her feet in a hideous pair of fluoro yellow sneakers.

'Hi,' he said. 'Like your shoes.'

She shook her head briefly, discarding the flippant comment, expression stern. 'Calypso came back without Rod.'

'When?'

Not good. He'd be a very competent horseman. He followed her into the stables. The wind was still blowing but lighter than earlier in the afternoon, easing the fire danger a notch but not the smoke haze.

'A couple of hours ago. I walked around this back paddock but I didn't know which direction or how far he went and I wanted to stay close enough so I'd see you arrive.'

'Is Calypso injured?'

'Not that I can see. She's here.'

A saddle and bridle lay dumped on the floor outside the stall. The mare stood quietly as he ran his hands down her legs and checked for cuts or bites.

'You're right. She's fine,' he said. 'She's a beautiful animal.'

'Bit different to Archie now I've seen them both up close.'

'Yes, but close enough to fake it for a while. I can take the car around the paddocks and look for him.'

Oliver hurried out to unhitch the float. Krista hovered, watching. 'Shall I come with you?'

'Might as well. Open the gate.' He got into the car and started the engine.

She ran across to the gate into the paddock that ran beside the driveway up to the road. He hadn't seen anything on the way in but he hadn't been looking.

He stopped at the gate and she wrestled with the passenger door, but gave it a good yank to open it and a hefty slam when she was in.

'What colour shirt is he wearing?'

'Dark blue.'

'Pity it's not bright red.' He smiled and glanced at her shoes. 'Or yellow.'

This time she smiled. 'They're all I could find. I can't imagine why Mama had them. But I know why she left them.'

'No sign of Lola?'

'No. Do you think we'll disappear too?'

'A black hole in the paddock?'

'Or abducted by aliens.'

The ground sloped away to the right the closer they came to the fence along the road. Oliver swung the car to head downhill towards a windbreak of trees on the far side.

'Is this the boundary?'

'Yes. The property widens out behind the house and on the other side.'

'Nothing here.'

'No. I walked about halfway so I could see the fence. He'd never hear me calling, not with the wind.'

He drove close to the tree line and turned to the right. A few branches had come down, a couple of them squashing the fence.

'They'll need clearing.'

When he reached the fence that ran across to the stables, Krista jumped out to open the gate leading to the rear paddock where the post-and-rail yards adjoined the building.

'Calypso came in here,' she said.

Oliver clamped his mouth firmly on a sharp retort. Why the hell didn't she say so and they could have started looking in the right paddock? Horses couldn't open gates as far as he knew. Not these gates.

'Oh!' She gasped. The penny must have dropped 'How stupid. I'm sorry. I'm not thinking straight.'

'Okay. So how far did you go in this one?'

'Till I could see down to the trees from the rise. It's much, much bigger. I couldn't walk it.'

'I take it you tried phoning him?'

'Yes. Voicemail.'

So he couldn't answer, which could mean he was injured, had lost or dropped the phone or it was broken. Injury was certain. He could have walked back within half an hour otherwise. There was no way of telling how long Calypso took to come home.

'Is this paddock isolated from the others? Would the gates be closed?'

'I don't know. The gate closest to the stables is shut but I've never been this far down. I don't think they let the horses loose in here very often.'

Oliver accelerated over the clear, dusty ground towards the copse of gumtrees, which stretched for a hundred metres or so. More branches had fallen.

'Do you think Lola would come this far?' he asked.

'I've no idea. She might have chased a rabbit or something.'

He glanced in the rear-view mirror. The buildings were almost out of sight behind the ridge. He ran the car slowly along beside the trees but not so close a falling branch would land on them. At the end he swung wide and followed along the other side.

'There he is,' shrieked Krista. 'Stop.'

She was out of the car before he'd stopped, running into the trees. Stumbling over fallen branches, twigs and leaf litter, he followed her towards the figure lying motionless, facedown on the ground, legs obscured by a jumble of leaves. The jagged broken end of the branch protruded from the tangle, thick and heavy.

Krista knelt beside Rod. 'Can you hear me? Rod?'

She looked up, pale faced. 'Is he alive?'

Oliver checked for a pulse. 'Yes. Call an ambulance. I don't think we should move him but we can get the branch off.'

'Thought you'd never come,' Rod murmured. 'Calypso...'

'Smart girl went home. She's fine. That's how Krista knew to look for you.'

While Krista made the call, Oliver studied the situation. It would take both of them to shift the branch and it would need to be lifted off cleanly and moved aside. Was she strong enough? Dropping it or scraping it over his body would be disastrous.

'It'll be half an hour.' Krista jammed the phone into her jeans pocket.

'Help me get this branch off him.'

Oliver broke off as many smaller pieces as he could manage by hand. 'You grab that end and I'll take this bit.' He took hold of the thick, broken end and gently tested the weight. Heavy but doable. 'On three, lift and turn to your left, clear of his feet.'

She bent her knees and grasped two thicker pieces branching from the main trunk.

'One, two, three.'

Oliver sucked in air and strained hard to lift the branch away from Rod's body while she swung around and took two steps to the side. He staggered over the rough ground, hanging on with muscles straining until there was at least a metre clearance.

'Okay.'

The deadweight crashed down.

Rod groaned and tried to move his head.

'Take it easy, mate. The ambulance is on its way.' Oliver spoke softly as he did a rough assessment of the damage to the lower body. One leg looked bad, the ankle bent at an odd angle but he didn't dare move him.

'Krista, there's a blanket and a couple of towels in my car. Get them, please, and the water bottle in the driver's side pocket.'

She scampered away to return minutes later with laden arms.

'Put the blanket over him.' He folded a towel and slipped it under Rod's cheek as a pillow. Carefully he held the bottle to the parched lips, allowing a few drops at a time to moisten his mouth. With the remaining towel he wiped away dirt and sweat from his face. No blood on the head was a good sign but the leg of his jeans was stained red.

'Can you feel your legs?'

'Damn right,' came the hoarse reply. 'Hurts like hell.'

'Your left leg is broken.'

'Branch fell. Knocked me for six.'

'Yes. Lucky it didn't hit you on the head.'

'Fire?'

'The wind has died down so we're not in danger right now.'

'Call Amy.'

'What's her number?'

Krista typed as he recited. When Amy answered, she gave her a quick rundown then put the phone to Rod's ear so he could reassure her he was alive.

'She's coming home,' said Krista. 'She'll be here some time tonight.'

Oliver nodded. 'Take the car and go back up to the house so you can show Fiona where to bring the ambulance.'

'Fiona?'

'It'll most likely be her. Could be Eddie.'

'All right.' He handed her the keys. 'Can you drive a manual?'

'Of course.'

She gave him such a scornful look he said. 'Sorry.'

'My dad was a Formula One driver.'

'Really?'

'Yes, really.'

She turned to go but Rod croaked, 'Angus said you were three when he died.'

Chapter 10

Rod's left leg was broken just above the ankle but Fiona's initial appraisal was that an X-ray would probably show it was a relatively straightforward break. He had numerous scrapes and a cut on his thigh where a sharp, splintery piece of tree had ripped through the denim pants.

Krista, with Oliver beside her, heaved a sigh of relief when the ambulance disappeared down the driveway.

'Sounds like he'll be okay,' he said.

'Thank goodness. I need a drink after that. How about you?' A shower and food as well.

'It's getting late. I should go home.'

'But...' He couldn't leave her here all alone. Surely he realised that?

'What?'

'What if the fire comes? I can't load the horses by myself. And Lola is still missing. I can't leave without her.'

Oliver planted his hands on his hips and gazed at where the sun was slowly heading for the horizon, a glowing red ball behind the curtain of smoke. He came to his decision and turned to face her.

'I'll take Firebrand and another horse to my place. I'll settle them in and do a few chores, then come back. Okay? We can't move the others without someone to settle them and stay with them at the showgrounds.'

Weak with relief, she could only nod.

'I'll take Calypso,' he said.

She found her voice. 'Thank you. I'll cook dinner. Will you stay overnight? There's plenty of room,' she added hastily in case he thought she was attempting to offer some sort of bonus. Or a bribe.

'Not much point coming back if I don't, is there? Specially if we have to get out in the middle of the night.' Was he annoyed with her again? She couldn't tell by the impassive tone.

'No, I guess not. No. Thanks.'

'All right. Come and help load them, and you'll need to feed the others and check their water.'

'What do I feed them?'

The enormity of the situation slammed into her. She was the only one here and she would have four valuable horses to care for, two of which belonged to other people who Rod had assured would be well taken care of and safe. Goodness knows how long Rod would be gone, and even when he did come home he couldn't work. Amy would go straight to Wagga to the hospital and stay there with him. Might be days before they discharged him.

Would she be able to handle it? She'd have to, there was no-one else and Oliver wouldn't be able to stay here with her for long. He was already doing her a massive favour. Another one.

'Not sure but I'll mix up a basic feed bucket and you can watch me and do one each for the other three.'

The shower and drink vanished into the future.

Oliver didn't return for nearly two and a half hours, during which time Krista took care of the horses, a task she discovered was quite enjoyable, checked there was enough food to put together a decent meal, made up the bed and cleaned the ensuite in the spare room where Hugh's brother had stayed. Gemma, the maid, hadn't changed the sheets or cleaned the bathrooms before they all left. She wouldn't have had time. She'd also dragged her suitcase from the car and back upstairs to her room.

When Oliver came in through the sliding door to the garden, calling out, 'I'm back,' Krista was newly showered and in her skirt and last clean tank top. She'd need to do some washing later, having only brought clothes for a few days, most of them totally impractical for what lay ahead and all of them impregnated with the odour of smoke. The fluoro sneakers had given her blisters. Maybe Amy would lend her socks.

'In the kitchen,' she called.

He'd changed too and carried a backpack, which he dumped on the floor by the door.

'Can I help?'

'No, you've done enough. Sit down. Like a beer? Or there's plenty of wine.'

'A beer, thanks.' He perched on a stool at the bench.

She gave him the beer and slid a plate of antipasti across before coming to sit beside him. 'There's a fair bit of food leftover. Do you mind steak again?'

'Eating leftover steak? Not at all.' He ate an olive. 'Any of that chocolate mousse left?'

She smiled. 'Yes. Enough to make you sick.'

He raised the beer bottle. 'Cheers.'

She clinked her wine glass against it. 'Cheers.'

'I was listening to the radio on the way back and they said they have that main fire front under control but they're worried if the wind comes up again they'll lose it. Might get breakouts in other areas.'

'So we could still be in trouble?'

'Yep. Can't rule it out until the end of the fire season. Trouble is, that's getting longer each year.'

'But the paddocks are so dry there isn't much to burn.'

'There'll be enough. You've got trees all along the fences and the wind carries burning leaves and twigs for a long way. That's how it jumps ahead. If that happens you have to put the spot fires out. At least you've got green gardens round the house.'

'But won't we be out of here by then?'

'Should be. I'm just saying...'

'Is Taylor's Bend safe?'

'Nowhere is really safe but the Bend has never been burnt out. We've had a couple of grassfires but nothing completely out of control. The town is tucked away in the hills, a bit sheltered, and the river acts as a firebreak of sorts.'

Krista took a cracker biscuit with a piece of camembert. 'What a day.'

'Have you found Lola?'

'Gosh! No. I'd forgotten all about her. I've no idea where she could be.'

'Maybe she got shut in somewhere the night of the party when everyone was packing up.'

'Maybe. But she'd bark.'

'Not necessarily. We should take another quick look around the garden. I will, if you like. Fresh eyes.'

'I'll come too.'

Oliver took some crackers and cheese then headed for the door. The dog had been missing for over twelve hours. If she wasn't injured she'd be all right. Thirsty and hungry but not in danger. If she'd been bitten by something she was unlikely to be alive. Did Krista realise?

'Krista,' he said. 'If she was bitten by a tick or a snake she may not have survived.'

'I know.' She flicked him a tiny smile. 'But thanks.'

The sun was just disappearing behind the stables, casting an eerie red orange glow over the garden. Smoke hung in the air but the wind had almost died away.

'I hate that smell,' she said. 'It's in everything.'

'Yeah, it stinks. You've checked all the bushes, I suppose?' he asked.

'Yes.'

'Any sheds in the gardens?'

'None in this area but the garden shed is around to the side. She couldn't get in there. The gardener hasn't been here since Thursday.'

'Did you look?'

'I opened the door and called her. The same with the pool house. I'm the only one who swims and I don't go in there. No-one else was using that.'

'That you know of.' Nothing that crowd did would surprise him. They were like square dancers—change your partners and do-si-do.

Krista threw him a startled look. 'I suppose any of the guests could have gone in.'

'Let's check the shed first.'

Oliver peered into the gloomy interior. Krista flicked a switch on, bathing the contents in bright light. As far as garden sheds went, this one was the deluxe version and totally unlike any sheds he'd ever seen. Everything was arranged neatly on shelves and the larger equipment like the mower, two chainsaws, an edger and a whipper snipper were ranged along the far wall. He walked in and moved some sacks of fertiliser aside, pretty certain Lola wasn't here but making the effort anyway.

'You're right.' He turned off the light.

'The pool is around the corner.'

An inviting expanse of water lay before him in a twenty-five-metre rectangle, surrounded by paving. 'Wow. Nice.'

'You can have a swim if you like.'

'Might take you up on that later.'

He skirted around the water to the white-painted cabana on the far side, tucked into the corner with a slate terrace, bare now, save for a deck chair and two sun lounges.

'We should put those inside,' he said.

Krista took the cushions off the lounges while Oliver folded the deck chair. She helped him carried the lot in to the pool house.

Inside was a tiled room furnished with cane chairs with big padded green cushions, a table, a bar in one corner and three closed doors opposite the entrance.

'I didn't open those,' said Krista. 'I assumed she couldn't get in there.'

Oliver strode across and flung one open. 'She probably couldn't but you never know. If someone came in she might have followed without them knowing.'

The room had a bed with rumpled sheets and pillows out of place. Two empty champagne bottles lay on the floor and empty glasses sat on the bedside table.

'Visitors, I'd say.' He threw Krista a grin but she was already in the room, flinging open the wardrobe door and almost climbing in to look.

'Not here.'

An adjoining door led into a small bathroom with a shower and toilet. Nowhere in there for a dog to hide. Oliver went back into the main area and opened the remaining door. It was a walk-in linen press with shelves holding towels and scuffs, and a couple of robes in the hanging space. Curled up on the floor was Lola.

'She's here.' He squatted down to examine her. No injuries but fast breaths, listless and hot.

Krista squeezed in beside him. 'Is she alive?'

'Yes. Dehydrated but she'll be fine.'

He scooped up the little dog and took her to the bathroom. She licked the water he dripped into her mouth while Krista watched, hands tightly clasped.

'Good girl, Lola.' He glanced at Krista. Tears shimmered on her eyelids. 'Hey,' he said softly. 'She'll be fine.'

She ran a hand across her eyes and smiled, reaching out to pat Lola gently on the head.

'Let's get her to the house. I've got some rehydration sachets in my bag.'

'I'll get it,' she said. 'Where is it?'

'In the car, back seat. Black leather.'

***

Fortunately Lola drank the liquid Oliver prepared, and as he suspected it would, the electrolyte replacement worked well. Krista had brought her blanket in and folded it in the corner for her to lie on.

'It's lucky she was indoors,' he said, looking down at her as she lapped up the quantity he'd given her. 'It was cooler and the air is clean in there.'

'Someone must have shut her in deliberately,' said Krista.

Satisfied Lola was in recovery mode, she'd finally got up from the floor beside her where she'd been offering encouragement and begun to grill the steaks on the hi-tech stovetop. He hadn't wanted to prompt her by suggesting he cook but he was starving and it had been a long, long day. The platter of antipasti was gone, but olives and a few bits of salami and cheese barely hit the sides.

'She might have barked too much when they were trying to be secretive.' Oliver drank his neglected beer. Warm. He put it in the massive fridge and opened another bottle. There was enough food in that thing to withstand a year-long siege.

'So they shoved her in the cupboard and forgot to let her out.'

'Probably too drunk.'

Krista snorted. 'I hate those people. If Mama divorces Hugh I won't have to see any of them ever again. I hope she does.'

'You don't need to see them anyway, do you? You must have your own friends.'

'I do but...'

'But?'

'I don't know if I have anything much in common with most of them. My best friend, Trudi, got married last year and they moved to Switzerland.'

He cast his mind around for a positive comment. 'That guy at our table seemed okay. The older one you danced with.'

'Jack. Yes, he's nice.'

'And I met someone earlier. An elderly lady in pale purple. I've forgotten her name but she was nice.' About seventy but still ... a nice lady.

'I don't know who that was. All sorts of people came who had nothing to do with them personally.'

She turned the steaks over in a sizzle of steam and the delicious smell set saliva flowing. Lola, having finished the fluid, looked up from her blanket and sniffed.

'She's feeling better,' he said. 'We can give her a bit of soft food in a little while.'

'You know what I think?' she said. 'I think Hugh and Gwen were in that room. Lola would probably follow Hugh, and if Mama had already left she'd stick with him. He doesn't like her much.'

Oliver sighed. 'Krista, I don't know what to say. I don't know these people. I'm sorry you're in the situation you're in, but I think you should look on it as an opportunity to make some decisions for yourself. Be you.'

'I think these are ready.' She put the steaks on a plate and covered them with foil. 'They should rest for a few minutes. I'll set the table in the other room.'

Here came the ice maiden again. Whenever he suggested she be proactive instead of being the victim, he could almost see the frost forming. He didn't care if the steaks rested or not but he wasn't arguing with her in that mood.

He took their glasses and obediently went in the direction she pointed.

Krista ate slowly despite being hungry. Oliver had attacked her again and his words hurt. Couldn't he see she was trying? At the moment she had no choice but to assume Rod's role and attempt to take care of Hugh's property and the horses. How could she make plans for her own future in these circumstances? He knew she couldn't go home to her apartment. What did he expect?

He said, 'I'll give Abbie a call after dinner and see if she needs help painting sets.'

'What?' She looked at him blankly.

'You said you'd like to help out with the show. *Patience*.' He cut off a lump of meat. 'Great steak. Thanks.'

'Right. yes. Thanks, that'd be good.'

He sat there so calmly, enjoying his dinner. Life was simple for him, doing work he loved, in a community he loved.

'I need to call my brother too,' he said. 'He broke his leg somehow. Mum phoned to tell me just before I came out here.'

'Gosh, him too? Are broken legs the fashion?'

He laughed. 'These things are supposed to come in threes. We'd better be careful.'

'We could count Angus as the first. He cracked a rib and sprained his wrist in the accident.'

'We're safe then.' His gaze caught hers and stuck. Her hand froze on the fork she was holding, breath stalled in her lungs. He smiled and her mouth curved all by itself. How did he do that? One minute she was angry and hurt by his words, the next he'd moved on and made her laugh. He didn't hold a grudge, that was for sure. Did she?

He'd begun eating again, piling potato salad onto his plate, oblivious to the turmoil he aroused across the table.

'How many brothers and sisters do you have?' she asked. He knew a lot about her disastrous family, she knew nothing about his.

'Just Julian. He's older. He's a very successful lawyer in Sydney.'

'Is he married? Do you have nieces and nephews?'

'No. He swore off women a few years ago when his fiancée dumped him. They met at university and he was devastated when she called it off.'

'Poor man.'

'Better before than after.'

'Not much consolation.'

'S'pose not.'

What about Oliver? Did he have a lost love? A broken heart? Or did he break hearts? No, not that, not deliberately. He was too kind, too honest.

'And what about your parents?' The vague reference he'd made at the party last night popped into her head. What was it he'd said? Something about his father. That Hugh's friends reminded him of his father. In what way?

'My father is one of the most eminent cardiologists in the country. My mother runs the house and looks after him.'

'They must be proud of you and your brother.'

He nodded but something in his expression made her ask, 'What did you mean when you said those people reminded you of your father? I mean Gwen and Felix and the Trues.'

'Snobs,' he said. 'They think the money you earn defines you and your place in society. Worse than that. Defines you as a person, your value as a person. My father wanted me to be a doctor like him. He thinks being a vet is a waste of my talent and living out here is completely insane.'

'But that's ridiculous. How could anyone think that? Especially a parent whose child is happy, well-educated and employed?'

He shrugged. 'I'm sure a lot do—parents who think their children are a disappointment. They might not say so but they often don't have to. The children know.'

Angus was a perfect example and Hugh made no secret of it. A pang of sympathy for her stepbrother took her by surprise. For all her faults, her mother never gave her the feeling she was a disappointment.

'What about your mother?'

'She rarely has an opinion of her own. She follows my father's lead in everything.'

Krista sipped her wine as understanding dawned. No wonder Oliver had been so vehement about a woman's reason for marrying. And so forthright when he encouraged her to find her own way in life. But it needn't be all bad, need it? The homemaker role as a wife was a choice. A choice few women could afford to make these days when she remembered the juggling act of those women with young children in her various workplaces.

It was something she'd never have to consider from a financial aspect.

'Is she happy?

'I think so. To a point. But if she wasn't, I doubt she'd have the strength to leave.'

Was he trying to tell her his father was physically abusive? Surely he and his brother would intervene if that were the case?

'He's not violent, is he?'

'No, no! He'd never hit anyone.' He smiled but it was sour, quite unlike his usual crinkly eyed grin. 'His hands are too precious to risk damaging. No, it's more that he sees his way as the only way. I'm sure he loves Mum and she loves him.'

'That's like Hugh. His way is the only way.'

Then Oliver caught her offside again. 'Krista, I'm sorry if I bully you about finding your own life. It's just that ... my mother has never had the opportunity to explore what she could be. She's always subjugated her own wants and needs to my father's. They were engaged very quickly after they met. He'd just graduated as a doctor and she had an office job she didn't like much, so when he suggested she stop work and bring up their children she did. Now that we're grown and gone, she only has my father and his career. I think she drifted into it without realising she was disappearing as a person in her own right.'

'Oliver, she might be perfectly happy with her life.'

'She says she is.'

'Why not believe her?'

'Because there's never any discussion about the major decisions in their lives. He chose the house, he chose the car she should drive and the colour, he decided two children were enough when she wanted four. She always wanted a daughter. He thinks holidays are a waste of time so he never takes her away on one. She likes opera and musicals but he hates them so she never gets to go unless it's a charity event or something, and he's given tickets and has to put in an appearance.'

Krista listened intently to the eye-opening rant. It was clearly a subject that affected him deeply and touched emotions she'd had no idea were lurking beneath the laidback exterior. Was she the first person to hear all this? If so, it was a humbling privilege she really didn't deserve and had no idea how to respond to.

He stopped talking abruptly. 'Sorry.'

Krista shook her head. 'Don't be.' She toyed with the stem of her wineglass, forming and discarding sentences in her mind. 'You know, when I was young I always envied my friends and other kids with two parents at home—who had a proper family. But now I know everyone has their own problems. No-one has the perfect family. At least not that I've come across yet.'

What a hopelessly inadequate thing to say. And so depressing, rather than uplifting or encouraging.

Oliver smiled. 'You haven't met Dot and Laurie. They run the General Store in town. They're both in their eighties and they're totally devoted to each other. They have daughters who've married and live in the area and they're always visiting Dot and Laurie with the grandchildren.'

'I'd love to meet them. I need to boost my faith in families.'

'Maybe you just need to meet a few normal people. Get involved in the musical and you'll see what small town community is all about.'

While Krista stacked the dishwasher and cleared away, a task she insisted on doing alone, Oliver filled Lola's bowl with water. The little dog was doing well. Lucky they'd found her when they did, before she became dangerously weak. As it was, she'd be fine by the morning.

He phoned Abbie about the sets.

'Rupe told me about her,' she said without elaborating. 'Is she in town for long?'

'Hard to say. At least a week, possibly more. She's keen to help.' He walked outside to the garden terrace. A light breeze stirred the treetops, rustling the leaves. 'She's had a rough couple of days—family trouble—so it'd be good if you could find something for her to do.'

'Sure,' she said. 'I'll be at the Arts Centre most mornings from about nine this coming week, and so will Maureen, doing the costumes. She's sure to need help with something.'

'Great. Thanks, Abbie.'

'So she's nice, is she? Rupe said she was a bit abrasive.'

'She's okay,' he said cautiously. 'Like I said, she has some bad family stuff happening.'

'Right. I look forward to meeting her. See you, Oliver.' Was she laughing quietly at the other end of the line? One thing he could count on with Abbie, she wasn't a gossip and she'd endured more than her share of troubles before settling down with Rupe.

He went back inside.

'Abbie said she'll be at the Arts Centre in town from nine every morning and can do with some help. Maureen will be there too, doing costumes, and Abbie said she'll probably have things for you to do.'

She turned from wiping down the bench and her lovely wide smile said it all, stopping him in his tracks, stopping his brain.

'Thanks. That's great.'

He gulped and swallowed and got his vocal chords working again. 'I wasn't sure how long you'd be in town but I thought at least a week.'

'It depends on Rod. Amy can't manage on her own for too long but with two of us we should be okay. And there's the fire.'

'Yes, there's that.' He grimaced. 'Fingers crossed.'

'How's your brother?'

'I'll call him now.' He went to the terrace room where he'd sat with the obnoxious fat man and the elderly woman ... Eleanor—the name flashed into his head.

Julian was surprised.

'How did you know?' he asked.

'Mum called me.'

'I told her not to.'

'Why?'

'I'm all right. No need for her to make a fuss.'

'Telling your brother is hardly making a fuss. I'm glad she did. How are you?'

'I have to keep my leg elevated and no weight on it for weeks. It's bloody ridiculous.'

'It must be necessary or they wouldn't say it. If you don't follow the instructions you'll delay your recovery, Julian. Do what you're told.'

'You sound like Dad.'

'For once I agree with him.'

Julian grunted the way he always did when he didn't agree but accepted the decision. 'How are you getting on anyway? Heard there are fires in your area.'

'So far so good but it can change very fast.' The fact his brother had registered the fires and that he may be in danger was unexpected, to say the least.

'Look after yourself. I only have one brother.'

'And I don't plan on you being an only child. Thanks, though,' he added awkwardly, touched by the concern. 'How's Mum? She said she was tired when I asked how she was this morning.'

'She didn't say anything when she visited me and she seemed normal. Bit pale. Maybe she is just tired. She said they'd been out a lot lately and she's been helping organise some hospital fundraiser thing.'

'Maybe she should see her doctor. Has she had a check-up recently?

'No idea. She won't go just because I say so.'

'Try. You know Dad won't notice anything unless she drops dead at his feet and he doesn't get his breakfast.'

'She'll be fine, don't worry. Thanks for calling, Oliver.'

Krista was sitting on the floor again with Lola.

'Should we give her something to eat?'

'Not too much and something soft.'

'She has canned food.' She opened the fridge and showed him a tin of Gourmet Lamb Dinner. 'At home Mama has food cooked specially for her but when they come here she brings these.'

She spooned a small amount onto a saucer. Lola sniffed and licked and nibbled a tiny bit.

'Leave it with her and she'll eat when she feels like it.'

Krista patted Lola's head and stroked her body. 'Good girl,' she murmured. 'You can sleep in my room tonight.'

'Talking of sleep, we should probably have an early night.' Oliver yawned. Last night's party had meant a later night than he was used to and the day had been packed with activity. 'I'll need to get going early tomorrow.'

'Okay.'

Krista took him upstairs to the room she'd prepared. 'My room is two doors along,' she said.

'It's a big house.' Not only big but luxuriously furnished. He felt like a big lumbering clodhopper walking along the cream-carpeted corridor, and when she showed him his room...

'Wow.' Five-star hotel standard. A king-size bed and an ensuite, walk-in wardrobe. TV.

'Makes my place look shabby.'

'But I liked your house. What I saw of it.'

'I like my place too, but this is something else.'

He put his backpack on the floor, glad he'd given it a brush to remove any dust and grass seeds leftover from its last outing.

'It doesn't feel like a home. No-one really lives here except Angus, and Rod says he's hardly ever here.'

'Christ, I'd forgotten about all that. When's the deadline?'

'I'd forgotten, too.' Krista gazed at him in alarm. 'Tomorrow, but Hugh reckons they won't do anything.'

'I wouldn't count on it but I really hope he's right.' Oliver stifled another yawn. 'Anyway, there's nothing we can do about it right now.'

'No, I suppose not but I'll lock all the doors.'

'What about the stables?'

'There are security lights and I locked the main doors and the office but I probably didn't need to. Calypso isn't there.'

'I wouldn't trust that pair we met.'

'No.' She turned to go but stopped. 'Thank you for staying.'

She took two quick steps forward and her lips brushed his cheek, light as a feather but indelible as the brand on a steer.

Chapter 11

Krista took Lola and her blanket and water bowl up to her bedroom when she'd secured all the doors and downstairs windows.

She very much doubted Moran would send anyone to rob the house in the night. He'd set a deadline and it had sounded very much as though he expected it to be kept. The fact that he'd come all the way out here to talk to Hugh must mean something, too—like a certain amount of respect. Surely he wouldn't send his goons in early? Wasn't there some of weird honour code going on in those organisations?

Lola settled down and went to sleep after licking Krista's fingers as she stroked her.

Krista lay awake.

The man in the room two doors along occupied most of her thoughts. Far from her initial impression of a chunky, not particularly physically attractive man, he'd morphed into ... what? Those clear blue eyes had immediately drilled right through the veneer of sophisticated confidence she'd spent her life cultivating and reached the messy core of self-doubt. It didn't turn him off, which in itself amazed her; he recognised the problem and gave her advice on how to improve her life.

He defended her against attack from not only those two men but also Hugh, Gwen and those other people at her table. Why would he do that? She hardly knew him. And yet he knew more about her than her family did.

He was an extraordinary man. He was a healer of animals and also of people, but he struggled with his own family issues. Typically for a man, she suspected he buried them deep inside and tonight's outburst would be something he'd regret.

He made her want to help him, too. How, she had no idea.

The thoughts muddled about in her head until...

'Krista! Wake up.'

Her eyes sprang open before her brain locked into gear. 'What? Who is it?' Had she slept?

'It's Oliver. Get up. We have to go. The fire changed direction in the night.'

She sat up, blinking. Sunlight streamed through the window. 'What time is it?'

'Six-thirty. Get up. I've hooked the float to my car but we have to load the horses. I just hope my car can pull the load.'

'Why not use Rod's?'

'I can't afford to be without mine if this place goes up. Get Lola. She's in the kitchen eating breakfast.' He was already out the door his backpack on his shoulder.

Five minutes later Krista bounded downstairs. Thick grey smoke billowed on the horizon. The wind had picked up and blew briskly through the trees in the driveway. Charred leaves skittered across the gravel. She flung her bag in her car, put Lola carefully on the back seat and ran to the stables. Oliver was leading a horse out.

A yellow fire truck roared down the drive and came to a halt in a wave of dust. The horse danced about, backing away, tugging at the lead rope, but Oliver calmed it. A fireman jumped out and came across.

'G'day mate. It's a mandatory evacuation,' he said. 'We're checking properties.'

'We're leaving now. Taking the horses to the showground,' Oliver called.

'Right. Anyone left here? Any animals?'

'No.'

'Okay. Good luck.'

'And you. Thank you.'

He waved and climbed back aboard. The engine roared, the truck turned and was gone.

'Get the next one,' Oliver said. 'Clip a leading rope onto the halter.' He led the horse into the float.

Krista's phone rang.

'Hello.'

'Krista, it's Amy. Rod's worried about the horses. He's checking the fire status every five minutes. We were supposed to come home this afternoon.'

'Tell him they're fine. Firebrand and Calypso are already at Oliver's place in Taylor's Bend and we're just leaving now with the rest.'

'Okay, listen, do you have time to collect the computer from the office? And if you could, there are some photos and papers in our house. Only if you have time but...'

'We do. What do you want?'

'The photo album from the bookshelf in the living room and in the spare room there's a cardboard expanding file. Just grab that.'

'Okay.'

Oliver grimaced when she relayed the request but he said, 'You go to the house. I'll get the computer.'

Krista ran. She bounded up the wooden steps and flung the door open, scanning the room quickly before spying the bookshelf. She grabbed the album and also a wedding photo on display then ran down the corridor. The house was small, two bedrooms, and the first door she opened was the right one. She stood frozen for a moment. Where was the file? She opened a cupboard and found a stack of jigsaws and games, spare pillows and a suitcase. A table stood under the window with papers on it. On the floor underneath it was the blue file holder. She dragged it out, shoved the album and photo inside, picked it up and raced outside.

A red ute was parked in front of Oliver's car and the float, blocking the way. A familiar red ute, the one that came with those two thugs.

Krista slowed. Where were they? Where was Oliver? Raised voices came from the stables. Heart pumping hard, she put the file case down crept along the stable wall to peer round the door. Oliver had the second horse on the lead rope. The outlines of the two men were unmistakable. Tall and thin, short and solid. Short guy was facing the open door and she drew back hurriedly pulling her phone from her pocket with shaky fingers.

Hugh. She should call Hugh. She had trouble scrolling for his number her hands shook so much.

'Good morning.' The voice startled her so much she dropped the phone. 'Who are you calling?'

Short guy bent and picked up the phone but didn't return it. He glanced at the screen then dropped the phone and ground his foot down on it.

'What are you doing? What do you want from us?' Her voice burst out in a shrill scream.

From inside, Oliver yelled, 'Krista?'

Steely fingers dug into her arm. 'Get in there.' He propelled her into the stables where the thin man waited with Oliver. The big brown horse stood, ears pricked, nervously blowing air through wide nostrils.

'What do you want?' Oliver asked. 'We have to go, there's a fire coming. We've been evacuated.'

'There's time.'

'Didn't you see the fire truck, you morons?' he shouted. 'This isn't a joke.'

Quick as a flash, the thin guy's arm shot out and struck Oliver in the stomach. He doubled over with a cry of pain and the horse backed away in fright, yanking the rope free from his grasp.

'Why are you here?' Krista demanded.

'We don't like being made fools of. We told you you'd be sorry if you lied to us so here we all are.'

'But the deadline isn't up yet.'

'This is between us,' he snarled.

'You'll be sorry if we get caught in the fire,' gasped Oliver. 'We have to leave now!'

'You're not going anywhere.'

'That's crazy. Let me go.' The grip on her arm tightened but Krista stamped as hard as she could on the guy's foot with her heel. He grunted and swore but instead of releasing her gave her a backhander with his free hand.

Oliver roared with rage and shoulder-charged the thin guy, knocking him into the side of the horse. It plunged aside and ran for the open door while Oliver barrelled for short guy like a rugby player. Krista elbowed the man in the ribs, which distracted him enough to let her go, but then the thin guy straightened and joined the fight, throwing some well-aimed punches at Oliver's head. Both of them attacked him, giving him no chance to defend himself other than by protecting his head.

Frantic, Krista cast around for a weapon and spotted an empty feed bucket. She swung it wildly and connected with the thin guy's head. He staggered, giving Oliver enough time to straighten. Krista gave him another whack but now short guy grabbed her arm and shoved her away. She stumbled and fell heavily on her behind onto the floor.

Dark grey smoke billowed in through the big open doorway. Thicker and heavier than before, choking her lungs and stinging her eyes.

'Fire,' she screamed. 'The fire's coming.'

'Let's go,' yelled the thin guy. He staggered out into the smoke-filled yard, closely followed by his mate. Doors slammed, the engine started and Krista caught a glimpse of red as the ute turned and accelerated away.

Krista stumbled to her feet. Her hip hurt and her ankle hurt but she was mobile. They had to get out.

Oliver was upright but swaying unsteadily on his feet, holding his left arm cradled across his body.

'The horses,' he croaked. 'Load the horses.'

'Are you all right?' Tears streamed down her cheeks, part relief, part fear, part smoke induced.

'Get the horses. I'll catch the one...' He staggered for the door.

Krista hesitated but adrenaline surged and she burst into action. Both remaining horses were wheeling about in their stalls and snorting their fear. She drew a deep breath, opened the closest stall and approached a big grey, trying hard to copy Oliver's calm manner when he dealt with Arch Rival.

'Calm down, I'm taking you outside. Saving you. Just let me...' She clipped the lead rope to the halter and the horse followed her relatively quietly.

Outside it pranced about, as upset as Krista by the heavy smoke, wind and the swirling scorched leaves and the dust. Oliver waited by the float, leaning against it for support.

'Bring her up the ramp and tie her next to the other one,' he said.

Luckily the grey was happy to step up the ramp and into the shelter of the float. It fidgeted as she secured it but didn't complain.

'Did you catch that one?'

'No, but she's by the fence. Get the last one out and onboard first.' His voice was hoarse with pain but there was no time to waste.

Swallowing the rising panic, Krista raced back into the dim interior. The remaining horse was frightened, whinnying and tossing its head, but when she snatched the lead rope from a hook by the door and opened the stall, it stood quietly long enough for her to attach the rope.

As soon as it reached the doorway it gave a sudden rush forward. The rope burned as it slid through her palms but she clung on and the horse slewed round, pulling her off balance.

'Hang on to her.' Oliver managed to stagger over and grab the rope with one hand, lending enough extra strength to control the panicky animal and manoeuvre it up the ramp.

The three horses stamped their feet and moved nervously but at least they were secure and ready to go.

'Where's the other one?'

'By the gate.'

Krista approached the horse as calmly as she could, talking as she went.

'Come on, you stupid thing. If we don't get you out of here you'll burn.

Do you want that? No, you don't. Come on.'

The horse took a step forward but a skittering clump of burning leaves came through the fence and it sidestepped away, trailing the rope. Krista cursed under her breath but maintained the calm tone through gritted teeth.

'Don't do that. Let me catch you, for God's sake.'

This time she managed to get within arm's reach but it backed away. Luckily it was now cornered by the fence and the wall of the stable, so she was able to grab the rope and lead it to the float.

'Good work.' Oliver smiled but it turned into a grimace as he tried to lift the ramp.

'Sorry. You'll have to do it.'

Ignoring the pain in her hip, Krista bent and lifted. The ramp came up easily when it got going and it was a quick matter to lock it in place.

'Shut the main doors,' he said. 'Stop random burning leaves blowing in.'

She scampered to close them.

'You'll have to drive,' Oliver said. 'I can't change gears.'

'What about my car?'

'Automatic?'

'Yes.'

'I'll drive it. Careful going out the gate with the float. Extra wide turn. You'll be slow up hills.'

'Okay. You follow me. What about the house?'

'It takes its chances. Go.' He turned away.

Through the smoke, she watched him get awkwardly into her car. How much pain was he in? Would he manage? No time. Go.

Heart in mouth, Krista got into Oliver's car and started the engine. The big float loomed in the rear-view mirror. She'd never towed anything in her life. She put the car in gear, released the handbrake and clutch and nothing happened. The engine roared.

'Come on. Go.' She pressed harder on the accelerator, urging the car forward. Gradually the wheels gained traction. She was moving, slowly, but moving. 'Thank God.'

The trees along the drive thrashed furiously in the wind. If one came down they'd be stuck. Even more frightening was the fact she could barely see ahead through the dense smoke. She found the lights but they didn't help much. A dull red glow lit the sky away to the right. How close was it? Perspiration ran down her cheeks and made her hands slippery on the steering wheel. She accelerated, anxious to get out onto the main road, clear of the trees which had now become threatening rather than welcoming.

Burning twigs and leaves landed on the bonnet and stuck against the wiper blades. She switched the wipers on and the trapped pieces flew away. Suddenly the intersection was in front of her. She braked and felt the momentum of the float continuing behind her, pushing the car on. She braked again and this time the whole lot slowed enough for her to begin the turn. Slowly, Oliver said and now she knew why, and she also knew how Angus had ended up in that ditch.

At least Oliver's car was slow because it was struggling with the load. She straightened the car on what she thought was the correct side of the road. The centre line wasn't visible and the guide posts were hazy on the edges of verge. She still had to be very careful on curves and especially going down those two hills. Her fingers gripped the steering wheel so tightly she had to consciously force herself to loosen the grip.

She peered into the wing mirror to see if Oliver was in view and glimpsed lights which she hoped were the headlights of her car. All her bearings had gone with the visibility. She had no idea how far she'd driven and it wasn't until the car began to slow on the first hill that she realised she was only about a third of the way to town. The whole run took her about twenty minutes in the BMW, breezing along a few k's over the ninety-k speed limit. Quite a few k's on the straights. Now she was probably averaging thirty, if that. This would take hours.

The pace slowed as the rise continued, but the car chugged on bravely with her verbal encouragement and a few pats on the dashboard. Finally the strain decreased and another problem became apparent. As it had when she braked for the intersection, the weight she was towing created a power all its own and if she wasn't really careful it would be out of control in an instant. She knew at the bottom of this hill the road curved right and then left, in two sweeping bends, before crossing the river on a single-lane bridge.

What did cheer her marginally was the decrease in burning leaves and twigs showering onto the car. The smoke had thinned too. Suddenly, with a couple of toots on the horn, a vehicle rushed past, coming up behind her out of the gloom and disappearing into the haze ahead, the tail-lights glowing red and then fading.

Somehow the sight of another vehicle boosted her spirits, and it was with renewed optimism she guided the car around the first of the bends and then the next. The white sides of the bridge came into sight next and she rattled across, confident no-one would be coming the other way. The next hill wasn't as steep or as long and when she reached the top, the first of the orchards outside Taylor's Bend were visible at the bottom of the slope. Here the smoke was a lighter bluey grey colour, and sky was visible when she looked ahead.

Tears ran down her cheeks and this time they were pure relief. When she reached the town proper she wasn't sure where to go. The showground wasn't on this road she'd come in on and it wasn't to the right, out where Oliver lived and Angus had crashed. She didn't remember it on the other road in either but she'd only driven that way once and that was over a year ago. A showground wouldn't have registered. She slowed and pulled to the side of the road near the primary school, waiting for Oliver to overtake and lead the way.

He stopped level with her and she waved him past. He nodded and continued on, turning left at the main street. The Arts Centre was on the left a few doors from the pub, but that was the only thing she noticed as now there was traffic to negotiate and when she stopped at the lights and then waited at a pedestrian crossing, it took ages for the car to get going again.

Nobody seemed to mind though, and a few people even gave her a wave as she went slowly by. Oliver turned right three blocks along from where they'd come in. She made the turn carefully, conscious that cars were waiting, but again no-one honked or yelled at her to get out of the way and again a couple of people smiled and waved.

About five-hundred metres along, a big sign announced the 'Taylor's Bend Showground and Sports Field'. Oliver drove through the gate and round the large dry, brown oval to buildings on the far side where cars, a few caravans, tents and people were visible. When she reached the area, a woman appeared in jeans, a red-checked shirt, big sunglasses and a wide-brimmed straw hat. She had a clipboard and a friendly smile on her round face.

'G'day. I'm Di Fuller.'

'I'm Krista Laatonen. From The Grange.'

'How many horses have you got there, Krista?'

'Four.'

'Bad out your way? Looks like it. Your rig's covered in ash.'

'I think so. It was...' Words failed her and she had to wipe her eyes.

'Don't worry, darl. You're here now and the firies are doing their best. Drive along there to the stables.' She pointed. 'Stalls four, five, six and seven. Okay? Les will help you unload. Are you on your own?'

'No, Oliver is there. In my car. The blue one. He's hurt.' Not blue now. Filthy. But they'd made it.

'I'll take care of him.' Di smiled. 'Don't worry. Take care of your horses and come back here for a cuppa and some brekkie when you're done. Okay, darl.' She stepped back.

'Thank you.'

Krista followed her instructions and drove carefully along the first row of empty stalls to the far end. Two empty floats were parked against the fence to the rear and two curious horses poked their heads out of the wooden stables. An elderly man in shorts sat on a camp chair next to a battered old truck and a camper trailer, reading the paper and nursing a cup of tea. A brown dog lay sprawled in the shade nearby.

She switched off the engine and sat for a moment, eyes closed, weak with relief, relishing the quiet and the relatively sweet freshness of the air coming through the open window. Safe.

'Need a hand, love?'

The wiry, tanned paper-reader was next to the car, displaying missing teeth in a friendly smile. Close to eighty?

Krista got out, wincing as her hip complained about the change of position. 'Yes, please.'

'Got a full load?'

'Four.' Where was Oliver? She shaded her eyes and looked back. Her car was still parked near where she'd talked to Di but no-one was in sight. Was he all right? She couldn't tell when he passed her in town.

'Let's get this back down.' He was already unlatching the rear door. 'From The Grange, are you?'

'Yes. Are these two your horses?'

'One is. Old Blackie there. Brought the milking cow in too. And that lazy dog.' He jerked his thumb in the direction of the camper. 'The missus has taken the car in to Dot and Laurie's to get some supplies. Might be here for a while.'

Now she looked more clearly, his truck was loaded with possessions. He stood to lose everything yet here he was helping her and sounding as though he was on a camping trip.

He expertly lowered the back and made sure the ramp was steady. Krista untied the first horse, the brown one with the white strip on its nose. The one that tried to escape.

'See,' she said. 'You're safe now.' It nuzzled at her shoulder as she led it to a stall. 'Now you're all friendly, aren't you?' She stroked its neck and let it loose, closing and latching the half door carefully.

Her other new friend was already leading the second horse out and within a few minutes all four were assessing their new surroundings from their temporary accommodation.

'Sorry, love. Name's Les,' the man said, holding out a gnarled hand.

She shook it firmly. 'Krista. Thank you very much, Les.'

'Hope your property makes it through. They've evacuated Jindalee.'

'My goodness. I hope yours makes it too. Where do you live?'

'Out your way but not as far. Just before the bridge. You left it a bit late.'

'I know but we got held up catching a horse, and then it was very slow driving. I couldn't see much.'

'Yeah, it wasn't too bad when we left. We were ready to go last night but Sal couldn't sleep so we got going at four-thirty this morning.'

'Do you think the fire will get as far as your place?'

'Hard to say. The firies will do what they can but it depends on what the wind does. How close was it to The Grange?'

'I don't know. There was an orange glow off to the right but not close ... I think. I don't know. Burning leaves were blowing around. It's terrifying.'

'You're safe here, love. And you got your horses out.'

Krista wiped a hand across her eyes, conscious of her hand shaking uncontrollably, and the increasing ache in her hip.

'Isn't that the vet's car?' Shrewd eyes studied the car and then her.

'Yes.' She sucked in air and focused. 'He drove my car in. It's an automatic. He hurt his arm and couldn't change gear.'

Where was he? How badly was he injured? Those two men had been vicious in their attack.

'Like me to unhook her for you?'

'What?'

'The float, love.' He grinned. 'Can you back her up against the fence out of the way?'

'I doubt it. It's the first time I've towed anything.'

'You did well. Give us a sec.' He hopped into the car, took all of five minutes to position the float neatly against the fence, then got out, bent over and fiddled about with the connection. 'Drive her forward a bit,' he said.

Krista got in and edged the now responsive car clear of the float. She leaned out the window.

'That was impressive parking. Thanks very much for the help.'

'No worries. I'll keep an eye on the horses for you.'

Did he swagger a little as he shrugged the praise off and went back to his tea and paper?

Krista drove back to where her car was parked. Oliver wasn't inside and neither was Lola. She got out and stared around at the parked cars and sundry caravans. A couple of goats and alpacas were housed in the open yards, along with three cows, two ponies and a donkey. Another horse float drove through the gate.

Di came out of a white tent with her clipboard.

'Oliver's in here, darl,' she said. 'Looks like he's been in a fight. So do you, for that matter. I rang the doc and told him to expect a visit. Reckon you should give Rupe a call too.' Her eyes narrowed and her tone sharpened on the last comment. Did Di think she and Oliver had been fighting each other? What had Oliver told her? She must look a mess.

'Um ... thanks.'

Krista pushed through the tent flap, blinking in the darker interior. Even though it was in the shade, the inside was hot and stuffy. Lola trotted across, wagging her tail.

'Hello, little girl.' Krista knelt to pat her and received a lick on the cheek. One bright note in the overall gloom of recent events.

'G'day.' Oliver prised himself off a folding chair. Dirty, dust in his hair, his left arm held uncomfortably in front of his body, the wrist swollen, a streak of blood on his cheek along with rising bruises, he looked ... wonderful.

'Hi.'

A rush of emotion propelled her forward. She wanted to fling her arms around him and hold him as close as she could but his arm was a barrier so she stopped, unsure and suddenly embarrassed. What if he didn't want...

'Come here,' he said gruffly and pulled her in to a hug with his good right arm—surprisingly firm and surprisingly, gratifyingly intense. She wanted to bury herself in his embrace but she slipped her arms carefully around his body and held him as tight as she dared, given he'd been punched in the stomach and generally beaten up.

'You smell of smoke,' he murmured into her hair.

'So do you,' she whispered. 'And you're filthy.

'So are you but I don't care.'

'Neither do I.' She sniffed hard at the tears clogging her throat and nose. It was true. For the first time in her life she genuinely didn't care how she looked. And this man genuinely didn't care either.

He released her way too soon but she relinquished her hold, knowing he was probably in all sorts of pain.

'Di said the doctor is expecting us,' she said.

'Yes. I didn't have the energy to argue. Are the horses all right?'

'Yes. Someone called Les said he'll keep an eye on them for me. He and his wife have a camper there.'

Oliver nodded. 'Les and Sally. They'll be fine then. Have they got water?'

'No, the buckets are in my car.'

'We should fix that before we go, and they'll need a feed, too.'

'I'll do it. You wait here.' She turned to leave.

'Krista...'

'What?'

'You're a champion.'

The flood of pride was so intense she could only smile at him like an idiot. She ducked her head to hide the heat rushing to her cheeks, and after a little tussle with the tent flap, hurried to feed and water the horses.

Chapter 12

Krista left a bucket of water in each stall and fed the horses the mix Oliver had shown her the previous night. She parked her car next to the float, took her suitcase and handbag and walked back to where Oliver waited, leaning on his car. She'd have to drive to the doctor and then take him home. Then what? Borrow his car and try for a room at the motel or the pub?

Should she stay here overnight? She had nothing to sleep in or on. Was it necessary? Perhaps it was. Those horses were valuable and two belonged to other people. They should come and collect them. She'd phone Rod later. And Hugh should know what had happened here.

Oh! Her phone was lying smashed on the ground at the stables with all her contact details in it. Possibly even melted by now.

Oliver straightened when she came near. Lola sat at his feet, waiting. 'Do you want tea and something to eat?'

'Not yet. You should see the doctor. Your eye is swollen.'

'I can see all right. I think it's just bruising.'

'Maybe you can see but I'll drive,' she said.

'Thanks.'

'How are you feeling?' he asked when they were heading for the gate, but winced and hissed in air as the car bounced over the rough track.

'Not as bad as you, but I think I hurt my ankle and my hip when he knocked me over.'

'What about your cheek? He hit you pretty hard, the bastard.' His hand landed on her shoulder briefly with a consoling squeeze.

'It's a bit tender. I haven't thought about it. How are you?'

'Bloody terrible. They were used to beating people up. I'm not.'

'It was two against one, the cowards.' She gave a low chuckle and glanced across to catch his curious eye on her. 'I gave him a good whack with that bucket.'

'Ha! You sure did.'

Her laughter died. 'What would have happened if the fire hadn't frightened them off?'

'I reckon we'd be a lot worse off than we are,' he said grimly. 'I'll give Rupe a call and get him or Shannon to drive past my place.'

'Do you think they'd go there?'

'Hope not but you never know. Go left on the main road and two blocks down, left again.'

He made the call and gave an edited version of events, answered a couple of questions and finished with a description of the red ute.

'He'll put out an alert for it but it's pretty chaotic at the moment with the fire.'

'Any news on that?'

'They've closed the Jindalee Road but he didn't know any more details about properties along there.'

The doctor's surgery was a squat red-brick building with big blue hydrangeas along the wall, wilting in the heat. A white sign stuck in the garden by the gate said 'Doctor Gustav Jensen' followed by a string of initials.

'Danish,' said Krista as they walked up the white concrete path to the steps with Lola trotting along behind.

'Is it?'

'Yes, it's a very common name there.'

'He's been here forever.'

Krista pushed open the door and held it for Oliver. The waiting room was empty but a sharp-featured woman of indeterminate age, with bright red lipstick and a crisp white blouse, sat behind the reception desk under a pile of fifties-style teased blonde hair.

'Morning, Penny.'

'Good grief, Oliver, what have you been doing?' she cried. 'Di said you'd been fighting.'

She came out from behind the desk all fussing and clucking in a swirl of floral-print blue skirt, fifties-style. 'Sit down, the doctor will be with you in a jiffy.' She guided him to a chair and Oliver subsided into it with a grunt. Lola sat beside his feet, panting.

Penny gave Lola a frowning look but retreated behind the desk.

'It's too hot to leave her in the car,' said Oliver with a touch of authority.

'Of course.' She swung her attention to Krista but with far less sympathy, eyeing the filthy jeans, dirt-and-soot-smudged top and yellow sneakers. 'You've been in the wars too.' It sounded disapproving applied to her. 'I'll need you to fill out this form, please.' She held out a clipboard with a paper and pen attached.

'I don't need to see the doctor,' Krista said.

'Are you sure?' Penny frowned at such wilful disobedience.

'Yes, thank you.'

'Maybe you should get him to look at your ankle,' said Oliver.

'It'll be fine. I'll ice it later.'

'Suit yourself,' said Penny with a disapproving sniff. 'But Doc Jensen is a very good doctor. Every bit as good as your city ones.'

'I'm sure he is.' Krista sat beside Oliver. 'I don't need to waste his time, that's all. Oliver needs his attention, not me.'

'We never see The Grange people.' She fired the comment into the silence.

Oliver shifted beside Krista. 'Maybe they don't get sick,' he said.

'I meant in town,' snapped Penny. 'So what happened to you out there?'

'We had a bit of trouble with a couple of blokes.'

'Not surprising at that place. What on earth were you doing there so early, Oliver?'

'That's none of your business, is it?' Krista said before Oliver could open his mouth and encourage this obnoxious woman.

Fortunately the doctor's door opened, and a grey-haired, gaunt-faced man in his fifties appeared.

'Oliver, come in.'

He held out his hand to Krista. 'Hello. We haven't met.'

'*Hej. Jeg hedder* Krista Laatonen.'

He laughed. '*Rart at møde dig.* That's about the extent of my Danish these days.'

'Mine too. I'm Finnish by birth.'

'And I haven't spoken Danish for thirty-five years. You'd both better come in by the look of you.'

'She said she doesn't want to see you,' piped up Penny.

'I said I don't need to,' said Krista.

'Won't hurt to let me check that cheek.' Dr Jensen gave Oliver a surreptitious wink, which he acknowledged with a tiny smile. What was that about?

'See Oliver first.'

'Okay. Krista, you can have a wash if you like. Through there.' He nodded at a door marked Toilet and ushered Oliver into his office, leaving Krista with a glowering Penny and a happily grinning Lola.

***

'You've got yourself a very stylish girl, there, Oliver, underneath the dirt,' Doc said as he peered at the cuts and bruises on Oliver's face. 'Your eye seems okay. Any vision problems?'

'No. She's not my girl.'

'Well, you won't mind if I invite her out for a coffee and Danish.' He applied something to his eyebrow that stung like a hornet.

'Christ almighty—what was that?'

'Bit of disinfectant.' He continued dabbing. 'It won't need a stitch. So what? A herd of horses ran you down, did it?'

'Two thugs were threatening Krista. They were really after her stepbrother but he's cleared out. The rest of the family left yesterday.'

'Nice family.' Doc put a tape on his eyebrow. 'Follow my finger but don't move your head.' Oliver obeyed. He shone a light in his eye, grunted and flicked it off. 'Now, let's have a look at that arm. What happened?'

'Not sure. I think it got kicked or maybe it was from defending myself. They were both laying into me.'

'Any other pains?' He studied the swollen wrist and lower arm, now turning dark purple.

'Bruises. I got a punch in the stomach.'

'Can you move your fingers and thumb? Bend your wrist up and down?'

He tried the movement carefully. 'Yes.'

'It's not broken. I can send you for an X-ray if you want but I'm pretty sure it's just very badly bruised. The joint itself is undamaged but you can use a sling for support.' He went to a cupboard and produced a length of fabric, which he proceeded to tie around Oliver's neck and arm.

'Thank goodness. I don't want to miss too many rehearsals for the show.'

'Got roped in, did you? What have they got you doing? Leading man?'

'Playing cello in the orchestra. Are you involved?'

'Ha. No. They tried but it's not my thing at all. Penny's in the chorus. I hear all about it. That's enough.'

'How long will this take to heal?'

'A few weeks and you should be fine. It'll be sore though. Take some painkillers if you need to and take it easy. Get your girlfriend to look after you.'

Oliver got to his feet slowly, every joint and muscle yelling at him to stop. 'Thanks, Doc.'

'No worries.'

Doc opened the door. 'Ms Laatonen.'

Krista went in obediently, mainly, Oliver suspected, to spite Penny who sat glaring at the door as it closed. Krista had washed her face and run a comb through her hair but hadn't attempted to conceal the red mark on her cheek. That bastard had hit her hard, not with a fist though, which was something. She'd have a broken jaw if he had.

Oliver pulled out his wallet but Penny plastered on a smile and said, 'No charge.'

'Who says?'

'Doc.'

He frowned. 'But...'

'Nothing I can do,' she said. 'I just work here. Do you need another appointment?'

'No, thanks.'

She tapped something into the computer. 'Whose dog is it?'

'Krista's mother's.'

'Is she staying with you?'

'Who, the mother or the dog?'

'The blonde.' She gave him a scathing look.

'I don't know.' Oliver spoke as carefully as he could, given the anger bubbling more and more violently inside the longer her cross-examination and insinuations continued. 'Penny, we've been attacked and we just barely escaped being caught in a raging, out-of-control bushfire. Krista drove four horses to safety after being hit in the face and knocked to the ground. The horses don't belong to her and she doesn't live at The Grange. Give her, and me, a break, please.'

A flush stained her throat and worked its way upward. 'I'm just saying. I don't see why those people should involve the town in their goings-on.'

'What goings-on exactly?'

'Well, all those rich sorts go there ... and...'

'And what?'

She clamped her mouth tight shut.

'You were complaining earlier that The Grange people never come into town and now you're saying they involve the town. Make up your mind or better still, get some facts straight first. Tell Krista I'll be outside.'

Too angry to remain, he flicked his fingers at Lola who sprang to her feet, tail wagging, and pattered after him as he strode for the door.

How dare Penny? Being one of the town's biggest gossips was her main claim to fame, along with her mania for Elvis, and he was under no illusions that she wouldn't be on the phone before he'd reached the car, passing on her version of what just happened. Normally he ignored her attempts to involve him in her speculation and innuendo because he wasn't the slightest bit interested but *this* ... under the circumstances, this was plain mean-spirited and blatantly unfair.

How Krista would react was another matter but she'd pulled out her ice-queen voice and shut Penny up pretty effectively by offering no explanation of his presence at The Grange. And speaking Danish to Doc was a deliberate and brilliantly calculated piece of one-upmanship appreciated by the man himself. In fact, maybe he liked it too much. What was that crack about coffee and Danish? Hard to tell with Doc sometimes, whether he was joking or not.

Anyway, Krista could hold her own with the gossips.

Where *was* she going to stay?

He leaned against the car while Lola sniffed about in the patchy grass on the nature strip. She'd made a good recovery and was coping well with the switch from pampered pet to refugee.

His phone rang. Margie. She'd be at his place, locked out.

'Hello, Margie.'

'G'day, Oliver. Are you dead in your bed or are you out on a call? The gate's locked.'

'Neither. Sorry, it's a long story but I'm on my way home now. Cancel any appointments will you, please?'

'Okay. I'll climb over the gate. See you soon.'

'Don't do that, you'll do yourself a mischief. Ten minutes max.'

She laughed and disconnected.

Five minutes later, Krista came down the path. Lola scampered across to greet her and got picked up and cuddled for her trouble.

'What did he say?' she asked.

'Bruised but not broken. Same with the eye. You?'

'Like I told Penny. Ice on the ankle. Bruised hip. What's her problem by the way?'

'She's the town gossip and she regards the doc as her property.'

'Goodness. What a frightening thought. Does he know?'

'Probably, but he wouldn't care one way or the other unless it interfered with her work. He generally keeps to himself.'

'She seems to regard you the same way.'

'Hardly.'

Now that really was a frightening thought. According to Margie, Beryl only brought Claudette in as an excuse to see him and now Krista was saying much the same thing about Penny. Rubbish. Their paths rarely crossed since her old cat had died a couple of months ago.

'Don't you know you're the town's most eligible bachelor?' She smirked. 'I'll drive you home.'

'Keep going on this road, it'll take you right round the back of town to my place. Who told you that?'

'Word gets around.'

How could she hear something like that? No-one told him. There must definitely be some women's network he didn't know about.

'Oliver, could I borrow your car, please? I need to find somewhere to stay and I also need to buy some socks, maybe some T-shirts and a phone. Is there somewhere in town?'

'Not sure about the phone. I think you'll need to go to Willoughby for that, but the supermarket will have socks and there's a dress shop in the main street. Tina will probably have shirts or something. Not the sort of thing you're used to, though.'

Her mouth tightened but she didn't say anything. He nearly added that the jeans and slacks Tina sold didn't have rips in the legs but he had scissors she could use, then decided better not.

'You can stay with me if you like,' he said, much more casually than he felt.

'Thanks but there's a motel, isn't there? Some of the staff who came for the party stayed there.' No hint she'd taken any inference of an ulterior motive from his offer. Not that there was one.

'Yes, and a B & B and two pubs. You can give them a call from my place. Could be full up with other evacuees.'

'Rod and Amy will need somewhere to stay, too. My God, I hope they haven't lost their house and car.'

'Me too but we couldn't drive three vehicles. I could fit them in at my house as well. There are three bedrooms.'

'Would you?' She flashed him a smile.

'I'll need some help with the horses. Three of them do belong to The Grange.'

'Yes, of course. And you can't drive.' She drove in silence for a few minutes. 'Maybe I should stay—to help.'

'It would certainly be handy.' He turned his head to look out the side window, to hide the pleased smile he couldn't stop.

Margie hadn't attempted to climb the gate. She was leaning against it, staring at her phone.

'Gosh, look at the smoke,' said Krista.

The road rose as it swung round the outskirts of the town, and he usually had a fairly clear view to the north and west from this direction. Huge billowing waves of dirty grey smoke blocked the whole sky to the north, where Jindalee and The Grange lay. Overhead, patches of blue were visible in a bizarre delineation of catastrophe and relative safety.

Krista stopped behind the small car blocking the driveway. Margie came to the window and peered in.

'What on earth have you two been doing?'

'Open up and we'll tell you,' said Oliver. He handed her a bunch of keys.

***

Margie took charge once she'd heard a summary of events. She helped bring in Oliver's and Krista's bags, put the kettle on, ordered Krista to the bathroom to wash and change into one of Oliver's T-shirts because hers all needed a wash, made Oliver wash his hands and face, then sat him down with toast and tea for starters and went to the office to cancel appointments.

'I'll be back in ten minutes to cook a proper breakfast and feed the dog while you have your shower,' she said.

Oliver switched on the radio for a fire update. The local ABC station was a critical resource for on the spot emergency information.

'...are closed between Smith's Gully, Andamook, Cleary and Farleigh Creek. Jindalee Road between Taylor's Bend and Jindalee is closed. The town of Jindalee has been evacuated but the main fire front is several kilometres west of the town. Firefighting resources have been focused on protecting the town and are so far successful in slowing the progress. There have been no new reports of property loss but fire crews have not been able to access some areas to check. It's believed all properties have been evacuated. The tally stands at no loss of life, two injuries to firemen, one serious but not life threatening, three houses and outbuildings destroyed in the Fairlight area. Stock losses are unknown at this stage.*

*Fire Chief Brett Green said a short time ago that if the wind remained light he was hopeful the main front threatening Jindalee would be brought under control by this afternoon.'

He switched it off. West of Jindalee meant the fire was well away from the

National Park, which ran along behind Taylor's Bend and was also well away from The Grange, which lay south of the town. That didn't mean other fronts couldn't start up. At least the weather was better today.

What a bloody nightmare. His arm throbbed. Now he was at home with time to think, the adrenaline that had carried him through the previous hours was fading. An intense weariness settled over him. He couldn't sleep now though, he needed to shower and change out of the smoke-stinking clothes. All one-handed and awkward.

How was he going to work? He couldn't handle animals with one arm out of action. He'd have to take time off and close the practice. First time in five years. He never got sick.

Krista came out of the bathroom wearing his black T-shirt and a skirt, her hair washed but still wet. The bruise on her cheek stood out stark and red on the pale skin but she was smiling. She was beautiful. She was fragile and strong and vulnerable and brave. She stole his breath and his ability to think straight and kept them as her own.

'Your turn,' she said. 'Stinky.'

'That's what I get for being gentlemanly and letting you go first?'

He rose with a groan as muscles grumbled, and headed for his bedroom.

'Can I use your washing machine, please?'

'Sure.'

'Need any help?'

He stopped. 'What with?' Was she going to help take his clothes off?

She shrugged. 'Your shoes? Unbuttoning your shirt?'

'I reckon I can manage, thanks.'

'I'll wash your clothes too if you want.'

'Okay. No need now, though.' He grinned and continued to his room.

Krista took her bag to the laundry and dumped most of the contents into the machine. Margie came back while she was studying the controls and deciding which cycle to choose.

'If you hang those outside they'll smell of smoke,' she said.

'Gosh, you're right. It's mainly underwear and tops. It'll dry inside.'

'You up for eggs and bacon?'

'Yes, but I can do it, Margie.'

'You need a breather. Come and sit down.' She disappeared into the kitchen. A drawer opened closed and she said, 'Now, little doggy, what do you think of this? It's special food from the vet.'

Krista pressed the Start button. Stupidly, she had an overwhelming desire to cry, rising up from nowhere, for no reason at all, except maybe Margie's matter-of-fact kindness. She rubbed a hand over her eyes and waited for the teariness to subside, then went through to the kitchen.

Lola had her nose in a plastic bowl, guzzling something down.

'I didn't think of bringing her food,' she said.

'No worries. There's plenty in the surgery storeroom. I've given Sandy a call, got her to come over and feed the horses.'

'Thanks. I'd forgotten about that too. I fed the ones at the showground, though, before we left. Will they be all right there?'

'Yeah, I reckon. Sandy can feed them this evening too, probably. She knows them all and she's good with horses. All animals, really.'

'I met her. She's nice.'

'Yeah, she's a good kid.'

'I need to phone my stepfather and tell him what's happened. And Rod.'

'Eat first, love.'

Krista sat at the red formica-topped table while Margie tended a large frying pan that sent out mouth-watering aromas. Toast popped in the toaster and she whipped the slices out and applied a slab of butter to each before putting two more slices of bread in.

In between poking at the bacon, she made a pot of tea and fixed more toast with effortless efficiency. She placed a heaped plate in front of Krista. Two fried eggs and a couple of rashers of bacon all sitting on lavishly buttered toast. Cholesterol hotel.

'Thank you.'

'You're welcome, love.' Margie went down the hallway to the bathroom door and yelled, 'Are you okay in there. Need some help with your pants?' She turned and grinned at Krista's astonishment.

Oliver's reply was muffled but clearly negative because Margie came back to the kitchen.

'I've got three boys who play footie and a husband,' she said. 'One or other of them has always broken something or hurt themselves. I've seen it all.'

'I offered to help him take his shirt off but he refused.'

Margie gave a burst of raucous laughter. 'He's a bit shy.'

Krista tried a mouthful of toast and egg. Her stomach gurgled in anticipation and her tastebuds danced with glee at the onslaught of eggy fat. Once wouldn't hurt.

'I didn't realise how hungry I was.' Next came bacon followed by a slurp of tea. Then more egg, more toast. Delicious.

A door opened and another closed.

'He's made it through the shower.' said Margie, and cracked two more eggs into the sizzling pan.

Oliver came in, fresh and clean, newly shaved and smelling of soap, his arm in the sling. 'That smells fantastic. Thanks, Margie.'

'No worries. Sandy's coming over to take care of the horses.'

'Good idea.'

His eyes rested on Krista for a moment, soft, smiling, making her skin prickle with heat and shattering her composure.

'Do you have Rod's number?' she asked.

'Yep. We can give him a call after breakfast.'

'How's your arm?'

'Sore but I can use my fingers a bit so I'll manage.'

She nodded, incapable of coming up with anything intelligent to say. He was too close and too ... desirable. Was she in danger of becoming another Penny? Was she falling for this man simply because he was nice to her? How pathetically needy was that? She'd known him less than a week, for goodness sake, and her real life was in Melbourne. All this was an aberration. She could leave any time she wanted now that the horses were safe and Rod and Amy were coming to take charge.

Except for damned Angus and her keys. Where would they be delivered now? Not that it mattered. But Mel had a key and she could contact her through the agency. Why hadn't she thought of that earlier?

'What will happen to The Grange mail?' she asked.

'The mail?' Oliver shrugged. 'No idea. They'd hold it at the local post office I suppose.'

'Here?'

'Jindalee, I'd say,' said Margie. 'That's closest to them. You expecting something?' She served Oliver a heaped plate, sat down and poured herself a cup of tea.

'The keys to my apartment.'

'Jindalee's closed off,' said Oliver. 'Are you in a hurry to leave?' He sounded disappointed. Was he?

'There's no reason for me to stay once Rod turns up and I talk to Hugh.'

'Might be a while before you track down the keys.'

'It doesn't matter,' she said. 'I remembered my cleaner has a key.'

'Right. Your cleaner.'

'Wish I had a cleaner,' said Margie.

'A cleaner's the last thing I'd spend money on,' said Oliver.

'You don't have three boys and a husband,' said Margie.

He smiled. 'That's true.' But he glanced at her as if to say 'But neither does Krista'.

'If I could afford one I'd get one, believe me,' said Margie. 'Even if I did live by myself.'

Krista concentrated on mopping up egg yolk with her last piece of toast. Again she didn't know what to say. How could she defend herself against the implication she had too much money? She did. She had Mel come in because she hated cleaning and she could afford not to do it herself. Was that wrong? Oliver seemed to think so. How strongly did he feel about it? How spiky was this exchange going to get? Hugh and her mother would be at each other's throats on a topic like this. She put her knife and fork neatly together on her plate and took it to the sink.

'Take no notice of him,' said Margie. 'If he enjoys cleaning the toilet so much he can come and do mine.'

Krista smiled warily and slid a glance at Oliver who was grinning as he shovelled in bacon. She sat down. Thank God the conversation hadn't escalated the way most of Mama's and Hugh's did.

Chapter 13

Rod and Amy arrived later that afternoon with Rod clumping along on crutches, his leg in a cast. They both thanked Oliver profusely for taking them in and for saving the precious photo album and files.

'The car's insured,' Amy said when Krista apologised for leaving it behind. 'You couldn't do much else. You saved the horses and yourselves, that's much more important.'

'Hugh's been on the phone,' said Rod after they'd settled into their room with what meagre possessions they had, and rejoined Oliver and Krista in the kitchen for a cold beer. 'He's going to sell The Grange.'

'Is he? Why?' asked Oliver.

'He's a businessman. He's good at cutting his losses,' said Krista. 'He's lost interest in being a rural gentleman, Angus was hopeless at running the place, the bushfire has caused big problems he doesn't want and he'll be concentrating on Viivi and what to do about the marriage.' She shrugged. 'He doesn't mess around with lost causes.'

He'd been furious when she reported in that she and Oliver had been attacked. 'Leave it with me,' he said, which was what he'd said before. But he hadn't mentioned selling The Grange. Maybe her phone call was the final straw.

'What will you two do if he sells?' asked Oliver.

'See what happens. It depends if the place is still standing. If the house has gone it'll be a land sale. If it survives – who knows? A new owner can do anything or nothing with it,' Rod said.

Amy leaned forward, pushing a strand of brown hair behind her ear. 'We'd really like to buy it and run it properly as a stud farm.'

'Might be a good time,' said Oliver. 'Get in while the price is down. People will be reluctant to invest out here for a while.'

'That's what we thought.' She glanced at Rod. 'Our parents would help us.'

He nodded. 'My family are all into horses.'

'Good luck with it,' said Oliver.

Krista and Amy dropped Rod at the showground to meet Sandy and check on the horses then went to the supermarket for supplies.

'What's been going on with Hugh and your mother?' Amy asked when they were alone in the car. 'Roddy was very sketchy with details.'

'They had a massive fight at the party. At dinner in front of all the guests. Mama slapped his face and stormed off. She's accused Hugh of having an affair.'

'Was he?'

'Probably.'

'That's sad.'

Krista glanced at her, surprised. No-one had said that before. People usually launched into an opinion of the marriage or who was at fault.

Amy said, 'I always think divorces are sad. People don't go into a marriage thinking of splitting up.'

'I suppose not. Although Mama has had plenty. You'd think she'd be a bit wary by now. Or smarter.'

'The triumph of hope over experience.' Amy sighed. 'How about you? Are you okay? You've had a rough time of it.'

'Thanks ... it was a shock when it happened. I knew they'd been fighting a lot but I didn't expect her to leave like that. I've never seen her so upset.'

'Do you think they'll sort it out?'

'I doubt it. Mama's not a forgiving person.'

'That bruise looks painful.'

Krista touched her cheek lightly. She'd covered it as much as possible with foundation but the darkening colour and the swelling was difficult to hide completely. 'It's not too bad. Oliver was hurt much worse. I feel so guilty. It's all my fault he got involved.'

'He doesn't seem to mind. I mean, he obviously minds being injured and not being able to work, but he didn't need to be involved if he hadn't wanted to be. Not with the horse affair and those two bully boys. Anyway, that's all Angus's fault, not yours.'

'I bet he does mind! He's just too nice to say so.'

'He is a very nice man, isn't he? Good looking too. Quite the catch.' Amy smiled but it had a subtly suggestive edge to it and chimed exactly with her own thoughts, a fact which Krista tried to ignore.

'Sandy told me he's Taylor's Bend's most eligible bachelor since the policeman got married.'

'I haven't seen the cop but judging by the other blokes I've seen around town, I'm sure he is.'

'The Doc's receptionist is a big fan of his. She was very prickly when I walked in with him.' Krista snickered. 'When I told him what Sandy said, he was embarrassed. Most of the guys I know would boast about it.'

'It's different in the country.'

'I'm beginning to see that.'

'Roddy and I couldn't live in a city again.' Amy swung the car into a parking spot at the supermarket.

'I'm not sure I'd go that far,' said Krista. 'I have no idea what I'd do here. There's only one dress shop and what about entertainment?'

'There's lots goes on in these places. Rod and I are just too tired at night to make the effort to go out.'

Amy got out of the car and took shopping bags from the back seat.

Krista said, as they walked to the sliding doors at the front of the supermarket, 'Oliver told me they're putting on a show in June. He plays the cello, of all things.'

'Goodness, is there no end to his talents?'

'Seems not. Someone called Abbie said I could help her with the sets if I wanted while I'm here.'

'That sounds fun. I didn't know about the show. I wonder if they need more people in the chorus.'

'Come with me in the morning and meet her. I need to buy some clothes tomorrow too. I only brought a few things with me.'

'How long are you staying?'

'I thought until my keys arrived, but with the fire who knows when that will be? If Angus ever posted them. But I remembered my cleaner has a key so I can leave any time.'

'So there's no need to buy clothes,' said Amy. She dragged a trolley from the row and set off down an aisle, list in hand.

Krista trailed after her. She was right. Not about buying clothes because she needed socks and sneakers, and clothes shopping was always a good idea, but the implication was why stay? The horses weren't hers, apart from Calypso who'd always been cared for by The Grange staff.

A new question arose. What would happen if Hugh sold up? She'd have to sell Calypso or pay to board her somewhere, which seemed crazy when she didn't ride. She really should be paying board for her at Oliver's.

She'd made assumptions all her life based on her mother's and, more recently, Hugh's example—ask for help but don't consider the cost to the giver. Amy wasn't making that assumption because she was used to paying her way and counting pennies. She'd made it clear they were accepting the bed but not free board from Oliver by charging off to the supermarket for provisions. It hadn't occurred to Krista at all.

The least she could do was pay for the food they were loading into the trolley. Rod wouldn't be in his situation if she hadn't roped him into finding Lola. The dog wasn't his responsibility. All these people had suffered because of her and her family and their lack of consideration. Angus had started it but she'd continued with the wreckage. No wonder the locals viewed them with disdain.

Amy turned with a packet of cereal in her hand, glanced at Krista and said, 'What's up?'

'All this is my fault. Rod's leg, Oliver...'

'You didn't start the bushfire, did you?'

'Of course not.'

'And you don't control the wind and the weather.'

'But Lola wasn't Rod's responsibility. He was trying to get the horses ready and I nagged at him about her.'

'So what? She's not your dog either. He wouldn't leave a dog to be burnt alive and if you'd said go without her it would have been the other way round. He'd have been insisting you find her first.'

Krista stared at her, wanting her words to be true. 'But...'

'Shut up and let's get moving. Roddy and Oliver will want their dinner.' She turned and continued on. 'Go and find ice cream.'

In the face of such a thorough dismissal of her attempt to apologise, Krista did as she was told. Amy was a force to be reckoned with.

***

After dinner, news came through that the fire was under control and residents could return home in the morning to assess the damage to their properties.

'They haven't said anything about the extent of damage,' said Amy.

'They won't have been able to cover every house yet if it wasn't directly in the path of the fire,' said Oliver.

'So The Grange should be safe?' said Krista.

'With any luck.' Rod smiled. 'We'll go out first thing and then come back for the horses if it's okay to go home.'

'I'll come too.' Krista looked at Oliver, who was holding an icepack against his swollen arm. 'Can I leave Lola here, please?'

Lola, lounging on the floor by her feet, wagged her tail at the mention of her name.

'Of course.'

'She's enjoying herself being a proper dog,' said Rod.

'She's sure had some adventures lately.' Krista stroked the silky head.

'She's not alone,' said Amy. 'I'm the only one in this crew who hasn't been locked up, dehydrated, beaten up or squashed by something.'

'How did you get hit by that tree, Rod? Calypso wasn't hurt,' Oliver said.

'I went into the trees to have a look on foot and she took off. Spooked by the wind.'

'If Hugh sells The Grange, I'll have to decide if I want to keep her,' said Krista.

'Unless that Mafia type comes to claim her.' Oliver grimaced. 'The deadline has gone by.'

'Do you think he'll turn up again?' Rod frowned. 'At The Grange?'

'If he does, or any of those men do, I'm calling the police,' said Amy.

'The police are already on the lookout for that red ute,' said Oliver. 'I doubt that pair will come back unless they're much, much thicker than we think they are.'

'When I told Hugh what had happened, he was furious,' said Krista. 'He'll be talking to Stefan Moran about it.'

'So much for "I'll take care of it" and "don't worry".'

Krista glanced at Amy's stern expression and clamped down on the desire to apologise yet again for causing such trouble.

'I wonder if Angus will be game to show his face here again,' she said instead.

'If he has a suitcase of cash he'll be welcome.' Oliver gave a short laugh.

'That's not going to happen,' said Rod.

'Where do you think he is?' asked Amy.

'No idea,' said Krista.

'Probably in Vegas playing the poker machines,' said Rod.

'I think he's a bit more high-stakes than that or we wouldn't be in this mess.' Krista exhaled and slumped deeper into the lounge chair. Oliver's furniture was well worn and old-fashioned and far cosier and more comfortable than her modern designer-styled suite. Her apartment was toned in grey, black, silver and glass. Cold and unfriendly by comparison. Functional but unwelcoming.

Oliver's phone rang, shattering the silence that followed her remark. Krista straightened as he answered. No way could he go out on a call. Whoever it was would have to phone another vet. He'd have to put a message on his phone saying he was closed for business.

'Hello?'

Frowning, he looked at Krista and mouthed, 'It's them.'

With a chill of fear working its way through her body, she moved close, trying to hear the caller.

'Krista's phone was smashed by one of your men when they came to beat us up this morning,' he said.

Stefan Moran? Why was he phoning Oliver?

Oliver put his hand over the phone. 'It's that bloke Stefan Moran, the boss. He wants to speak to you.'

'I'm calling the police,' said Amy in a low voice. She got up and went into the kitchen.

'Wait a minute,' said Krista. 'I'll see what he wants first.'

Amy reappeared. Krista took the phone from Oliver as the fear turned into icy determination. Enough was enough.

'Hello.'

'Good evening, Krista, Stefan Moran speaking.'

'Why did your men attack us this morning? The deadline was this evening.'

'They acted without my knowledge,' he said. 'As you say, the deadline has passed and you have failed to honour your side of the deal.'

'There was no deal, Mr Moran, and as far as I'm concerned I owe you nothing. Even if I did, the actions of your men negated any deadline or arrangement you might have made. The police have been informed of the attack and I fully intend to press charges when they are arrested. If you want to distance yourself from their actions, I suggest you leave me and Oliver Johnson alone.'

She disconnected and handed the phone back to Oliver.

'Wow!' Rod began applauding. 'Go Krista. That's telling him.'

'Are you sure that was a good idea?' asked Oliver.

'No, but I suddenly got really pissed off with feeling like a victim when I haven't done anything wrong. Men like him make me furious. He holds me accountable for Angus's stuff-up, which I had absolutely nothing to do with, but takes no responsibility for what his men do in his name.'

'Typical hypocrite,' said Amy. 'But he's dangerous, isn't he?'

'Yes,' said Oliver. 'Very.'

'He won't want to be involved in a court case with that pair,' said Krista. 'They'll say they were acting on his orders and he'll deny it and leave them hanging. But if Hugh and I add our story, he'll have a few questions to answer.'

'I hope it works.' Oliver sucked in a deep breath and exhaled slowly. 'What if those two don't get caught?'

'I don't know.' Krista grimaced. 'I hadn't thought of that.'

***

Amy and Krista were busy in the kitchen when Oliver surfaced the next morning. He heard their voices and breathed in the smell of toast and bacon on his way to the bathroom. Muscles ached he'd never realised were there and when he looked at his face in the mirror, the darkening blue and black bruises made him blink in astonishment and peer more closely at the unfamiliar reflection.

'That's enough to scare the horses,' he murmured.

His forearm was still swollen but not as badly as yesterday even though the colour was deepening to rival that of his face. The icepack had helped a lot but he'd been woken at intervals during the night with the throbbing pain.

He flexed his fingers carefully, wincing as all the tendons complained. Showering and dressing took longer than usual, but a T-shirt was far easier to pull on than buttoning a shirt, and trackpants were easier than jeans.

The women sat at the table with cups of tea and empty cereal bowls. They must have bought that yesterday because he never ate cereal. Amy was eating toast, listening to Krista talk about hairdressers. Oliver poured himself tea and put bread in the toaster.

'I'll cook your eggs or you'll have an accident,' said Krista. 'Sit down.' She'd covered the worst of the bruise on her cheek with make-up and dressed in her own clothes. Reverting to herself, the rich stepdaughter of a billionaire.

Rod hobbled in from checking the horses.

'Fred's much better. We can take him home with the others,' he said. 'We'll go and check it out as soon as you're ready, Amy.'

'I'm ready now.' She drained the last of her tea and stood up.

'What about breakfast?' asked Oliver.

'Mate, I ate ages ago.' Rod laughed. 'You deserved a sleep-in. We'll phone and tell you what's happening, Krista. No need to come out there yet. Sandy's feeding the horses at the showground.'

'Okay. There's a lot of food in the fridge in the main house you should have. If there is a house.'

'You could bring some chocolate mousse back,' Oliver said.

'Chocolate mousse? You're kidding.' Amy grinned. 'You'll have to fight me for it.'

'That wouldn't be a fair fight,' he said indignantly.

Krista cleaned up in the kitchen while Oliver went to unlock the gate. Margie would arrive in half an hour to do some work in the office and then they'd do the ordering of supplies.

Would Krista stay? She'd said she would but there was no reason to now that Rod and Amy were back. Sandy would be happy to help them at The Grange. Horses were her main passion whereas Krista knew next to nothing about them and couldn't ride. The Grange wasn't her home. She was a city girl.

If the place had been destroyed there was even less reason.

If she wanted to leave she'd leave. He wasn't going to beg her to stay.

He waved to Amy and Rod as they drove by then went to say good morning to Billy and Calypso. They had their heads in their feed and barely deigned to acknowledge him. He checked on the black stallion and Rod was right. He was brighter this morning with no nasal discharge. The fresher, cleaner air would help with his recovery. The smoke haze had cleared overnight although looking across to the north where the fire had burned strongest there was still a thick pall. Fires would be still be burning here and there and unless it poured with rain for a few days some could smoulder on for weeks.

In the kitchen, Krista was putting the last of the washed and dried dishes away in the cupboard. She looked at home in his house. He liked that she fitted.

'You didn't have to do all that,' he said.

'What, were you going to do one-handed? You'd end up with no crockery.' She laughed. 'Don't worry, I know you're not expecting me to be the kitchen drudge.'

'Anyone less like a kitchen drudge I've yet to meet.'

'It's the least I can do, Oliver. You've just let three virtual strangers stay in your house. If The Grange is still standing I should go there.'

'Why?'

'I don't belong here.'

'You don't belong there either, do you?'

'No, I suppose not. I should go home to Melbourne.'

'What will you do there? What about helping Abbie?'

She sighed and slumped onto a chair, leaning her elbows on the table and cupping her chin in her hands.

'I don't know what to do. I keep changing my mind.'

He pulled out a chair and sat down opposite her. 'What do you really want to do? Forget what you should do or what you think you should do. Or what you think I'll think about it, or anyone else for that matter.'

She straightened, brow furrowed, as she thought about what he'd asked.

'I want to stay.'

His heart thumped harder. What was she saying? She wanted to stay with him? Here in his house?

She hadn't finished. 'I like Taylor's Bend. I didn't think I would but the people here are really friendly and kind. For the first time in my life I feel as if I might be able to belong somewhere.'

'You've forgotten Penny,' he said with a laugh to cover the great leap of exhilaration. Staying in town was good, very good. Excellent, in fact. She wouldn't walk out of his life and disappear, leaving a hole the size of Australia.

'Gosh—yes.' But she didn't laugh. She watched him with apprehension in her eyes.

'But that's ... good,' he said cautiously. 'Are you thinking long-term?'

Her face crumpled again. 'I don't know. You asked me what I really wanted...'

'I did.' He smiled. 'You could start a fashion clothes shop. Or open a classy restaurant.'

Her eyes widened. 'I doubt it.'

'There's sure to be some sort of work around to tide you over until you decide what you want to do. The point is, knowing where you want to live is a good start. The rest will sort itself out.'

'Are there places to rent here?'

'Houses, yes. No apartments. There'll be a few rentals about.' Not the quality she was used to though.

'I don't need a whole house.'

He laughed. 'You can rent a room from me if you like until you decide.' He almost held his breath as he watched her reaction. Surprise first, then considering, followed by doubt, a frown...

'Can I?'

'I was joking.' Giving her an out if she needed one.

'Oh.'

She didn't. Her expression was pure disappointment. 'You wouldn't need to pay rent.'

'I would!'

'Okay.' He shrugged. 'We can work something out.'

'Are you serious?'

'Are you?'

She paused for a couple of beats, holding his gaze, then that glorious smile appeared.

'Yes.'

He held out his hand and she shook it solemnly.

'Done.'

He smiled and she sprang to her feet and ran around the table to kiss his cheek. 'Thank you. I'll have to go back to Melbourne and collect more clothes and things.'

'When?'

'Tomorrow. I have to get a new phone today. Will you come with me? I don't know where to go.'

'If yours isn't melted, you might be able to retrieve the data.'

'That's right! Although he did grind his foot onto it, the bastard.'

Half an hour later, Rod and Amy parked their big ute next to the office. Krista, with Lola trotting by her side, came out of the house to greet them. She'd been waiting anxiously for the phone call, unwilling to bother Oliver and Margie at work across the yard but in a fever to know if The Grange had survived. Not the main house, although that would be a big loss, but Rod and Amy's little cottage and their car. That house was a proper home, their lives were there.

'Everything's fine. That copse where I was injured has a few singed bits but nothing came closer.' Rod's voice and expression said it all. 'We'll go and collect the horses from the showground first and come back for the three here. I called Sandy to let her know.'

'I'll come with you and collect my car,' said Krista. 'I'll tell Oliver.'

'I'll collect our bags.' Amy jumped out of the driver's seat and hurried into the house.

Oliver and Margie were in the storeroom, she with a clipboard and he staring at a shelf of different sized boxes.

'Four of the medium and one small, left,' he said.

'Sorry to interrupt,' said Krista. 'The Grange is fine. Rod and Amy are here and they're going to the showground to collect the horses. I'm going with them to get my car.'

'That's great news,' said Margie. 'Means Sally and Les will be okay, too. They're closer in than The Grange.'

'Yes, I met Les. He helped me unload the horses.'

'Are you going out there?' asked Oliver.

'If they need a hand I will, but Sandy's more use than I am.'

He smiled. 'Okay, see you soon.'

Margie stood there grinning from one to the other.

'What?' he asked.

'Nothing.'

'See you later.' Krista escaped before the pinkness rising up her throat and neck reached her face. What was Margie? Psychic?

She collected her handbag from the house and met Amy coming out with a suitcase.

'I found your phone,' she said. 'It's completely smashed. Maybe a horse trod on it as well.'

'Thanks.' Krista took the shattered wreckage. An expert might be able to recover something. She could ask when she bought the new one. She had her laptop and iPad at home with the same information on them, so apart from a few phone numbers it wasn't crucial. If she was starting her new life she wouldn't need a lot of those numbers, she'd have new ones.

Chapter 14

By early afternoon, all The Grange horses had gone home with the exception of Calypso.

'She's not your responsibility,' said Krista when Rod objected. 'She's mine, and apart from that I don't want to give Moran any excuse to go to The Grange and cause trouble. If she's not there you don't have to lie. Tell him where she is if you have to.'

'I'll be straight onto the police if they turn up,' said Amy.

'Me too,' said Oliver.

After they'd gone, Oliver went with Krista to the neighbouring larger town of Willoughby for a new phone.

'How's your ankle?' he asked from the passenger seat.

'Not bad. It only hurts if I move it a certain way. My face is worse.'

'Is it painful? The bruising will take a few days to fade.'

'No, not really painful unless I press on it, and my jaw is a bit stiff. It's just ... ugly. Mama always used to say my looks were my best, my only, asset. I wonder what she'd say if she could see me at the moment.'

'Do you believe that?'

'She might be right.'

Dark glasses and heavily applied foundation weren't really doing the job of covering the dark, now turning multicoloured, stain spread across her cheek. She'd considered cancelling the outing, acutely conscious that going out in public meant people would see her and stare. Strangely, it was only today, this afternoon in the bathroom, she felt that way, when she was changing and preparing to go shopping, doing her make-up.

Les and Di saw her at her worst, as did Penny and Doc. She'd been make-upless, filthy, sweaty and battered, but even though Penny wasn't friendly she didn't stare at her as though she was somehow disfigured. They all knew what had happened. Margie wouldn't care what she looked like. Oliver ... well Oliver had tried to protect her and had his own problems as a result.

'Does it worry you?' he asked.

'What?

'Having a bruised face. That people might stare.'

'People always stare at me. Different reason though.' She gave a tiny laugh. 'They'll think you've hit me.'

He lifted his arm in the sling. 'Likewise.'

'Quite the fight,' she said and he laughed.

Oliver gazed out the window at the scenery rushing by. What was it like to be constantly stared at? He had no idea. Her mother's comment about her looks being her only asset was horrifying but explained a lot. What sort of woman would demean the self-worth of her child? Maybe she thought she was giving her daughter a tip. Use your looks to get you where you want to be, to get what you want from men because they're the ones who'll support you.

Straight out of the nineteenth century.

'Your looks aren't your only asset,' he said. When she didn't reply, he glanced at her and was surprised to see her wipe a finger across her cheek below the dark glasses.

'I need to find some other shoes while we're in Willoughby,' she said. 'Sneakers.'

'Do you need to if you're going home tomorrow?'

'Yes.' Her tone implied he was completely clueless. He was. He only bought new shoes if he needed them because the old ones had worn out. His trainers worked for tennis and cricket, he had good black shoes he rarely wore, a pair of slip-on loafers, thongs, workboots and gumboots.

While the phone-shop man studied the wreckage of her phone with a view to salvaging data, Oliver took Krista down a side street to Willoughby's small shopping mall.

'There's a shoe shop in here,' he said. 'But it'll be pretty basic.'

'I only want basic,' she said.

'I'll wait in Clancy's Bookshop. It's two along from the corner with the main street.'

'Okay.'

Out on the street, Oliver suddenly remembered he needed to tell Gina he couldn't play at *Patience* orchestra rehearsals until his left arm and fingers could cope. Tennis was off the agenda too, dammit, but only till his battered body was up to strenuous activity. He was right-handed so apart from the ball toss he didn't need his left hand to play. Calls made, with the ensuing explanations and apologies on his side and shocked sympathy from the others, he continued on to the bookshop. He'd have time to read if he wasn't working, which was a small consolation.

Half an hour later, Krista joined him with two shopping bags swinging from her hand.

'So you found some shoes?'

'Yes, two pairs, different colours. And I got the new phone. He was able to save everything.'

'Good.' Two pairs of the same shoe? Why? 'Ready to go?'

'Yes. Are you buying books?'

'Just one.' He showed her the thriller he'd chosen. 'Do you read?'

'Not much. I watch TV sometimes and movies.'

'I don't watch TV very often, apart from the news if I'm home. Other things to do.'

'You must get called out at odd times.'

'Yep. It's part of the job. People are pretty considerate. They only call me after hours if it's really urgent.'

'You're needed here, aren't you?'

'Me or someone like me. A vet, certainly.'

'Doesn't your father understand that?'

The questions surprised him. 'I don't think he thinks much about it. Or me. Not anymore.'

'Who'd have thought we'd have something in common,' she said and slid him a tentative little smile.

***

Krista left for Melbourne the next morning. She had on her ripped jeans, new pink sneakers and the same pink blouse she'd worn that first day. Exactly one week ago but what a change she'd undergone in that week. As had he.

'I'll be back in a few days,' she said, standing by her car, the door open, ready to slide in behind the wheel and drive away. 'It might take a bit longer but I'll definitely be back.'

'You might change your mind when you slot into your real life and see your friends again.'

Could he believe her? He believed she believed herself. Right now, as she spoke ... but later? Why would she return to a small country town with nothing to offer a girl who liked clothes and shopping, overseas holidays, went out with friends to restaurants and shows. Rich people with expensive tastes and lifestyles. He'd seen them in action at The Grange. They may have been Hugh's friends and colleagues but their children were her peers.

'No, I won't.' She looked straight into his eyes as she said that. 'I won't,' she repeated softly. 'I want to come back here.' She hesitated. 'To you.' She placed her palm gently against his cheek. 'You need looking after.'

'I won't be like this forever,' he said.

'No, but you'll still need looking after.' A shadow flitted across her face. Doubt. With her so close, her voice and expression so intimate, his own doubt was fading fast, but enough remained to prevent him dragging her back into the house to explore what he'd only dreamed might be a mutually consuming attraction.

'So do you.'

He stepped closer but she didn't move away, she slipped her hand around his neck and her lips landed on his. Still unsure what she meant by this kiss, he kept a tight rein on the surge of passion. The last thing he wanted to do was bugger things up by coming on too strong and scaring her off. She'd told him many times how men assumed she was available for the taking, how she despised them for it. Her kiss could be of the friendly 'thank you for everything, see you soon' variety.

Even though it nearly killed him, he hoped he gave her enough to show he wanted to kiss her but not too much of the raging desire coursing through his body, the desire to tear both their clothes off and make love right there in the yard. By her face when she drew away, he may or may not have succeeded.

'I'll be off,' she said hoarsely.

'Krista,' he began but her fingers prevented more words, sealing his mouth gently.

'Don't,' she said, slid in to the driver's seat and closed the door. She gave a little wave, jammed her dark glasses on, started the engine and turned the blue car for the gate.

'I think I love you,' Oliver said helplessly, and watched until the car disappeared from view.

***

Krista drove with damp cheeks. She stopped when, out of sight of Oliver's place, she reached the turn into the main street, opposite the house with tyre swans in the yard, and pulled out a tissue to wipe her eyes and blow her nose. How could she have fallen so hard and so fast for that man? And wasn't it just typical that when the perfect man turned up, he was one of the very few who was resistant to her looks. He was more interested in personality and what a woman was like, her brain and what she could do. She wasn't anywhere near up to his standard in that department. She didn't know where to start when it came to using her brain to attract a man. Or using her brain for anything important. She was a brainless bimbo. Her mother was right.

She continued on slowly through the town, noting the Arts Centre and remembering she hadn't followed up Abbie's offer to help. There was another example of her superficial approach to life and commitment. But she had meant to help Abbie and when she came back she would.

At the far end of the main street, she passed the General Store. Oliver mentioned the owners but she'd forgotten their names. An elderly couple married for ages, he'd said. On impulse, she parked and went in on the pretext of buying a bottled of cold water to drink on the way. A black dog lay half across the doorway and thumped his tail twice when she edged around his bulky body.

A grey-haired old man smiled at her from behind the counter. 'Hello there, Krista, isn't it?'

'Yes, it is.' How one earth did he know that?

'Laurie's the name. Dot and I've owned this place for fifty years.'

'Gosh.' She shook the proffered hand.

'Saw you walking that big horse to Oliver's last week. Glad you made it safely.'

'You stopped and asked if I needed help!'

'Guilty as charged,' he said.

'Thanks for stopping.' She could say that now and mean it. She understood.

'No worries. You were lucky The Grange didn't get hit by those fires.'

'Yes, I know. It was scary though. Les and Sally are on that road too and they should be all right. Les helped me at the showground with the horses.'

'Right as rain,' he said. 'Sal was in this morning picking up a few things on their way home. She told me you and Oliver had been attacked by a gang of thugs.'

'Two thugs, but yes.'

'Looters. Those bastards. Reckon they thought The Grange would be easy pickings and worth the risk.'

'Probably.'

'Fancy hitting a woman,' he went on. 'What sort of man does that?'

'I hit one of them with a bucket, twice,' she said. 'To stop them beating up Oliver.'

'Good for you, love. Those types should be thrown in jail and never let out. We don't like that sort of thing around here.'

'The police have put out an alert for them but we haven't heard anything yet.'

'They'll be from Wagga, probably. Not local.'

So he didn't know everything but she doubted she'd be able to tell Laurie anything new. Except ... 'The stable manager and his wife are home now so I'm on my way back to Melbourne. I've stopped in to get some water.'

He nodded and pointed to the drinks fridge.

'Word is your stepfather is selling up,' he said. 'So we may not see you around here again.'

'I'll be back in a few days,' she said. 'I need to collect a few more things from home and tie up some loose ends.'

That was definitely news to Laurie. She almost saw his ears prick up.

'Oliver got anything to do with this?' he asked with a cheeky smile, which made her laugh. 'He's a handsome young feller.'

'How much do I owe you?'

She gave him the coins. 'Nice to meet you, Laurie.'

'Likewise, love. Call in when you get back.'

'Will do. What's your dog's name?'

'Banjo.'

Krista drove on with a lighter heart. The Taylor's Bend residents assumed she and Oliver were shaping up to be a couple even if they themselves were in a weird sort of limbo. If Doc, Laurie and Margie were random samples of popular opinion, it seemed she'd gained their approval. Laurie hadn't commented once or even looked twice at her bruise. His reaction was sympathy and disgust at who would so such a thing. Somehow she'd worked her way into local life without even trying. Somehow these people accepted her.

Oliver obviously hadn't told a soul about the Calypso exchange. Had he put out the looters theory or had that arisen like water to fill a hole in local knowledge? Gossips were the same the world over. If facts were scarce, make them up.

Two hours later, she stopped for petrol and a break. She'd taken a rest at the same place on the way to Taylor's Bend, dreading the stultifying weekend ahead of her, but the events that transpired were extraordinary—from being threatened by gangsters to escaping a bushfire to falling in love with a most unlikely man. Unbelievable, really. She would have sworn on her life that she'd never want to live in Taylor's Bend or anywhere like it. Now she was seriously considering the move. She wasn't taking any drastic action like selling her Melbourne apartment, or even renting it out, but she would stay for a few months and see what happened. Not least of the reasons why was, as crafty old Laurie had thought, Oliver.

Oliver. She might be in love with him but how did he feel about her?

Now that she was away from him and the drama of the preceding days had faded, it was easier to think clearly. Staying in his house probably wasn't a very good idea. Not for more than a few days. She'd look for somewhere to rent as soon as she got back, or, more sensibly, she could stay at The Grange. Learning about the horses would be useful, and until Rod's leg was out of the cast Amy would bear the brunt of the workload. She really should be there to help.

What she mustn't do was trail uselessly around after Oliver. She needed to be independent, just as he'd said. 'Make your own decisions.' He didn't need looking after, not really, not in a practical day-to-day sense. That was her own desire talking. Margie would be there and she was far more efficient and experienced at what was necessary than Krista would ever be.

If he was the man she thought he was, she had to be cautious and she had to prove to him she was worthy of loving and not a liability. That would take time and she had plenty of that. By the time she arrived outside her apartment block, she was fairly sure she'd made the first grown-up decision of her adult life. In other words, she'd resisted the urge to leap in headfirst and made a rational, considered plan of action all by herself and for herself.

She'd rung Mel, the cleaner, on her way in and arranged to meet her at five with the keys. Luckily she was cleaning other apartments in the same complex so there was no problem. Until she had the keys, she couldn't park in the underground area so she circled the block until Mel appeared, then parked illegally during a quick exchange of greetings and thanks.

'I'm moving to the country for a while,' she said, although she knew Mel wasn't the slightest bit interested in her doings. 'So I'll be in touch when I need you again.'

Krista hadn't bothered bringing anything with her except her toiletries. She had more than enough clothes and shoes to choose from at home. The problem would be deciding how many bags to pack and what to take. She rode up in the lift from the underground-parking garage, turning her choices over in her mind. Jeans, shorts, solid shoes and maybe workboots of some sort. Elastic siders, perhaps? She'd need to go shopping for those. T-shirts, blouses and shirts. Leave the work clothes and upmarket party dresses and high heels behind. Think practical, outdoors, serviceable. Take her tennis racquet and gear for when Oliver recovered. Maybe take a couple of dressy outfits just in case. The pink floral? Teal sheath? A couple of light cotton summer dresses. Jacket and anorak for when the weather changed.

Humming to herself happily, she opened her apartment door, eager to get started right away on the packing. She'd call Oliver to let him know she'd arrived but not right away. Maybe a text would be better. More low key. A simple, 'I'm home' would do. Be cool.

She dumped her bag on the nearest chair and looked around the familiar space. As sparse and clinical as always. It didn't have the lived-in feel of Oliver's sprawling old house or the cosy family feel of Rod and Amy's cottage. Even The Grange had an air of being lived in.

First she needed a cold drink. Melbourne was as hot as Taylor's Bend but with the grime of the city replacing the dust and smoke. In the kitchen,

Angus had left dirty dishes on the draining board. What a slob! The least he could do was clean up his mess, having invited himself into her home without permission. Where was he hiding? Did he think his debt would go away magically?

She took her glass of chilled juice to her bedroom. Angus wouldn't have dared sleep in her bed, surely. No, he hadn't. A quick look into the second bedroom with its rumpled bed confirmed it. Just as well.

Half an hour later, in the midst of trying to decide which shoes to take and which to leave, the buzzer sounded for the street door access.

'Yes?'

'Delivery for Ms Laatonen.'

'What sort of delivery?'

'A package.'

'Is there a sender's name?' She frowned. Had she ordered anything online recently? Not that she remembered.

'Littlejohn.'

'Okay. Twelfth floor.' She pressed the door opener. Which Littlejohn? Possibly Mama. Maybe Hugh. Not Angus.

She suppressed a tingle of alarm. This was a delivery, she received them all the time, but she waited for the knock and looked through the peephole rather than open her door. A man in a black polo shirt and cap stood there, blank faced, holding a largish box. He was alone and he looked vaguely familiar. A courier.

'Krista Laatonen?' He pronounced it like Late-nen. 'Sign here, please.'

'Thanks.' She scrawled her signature quickly and retreated inside. The box was light but bulky. The sender was V Littlejohn. Mama. Still using her married name, which was a good sign. What on earth was Mama sending?

Lola's lead, food bowl and blanket. Good grief. A note on top said *Lola will need these or she'll pine. I'll be in touch when things are better. Love Mama.*

Far from pining, Lola was having the time of her doggy life and who better to care for her than a vet? By the sound of that last sentence, Lola would be visiting for quite a while. Typical of Mama to assume Krista wouldn't mind.

After dinner, Krista sent Oliver the text she'd prepared in her head. Short and to the point. *I'm home. Not sure when I'll be back but will probably stay at The Grange.*

His reply came in five minutes later, shorter and even more to the point. *Okay.*

Krista spent the next day sorting through her clothes. She had barely anything suitable for a working country life. A shopping expedition was definitely necessary for plain jeans and boots. There wasn't a lot of food in her kitchen but she'd take the fruit, cereal, eggs and vegetables. And a few jars of her favourite olives and water crackers.

She texted a couple of friends saying she was back in town for a few days and that a get-together would be nice to say goodbye. Not that there were many people she'd miss. No-one close. She'd never been the 'best girlfriends' type of girl. Moved around too much to form close relationships and never wanted to—apart from Trudy. She was a loner.

Clea and George responded, suggesting dinner at a restaurant in the city and that they'd put the word around. *Saturday at 8.*

See you then. Xxx, she responded.

So if she spent Friday and Saturday completing her packing and shopping, she could leave on Sunday. She wouldn't tell Oliver or anyone else, she'd just turn up and surprise them. Rod and Amy would be pleased to see her. Oliver ... probably would.

Surprisingly, Hugh phoned her on Friday when she was shopping but he didn't seem to have much to say beyond asking how she was.

'I'm fine. How are you?' she countered.

'I miss your mother.'

'Does it serve you right, do you think?'

'Probably.' He sighed heavily. 'I want her back.'

'She was very angry and hurt, Hugh. I've never seen her so upset.'

'Do you think she'll forgive me?'

'I'm sorry. I really don't know.'

'What are your plans, Krista?' he said with an effort at stepfatherly interest.

'Dinner with friends tomorrow night.'

'Enjoy yourself. You know I'm very fond of you. Take care.'

'Thanks Hugh. You too,' she replied, touched by the unexpected call.

On Friday afternoon, she lugged one of her large suitcases down to the car and heaved it into the boot. She eyed the remaining space. If she put half the back seat flat, she'd get the other slightly smaller one in next to the first, and her other bags could go in the gaps and on the back seat and passenger side floor and seat. She shut the boot and headed upstairs to bring down the second one. A bit of juggling later and both were stowed in the BMW.

Maybe she should have hired a van. Her car wasn't used to being a carthorse. 'Welcome to your new life,' she murmured and turned away for the lift.

Chapter 15

On Saturday, Oliver decided he could return to work on Monday despite ribs that ached and a badly discoloured forearm. His hand had enough strength to hold a cat or dog and anything he couldn't manage he'd redirect to Willoughby. He could give an injection and dress a wound and he could drive—just. And he was bored. He'd finished the thriller he'd bought and he'd read the paper each day and done the puzzles. He'd pottered about in the house and caught up on a few domestic chores and he'd waited for Krista to come back.

She hadn't texted since her initial message. Staying at The Grange was probably a better idea than staying here, disappointing though that was. Distance and space had allowed some perspective into what had been a fraught and emotionally heightened situation. Was he losing interest in her? No way. He missed her like a piece of himself.

The kiss she'd so surprisingly bestowed on him had sealed his love, and the memory sustained him during the ensuing empty days. Several times he'd picked up his phone to ask her if she'd decided when she'd return, and every time he put it down unused.

On the pretext of checking how things were, he called Rod on Sunday evening.

'I'm hobbling around doing what I can. It's good to be back though. Amy's been fantastic and we're managing okay. How are you?' No mention of Krista.

'Much better. I'll start work again on Monday.'

'Good. Fred's recovered. You were right about it being a cold and none of the other horses got it.'

'Excellent. Listen have you heard from Krista? Any idea when she's coming back?'

'Not a thing. I reckon you'd be the one she'd call, mate.'

'I don't know about that ... she said she'd probably stay at The Grange. And I've got Lola and some of her things here. Not that that's a problem. Lola's been good company while I had nothing to do.'

'Have you called her and asked?'

'No. I thought I'd leave it to her. She'll come when she's ready.'

'Okay. But I reckon she'll be back. Don't worry.' Rod laughed. 'Gotta go, dinner's ready. See you, mate.'

Oliver hung up then called Krista. Voicemail. He hesitated but didn't speak. She'd see the number and know it was him.

'What do you reckon, Lola? Is she coming home to us?'

Lola wagged her tail and he scratched her ears.

While he was eating dinner, his phone pinged. A text. He snatched it up. Krista.

Decided to go away for a few weeks.

What the hell? He called the number again. Voicemail.

He texted, frowning.

Call me.

He finished eating, cleared away the dishes, watched some TV, but she didn't respond and she didn't call.

Monday dragged. Morning surgery was quiet and he only had two calls in the afternoon, neither of which involved anything too demanding. Margie insisted on closing early, saying he shouldn't overdo it and he looked tired. He was. He was also distracted—worry was making inroads. Where was she and why the silence?

He considered phoning Rupe but dismissed that as a waste of his time. What could he do? He'd say she was an adult and could do what she liked, that Oliver barely knew her and since she'd gone back to the city she might have decided Taylor's Bend was what she'd originally thought it was. Boring. That text could be her way of saying she'd changed her mind. Rupe would tell him to forget her. He would have believed the woman he'd first encountered could act so dismissively, ignoring the fact he was minding her dog, but he did know her now, much better and she wouldn't do that. He went to bed but he couldn't forget her and he couldn't still that nagging little voice in his head telling him something was wrong.

His ringing phone woke him from a sleep disturbed by dreams and periods of wakefulness. He snatched it up, his fuzzy mind flying immediately to Krista rather than the more likely worried animal owner.

'Hello.'

'Is that Oliver Johnson, the vet?'

'Yes.' He sighed and swung his legs out of the bed, ready to get up and going. Morning light streamed in. He was late.

'It's Angus Littlejohn. Is Krista with you? Her phone is off.'

Oliver sat up, ignoring the protest from his bruised stomach muscles. 'No, she's in Melbourne, at her apartment.'

'She's not.'

'Where are you? Are you overseas?'

'I'm at her apartment. I just got in. Rod said you might know where she is.'

Wide awake now, anger surged. 'I don't. You've got a hide, you know that? Have you any idea of the trouble you've caused. We both got threatened and beaten up because of you, you bastard.'

'I'm sorry.'

'Sorry isn't good enough. Pay back the money you owe that man and get him off our backs.'

'I will. I'm going to.'

'How?'

'I've just got back from Macau.'

'What? You've been gambling in Macau?' Unbelievable. Oliver could only shake his head as his mind groped for words.

'Yes, and I won. I'll pay him everything I owe.' He actually sounded proud of himself.

'Does he know that?'

'I'm going to see him today.'

'So what's happened to Krista?'

'No idea. That's why I'm asking you. I want to tell her not to worry.'

Oliver's brain kicked into gear. 'Is there any sign of her there?'

'There are some things in a couple of carry bags and her make-up and stuff is in her bathroom. It's a bit weird.'

'What is?'

'There are clothes on her bed and the cupboard doors are open as if she'd been packing or something and her handbag is in the living room.'

'She was packing. She was planning to stay in Taylor's Bend for a while.'

'Why? She hates it there.'

'Long story. Is there an underground car park?'

'Yes.'

'Is her car there?'

'Don't know.'

'Go and have a look and call me back.'

'Can I have a shower and change first?'

'No. Do it now.'

In a fever of impatience, Oliver went to the kitchen and started making breakfast until his phone rang.

'Her car's there but I don't have a key. It looks as though she was loading it up with her things though. There's a suitcase and some carry bags on the back seat. Looks like some of Lola's stuff.'

'Do you know her friends?'

'Not really.'

'Think, Angus.'

'Why are you so worried about her? She probably spent the night with some guy.'

Oliver ground his teeth. 'She left last Wednesday and texted to say she'd arrived and would be back at The Grange in a few days. I rang her earlier today and got voicemail, but a little while later a text came saying she was going away for a few weeks.'

'And you don't think she has?'

'No, I don't. Do you? Why would she leave her car behind with her stuff in it? Her suitcase. And as far as I know, women don't leave their handbags behind.'

'The keys aren't in it, I looked. She has more than one handbag and more suitcases.' Angus paused. 'But she would take her make-up and toothbrush. What do you think has happened?' Mild interest now.

'I think your mate Moran abducted her.'

'Christ! He wouldn't do that.'

'Have you any idea what he's capable of?' Was he really so dense? Who did he think the man was? Some benign, friendly old mate of his father's?

'Dad wouldn't let it get that far.'

'Are you sure? He was furious when you cleared out, and he washed his hands of your debt. Moran holds him and Krista responsible instead. And with your father refusing to play along, Krista was left holding the bag. And me.'

'Why you?"

'For God's sake, Angus! I had Arch Rival at my place when they came to collect her thinking she was Calypso. Did you really think you'd get away with that pathetic trick?'

'I was desperate.'

'Call Hugh and tell him what's happened.'

'But if I pay back the money, Moran will let her go and Dad needn't be involved.'

'If she's still alive.'

'No. He won't dare kill her. No, don't say that.'

At last he'd struck a nerve in that egotistical, overgrown child. 'Call him and find out.' Oliver hung up.

Still shaking with rage, he showered and dressed. There was no way of figuring out when Krista was planning to leave Melbourne and no way of figuring out how long ago she'd been taken. If ransom was the plan someone would have heard by now, most likely

Hugh. If so, why hadn't he phoned Oliver?

He snatched up the phone.

It rang for some time. He'd bet the man was up making a few millions before morning tea. He was right. He was up.

'Oliver Johnson,' he barked. 'What can I do for you?'

'Have you heard anything from Krista recently?'

Breath feathered into the receiver. 'Why do you ask?' The tone was even and controlled, very like his father's when he was dealing with a distasteful subject but not wanting to give away his opinion.

Oliver was in no mood to pussyfoot around. 'I think Moran has abducted her.'

'Why would you think that?' Again the smooth tone.

'I haven't heard from her since Wednesday.'

'Is that unusual? Would you expect to hear from her?'

'Yes, I would. Her phone's off. She went home to pack up her things and move back to Taylor's Bend. She said she'd be a few days and it's nearly a week. Angus is back and he said her car is in the garage packed up ready to leave but she's not there.'

'When did Angus get back?'

'Early this morning. He rang me asking where Krista was. He has the money and is going to pay his debt.'

More silence then, 'How long do you think she's been missing?'

'I'm not sure but it would have taken her a while to pack so it could be since yesterday, or even Friday.'

'And you've had no contact from anyone?'

'No. I got a weird text from her phone on Sunday night saying she was going away for a few weeks but I'm sure she didn't send it. Have you been contacted?' Suspicious now. Hugh was holding something back; he was sure of it. 'Tell me the truth, dammit!'

'I received a photo of her. It was taken in the city on Friday morning and sent straight away. She had a shopping bag in her hand and she was coming out of a department store.'

'And? Who sent it?'

'I don't know.'

'What did you do?'

'What could I do?'

'Trace the email?' What couldn't he do if he wanted to?

'Of course, I got my IT man onto it but the phone was a prepaid throwaway.'

'It was a threat. Did you warn her?'

'I called to see if she was all right but didn't tell her why. She was still out shopping and was fine. She didn't mention going back to Taylor's Bend but she did say she was meeting friends on Saturday night for dinner.'

'Did she?'

'I've no idea.'

'I'm calling the police,' Oliver said.

'No, I'll take care of this.'

'The way you took care of the debt? No thanks.'

'How can Angus pay off his debt?' Hugh asked suddenly.

'He said he won the money in Macau and he's telling Moran right away. Will he let her go if the debt is paid?'

'It's more than the money to a man like Stefan Moran.' Hugh sighed heavily. 'It's an honour thing. It involves his pride and making her an example for others who might try to step out of line.'

'An example how?'

Hugh's silence was enough to chill him to the bone.

Oliver phoned Rupe. After listening to his story, he said, 'I can contact the Melbourne police and ask them to do some investigating. They should be able to track down the friends. And if she has her phone with her, they can track its whereabouts.'

'Thanks. I'm positive something's happened to her.'

'Is this connected to that beating you took? You have to tell me everything, Ollie. We can't operate on half-arsed information.'

'It could be. I think it is.' He gave Rupe a quick rundown of events, knowing exactly what his reaction would be, finishing with, 'I didn't have any real proof and Moran hadn't actually done anything.'

'Right,' he said. 'Apart from threaten you both and send those goons in to give you a beating.'

'They said he didn't, that it was their idea because we made them look stupid in front of the boss. Have you found them yet?'

'We found the vehicle, burnt out. At least we think it's the right one. All the identifying info had been removed. Okay. I'll get onto this right now. Sit tight and don't do anything stupid. These people aren't playing games.'

'If Angus repays his debt they'll let her go though, won't they?'

'I hope so, but if they haven't contacted anyone to say they have her, they might have a different plan.'

'Not a ransom?'

'Doesn't seem so.'

Which left revenge. But whose revenge was it? Moran's or their two attackers?

***

By lunchtime, Oliver was so wound up he could barely function. He'd had to force himself to focus on treating the cut on the hind leg of Carly Smith's pony that morning, but it wasn't a bad wound and he managed the antiseptic and bandaging as near to normally as was possible. He declined the offer of tea and shortbread and headed home, glad that at least a few hours had been occupied while he waited for news that didn't come.

Surely Angus had contacted Moran by now, it was nearly twelve. And what was Hugh doing?

Margie was on the phone when he walked into the surgery.

'Beryl,' she mouthed.

He grimaced. The last thing he needed was Beryl with her false alarms. Normally it didn't bother him but today...

'You'd better bring her in,' Margie said. 'Yes, he's just come back. Bye.'

'Margie, I don't have the time or the energy to deal with Beryl.'

'I think it's real this time. Sounds like a tick. Back legs are paralysed and Beryl was visiting friends in Sydney over the weekend—Dee Why.'

'Okay.' He nodded. Plenty of ticks in the Northern Beaches areas of Sydney. 'I hope for your sake it is and for Beryl and the dog's sake it's not.'

'She'll be back,' Margie called as he stomped into the consulting room to prepare.

'She always comes back, that's the problem.'

'Not Beryl, Krista.'

'Krista?' He came to stand in the doorway.

'Yes, the reason you're so grumpy.' She eyed him with an infuriating smirk.

'That's not...' He rubbed a hand over his face. 'She's missing.'

'Missing? What do you mean missing?'

'Her phone's off and she hasn't contacted anyone since Saturday night.' Once he started, the words kept coming. 'Angus is at her apartment and he said she's gone but her personal stuff is still there. Her car's in the garage there half packed. She was coming back.'

'Have you told the police?'

'Yes.'

'Cripes, no wonder you're worried. I had no idea, I'm sorry. Shall I put Beryl off?'

'No, you might be right about a tick. Better not. It'll take my mind off ... the other. I'm waiting for Angus or Hugh to call.'

'Any idea what might have happened?'

'It could be connected to those two men who attacked us.'

Her expression said it all. Oliver couldn't face the reflection of his own fear. He turned and began mindlessly preparing to treat Beryl's dog for a tick, just in case.

***

The first thing she became conscious of was her head aching with a relentless, dull, throb that resonated through her body. Her mouth was parched but a thick wad of cloth prevented her from moistening her lips with her tongue. A gag. Swallowing was difficult and she almost choked.

She opened her eyes slowly, blinking, straining to see something but the darkness was the same with eyes closed or open. An oily smell suffused the air. Like a mechanic's workshop. But she was in the back of a van, lying on some sort of thin foam layer that smelled mouldy. Night-time? She tried to sit up but her ankles and arms were tied and when she moved her head, the throb became a pounding and she had to lie still until it subsided.

She tried to remember what had happened but her brain was like cottonwool with snippets of memory caught like dust in the soft strands. Packing her car. Oliver. Her eagerness to leave. Dinner in a restaurant. White tablecloths. Clea was there and Malcolm. After that? Walking. Warm night. A taxi?

Then what? She closed her eyes in an effort to visualise but failed. Her feet and legs were bare. Where were her shoes? Her arms were bare, too. She had on a dress. She'd worn a dress to dinner. It came in a flash, like a photograph. The black dress with a purple and yellow floral-print, floaty skirt, ruffled hem and sleeves. The soft fabric felt familiar against her arms.

She hadn't made it home.

Voices sounded outside. Men talking low but urgently. Suddenly the side door slid open with a rasp of metal on metal, a square of dim yellow light in the darkness. A torch blinded her and she turned her head, after images dancing in her eyes.

'She's awake.'

A dark figure leaned in and she tried to shrink away as it loomed over her but she was against the wall of the van, trapped. Black featureless face. Rough hands removed the gag and she gulped deep breaths. He held her head up. Another smell mingled with the oiliness—cheap aftershave and sweat. In the light from the torch she glimpsed a plastic water bottle as he brought it to her lips. She swallowed gratefully and her mind began to clear.

'Who are you?' Her voice barely worked.

'Your teachers.' The water bottle was removed. 'If you're a good girl I won't put the gag back on.'

'What do you want?' Teachers? What?

'No yelling. No-one will hear you anyway. Except us.'

'What are you going to do to me?'

'The boss says you need to learn some manners.'

He straightened and the door slammed shut.

Moran. Tears trickled down her cheek. She'd angered him, disrespected him and now he was teaching her a lesson via this man and his offsider. This so-called teacher wasn't one of the pair that claimed Calypso. This was someone else and he was much more frightening with his casual, disinterested tone.

Hours later, the light increased enough for her to make out the interior of the van. The rear window was tinted but part of the windscreen was visible between the two seats and the partial panel and wire mesh separating the two areas. She could make out a wall, a shed or a garage wall. Her head wasn't as painful now the drug had worn off, and she was able to move without a sledgehammer attack on her brain. Her shoulders and legs were stiff and cramped and her left arm had lost all feeling but she managed to shuffle her body and struggle into a sitting position with her back against the wall. Excruciating pins and needles made her gasp as the blood rushed into the deadened arm.

Her shoes lay in the far corner, tossed in as an afterthought. She stared at them, willing herself to remember, but nothing came after the fragmented pieces of finishing dinner and walking with Malcolm to hail a cab. Had she gone in it? No. She remembered watching as his cab drove off. She'd walked the couple of blocks to the restaurant. She must have meant to walk home. It wasn't late, there were people around.

What had happened next? She must have been abducted on the street. Wouldn't someone have seen? They must have. Someone would have called the police and they'd be looking for her. But what if no-one had? Who would know she was missing?

No-one. Oliver would think she'd changed her mind or be taking longer than she expected. He wouldn't worry about her. He might try to call after a while because Lola was with him and he'd want to know what to do with her. But that might take him a week. Or never. He'd take her to The Grange and leave her with Rod and Amy. The end.

More tears trickled down, dripping onto her throat and running down onto her chest but she couldn't wipe them away. The best she could do was bend her head and lift her shoulder to blot her cheek, but she was so stiff it hurt. She drew her legs up clumsily in an effort to regain some circulation and realised she could bend forward and wipe her face on the skirt of the dress rumpled over her bent knees.

The door scraped open again. The men had balaclavas on, the thick wool incongruous with black T-shirts, and why she'd thought the face had no features. One of them grabbed her legs and dragged her to the opening. He pulled out a knife and before she could react he'd sliced through the tape on her ankles.

'Stand up.'

She slid her bottom forward so her feet touched the ground. Rough concrete, cool underfoot, but the air in the shed was stuffy and hot. It was a garage. Tools hung on the walls in neat rows and a work bench ran along the side nearest. A roller door was closed but sunlight sneaked in through the chinks around the edges. The man steered her stumbling steps to another door at the far end of the space.

The other one flung open the door onto a grimy toilet. The first man cut her hands free and shoved her inside. The room was so small she had to close the door to use the toilet.

'Don't lock it and be quick,' he said.

Trembling, Krista did as she was told. After she finished, she turned the tap on the small washbasin and the trickle of lukewarm water was enough to drink and wash the dried tears and sweat from her face and neck. With the refreshing water came a sliver of hope. If they were letting her use the bathroom, they weren't going to kill her. She clung to that thought.

'Out,' came the voice.

The other man had gone. This one retaped her hands, but instead of pushing her back into the van—white she saw now, common but she didn't remember the make—he took her through another door, into a corridor and along to what appeared to be a small storeroom, windowless. Shelves lined the walls but it was empty save for a single chair.

'Sit down.'

She did. He stared down at her. She stared back. Details, she had to remember details. His eyes were grey with long pale lashes. He was the same man who came in the night and gave her a drink. She'd know that aftershave, his body smell, anywhere. He was about Oliver's height and build. He had no visible tattoos on his bare arms but the other one did. What was it? Where was he?

'If I free your hands will you be a good girl?'

She nodded. He had no particular accent and he spoke and acted as though he was bored with the whole thing. Like a shop assistant who'd rather be somewhere else. Like someone waiting for something, or someone. Waiting for time to pass.

The knife was on his belt and again he whipped it out with practised ease and cut the tape.

'Thanks.'

The door opened and the other man appeared. He had a takeaway cup, a bottle of water and a small, white paper bag. He put them on a shelf by the door, flicked on the light and both men withdrew. The door closed and the lock clicked firmly into place. There was no handle on the inside.

She stood up, flexing her fingers and rotating her protesting wrists and shoulders. They'd brought her food and drink. She drank some of the water and sniffed at the mug. Coffee. Milky and too sweet but welcome. The paper bag had two Danish pastries, which almost made her laugh, they were so unexpected, but didn't. She ate one slowly, not really hungry, but she needed the energy for whatever they had in mind, especially if she was to attempt an escape. How she could manage that she had no idea, but if she didn't have a go, who would?

She had no idea how long she'd been in the storeroom before footsteps sounded outside and the door opened again. Hours. This time they took her to the bathroom and brought more water and a hamburger.

'How long are you keeping me here?'

'Till the boss says enough.'

'Can I talk to him?'

But neither answered and the door banged shut again. The skinny guy had a tattoo of a cross on his forearm. A cross with flames behind it. His eyes were pale blue and flitted about like moths.

More hours dragged by. She turned off the light and waited for her eyes to adjust. Light came through under the door, just enough for her to find it in the dark. She lay on the floor and tried to sleep but it was hard concrete and impossible to be comfortable.

With the light back on, she examined the ceiling and shelves but found no convenient air vents or structural weaknesses. The door was too solid to break down and she had no shoes to protect her feet if she tried kicking it. The chair was plastic. One of those cheap stackable ones. Useless as a weapon. She could only wait and try not to panic.

Yoga filled time. She practised as many positions as she could remember and her body felt better for it. She sat on the chair and did a meditation exercise, not quite as successfully, but she'd never been very good at calming her mind at the best of times.

When would Oliver start to wonder where she was? When would anyone?

When would Moran decide she'd learned her lesson? Was this it or was he softening her up for something else? Was this lack of information part of it?

Much later the men came back, took her to the bathroom and gave her another hamburger and more water.

'What day is it? What time? How long have I been here?'

No answer beyond the slamming of the door.

It must have been night because the next time they came it was the longest stretch without contact. The air in the enclosed space had become thick and heavy and she lay on the floor in the darkness, too exhausted to keep awake. Sleep came in fit and starts until she woke trembling, unsure if she was dreaming as her mind ran through the various scenarios for a final scene, none of them good, none of them with a happy ending. She sat up and rubbed her hands over her face.

Moran could keep her here indefinitely if he wanted. He probably wouldn't but he could. For all Hugh's bluster, he'd been completely ineffectual in stopping the man taking action. All over money. If that's what he wanted she'd give it to him, and if she got the chance she'd grovel and apologise. Anything to be let out of this hideous cell before she lost her mind. Already she could feel her grasp on reality beginning to slip. Time had become meaningless. They could be feeding her at three in the morning and the middle of the afternoon for all she knew.

When the door opened and the same bathroom and food procedure began again, she said, 'Tell your boss I'll pay him the money.'

No reply.

She ate the food, more Danish pastries and coffee. What did Moran actually want from her? Surely he'd want his money? How long did he propose to keep her here?

They must have relayed her offer because when they reappeared countless hours later, they took her to the bathroom then, instead of taking her back to the storeroom, they taped her wrists, led her to the van and pushed her in.

'Where are you taking me? I want to speak to Stefan Moran.'

'Shut up or I'll have to gag you.'

Krista clamped her mouth shut. She sat on the foam with her back against the wall. Luxury softness after the harsh concrete floor. They hadn't taped her ankles this time so moving was easier and she shuffled around so she could see out the front. Both men got into the cab and the engine started. The roller door rattled up and the van backed out into dazzling sunlight.

From what she could see and hear they were in a quiet area with no high-rise buildings. Not in the city. It could be anywhere in the outer Melbourne environs. Each time the van turned a corner she swayed and lost her balance until she worked out how to brace herself with her feet and stay more or less upright. Then they were on a straighter stretch with louder traffic noise and the driver accelerated. A freeway. Which one?

She tried to work out the angle of the sun and from that the direction they were headed, but her view was too limited. It wasn't early though, the sun seemed to be high overhead and it was already baking hot in the back where she sat.

They only stopped once, in a rest area, for the driver to get out. Then they were on the road again. Someone's phone rang but she couldn't hear any conversations in the front seat over the roar of the tyres on tarmac and the engine noise, which reverberated in the empty space.

Then, when she was on the brink of calling out for a drink, parched and wilted in the heat, with drops of sweat running down between her breasts, her bottom, and her back sore from sitting, the van slowed and stopped. The sun shone directly through the windscreen now, low and red, sinking into the horizon. Sunset. Both men donned their balaclavas and got out. The sliding door opened. Fresh air rushed in and she drew deep, grateful lungfuls even though it was still hot.

'Get out.'

She shuffled herself to the open door and swung her legs outside and onto the ground. They were on a dirt road with trees lining the fences and dry brown paddocks stretching away on either side in the gathering dusk. The skinny guy pulled her away from the van while the other one crawled inside. He reappeared with her shoes and dropped them at her feet.

'Put them on.'

She fumbled her feet into the sandals. The red ones Oliver had been so scornful of. They were just as useless here as they had been then but it was better than going barefoot on this stony rough road. Were they letting her go? Here in the middle of nowhere? As she straightened, the skinny guy stepped behind her and held her head between both hands. Aftershave guy stood in front of her. He had his knife in his hand.

'The boss wants to give you something to remember him by,' he said in that same casual tone which was terrifying now. 'So you don't make the same mistake again.'

His fingers stroked her cheek softly as he raised the knife with his other hand.

'Such a shame,' he murmured but the cold hard look in his eyes belied the words.

The breath stalled in her throat and she struggled helplessly against the hands gripping her head. A whimper escaped from her lips but he ignored it, and the screams that followed.

Chapter 16

Oliver was picking lettuce leaves in his garden to have with dinner when he heard what sounded like screaming. Faint but clear enough in the still evening. Sounded like a woman, but stopped abruptly.

'Did you hear that?' he asked Lola, who was busily snuffling about in the garden. She looked up and wagged her tail.

A car engine broke the silence, revving and accelerating until the sound died away. Another cry came but it was more a wail than a scream. It came from the road on the far side of the horse paddock. No-one lived along there. Oliver hurried into the laundry and snatched up the torch.

'Come on,' he said. Lola bounded after him as he strode up to the gate. A purple and orange tinge in the sky above the hills to the west marked the last of the sun but the darkness was intense here, away from street and house lights. Out on the road he paused, listening. Lola sniffed the air and ran purposefully off to the left. He followed, shining the torch ahead of them both. The road rose slowly, and then when it crested the hill swung left on the run down towards town. Trees lined the roadside, casting deeper shadows now the westerly glow had faded. Lola yipped and increased her speed.

'Anyone there?' he called. 'Hello.'

'Oliver?' Her voice. Desperate, exhausted, filled with pain and fear.

'Krista?' He swung the torch wildly, adrenaline surging. 'Where are you?'

'Oliver.' A figure stumbled out of the darkness of the trees. Pale hair shone in the torchlight. She tripped and almost fell but he lurched forward and caught her in his arms while Lola whimpered at their feet.

Krista clung to him as though she'd never let him go but he loosened his grip to hold her away slightly. Blood stained her face and neck. Fresh, sticky blood coming from a gaping wound in her left cheek.

'My God. What happened?'

'He cut me...' She sagged against him and he staggered under the sudden weight as her legs gave way. He lowered her to the ground and yanked out his phone.

'Hello. Doctor's surgery.'

'Doc? Emergency. It's Krista. We're on the road about two-hundred metres past my place on the way into town, your side.'

'What's happened?'

'She's bleeding badly from a facial wound, knife cut, I think. Can you come? I can't leave her to get the car.'

'Be right there. Does she need an ambulance?'

'I'm not sure.'

He pulled off his shirt and held a pad of the fabric to her cheek, gently trying to stem the flow of blood then, keeping it in place, he sat beside her and held her close. 'Doc's on his way,' he said.

What the hell had happened? Moran was a monster that he would do this to her. But she was alive and she was here safe in his arms. They must have dumped her. He'd heard the car.

'What sort of vehicle was it? Krista? Was it a car?'

'White van,' she murmured. 'Two men.'

He rang Rupe.

'I'll get onto it,' Rupe said. 'I'll need to talk to her. Where will you be?'

'At Doc's but she may need the hospital.'

'I'll meet you there.'

***

Krista was dimly aware of Oliver and Doc lifting her into a car. Lola was there too, climbing onto her lap as she sat in the back seat until Oliver told her to stop it. She nestled into his arms, eyes closed against the pain, giving up the fight, brain in limbo now that she was safe, letting herself slide away on the sedative Doc had given her.

The handsome policeman was there next, leaning over her asking questions she couldn't answer even though she wanted to and tried to make sense for him. He smiled and said he'd see her later. He and Oliver murmured together while Doc touched her face with light fingers and gave her another injection in the arm. Tetanus, she heard through the fog.

When she woke, she was in bed in a hospital. It was dark outside but the door to the corridor was open and soft yellow light shone in reassuringly. She was attached to a drip and when she touched her cheek she felt the thick padding of a bandage. The side of her face was numb. Her eyes closed.

A nurse woke her by attaching a blood pressure cuff. Daytime. Voices and the sounds of people at work came in through the door.

'Good morning,' she said. 'How are you feeling?' She had a lovely lilting Irish accent and a cheery face under a pile of ginger curls.

'Better.'

'Any pain?'

Krista ran her mind over her body. 'I'm not sure.'

'Can't be too bad then.'

'My face ... what happened?'

'You had a nasty cut. Do you remember? Doctor put in stitches last night when you came in.' She undid the cuff and straightened Krista's sheets.

'How bad is it?' Her stomach sagged. Stitches. Scarring?

'Doctor will be around to see you shortly and you can ask him yourself.'

'When can I go home?'

'Later today, I think, but doctor will have the final say. You have a friend here. He's been waiting to see you.'

'Oliver?'

'I'll send him in. There's a policeman too.'

'Can I see Oliver first?'

Oliver was in the corridor outside Krista's room talking to Rupe, who'd just arrived, when the nurse came out. She smiled at them both.

'Krista's awake now and she'd like to see Oliver first, if that's all right?' She directed the last part at Rupe.

'Two minutes,' he said.

Oliver went in, heart thudding. What had happened to her these last few days? How would she cope with it? How could he help and would she want his help? He and Doc had brought her here to Wagga Hospital and when, after she'd been treated, he wanted to stay all night Doc had insisted he go home, change, eat, and return in the morning.

Which he had done, arriving at six to find her asleep.

Rupe had turned up fifteen minutes later and just after he arrived she was awake.

When she saw Oliver enter the room her eyes filled with tears, the last thing he expected.

'Hey.' He hurried to the bed and leaned down to kiss her gently on the undamaged cheek. 'Don't cry. What sort of welcome is that?'

'I'm so pleased to see you,' she said and sniffed. 'I wasn't sure if you'd stay.'

He drew a chair closer and sat down, keeping tight hold of her hand.

'Of course I'm here. How are you feeling?'

'Good, now.' She attempted a smile but it was lopsided due to the anaesthetic and the bandage covering the left side of her face. 'How did you find me last night? Where was I?'

'I heard you scream and I heard the van drive away. Lola and I went to investigate. They left you just up near the horse paddock.'

'Close to your house?'

He nodded, lips firm. 'You should be let out of here soon.'

Her eyes filled again. 'Where can I go?'

'The Grange? Amy will take care of you.'

'Yes, I suppose that's best.'

It was on the tip of his tongue to offer his place but The Grange was her previous choice and it was better. Probably.

Rupe tapped on the door and walked straight in without waiting for an invitation.

'Hello, Krista. How are you feeling?'

'Better, thank you.'

'I need to ask you some questions.'

'Okay. I'm sorry I wasn't much help last night.'

'That's all right. We picked up the van at around midnight. It had been dumped and partially burned. Stolen, of course, but forensics may get something useful.'

'That's good, isn't it?'

'Yes, possibly. Can you tell me exactly what happened leading up to and including the abduction?'

'I can't remember much. I tried all the time I was locked up but only bits were there. I went to dinner at a restaurant in the city—a couple of blocks from my apartment so I walked. I was with my friends and then, at about eleven, I walked with Malcolm to a taxi rank and he went home. I remember watching the cab leave, then I started walking. I don't remember after that until I came to in the back of the van, my hands and feet were taped and I had a gag.'

'They must have drugged you but it's probably too late to find anything in the blood sample the hospital took last night. Your dinner was on Saturday night according to what your stepfather told Oliver. Did you see the people who did it? Two, you told us.'

'Yes.' She closed her eyes as she described them. 'They wore balaclavas and black T-shirts, blue jeans. One of them was skinny with pale blue eyes and a tattoo of a cross and flames on his forearm. The other one was about Oliver's build, grey eyes, and he wore strong aftershave. Cheap and nasty. He smelled bad. Australian, no accent. He didn't say much and the other one never spoke.' Her eyes opened.

'That's terrific,' said Rupe. 'Well done.'

'I tried really hard to remember details,' she said. 'I had nothing else to do.'

'Can you describe where you were held? Any sounds from outside for example, smells in the air? Anything else that might help us?'

'They brought takeaway coffee, hamburgers and Danish pastries. I thought the pastries were an odd thing. They were good, fresh from a bakery, I think.' She closed her eyes again as she spoke, describing the shed, concentrating, never letting go of Oliver's hand as if he were an anchor holding her in place.

When she finished, Rupe said, 'Do have any idea who kidnapped you? Or why?'

Her expression hardened. 'Moran's men, I'm sure. Not the ones from before. They said they were teaching me a lesson but they kept me locked up in a storeroom and didn't do anything and hardly spoke. Why did they do that?'

'Did they hurt you?'

'Not then. They brought the food and water and took me to the bathroom. But it was horrible. I think I would have gone mad if I'd been there much longer. I had to lie on the concrete floor.'

'I think Moran is showing you, and us, that he's in control and can do what he likes when he likes,' said Oliver.

She swallowed hard. 'Because I was rude to him on the phone,' she said hoarsely.

'I think so,' he said gently.

'I offered to pay the money,' she said. 'But that didn't make any difference, did it?'

'Angus paid him back,' said Oliver.

'Angus?'

'Yes. He was the one who discovered you were missing. He went to your apartment early on Tuesday and rang me because he thought you might be here. But your car was half packed and your handbag and bathroom things were still there. Did you know they sent me a text from your phone saying you were going away for a few weeks?'

'No. Where is my phone? And I had a small purse with me with my keys in it.'

'We haven't found either,' said Rupe. He turned to Oliver. 'Is Angus still at her apartment?'

'I think so. Are you thinking he should change the locks?'

Rupe nodded. 'No telling who has those keys. Get him to organise it.'

'He won't care,' said Krista. 'He only cares about himself. And he was supposed to have posted my keys back to me. The liar. This is all his fault. All of it.'

'He came through though. Maybe he's not so bad. He was upset when I rang him last night and told him what had happened to you.'

She didn't reply.

'It'll be difficult to pin this on Stefan Moran,' said Rupe. 'He'll have made sure there's no link to him.'

'What about this?' Krista touched her bandaged cheek. 'He said "the boss wants to give you something to remember him by". Then he ... he...'

An image of the blade glinting in the light from the setting sun. She couldn't look away. Hypnotised.

Oliver squeezed her hand.

'We'll do our best to nail him. See you later, Ollie,' said Rupe. 'Thank you, Krista.' He headed for the door.

'Thank you. Rupe?'

He turned. 'Will you please tell your wife ... Abbie... that I really mean to help with the show and I'm sorry I haven't yet.'

'I will, but don't worry about it. Things got messed around with the fires anyway.'

When he'd gone, Krista said, 'Oliver, how bad is this?' Her fingers hovered over the bandage, shaking, her eyes wide.

He rubbed his lips together. 'There was a lot of blood when I found you and it was dark. It was hard to tell. Faces bleed a lot.'

'But what did the doctor say?'

'He had to put in stiches but apart from that ... I don't know.'

'Will I be scarred?' Her eyes bored into him, relentlessly seeking answers. Seeking the truth.

'I don't know. He said he'd do his best to prevent it.' His actual word had been 'minimise'.

'Oliver, I can't have a scar. When's the doctor coming? What sort of hospital is this? I should go to Melbourne and find a specialist. A plastic surgeon.'

'The doctors here are very good. If there is a scar it won't be very noticeable,' said Oliver.

'But it'll be ugly. I'll be ugly,' she wailed.

He smiled, shaking his head. 'You'll never be ugly.' He wanted to add 'not to me' but knew that wasn't enough, not for her and definitely not at this moment.

'I'll be scarred.' She turned her face away, as he'd suspected, unconvinced.

The nurse came in and frowned at Oliver before fussing over Krista. 'The doctor will be in to see you soon. Are you hungry?'

'Thirsty, but my face is sore.'

'You're not due for your next dose of painkillers yet. Is the pain bad?'

'Not unbearable.'

'Let me know if it gets too much.' The nurse held a mug with a straw for her to take slow sips, wincing.

'Thank you.'

The nurse went out.

'Does Mama know?' asked Krista.

'Hugh does, he said he'd contact her.'

'What did he say about it?'

'He's furious.'

'He said he'd take care of Moran,' she said.

'That's what I said to him. Neither of them care about anything other than their own gigantic egos.'

The doctor came in a few minutes later, grey-haired and stern-faced. He studied Krista's details and turned to Oliver. 'Are you a relative?'

'No. Should I leave?'

'I want him to stay,' said Krista.

'I'm Glen McInnis, head of surgery. I treated you last night. You were lucky I was still here. These wounds are best treated as soon as possible. Half an hour later and I would have been at a dinner.' He smiled benignly. 'Lucky for me as well as you, Krista. I wasn't looking forward to it.'

Not waiting for a reply, he deftly uncovered Krista's wound and, adjusting his glasses, peered at his work. To Oliver's eye it looked as good as could be expected. A seven- or eight-centimetre line running from below her left eye and curving to finish under the corner of her mouth.

'Hmmm,' McInnis said. 'We're also lucky the knife was sharp.'

'Are we?' Krista asked weakly but Oliver knew what he meant.

'Nice clean cut,' said McInnis. 'Much messier if it's a jagged wound.'

'Will I have a scar?'

'I'm afraid so, but it will be a very thin line and will fade as time goes by. You'll be able to conceal it with make-up. He made quite a long, controlled incision, as if he wanted it to mark your face rather than cut you through anger.'

'He did.'

'Oh, I'm sorry. I wasn't given all the details. Domestic?'

'No. There were two men involved. It was an abduction and they were making a statement,' said Oliver.

'I see. Well, Krista, you'll need to rest for the next few days and take painkillers as you need. Your GP can monitor the healing so see him in a day or two, but if you are at all concerned, by all means make an appointment to see me. We've got you on antibiotics so make sure you finish the course when you go home.'

'Thank you,' she said.

'When is she able to go home?' asked Oliver.

'Given the circumstances you've just outlined I think it will do you good, Krista, to stay with us for another night in order to rest properly and to make sure there's no developing infection. There shouldn't be. I'll ask the social worker to have a chat with you this morning.'

'Why?'

'You've had a traumatic experience. It helps to talk about it. You may not want to just yet but these things can linger on and cause trouble. She can give you some information to follow up.'

He bestowed another of his benign smiles on her and left.

'I want to leave now,' she said with a grim edge to her voice.

Oliver said calmly, 'He's right. You need to stay where you are and give your body a chance to recover.'

'Can't I do that at The Grange?'

'You'll be well looked after here and Amy won't need to be worried about you.'

That comment must have hit home because she nodded.

'Would you do me a favour, please?'

'Of course.'

'Buy me another phone?'

He smiled. 'As long as you promise not to lose it. You've already gone through two in a week.'

That produced the lopsided little smile again but it didn't last long.

***

The nurse removed the bandage that evening.

'No need for this,' she said. 'As doctor said, the stitches will come out next week. You need to keep your head up so as not to put strain on them.'

In the bathroom mirror, Krista had her first look at the wound and had to clutch the basin for support as her body gave way. A horrifying, red, swollen lumpy suture line, held together with roughly tied black stitches, split her left cheek in two. How could they say it was looking good? It was nightmarish. She looked like Frankenstein's monster. How could she possibly let anyone see her?

With her new phone, Krista had called Amy and asked if she could possibly come to collect her the next day. That was before she'd seen her disfigurement. She wasn't going to be a burden, she didn't need looking after but she did need assistance to get home. A taxi would involve waiting and talking to the driver and it was a long way to The Grange. She couldn't possibly let Oliver see her like this.

'What time shall I come?' Amy asked immediately.

'They said about twelve.'

'Do you need anything?'

'Could you bring me some dark glasses, please? I have clothes. Oliver brought my suitcase in, the one I left at his place.'

He'd brought in the new phone, along with a new toothbrush and toothpaste, and offered to return for the pick-up but she declined even before the bandage came off. If he was offended he didn't say, but after he left she heard him talking to the nurse outside in the corridor. They moved away so she couldn't hear what was said but whatever it was it would be a well-meaning discussion about how to deal with the traumatised invalid during her recovery.

The full implications of her wound became clearer and clearer in her mind. She was no longer a beautiful woman who turned heads wherever she went. People would look but their gaze would flick away quickly. The bruises she'd sustained after the other attack were just a warm-up for this. This was a life-long blemish.

Oliver's kindness and sympathetic expression would become suffocating. He wouldn't understand that she didn't want him to see her ugliness, the raw red wound on her face marked with a row of stitches like black markers. He'd say it didn't matter but it would matter.

Her beauty had attracted him from the start, the way it did every man she met, but now she had nothing. She couldn't even bear to look at herself in the mirror.

Dr McInnis and the nurses were delighted by their work. He'd proclaimed himself well satisfied with the way it was shaping up and went away smiling. The social worker had come along and chatted and given her some pamphlets with phone numbers to call if she needed support later. She didn't. She wanted them all to go away.

It was a good thing she'd said goodbye to Melbourne, she wouldn't ever go back. She'd hide in her room at The Grange with her ruined face.

In the middle of the second night she woke with a start, sweating and trembling, shocked awake by a dark shadowy figure with a long shiny blade, bigger than the real knife, more like a butcher's chopping blade. The dim light from the corridor cast a reassuring glow but she was afraid to close her eyes, and kept them fixed on the light until sleep came again.

Amy arrived with the dark glasses and a smile, but she wasn't overcome with awkward sympathy. She looked but she didn't stare. She asked how she was feeling, gave Krista a brisk hug, picked up her bag and took her to the car.

'How's Rod?' Krista asked when they were on the road out of town and her tense muscles finally began to relax. Amy wasn't pretending, she was practical and she was honest and her opinion of Krista had been pretty low to start with.

'Hah. Clumping about like Peg Leg Pete but he's managing. We're pretty busy.'

'Oh, sorry. You should have said so.'

'Don't worry. It's fine.' Amy flung her a warm smile. 'We're really pleased you decided to stay.'

'I'm never going back to Melbourne. Not like this.' Krista stared out the window blindly. Her friends would be horrified. And Mama ... how could she face Mama?

'It'll heal,' said Amy. 'Like Rod's leg. It needs time. You need time.'

'Amy, I'll have a scar for the rest of my life,' she said harshly. Why didn't they understand? Any of them. This was her face. Her best asset. What did she have if she didn't have beauty?

Amy didn't reply. Krista closed her eyes against the tears which seemed to be coming more frequently lately.

'We met Les and Sally the other day,' said Amy. 'They called in to say hello and see how we, and you, were getting on.'

Krista opened her eyes. 'I never met Sally.' The bridge near their gate was fast approaching. 'Les helped me with the horses.'

'He was pretty impressed with you. They want you to visit.'

'I can't do that,' she said flatly. How could she go out looking like a freak? It was bad enough the people she knew saw her in this state.

The Grange had survived the fires by pure luck. Blackened grass was visible along the roadside past the gate when Amy slowed for the turn. The upper branches of the trees lining the fence on the far left of the front paddock looked as though a giant blowtorch had been along the row, singeing the tops.

'I didn't realise it came so close,' Krista said. The memory of her last terrifying drive on this stretch of road flooded back, momentarily blotting out the misery of the present.

'Spot fires. Luckily they didn't get going before the firies got to them. The trees where you found Roddy are burned but it didn't make it up to the house and yards. It's weird the way that happens. Must have been the wind or something.'

'Whatever it was, we were incredibly lucky. I was so worried you'd lose your home.' It seemed an age ago. Another life. But she had been worried for Rod and Amy, felt the heavy responsibility when she'd rushed in to retrieve photos and the files. The representation of their life together.

'You were fantastic, Krista. We're so grateful to you.' Amy stretched out a hand and grasped Krista's briefly.

Rod, with Lola sitting by his feet, was waiting by the front door of the main house and so, amazingly, was Angus.

'Surprise,' said Amy and got out before Krista could say a word.

He came forward, opened the door for her and helped her out. Then, to complete her astonishment he pulled her into a hug.

'I'm so sorry, sis,' he said.

Speechless she let him hold her. He'd never hugged her before. Lola was bouncing at her feet, yipping with excitement, so she eased herself from the embrace and bent to greet her. 'Hello little one,' she murmured and straightened because she'd forgotten the instructions and bending made her cheek throb. She wasn't supposed to lower her head.

Angus led her inside. Rod and Amy followed with her bag.

'We put your things in your room,' said Angus.

'What things?'

'I drove your car back from Melbourne,' he said. 'And I brought your handbag and make-up and anything else I thought you meant to bring with you.'

'Angus ... thank you.' Who was this person? It certainly wasn't the stepbrother she knew. That one wouldn't have hugged her, or thought about anything she might have been planning. Or thought about her at all.

'I'll put the kettle on while you settle in,' said Rod. 'C'mon, mate. Amy can help her.'

Upstairs in her room, Krista sat on the bed. Her cheek throbbed with a regular monotonous pulse of pain and the effort of climbing the stairs drained her energy.

'When did he turn up?'

'Last night. Surprised us too.' Amy smiled. 'Look, he's left your keys on the dressing table.'

'Amazing.' Her big red handbag was on the chair by the window.

'Yes. Maybe all this has jolted him a bit.'

'I doubt it'll last very long.' Krista heaved a deep sigh.

'Shall I help you unpack?'

'Just the small bag for now, thanks. I can do the others later. How long is he staying?'

'I don't know.'

Krista stood up and went into the bathroom for a glass of water to down a couple of painkillers. The two bathroom bags containing all her toiletries and make-up were on the vanity. How bizarre that Angus would be thoughtful. He must have an ulterior motive, or Amy was right and he felt guilty. Briefly.

When Krista and Amy joined them in the kitchen, Rod and Angus were sitting at the table deep in conversation.

'Where were you?' demanded Krista.

Angus turned to face her, smiling. 'In Macau.

'Of course,' she said in disgust. 'Gambler's paradise.'

'I won the money to pay off the debt. You should be pleased.'

How dare he be indignant? Did he ever listen to what came out of his mouth?

'You lost the money gambling in the first place. Don't you get it?'

'But it's fixed now.' He sounded like a bewildered child. He *was* a child.

'Fixed?' she yelled. 'Does this look fixed? I'm scarred, Angus. For life. I have nightmares. And it's your fault. Don't tell me it's fixed. It'll never be fixed.'

'I'm sorry,' he said helplessly. 'I tried to make it right. They let you go.'

'They'd have let me go anyway. This wasn't about your money, I offered to pay them when they had me locked up, and they ignored me. This was about me being taught not to defy your mate Moran. I pissed him off last week when I told him I wasn't paying your debt. It's about control. His control.'

'I didn't think he'd go that far.'

'Neither did I but he did. You knew what he was like, I didn't, not fully. For God's sake, Angus, grow up!'

Krista slumped onto a chair, breathing hard. Lola pattered across and leaned against her leg. Amy opened the fridge and began transferring containers of cheese, ham, salad and butter to the table for lunch. Rod got up and started making tea. Angus sat glowering in the growing silence.

A flicker of remorse sparked in Krista. She straightened slightly and said softly, 'I know you tried, Angus. Thanks for bringing my car and my bags.'

'I had the locks changed at the apartment,' he said. 'But I don't think anyone had been in except me.'

'Thanks.' She tried a tiny smile and he returned it eagerly.

'Would you mind if I stayed there, at your apartment?'

'Aren't you living here?'

'Dad's putting it on the market soon.'

She'd forgotten. If it sold she'd have to go somewhere else to hide. Where? To the Sydney house with Hugh? He wouldn't understand her desire for privacy and quiet. He'd expect her to snap out of it and take Mama's place at social functions. The idea filled her with dread. She wanted to stay here at The Grange. At Taylor's Bend.

What about Rod and Amy? Weren't they interested? Hadn't they said as much that last night at Oliver's place?

Krista looked at Rod. 'Have you told Hugh what you were talking about at Oliver's?'

He shook his head. 'Haven't had time to think it through.'

'What?' asked Angus.

'They want to buy The Grange,' said Krista.

'Great idea.' Typical Angus. The enthusiasm comes first and the calculations and planning later, if ever.

'It depends on how much Hugh wants,' said Amy.

'I reckon land prices will drop because of the fire and the drought in general,' Rod said hopefully.

'You should make him an offer,' said Angus. 'I think he'd be happy to get rid of the place easily. Once he makes up his mind about something, he likes to get it done.'

'That's what I said.' Krista nodded. 'Ring him and see what he says.'

'He likes you,' added Angus. 'As opposed to me.'

Rod and Amy shared a long look, one of those mysterious communications that happily married couples use to convey all sorts of things that are secret from onlookers.

'Now?' Rod asked.

'Might as well.' Amy smiled. 'See if we have any chance at all.'

'Use the phone in the study,' said Angus.

Rod drew a deep breath and headed out the door. Amy continued setting the table for lunch. Krista got up to help but Amy said, 'No.'

'I don't want you to feel you have to look after me,' Krista said.

'I don't, that's why we're having salad and sandwiches for lunch, but you've just come out of hospital so it's the least I can do.' She smiled. 'Special consideration for today.'

'Thank you.'

Rod came back in with a gloomy expression. 'He was about to go into a meeting so he couldn't talk for long but I got a figure out of him. Two million.'

'That settles that then.' Amy turned her back and finished making the tea Rod had begun, the disappointment evident in the droop of her shoulders.

'Is that a fair price?' Krista asked. It sounded like a lot to her. The land wouldn't be worth much but the house was big, new and luxuriously fitted out.

'I don't think so,' said Amy. 'It's worth what someone will pay and at the moment I doubt anyone would pay that.'

'It includes three horses,' said Rod. 'Not counting Calypso and Arch Rival. They belong to you two.'

'Could you afford it without the horses?' Angus asked.

'We'd have to buy more if we did that and Fred's in demand. He's a good asset. So are two of the mares, but one, The Ghost, is getting old.'

'How much are you short?'

'Angus, that's none of your business,' said Krista.

'We can come up with half that. But it's not worth two million. More like one seven, if that.' Amy put the teapot on the table with a thud and a face as miserable as Rod's. 'And please don't suggest you can raise the rest by gambling what we have.'

'I wasn't going to. But I did win enough to pay off my debt. Just saying,' he added when Krista groaned and glared at him.

***

Oliver's finger hung poised over his phone countless times when Krista went home from hospital, but each time he resisted and jammed the mobile back in his pocket. He had to stay away until she was ready, until she called him. Doc recommended he give her space to come to terms with what had happened.

'Don't crowd her,' he said in the pub when Oliver ran into him there on Saturday evening. 'She has to reassess her place in the world.'

'She thinks she's ugly,' Oliver said. 'She's not.'

'Of course she's not, but to her she is. She was a beautiful woman with flawless skin and in her world that kind of perfection was critical. Her life, as she sees it, is ruined.'

'There's so much more to her than that. I don't care that she has a scar.'

Doc's smile was sympathetic. 'I know, Ollie.'

'What can I do? Or any of us?'

'Nothing much as yet. Call her, ask how she's getting on. I'll see her next week for the stitches to come out.'

'Do you think the scar will be very bad? I wouldn't have thought so by what I saw but I'm used to animals with tougher hides. Her skin is so delicate.' And soft. Flawless, as Doc said.

'McInnis is very good so it'll be minimal. It's how she copes with it that matters most.'

'She told me once that her mother raised her to think her beauty is her only asset. And she believes it.'

'She has to be brought to see that's not so, but slowly, Ollie. Don't push.'

'When we made it away from the bushfire we were both dirty, smelling of smoke and bruised—you saw us—and she didn't care then. I thought she was changing, realising how superficial her perception of beauty is.'

'It was a different situation. You'd done it together and you'd survived. She was proud to have done something important, to have helped, and deep down she knew that dirt washes off and bruises fade. This won't, and this was an act done with the deliberate intention of frightening and humiliating her. Making her feel powerless, insignificant, worth nothing.'

'Her self-esteem was never strong,' said Oliver. 'Her mother saw to that, unintentionally I suppose, but still effectively.' That aloof disdain that so annoyed him when they first met was a front, a barrier to protect herself from being exposed as the deeply insecure woman she really was.

On Sunday, Oliver was feeding Billy when an unfamiliar white sedan pulled up and Angus called from the gate. He walked up to let him in. Angus had collected Lola and Krista's suitcase a few days ago, surprising Oliver with his concern for her. Given the trouble he'd caused, Oliver had been sorely tempted to give him an earful but figured Krista would do that.

'G'day.' He unlocked the padlock and let the gate swing wide. The car must be a rental because he'd driven Krista's back for her from Melbourne.

'Hi Oliver. I'm not stopping. I've come to say goodbye. I'm on my way back to Melbourne.'

'How's Krista?'

'Not bad physically, but she's pretty down. She has nightmares and doesn't want to go out, doesn't want to be seen.'

'The scar?'

Angus nodded. 'She thinks it's ruined her life. Don't know why. It's pretty ugly right now, but it won't be when they take the stitches out and the redness goes. She can't see that. She's always been obsessed with how she looks. Gets that from her mother.'

'She had a rough few days, Angus. Apart from the knife wound, she was held captive, remember? She was terrified. No wonder she has bad dreams.'

'Yeah, I know but she's safe now.'

'And we were both attacked a few days before that in the middle of a bushfire.' Was Angus as dense as he appeared? No wonder Krista always had a low opinion of him. And his father.

'Yeah, yeah. It must have been awful.'

'It was. I've still got bruises.' Mostly on his torso from being kicked. He'd managed a few minutes on the cello yesterday before his wrist ached too much, and that had been encouraging. He planned more practice today and possibly the rehearsal on Wednesday night.

'Anyway, Krista's letting me stay at her place.'

'So she's not going back to Melbourne?'

'No way. She's hiding out at The Grange so no-one sees her. Like in *Beauty and the Beast*, except she's not a beast. She just thinks she is.'

Oliver sighed and kept his mouth firmly shut. Who did that make Beauty? Fairy stories were about Angus's level.

'Has her mother been in touch? Or Hugh?'

'Don't think so. Dad said he'd tell Viivi but I don't know where she is. She might have called Krista. I spoke to Dad a few days ago. Rod and Amy want to buy The Grange but they can't afford it. Dad's hard-nosed when it comes to business.'

Oliver nodded. Hugh hadn't arrived where he was by being a soft touch and he'd proven that by his attitude to Angus and the Moran problem.

Krista would leave when The Grange was sold. Would she have recovered enough to survive without help? Maybe she'd see a counsellor when the stitches came out and the wound had healed. From what Angus was saying, she desperately needed support but would she accept it from anyone? From him?

Angus said, 'You should give her a call and tell her to stop being an idiot. She's the only sister I've got, you know, and I do care about her, despite what she thinks.' He held out his hand. 'Sorry for all this, Oliver,' he said breezily.

Oliver shook the proffered hand. 'Sure. Drive safely.' What else could he say? In Angus world the sun was shining again and the future gleamed bright and shiny.

Angus laughed. 'Don't worry. I've learned my lesson.'

He beeped the horn and waved as he drove away. That bloke was incapable of learning anything, but one positive had emerged from the mess. Angus and Krista had somehow come a little closer and the man was right about one other thing. Neither of them had other siblings and maintaining that newly appreciated bond was important.

Oliver went back to his chores, and after he'd finished and cleaned up he rang Krista but she didn't answer so he left a stumbling, awkward message. Then he phoned his own brother.

Chapter 17

Krista drove herself to see Doc to have her stitches removed. It was her first foray into public view since leaving hospital. Not that she was planning to walk down the main street and show herself off. Far from it. She'd asked for her appointment to be the first of the day. No-one in the waiting room and only that receptionist to deal with. She'd park right outside and go straight in and out. She'd manage.

Even so, her heart thudded wildly and sweat that wasn't from the day's heat trickled down her back as she pulled up in the gutter outside the surgery. Clouds had built up this morning, the first likely looking rain-bearers for weeks according to Rod. He and Amy hoped fervently for rain today but she found it hard to summon up more than a semblance of interest. A brisk wind tugged at her clothes and hair when she opened the car door and walked up the path.

The blonde smiled. 'Good morning. Please take a seat. Doc will be with you in a few minutes.' This time there was no acid in the woman's tone and her smile was pure friendliness.

Krista did as she was told, sitting with her face averted, back to the door.

'I'm really sorry,' the receptionist said.

Krista turned her head, gritting her teeth against a flood of sympathetic words that would mean nothing. The woman was coming towards her with a clipboard in her hand. 'I do need you to fill out the form this time.' No antagonism, no sense of a victory.

She nodded and took the clipboard with the form and pen attached to it. Doc appeared before she'd finished and exchanged a few words with the receptionist about organising another patient's tests.

'Thanks, Penny,' he said. 'See if you can get them to speed up the results.'

Penny, that was her name. Krista had forgotten, hopeless with names. She handed the clipboard back.

'Come in, Krista.' Doc smiled, ushered her into his office and closed the door. 'Nice to see you. How are you?'

'All right.' How could she possibly answer such a question? She was upright, she was breathing.

'Any pain?'

'Not as much now. It's sore to touch.'

'Yes, that's to be expected. You've been following the hospital aftercare instructions, I take it? Let's have a look.'

Brow wrinkled, Doc peered at her, touching her cheek with gentle fingers. 'Hmm,' he said. 'These can come out.' He reached for scissors.

Krista closed her eyes while he snipped. It didn't matter how carefully he did it or how brilliantly Dr McInnis had done his job, the fact remained that the ugly, red, lumpy wound disfigured her.

'You'll need to massage Vaseline or vitamin E oil into it three or four times a day. That will help minimise the scar and speed up the healing.'

He proceeded to demonstrate the technique, explaining as he applied Vaseline. 'Don't overdo it. Firm but gentle.'

Finished, he sat back, wiping his hands on a paper towel. 'It'll take a few months, Krista, but I promise you the end result will be a very fine line. Nothing like it is now. You'll be able to conceal it very well with make-up if you think it's necessary.'

'If I think it's necessary?' she burst out. 'Of course it's necessary. How can I show my face like this?'

'You can when you're ready. You have nothing to be ashamed of. I think you'll find the locals will be very sympathetic.'

'I'm sure,' she muttered. Pitying glances, faces dripping sympathy disguising relief that it wasn't them. The attitude locals had towards The Grange wasn't going to change because she was injured. Penny's may have, but some people would think it served the rich city blow-ins right.

'Krista, life is tougher out here. People judge others by their actions, not what they look like.' He chuckled. 'If looks were the only yardstick none of us would measure up. You've proven yourself already during the fires. You earned yourself a lot of respect that day. And that attack out at The Grange on you and Oliver made people really angry. Let alone this recent trauma.'

So apparently she was the current subject of discussion and interest here in Taylor's Bend. If she ventured out again she'd create a spectacle, stop traffic, enthral children as though the circus had come to town. The thought made her heart thud and her skin clammy.

'I don't belong here, Doc.' Her voice wavered. She swallowed and clenched her fingers tight against the tears. Her nails dug into her palms.

'Don't you?' His eyes were too kind, she couldn't look.

'This isn't my real life.' She had no real life, here or anywhere else.

'Ollie said you were planning to stay at The Grange.'

'If it sells I can't.'

'Until it does you can think about what you really want. Unless you have other commitments you have to deal with elsewhere.'

She shook her head.

'In some ways that could be a good thing. It gives you scope for a clean start. To reinvent yourself in a place where there are no preconceived notions about you.'

Something in his tone penetrated the fog of despair. Doc was a private man, Oliver said. Was he telling her something about himself? Had he come here for a clean start? Oliver had. He'd told her this was a chance to establish himself away from his father's critical gaze, to prove himself. But these two men had careers and goals. They were educated, cultured and intelligent and they knew what they wanted to do with their lives.

'Before ... this ... I thought I could do that. I was planning to change my life. To try, at least.'

'None of that has changed, Krista,' he said gently. 'This is a setback, not the end.'

'Thank you. I should go.' She stood up quickly.

'Krista, are you sleeping?'

His voice stopped her escape. She swallowed.

'I had bad dreams for the first few nights. Nightmares.'

'That's natural. Are you able to sleep at all? I can prescribe something if you want.'

She shook her head. 'No, I'd rather not. The last two nights haven't been so bad.' She'd allowed Lola to sleep on her bed and cuddled the warm soft body when she woke in blind fear. She looked into Doc's kind eyes. 'I let my dog sleep on the bed. I never thought I would do that.'

'That's good.' Doc stood as well. 'There's a counsellor in Willoughby you should visit if the nightmares don't fade within a few weeks. If that happens, he can help you and I strongly recommend you see him.' He wrote down a name and phone number and gave her the slip of paper. 'You could see him anyway.'

'I don't think so.'

'Give him, and yourself, a chance. Doctor's orders.' His gaze was as firm as his voice. She took the slip and put it in her bag.

'Goodbye.'

'Come and see me in a couple of weeks.' She nodded and he held the door open for her. 'Take care of yourself,' he said.

Penny printed out the account. 'Do you need another appointment?'

'Not at the moment.'

Krista tapped her credit card and waited for the receipt. The door opened and a burly man with a blue shirt straining over a beer belly walked in, limping badly.

'Morning, Bob,' said Penny. 'How are you?'

'Bloody awful,' he grunted and lowered himself onto a chair.

Penny handed Krista the paperwork. 'There you go.'

'Thanks.'

'By the way,' Penny said. 'While you're in town you might like to pop in and see Abbie. She's working on the sets at the Arts Centre this morning. She mentioned you'd offered to help and she certainly could do with it.'

'Yes, I did but...'

'You wouldn't need to stay this morning if you've other things on but she's keen to meet you.' Her eyes remained fixed on Krista's, insisting on a reply, waiting for a yes.

'Maybe.' Krista edged towards the door and made her escape.

Outside, she heaved a sigh of relief. See Abbie while she was in town? What did Penny think? That was she was in Taylor's Bend doing her shopping and making social calls after having the stitches removed? A car drove by and she averted her damaged cheek before getting into her own car. She started the engine. If she drove straight on she'd end up passing Oliver's place. She did a U-turn to go back the way she'd come. The Arts Centre was on the other side of the main street. She gave it a glance as she passed but didn't slow down.

Back at The Grange, Lola bounded to greet her and scampered in front of her on the walk to the house from the garage. The wind had dropped but the cloudbank was bigger now, covering half the sky with massed castles of white and grey; the temperature was heading up as usual. Most likely a thunderstorm was brewing. Rain would be a novelty out here.

Inside, she made herself coffee and took it to the terrace to drink. Lola lay on the warm tiles at her feet. 'We'll unpack another bag today.'

Lola's tail thumped a few times.

'You don't care what I look like, do you?' Krista said.

Her phone rang. She frowned. The number was unfamiliar.

'Hello.'

'Is that Krista? Hi, it's Abbie. I'm the artist doing the sets for the show.'

'Abbie, yes, hello.'

'I hope you don't mind me ringing but Penny said you were in town and I was hoping you might be able to call in. I'm swamped here. There's a lot to do and I'm minding my daughter's baby at the same time this week, which is ... well ... demanding.'

'Sorry, I came straight home.'

'Oh, okay. Do you think you might be able to come in this week?'

'I don't think so, Abbie. I'm sorry I can't...' To her horror, tears began streaming down her cheeks. She sniffed hard and groped for a tissue.

'Krista? Are you all right?'

'I'm sorry ... I'm ... I don't want to go out. Sorry.'

'Don't hang up, please,' Abbie said quickly. 'I'm sorry, I should have realised you'd be fragile at the moment. I don't know if you know, but my daughter and I went through a bad situation a while back. Similar in a way to yours. We were held hostage. It was terrifying.'

'I didn't know.' Oliver hadn't said a word. No-one had.

'Krista, if you would still like to help, how about I bring some of the smaller pieces out to you and you can work at home? There are shrubs and flowers and things like that to be painted. I can do the big backdrops here. I'd really appreciate it. Actually I'm a bit desperate. I have my own work to do too.'

'Well ... I've never done any painting.'

Abbie laughed. 'Think back to primary school art. It's like that. Nothing fancy. Paint between the lines is basically it.'

'All right. I guess I could try.'

'Great. How about I come out now? I'll bring everything you'll need.'

'Oh. I don't know...'

'I'll be there in about an hour. Wonderful! Thank you so much.'

Before Krista could object, she'd gone.

'My God, Lola. I can't do this. I'll have to call her back.'

She took her coffee cup to the kitchen. What could she possibly say to put Abbie off? She'd promised to help and now Abbie was on her way, grateful to her for agreeing, bringing everything all the way out here. Did she know how disfigured Krista was? Had Penny told her? Yes, she would have. So Abbie would be prepared and be able to hide her shock.

'I can't face her,' she said aloud. 'I can't.'

'Who?' Amy stood in the doorway. She bent to pat Lola.

'Abbie. She wants me to help with painting sets and she just rang to say she's bringing stuff out here so I can work at home. She's coming now.' The panic made her voice rise.

'That's good, isn't it? It'll give you something to do and you won't have to go out.'

'But she'll see me.'

'She'll understand. What did the doctor say? I see he took the stiches out.' She came closer and studied the scar. 'It's healing well.'

'That's what he said.' Krista moved away from the scrutiny.

'It won't be like this forever. It'll fade. No-one will notice it in a few months' time.'

'I will.'

'Of course you will, but it won't seem so important.'

Krista stared at her. Not important? How could she say that?

'You're still recovering from being kidnapped, remember. Give yourself a chance.'

'That's what Doc said.'

'Maybe you should see someone. Talk about it.'

'He gave me a phone number.'

'Give them a call.'

'Maybe.'

'Do it. You can't mope around here forever.' Amy sighed and raised her hands in a gesture of defeat before letting them fall to her sides. 'I'm sorry that sounded cruel ... but literally, you can't.' Her eyes welled with unshed tears but she bit at her lip and said, 'We've started looking for another position. Both of us will need jobs if we don't find something similar to this, and you'll have to leave too.'

'It might take a while to sell.' Panic bit into her with renewed energy. Leaving this haven was a reality she preferred not to face. Should she ask Hugh to reconsider the sale? Would he listen?

'Hope so. We really like it here. The place has such potential.' She sniffed hard.

'Me too.' And surprisingly that was true. She did like The Grange.

Amy's mouth drooped and she wiped a hand across her eyes swiftly. 'We really hoped we could buy it.'

'I'm sorry,' Krista said helplessly. She had no idea what else to say; she'd never seen Amy anywhere close to crying, she was always so strong and reliable. But what could she do? Hugh wouldn't budge on that price even if she did call him to plead their cause.

'No, I'm sorry, Krista. It's not your problem and you have enough to deal with. I shouldn't have said that about you moping.' Amy gave her a quick hug. 'Give yourself plenty of time. You're much better already.'

Krista spent the next hour in a fever of indecision. Should she phone Abbie and tell her not to come, she'd changed her mind, she wasn't feeling well, she was going away?

Lie.

Or should she pretend she wasn't home and not answer the door? Or ask Amy to meet her and take in the art supplies? Involving Amy wouldn't work. She knew Krista was at home and would think a new friend was a good idea but Amy would never understand what it was like to lose her self-confidence. The doorbell took her by surprise. Lola yapped and ran to the front door, giving her usual deafening welcome to visitors. So much for pretending she wasn't home. Abbie was early by at least ten minutes.

Krista stood by the door breathing hard, mind whirring but going nowhere. The bell rang again. Lola's yapping increased.

'Shush, Lola.'

She closed her eyes for a moment, opened them, grasped the handle and opened the door.

'G'day.'

'Oliver.' Her legs shook and she had to lean against the doorframe for support. What was he doing here? Why didn't he phone first? Her face ... he couldn't see her like this.

'Rod called me out for one of the horses. Thought I'd drop in and see how you are.'

'Uh ... I'm...'

'Had the stitches out.' He studied her cheek. 'It's a lot better than when I saw it last.'

She couldn't speak, she could barely stand. She wished he'd go. He shouldn't have come at all. Not without telling her.

'How are you?' He touched her chin gently. 'I've missed you.'

She wanted to lean into his hand. He was being nice. He always was.

'I'm okay.'

She hadn't returned his call. She'd listened and her heart had cried out for him but she couldn't make the move to dial. Like now. Couldn't move.

'Angus stopped by on his way out the other day. He's not so bad. A bit of an idiot but he has a good heart, I reckon. He cares about you.' He looked her directly in the eye. 'He said you're staying here.'

She nodded. 'Until Hugh sells it.'

'Might take a while.'

Another nod.

'I'm glad. I thought you might leave after what's happened. Go somewhere less...' He shrugged. 'I don't know. Somewhere more civilised.'

'No. I want privacy.'

'Privacy?' He frowned.

'From people.'

'Does that include me?'

She hesitated. 'I don't have anything you'd want.'

'I don't want anything from you.'

An unfamiliar white car slowed and parked. Oliver turned to look at it.

'That's Abbie,' he said. His gaze returned to her.

'Yes.'

He smiled but it was strained. 'Good. I'll leave you to it.'

Good what?

He strode down the steps and along the path. A red-haired woman was leaning into the rear of the car, unloading cardboard boxes on to the ground. She straightened and greeted Oliver. They were too far away for Krista to eavesdrop but they both turned and looked her way. Abbie waved. Krista raised her hand in a feeble response. Her stomach churned.

Oliver stooped and picked up a box. She loaded another on top and he walked towards the house.

'Where do you want this?'

She didn't want this at all. 'In the terrace room.'

'Get out of the way, Lola, or I'll tread on you,' he said as he disappeared into the house with Lola dancing in front of him.

'Hi, I'm Abbie. So nice to meet you at last.'

The woman, arms laden with flat sheets of plywood cut into odd shapes, stood on the doorstep. Her hair was pulled into a messy ponytail and her skin was smooth and unblemished, with a few crinkles around her eyes. Happiness radiated from her.

'Hello.' Krista stepped aside, keeping her bad cheek hidden as much as possible. 'Come in.'

'Thanks, and thank you for helping. You're a lifesaver. Where can I dump these? I've got my granddaughter in the car. She went to sleep on the way here but I can't leave her out there. Too hot even though it looks like a storm coming. Rain at last, with any luck.' A brilliant smile accompanied the barrage of words.

A baby? She was bringing a baby in? Why not the whole town?

'Down here.' Krista led the way to the terrace room, her stomach a lead weight.

'What a fabulous house,' Abbie said. 'Goodness, is that a Fred Williams?'

She'd stopped outside the living room door to study a framed sketch.

'I've no idea,' Krista said. 'If he's a famous artist, I'd say so.'

'He's one of Australia's best.'

Abbie stepped back, astonished. 'It is. How wonderful. It's lucky the house survived the fire. It'd be heartbreaking to lose it.'

'I had no idea. Hugh didn't say.'

'I wonder what other treasures you have here.'

Oliver was on his way back. 'Anything else?'

'A few more of these in the boot, and the baby.'

'You'd better fetch her.' He grinned and Abbie laughed.

Krista waited uneasily on one of the cane chairs while Abbie and Oliver ferried the remaining supplies in. How carelessly Hugh treated a valuable possession. If it had burned, he'd claim the insurance and buy something else. For Abbie the value was in the art itself. Her wonder and delight said it all. Did Hugh value anything away from its monetary value?

Abbie reappeared with a plump baby in her arms, pink-faced and in a little white singlet with a teddy bear on the front. She held a floppy, grey toy elephant by its trunk and studied her surroundings through big blue eyes.

Oliver propped the last flat shapes against one of the chairs. 'See you later, ladies,' he said.

Krista stood up.

'I know the way out, Krista,' he said. 'Take care.' He looked at her blankly then away to Abbie and the baby.

'Thanks, Ollie,' Abbie said. 'Wave to Ollie, darling.'

The baby stared at her, then at Oliver, who waved and headed for the door.

'Oh look, a doggy,' said Abbie. 'See darling, a doggy.'

She squatted down so the baby was at Lola's level. Lola's tail wagged like a flag and she sniffed the newcomers with great interest.

The baby pointed and giggled when Lola licked her hand.

'What's its name?' asked Abbie.

'Lola.'

'Lola, this is Charlotte.'

'How old is she?' Krista asked in an effort to appear interested. Babies were foreign objects to her.

'Nine months.'

The baby gurgled and squirmed in Abbie's arms, so she sat her down like a plump little Buddha while Lola examined her carefully.

Abbie stood up. 'Now. Let me show you what we're doing. Do you know *Patience* at all?'

'No.'

'I'll send you the video link Gina sent so you can listen to it. It has two acts and both are outdoor settings. One is outside a castle, the other is in a glade. I'm painting a castle wall and trees for the first and statues and trees for the second. I've brought you the shrubs and flowers for the second because it's really a garden. There's a lot of dark green involved.'

She took one of the flats and held it so Krista could see the shape of a stylised rosebush outlined on a white background. 'Georgia, my daughter, did the primer before our carpenter cut the shapes but she's had to go to Melbourne for a week. She's doing a master's degree. All you need to do is paint the colour I've marked in the relevant area. Painting by numbers.' She smiled. 'There's a list of the colours and numbers in one of the boxes with the paint and brushes. Not many. You won't get them mixed up. I'll leave the flower colours to you. Be creative. We have red, yellow and pink.'

It didn't look impossible. Abbie was already lifting a tin from one of the boxes. 'This is the basic green. It's water soluble so you can wash the brushes easily. And yourself. You'll need to wear old clothes and have a drop sheet for the floor if you work in here. An old bedsheet or an old shower curtain are good.'

Nothing old existed in this house, or any house Krista had ever lived in. Except antiques. But she nodded.

Thunder rumbled in the distance.

'Gosh, listen to that. It's getting quite dark. I'd better get a move on,' Abbie said. 'If you run out of paint give me a call, but I think you should be all right. Use a screwdriver to get the lids off and make sure they're on properly so the paint doesn't dry out. Wash the brushes in the laundry tub with water and detergent after every session. Any questions?'

'No.'

'Great. If you do a few each day, it shouldn't take too long. You could do all the green bits and then all the brown bits so it dries between colours. It's up to you.'

'How long have I got?'

'The show opens on the first of June but we want this done by early May, I think, so we know what we've got and they can rehearse properly as the date approaches. I've never done stage sets before so I've given myself a lot of time. Something's sure to go wrong when we start putting it all together.'

May. She had two months.

'Hugh is selling this place,' she said. 'I'll have to move when he does.'

'That can take a long time, what with settlement and all that,' Abbie said. 'He'd be lucky to have a changeover by June unless he has someone already lined up. The block of land next door to me took over a year to sell and it's closer to town than this. The house was old and rundown but the land is good farmland with river access.'

'I hope you're right.'

Thunder rumbled again. A prolonged growl, closer than the first.

'Right. I'm off. Don't want to be caught in it. Rupe said that bridge goes under sometimes in sudden downpours.

We have a bridge near us too. Water comes down from the mountains really fast.'

'I didn't know.'

Abbie scooped Charlotte up, ignoring the squeal of protest. Lola yapped and the baby stopped complaining to giggle. 'If it's not one thing it's another out here. Extreme heat, fires, floods, storms, dust. You name it we get it.'

Krista managed a little smile. 'Thank you for coming, Abbie.'

'No worries. Thank you for volunteering.' Her brilliant smile appeared. 'We'll find more for you to do, you know, now that you're on the radar.'

'I'm not sure...' Krista stopped.

Suddenly the smile faded. 'It seems overwhelming, doesn't it? I know how you feel. I lost almost everything and I had to start again. Twice really. The first was after I divorced my first husband.'

'Oh.'

'Rupe was my rock and so were the people I met here in town. They amazed me with their kindness. You're not alone, Krista.'

'I'm not a local, you are. It's different.'

Abbie shook her head. 'I'd only been here about a year. Less.'

A flash of lightning lit the room, followed by more growling and grumbling. Abbie headed for the front door. Krista followed.

'Gosh, it's dark,' she said. The sky was completely covered by roiling grey clouds. The wind had picked up again, blowing dust and dancing leaves across the gravel parking area.

'Thanks, Krista. See you later.' Abbie hurried to her car and strapped the baby into the rear seat. She shut the door and gave a quick wave before running to the driver's door.

Krista, with Lola at her feet, watched the car disappear down the drive. A crash of thunder right overhead made Lola whimper and run for the house. Krista gave an involuntary shiver. The temperature had plummeted. More lightning seared the gloom. She turned and ran after Lola.

Inside, she stood in the terrace room and surveyed the boxes and stacks of plywood flats with growing dismay. Why did she agree to this? She'd never get it all done and she'd ruin the show and upset Abbie, who was a lovely person. No wonder she'd landed that handsome policeman. How could any man resist such a beautiful, intelligent, charismatic and talented woman?

Abbie had instantly recognised that drawing as by a famous Australian artist Krista hadn't even heard of. She'd drunk champagne at gallery openings and gala events at museums but had no clue as to what was actually in those places. She should know cultural things like that but she didn't. She knew how to dress well and make small talk and which restaurants were in. None of that mattered in Taylor's Bend. None of that mattered in her new life.

The rain drummed down outside in a sudden onslaught so heavy the terrace and garden disappeared behind a thick wall of grey. More thunder cracked, this time directly over the house. Lola scrambled close to Krista, pressing against her legs, shaking and whimpering. Krista picked her up and cuddled her, staring out at the impenetrable mass of water.

'I hope Abbie made it past the bridge,' she said to Lola. She'd only been gone about five minutes but she could beat the storm if it was travelling in a different direction, and the river couldn't have risen that fast. Still holding Lola, she went upstairs to look out the windows with a view towards the town. No different. Rain pelted down and the sky was invisible. From here, the driveway was just discernible by the rows of trees thrashing in the wind.

What if a branch came down and Abbie and the baby were trapped along the road? Or if the car was hit by a falling tree like Rod had been? Her breath tightened in her chest and as if she'd conjured the reality from her thoughts, a tree at the end of the drive closest to the house crashed down in a swirl of leaves and tortured branches, crushing the fence, its roots rising in a dark and threatening mass.

She hurried back downstairs to find her phone but it was no use calling Abbie. If she was safe she'd be driving and it would distract her. She'd have to wait until either the rain died down enough to drive safely for her to take the car, and if the driveway wasn't blocked, check the road, or enough time had elapsed for Abbie to reach home. She put Lola down.

The boxes and flats had to be stowed somewhere else, out of the way.

'Let's sort all this stuff out,' she said. 'Where shall we put it?'

Lola wagged her tail.

Chapter 18

Oliver had to stop driving, the rain was so heavy when the storm broke. He nearly made it home but the road disappeared from view and the wipers couldn't keep up with the onslaught so he sat it out for ten minutes, deafened by the pounding on the roof of the car. Like sitting inside a big metal drum with a horde of maniacs beating on it as loudly as they could.

With any luck the rain would continue for the rest of the day. Too much to hope it would go on for a week but this would boost the dams and give the trees a drink, and the last thing anyone needed now was flooding.

Seeing Abbie at The Grange had been a surprise. Rod had told him Krista was hiding away and not wanting to see anyone. Understandable given the rough red wound on her face.

Why did Krista push him away? The question tormented him. When he'd found her that night she'd clung to him, not just as a saviour, he was sure. And when she saw him in hospital she was pleased to see him. She said so. What had happened since then? He'd given her some space, the way Doc recommended, but he hadn't expected such a chilly reception.

'Amy gets a bit frustrated with her sometimes,' Rod had said. 'But it's because she's worried about what we'll do when Hugh sells this place. She had her heart set on buying it.'

Oliver nodded. 'Disappointing.'

'Amy thinks Krista doesn't properly register that we'll have no home and no job. Those basic things aren't a problem for her. She doesn't need to work and she has an apartment.'

'Krista's had a rough time,' said Oliver. 'Bit of a shock for anyone, let alone a sheltered rich girl.'

'Yeah, I know, and so does Amy, don't get me wrong. She understands Krista's been through a terrible ordeal.' Sitting in the marooned car, Oliver pondered the truth of those words. Amy's viewpoint was understandable, but she was a practical, hardworking woman and a survivor. She and Rod would find another job. Krista was struggling to adjust to a complete upheaval of her comfortable existence with no support at all from her family. Angus was the only one of them who had shown any sign of caring for her wellbeing and that was driven by remorse. The trauma of kidnap and injury would take a while to overcome. It wasn't as simple as 'getting on with it' the way people in past generations expected.

The fact remained he wanted to help. They'd made a good team during the fire and forged a bond he was looking forward to strengthening when she returned from Melbourne. He thought she was too. How could she say he wanted something from her? Did she think he wanted her money? How could she? All he wanted was her love.

Maybe Abbie would be able to help where he couldn't. She knew firsthand what it was like to be in Krista's situation, she was kind and she had no personal involvement.

The onslaught had eased to a steady downpour; the storm had passed on, leaving a brighter sky to the west. He restarted the engine and eased the car back onto the road.

At the surgery, Margie was mopping the floor.

'What happened?'

'That side window was open. I was running around making sure the windows and the door at the back were closed and forgot this one. Did you get stuck in it?'

'I was about two k's out. Had to pull over. Big storm.'

'Sure was. Wonder if there's any damage.'

'I saw a few branches down when I came into town but nothing too bad.'

'At least the power stayed on.'

'Yes. I'd better check on Billy.'

'Sorry, I didn't think about him.'

'No worries.'

The yard had turned to slushy mud with large brown puddles but the rain had dwindled to a drizzle. Oliver pulled on gumboots and sloshed across to the horse yard and stables. Billy was on the far side of the paddock, sheltering under the trees along the fence. He raised his head and looked when Oliver called his name, then ambled across to say hello.

'You okay, mate?' Oliver asked.

Billy tossed his head. He was soaked through.

'You'd better come inside and get dried off.' He opened the gate and grasped a handful of mane to lead Billy into the yard. He released him and closed the gate.

'Come on.'

Billy followed him in to the stable and gave him a hard nudge in the back with his nose to speed him along. Oliver laughed.

'Stop it, you devil.'

He spent the next half hour with a towel and brushes. Soothing, rhythmical work that took his thoughts away from Krista and her troubled mind. If only people were as easy to understand and treat as animals.

Abbie phoned later that day. After exchanging pleasantries and opinions on the storm she said, 'Krista rang me just after I got back to town.'

His heart sank. 'Is she pulling out of the painting?'

'No. She was worried I'd be stuck in the storm somewhere with Charlotte. She was quite concerned.'

'That's surprising.'

'Yes and no. It was pretty violent, wasn't it? She said a tree came down in their driveway. It must have been worse out there. I left just before it got started. I had to pull over for a while.'

'So did I.'

'The thing is, Ollie, she was worried about me and I think that's a good sign.'

'I suppose so.'

'I like her and I can see why you do. I think the painting will be really good therapy for her. Give her something else to focus on.'

'I hope so, Abbie. I thought we might have something happening before she left for Melbourne, but now ... she doesn't want me around.'

'She's all confused at the moment. I was like that. Everything was totally overwhelming and if it hadn't been for Rupe...'

'But you didn't push him away.'

She chuckled. 'It wasn't as straightforward as you think.'

'Wasn't it? It seemed that way.'

'Believe me, it wasn't. Anyway, I knew Rupe for ages before we got together. Krista has only known you for a couple of weeks. She's lost all her bearings. I know what that's like too.'

'So what can I do?'

'Don't lose touch with her. Show her that you're here and that nothing has changed where you're concerned.'

'Wait, in other words.'

'Yes.'

'That's what Doc said.'

'He's right. I'll go out there again in a few days to see how she's getting on but I'll invent some other reason to do with painting.'

***

After she'd spoken to Abbie and confirmed she and the baby were safely in town, Krista, with Lola getting in her way, moved the flats to the far end of the terrace room in the corner behind the bar. The boxes of paint and brushes fitted neatly out of sight there as well. By the time she'd finished, the rain had eased to a trickle and the sun was trying to find its way through the clouds.

Rod knocked loudly while she was tearing lettuce for a salad and came in without waiting for her to open the door.

'It's me,' he called.

'In the kitchen.'

He appeared in the doorway. 'You okay? A tree came down in the drive.'

'I saw it from upstairs. I'm fine, thanks.'

'It hasn't blocked the road, luckily, but the fence is broken. I'll have to get someone in to fix it. Can't do it with this leg.'

'Is your house all right?' she asked.

'Yep. We got the horses in before it started. I hope Oliver got through okay.'

'Abbie left after he did and I just talked to her. She had to pull over but she's fine so he will be.'

'Right. Good.' He looked at her with a slight smile but turned away before she could comment. 'See you later.'

'Bye. Thanks for checking on me.'

'No worries. Listen, I reckon you should have some riding lessons. We've got that big arena, unused.'

'Oh, I don't think so.'

'Why not? Archie is perfect for a beginner. She's quieter than Calypso. I can't do much at the moment so teaching you would be a good way to fill in some time.' He lifted his hand to forestall her objections. 'Think about it.'

When he'd gone, Krista sat at the table, her salad untouched before her. Rod was trying to be kind. He and Amy probably cooked up that riding idea to give her something to do. She didn't want to learn to ride. She never had so why would she start now? Why couldn't they leave her alone? And why had she ever said she'd help Abbie with the sets?

She went upstairs to lie on her bed, staring unseeing at the ceiling, wishing the world would forget she existed. If she had the energy, she'd book herself into an exclusive hotel somewhere and tell them she wasn't to be disturbed. She'd live off room-service left at the door. The problem with that was she'd have to fly and she'd have to deal with people, people who would stare and mutter and comment to each other as she walked by. Lots of people, far more people than were here.

Lola scrambled onto the bed and licked her face.

'Gah. Stop it.' She shoved Lola's head away. 'You don't care, do you? You love me anyway.'

Oddly enough, she didn't mind Rod and Amy seeing her face. They didn't care how she looked. Neither did Abbie. Abbie said she understood how Krista felt and she believed her. She was an easy woman to like. To trust. What had happened to her? Whatever it was must have been bad if it meant she lost almost everything. Twice, she said. She had a grown-up daughter who had to be from the first marriage. She was young to a have a grandchild. The baby could easily be hers. She would have been young when she had her daughter. Were there other children?

Krista exhaled and closed her eyes.

She woke with her phone ringing insistently on the bedside table and picked it up without looking at the caller.

'Hello.'

'Krista, darling. How are you? How's Lola?'

'Mama?' A surge of relief brought tears to her eyes. For all her faults, her mother did love her and she hadn't realised until this moment how much she wanted and needed her support.

'Yes, of course it's your mother.'

'I'm so glad you called. Where are you? I thought...'

'I'm in Sydney.'

'Mama, can I come to stay with you?'

'No, darling, I'm about to leave, that's why I rang. Can you keep Lola permanently, please?'

'Yes, but...'

'Thank you, darling.'

'Mama, did Hugh tell you what happened?'

'He left a message. Two actually. He wanted me to call him but before I got around to doing that he rang back to say everything was all right and you were safe.'

'I was kidnapped.'

'My goodness, but you're safe now, aren't you? What was that about? Money, no doubt. Someone wanting a ransom. I lived in fear all through that marriage that someone would kidnap me. Not that he would have paid a penny to get me back. How much did they want for you?'

'Nothing,' she said hoarsely.

'Really? So they just let you go? Or did the police catch them first?'

'They let me go.'

'You were lucky. So no harm done and you're fine now?'

'Yes.' Her voice barely worked.

'Are you back in Melbourne now?'

'No, I'm staying at The Grange.'

'Why on earth are you doing that? I thought you hated the place. I certainly do.'

'Angus is staying at my apartment.'

'So he's back.' As usual Mama barely listened.

'Yes, he was in Macau.'

'And we all know why. He's nothing but trouble, that boy. I told Hugh over and over he needed straightening out but he never listened. Still, when the divorce comes through we never need lay eyes on either of them again.'

'Are you going through with it?'

'Of course, I am. He humiliated me in front of all my friends and he's going to pay for it.'

'I'm sorry, Mama.'

Her mother paused then said, 'So am I. We did have some good times.'

'Does Hugh want a divorce too?'

'He says not.'

'Is there a rush? Why not wait a little while?'

'I'm going to a retreat in India tomorrow. I'll be away a month, but when I return I intend to see my lawyer.'

'In India?' She hated the heat. 'What happened to skiing in Japan?'

'I need to clear my mind. Someone recommended this place to me. It's very exclusive and takes only a limited number of guests at once.'

'Good luck with it,' she said helplessly.

'Thank you. Take care, darling. I'll phone you when I come home.'

'Is Brenda going too?'

'No, she's having a month's holiday.'

The line went dead in her ear.

Why hadn't she told her mother what had really happened? Why hadn't Hugh? Because it wasn't worth the reaction. Somehow it would swing around to being about her and not Krista and she'd use the whole episode as a stick to beat Hugh with. They both knew Mama too well.

As usual with Mama, the conversation had torn through like a whirlwind and it was only now she realised what could have happened.

'Thank goodness. It looks like we're stuck with each other.' She scooped her up for a cuddle and received a lick on the ear.' If her mother had reclaimed Lola, she'd leave a gaping hole. 'You're my favourite girl. You keep the monsters away.'

The following morning the roar of a chainsaw dragged her from bed. Someone was working on the fallen tree. A red truck was parked in the driveway and a thickset man in khaki shirt and shorts, with ear protectors and a fluoro vest, wielded the chainsaw while another, smaller man dragged the debris away.

She'd slept in. A dreamless night. It was almost eight o'clock. The rain had gone and taken the clouds with it but everything had a new-washed sparkle in the morning sun. When she let Lola out, the pool beckoned. If she stuck to breaststroke and kept her head out of the water, there shouldn't be a problem. She went back upstairs and changed.

She should use the pool house and leave her swimming costumes there, along with sunscreen and hats and anything else she needed post swim.

After swimming, she went into the pool house, opened the windows and door and raised the blinds, letting in a flood of light and clean fresh air. The shut-up air inside had the faintest tang of bushfire smoke. She dragged the pool-side furniture back outside then showered and changed into shorts and tank top.

After breakfast, she went in search of a bedsheet to use as a drop sheet. The downstairs linen cupboard held a store of upmarket sheet sets. Upstairs yielded the same. Just as she'd thought, there was nothing old here and none of the bathrooms had shower curtains, they had glass screens.

She put a complete set of matching sheets and pillowcases in a shopping bag and went to find Amy.

She found Rod in the office, staring at the computer.

'Hi,' she said.

'G'day.' His warm smile washed over her.

'Is Amy around?'

'No, sorry. She went into town early to do some shopping.' He eyed the bag in her hand. 'Can I help?'

'Abbie said I needed a drop sheet for when I do the painting but I don't have anything. She said I could use an old sheet or a shower curtain but there aren't any in the house. I thought maybe you might have an old sheet I could swap for this.' Belatedly aware of how rude that sounded, she held the sheet set out in a shaky hand. 'Sorry, that sounded ... wrong.'

'We have plenty of old sheets,' Rod said. 'But I can give you a tarp instead. I use it when I paint. Or I could give Amy a ring and ask her to buy a plastic drop sheet while she's in town. She should find one at the supermarket.'

'Thanks. That would be great. I'm sorry, I didn't mean...'

'I know you didn't.' He smiled. 'I'm glad you've got something to do.'

'You won't need to give me riding lessons if I'm busy painting.'

'I was serious about that, Krista. You should learn to ride while you're here. Oliver said you were good with the horses. They responded to you and that's not always the case.'

She looked at him, astonished. Was he kidding? Somehow, she didn't think he was. He wasn't the type of man to say things for the sake of talking.

He went on, 'Archie is perfect, like I said. Angus didn't want her apart from his scam attempt. I've bought her from him.'

'Was she expensive?'

'No, peanuts, otherwise he couldn't have afforded her. He wanted her for her looks. She's well-bred but a failure as a racer, can't jump and is a bit too big for the average gymkhana rider. She's a nice, sedate ride though. I'll use her.'

'I like Archie.'

'I know. Let me know what you decide.'

'Thanks, Rod.'

***

Oliver resumed his regular cello practice and it took his focus off the subject that occupied the bulk of his waking moments. Krista. She lurked in every cell of his body and every pocket of his mind. She was in every room of his house, in his car, his surgery, the stables and on the farms and in the houses he visited.

Holding his cello and concentrating on the dots on the page, executing smooth strokes of the bow on the strings and accurately placing his fingers on the neck of the instrument gratifyingly filled his mind. Playing was therapeutic in the best possible way. It comforted and satisfied his soul the way no other activity could. His love of music wasn't the same as his love for Krista but it went a long way towards soothing the pain.

The first rehearsal after his injury had been reasonably successful and he discovered that he hadn't missed much in the two weeks he'd been unable to attend. His young cello-playing companion, Emma, was quietly delighted to see him, the evidence in her pink-cheeked fluster and her relief that he could play the difficult sections she was yet to master. The rest of the string section was struggling with the speed factor, resulting in intonation that reminded him of the noises emanating from some of his distressed patients. Cats, in particular.

The days chugged by and every morning he woke wondering if it was too soon to phone Krista and ask how she was. He'd seen her on Thursday, by Monday he figured it was about the right time. She took an age to answer. Had she seen his name on the screen and let it go through?

'Hello.'

'It's Oliver.'

'I know.'

'How are you?'

'Fine.'

'Really?'

'Yes.'

'That's good.'

'How are you? How's your arm?' She sounded as though she was struggling to maintain her interest in the conversation.

'Almost better. I've been practising again and I went to rehearsal last week.'

'That's good.'

'How are the sets coming along?' He held his breath, half-expecting her to say she'd given it away.

'Abbie seems happy with what I've done.' There was a tinge of surprise in her voice.

'That's great, she was really pleased you could help.'

'Have you been discussing me?' she said sharply.

'I was the one who asked her on your behalf,' he retorted. 'Remember?'

Silence. He thought she might hang up but she said, 'Yes.'

'Krista. I'd really like to come to see you,' he said.

More silence.

'Can I?'

'I don't think I'm ready.' Her voice shook. Was she crying?

'I can't stop thinking about you,' he said softly, tentatively. His empty hand curled into a fist, the fingers clenched tightly against this palm. Too much? Doc said don't push but he had to let her know.

'I ... I'm sorry.' The phone clicked in his ear.

Not ready. He sucked in air. Not ready was better than I don't want to. He wasn't going anywhere. He'd wait. Patience. How apt.

***

Krista discovered she enjoyed painting. After the storm, the temperature had dropped to bearable and more rain had fallen, mostly in the late evenings and overnight. She opened the wide terrace doors and put music on. Abbie had emailed a link the cast and orchestra had been sent and she played it as she worked. The jolly tunes and silly lyrics added to the experience and she began to feel she was making a contribution to something, a feeling that was reinforced when Abbie arrived a few days later with an extra tin of green paint and exclaimed over her efforts.

'Well done,' she said. 'I love the flowers. The colours look great. It's not too dull for you is it, doing this?'

'I like it. I need something easy. I'm not very smart.'

Abbie frowned. 'Who told you that?'

Krista rubbed her lips together. 'I didn't do very well at school.' Changing homes, countries and schools each time Mama remarried didn't help.

'That doesn't mean you're not smart. I was only interested in the art classes. I'm hopeless at maths and hated science.'

'But you're really good at art. I quite liked maths but I wasn't brilliant. Oliver said I could be whatever I liked, so did Brenda, my mother's assistant, but I don't have a clue. Oliver said I could open a fashion shop or a fancy restaurant.'

'You could if you wanted, but I think they require total dedication and passion and I'm not sure either would take off in this town. What else do you know about?'

'Mama organised PA jobs for me with her friends but they were favours, and all I had to do was book restaurants and things like that. I quite like cooking but I don't want to be a chef.'

'If you like painting you could try a drawing course.' Abbie smiled. 'No reason not to try a few things and find out what you like. Willoughby has some community classes in different subjects. Mind you, the attendees are usually the over-seventies crowd. And there's a technical college in Wagga that offers all sorts of things. Book-keeping maybe, if you're a maths person?'

That wasn't going to happen, not with her scarred face.

'Rod said I was good with the horses, that they liked me. I helped Oliver with his patients once. I've never thought of it before but I do like animals.'

'There you go. There are all sorts of jobs in connection with animals. You've got a stable full right here.'

Abbie's casual assumption that when Krista found something that appealed she'd be good at it was encouraging and unlike Brenda, she wasn't suggesting tackling something as daunting as a university degree.

A burst of gratitude made her say, 'Do you have time for coffee?'

'I do. Thanks.'

In the kitchen, Abbie sat at the table while Krista started the espresso coffeemaker.

'Where's Charlotte today?'

'Georgia came home last night so I dropped her off on my way here.'

'Don't they live with you?'

'When the baby was born, Georgia did for a while but now she has a house in town.'

'Is she a single mother?'

'Yes, and she's never told us who the father is.'

'Gosh.'

'She's a very independent girl, always has been.' Abbie pulled a face. 'She can be prickly so I don't ask.'

'What's she studying?'

'English. Creative writing.'

'That must be hard with a baby.'

'Yes, but she has us as backup and she found a good babysitter. She also works part-time for Arlo at the local newspaper. It's fairly new. It's called *Round the Bend*.'

'As a reporter?'

'Yes, and the photographer.'

'Is she helping with *Patience*?'

'She's in the chorus and she's helped me a bit.'

Krista handed Abbie her coffee and sat opposite with her own cup. 'I'm sorry, I don't have any biscuits or cake.' Georgia sounded an extraordinary person. Like her mother.

'I don't need anything to eat, thanks. It's great coffee.'

'Thanks. Hugh only buys the best coffee beans.'

Abbie smiled and took another sip. 'How long do they think it will take the scar to heal?'

Krista's hand froze halfway to her coffee. She couldn't speak. Chatting with Abbie had made her forget.

'It's looking better already,' said Abbie. 'A lot of the redness has gone since I saw you.'

'A couple of months, the doctor said.' Her voice came out hoarse and choked in her throat.

'Do you have to do anything at home? Rub cream in or something?'

'I massage Vaseline in four times a day.'

Abbie nodded. 'It's working. The healing power of the body is amazing. Apparently the face heals faster because of all the blood vessels there. More than other parts of the body.' She smiled. 'You're a beautiful woman, Krista.'

Krista shook her head as unwelcome tears dripped down her cheeks. 'I *was* beautiful, now there's nothing.'

'Who tells you this rubbish?' Abbie leaned forward and grasped her hand.

'My mother,' she whispered.

'She's wrong.' Abbie spoke with such confidence that for the first time in her life, a little glow of hope fought for existence. Was Mama wrong?

'You don't know me.'

'I know enough and so does Oliver.'

'He only thinks he knows me.' As she spoke, a little voice in her head told her that wasn't true. Oliver had seen right through her and found the vulnerable, sore spots easily.

'No-one ever really knows another person. I was married to my first husband for twenty years and he still surprised the hell out of me at the end. I had no idea what he was like all that time. Fortunately he wasn't a normal specimen of humanity.'

Her candour jolted Krista. What was the man? A serial killer? 'How did you trust Rupe enough to marry again after that experience?'

'He was too good to pass up through my fear of the unknown. The odds were in my favour because he'd been so wonderful and I had a fair idea

I'd be unlikely to have another chance. And I love him and I know he loves me.'

'You were brave. Braver than I am.'

'I was terrified. I was also a mess for weeks after the whole thing was over. The counsellor I saw told me not everyone gets PTSD. I didn't and you mightn't either. What you're going through now is part of the natural aftermath. Your brain and body need to process it all.'

Krista looked at the smiling confident woman across the table. Could she ever be like her?

'Doc said to see a counsellor if I felt I needed. He gave me a card.'

'Do you think you will?'

'I don't have the nightmares so often now ... just sometimes. And the panicky sweating has stopped.'

'No shame in seeing someone if you want to.' Abbie squeezed her hand. 'You know what they say—fake it till you make it. That's what I did and so can you. My art was a lifeline. When I paint, I forget everything.'

'I'm finding that too, and I listen to the music you sent while I paint.'

Chapter 19

After Abbie's visit, Krista tackled her painting task with renewed enthusiasm so when the phone rang she was annoyed, considered not answering, but picked it up to check the caller. Brenda.

'How are you, Krista? I'm so sorry I haven't called earlier but we were out of the country and well ... you know Viivi.'

'I do. Thank you for calling, Brenda. I'm doing okay.'

'It must have been a hideous experience. Do they know who kidnapped you?'

'Two of Stefan Moran's men. They locked me up to teach me a lesson for being rude to him. It was about Angus's debt. The police haven't told me anymore about it. The local policeman told me it would be difficult to prove Moran was involved and the men who held me wore balaclavas. I had no idea where they took me.'

'And what about Angus? Has he reappeared?'

'Yes. How much do you know about it?' she asked. Brenda sounded as unconcerned as Mama, which was unusual.

'Hardly anything. Viivi told me Hugh said you'd been kidnapped but released unharmed, so she didn't worry too much.'

'Unharmed? Brenda, they locked me a room for two days then cut my cheek open.'

'What?' she shrieked. 'Why didn't anyone tell us?'

'I thought Mama or Hugh might contact me to ask. Or even visit me.' She couldn't keep the acid from her tone.

'You poor darling. Is it bad? Are you being looked after?'

'They say I'll have a scar but it won't be very noticeable. I am being looked after. People here are very kind.'

'I'm so sorry. I feel so guilty. If I'd known I would have come straight away.'

'Brenda, don't tell Mama. She rang to see if I'd keep Lola but I didn't tell her anything. She's not interested anyway.'

'She's preoccupied with this India thing. Krista, I can come to stay with you. You need some company and someone to look after you. How about it?'

'Actually ... I think I'd rather get through this on my own. Not that I wouldn't love you to come, I would and of course you can—but later. I think I need to sort out who I am and I need to do it by myself.'

'Good for you. I completely understand. Let me know when you're ready for a visitor.'

'We may have to move from here. Hugh wants to sell, and Rod and Amy can't afford to buy it although they want to.'

'That's a shame. Will you move back to Melbourne?'

'No. I want to stay in Taylor's Bend.'

'Really?'

'I can't go back to what I was doing, you already know that.'

'Yes. Are there opportunities there?'

'Abbie, a friend I've met here, suggested I try a few courses and find something that interests me.'

'That's what I said. It's a good opportunity while you're recovering, to explore your options.'

'I know. At the moment I'm helping paint sets for their musical in June.'

'Sounds fun. And what about that lovely vet? I thought he was rather special.'

'He is but...'

'But?'

'Brenda, I'm ugly. This scar is hideous. I can't let him see me. I don't go out of the house.'

'Other people see you, don't they? Rod and Amy must, and your friend Abbie?'

'Yes, but they're different.'

'How?'

How? It was Oliver who was different. Oliver who was special. Oliver she wanted so desperately to love her.

'When I first met Oliver, he didn't like me at all and I didn't know why. He was attracted, physically, like men always are, but I realised after a bit that he knew immediately that I wasn't what he wanted. He wants a smart woman who knows things. He plays the cello and he's intelligent and he's a vet.

I can't do anything useful and now I'm not even beautiful.'

Brenda laughed softly. 'Did he say that?'

'He didn't need to.'

'Does he know you speak five languages?'

'No. What's that go to do with anything?'

'I speak one. English. You're as smart as anyone, Krista, you just know different things. And give the poor man some credit. He was only at that party because of you. He's smitten, believe me.'

'I thought he was, but that was before.'

'Didn't you go through that bushfire emergency with him and save the horses?'

'Yes.'

'That's hardly being useless. Hugh was impressed.'

'He didn't tell me.'

'Didn't he? I guess he was preoccupied. He was in Japan at those meetings. He told me when he got back.'

'Would he change his mind about selling The Grange?'

'I don't think so. Why don't you buy it from him if you like it so much? You've got the money.'

'Me? I can't run this place.'

'Talk to Rod and Amy and see if you can be partners. Go halves. I'm sure they'd be interested. You get on well, don't you?'

'Yes, we do. I've got to know them better recently.' Better than her Melbourne friends.

'Think about it. Talk to Hugh. He might be willing to negotiate. He wants your mother back and this might be a tick in his favour.'

'Do you think so?'

'Worth a try.'

'Thanks, Brenda. '

'Let me know when this show is on and I'll come to see it. What is it?'

'*Patience*.'

'Oh, that'll be heaps of fun. I love G&S. Haven't seen one for years.'

'I've never seen one.'

'Let me know how you're getting on, won't you?'

'I will. Thanks for calling.'

She hung up and wiped a couple of tears from her cheeks with the back of her hand. Brenda was more of a mother than Mama. And her idea of buying into The Grange was temptingly good. Why hadn't that occurred to her before? She had money and what better way to spend some of it than investing in a property and a home for not only herself, but also Rod and Amy?

She washed her brushes and packed up the painting gear, then, with Lola trotting happily alongside, went to find Rod.

'What do you think?' she asked after he'd called Amy to the office and Krista had outlined her proposal, standing, while the pair of them sat before her on the only two chairs. She felt like a schoolgirl presenting her work to the teacher.

Amy looked at Rod. Her expression was one of astonishment, but pleased or horrified, Krista couldn't tell.

'I can talk to Hugh and see if he's willing to lower the price if you think it might work. I'd be a silent partner. I wouldn't interfere in the way you run the place. As long as I can live here.'

Did she sound as desperate and hopeful as she was?

Amy stood up. 'Please, please call Hugh.' She flung her arms around Krista and hugged her tightly. When she released her, Rod did the same and then hugged Amy. Both had tears in their eyes.

'Thank you,' said Amy. 'I never imagined you'd want to be involved in this place.'

'Neither did I,' said Krista. 'But when Brenda suggested it, it was obvious.'

Rod and Amy went to finish off some chores in the stable while Krista made the call. Amy wanted to listen in but Rod pulled her out of the office and closed the door. Krista sat in Rod's chair and dialled the number.

'Krista, lovely girl. How are you?' Hugh boomed.

'I'm recovering. It's slow.'

'I've been making some moves. Moran won't get away with this even if the police don't catch those two men.' His voice changed. 'Did you know that pair who attacked you and your friend were found recently? They'd been shot.'

'No!' Rupe hadn't told her. Had he told Oliver?

'It's not surprising. That's how Moran deals with people who fail him.'

'He could have had me killed. Or Angus.'

'No, he wouldn't do that. He knows I can take steps to influence his businesses. And I will. He harmed you and he has to bear the consequences,' he said grimly.

'What will you do? Hugh, please don't upset him. What if he comes after me again?'

'He won't.'

'That's what you said last time.'

'Keep this quiet and don't tell a soul, but very soon all his businesses will be investigated by the government and the police. They'll be looking at corruption and under the tableland deals and contracts. They'll look at everything he owns and poke into every corner of his life.'

'How do you know that?'

'I know a lot of people and I have a great deal of influence in the right places. It's time to use them.'

'I hope you're right.'

'I am. Now, tell what's happening with you. Do you need specialist medical treatment? Plastic surgery? The top man in the country plays golf with me. Or we can go overseas.'

'I'm not sure yet. The doctors here told me it would take a couple of months for the wound to heal.'

'Wouldn't hurt to see Tony Tan. He has a waiting list as long as your arm but I'll fix it up for you. When can you be in Sydney?'

'I ... I'm not sure I can go. I have some things to do here and I'm not ready to go out yet.'

'Whenever you're ready, let me know.'

'Thanks, Hugh, I really appreciate it.'

'Krista, you're my daughter, or as close as can be, whatever happens with your mother,' he said, in a softened tone she'd rarely heard from him.

'I hope you can work something out. Maybe that retreat in India will help.' His infidelity wasn't something she wanted to hit him with right now, if ever. 'Hugh, I rang to ask ... I want to buy The Grange in partnership with Rod and Amy. What sort of price can you do?'

'That's straight to the point. I like your style. Hmmm. Two million is what I told Rod.' All business now.

'We don't think it's worth that in the current market. We think one million five is closer.'

'Krista, Krista, you know that's ridiculous. One nine.'

'One six.'

'One eight-fifty. A bargain and you know it.'

'One six-fifty.'

'One eight.'

'One seven. You know that's fair, Hugh, it gives you a profit and you also know it's much better to sell to us than go on the open market. No agent's fees, no advertising, no waiting. You also know we can pay.'

'Where did you learn to bargain?' She knew he was smiling.

'I've been to markets and bazaars all over the world. I can haggle with the best of them.'

Hugh laughed. 'You've got yourself a deal. Congratulations. I'm proud of you.'

'You've never said that before.'

'I should have, because I've always been proud of you even though I may not have shown it. I'm sorry for what you've been through. I hope The Grange will make you happy.'

'Thanks, Hugh. Love you.' She'd never said that before but it was true.

'You too, beautiful girl.'

***

Oliver called Krista every couple of days in the evening after dinner. He asked how she was, filled her in on his doings, kept her up to date with the *Patience* orchestral progress and even raised a laugh when he related some of the animal adventures he'd had during the day. His plan was to be a friend and gradually remind her what it was they enjoyed about each other's company, that he was interested in her as a person, what she was thinking, what she was doing, hoping and planning. He looked forward to the chats, and by the gradual opening up of her voice and conversation, she did too. At first she was reticent, but he persisted and she always answered his calls.

Her decision to buy The Grange in partnership with Rod and Amy surprised and impressed him, especially when she told him how she'd haggled the price down. She was bubbly and excited and eager to talk. For the first time he glimpsed the forward-looking Krista he'd kissed goodbye when she left for Melbourne.

'I bet not many people manage that,' he said.

'I think Hugh was playing with me but he wasn't going to give the place away. He wanted his profit and he got it. Smaller than he'd like but he wants to impress Mama and he feels guilty about me.'

Her other news shocked him as much as it had her.

'Did Rupe tell you anything about those deaths? I didn't know,' he said.

'No, it's horrible. Hugh said that's how Moran deals with employees who mess up.'

'Good God. It hasn't been in the news at all. You'd think two murders would be.' Krista could have been killed if that's how the man operated. A chill ran through his body and the urge to throw down the phone, drive to The Grange and hold her in his arms was overpowering. But disastrous if he succumbed.

'They might want it kept quiet,' she said.

'Maybe.'

'Those two were awful and stupid but they didn't deserve to be shot.'

'We don't know what else they've done,' he said.

'They acted on their own beating us up. Moran obviously didn't like it. He doesn't take kindly to being opposed, or ignored.'

'Thank God they let you go. You could have been...'

'No,' she said. 'I was warned. Hugh said Moran wouldn't dare kill me or Angus.'

'*He* says.'

'He's right though, isn't he? We're alive.'

When Oliver phoned her two days later, he had his own news. He hadn't told anyone, not even Doc, who would be the obvious person, but Krista was closer to him in many, more personal, ways and becoming more so each day. He hoped it was the same for her.

'Remember I told you about my brother, and my parents?'

'Yes, Julian with a broken leg. How is he?' The name had uncharacteristically lodged in her head, important to her because it was important to Oliver,

'Pretty good. Looking forward to getting his cast off.'

'So is Rod.'

'It's my mother. She never complains about her health but she told me she was tired and when I mentioned it to Julian he said he'd try to get her to see a doctor.'

'But your father is a doctor.'

'He wouldn't notice unless she stopped cooking his breakfast.'

'I'm sure he would.'

'I'm not. Anyway, Julian called today and said when she was visiting him this morning she fainted. He called the ambulance and she's in hospital. They're doing tests. He'll let me know when he knows anything.'

'Do they have any idea what's wrong?'

'Not yet. It could simply be low blood pressure.'

'I hope so. They can fix that, can't they?'

'Yes, but there's no use guessing until we get the test results.'

'Will you go to see her?'

'Yes, but not just yet.'

'Did I tell you my mother has gone to an exclusive retreat in India? For a month.'

'To be spiritually cleansed?'

'She hopes so. I can't see it working. She'll be bored after a couple of days. Especially if there's no champagne.'

'She might find nirvana.'

'My yoga teacher mentioned that once but I've forgotten what he said about it.'

'The ultimate goal of Buddhism. It's the state of mind where all suffering and desire is transcended.'

'That's right. You have to meditate.'

'Yes. Years and years' worth.'

'Nirvana would be something, wouldn't it? Maybe I should try meditation. I didn't really get into it before.'

'Worth a try.' Not his thing at all. Far too busy. Playing cello was his spiritual escape.

To his surprise Krista phoned him the following day, asking after his mother.

'They think it's her heart,' he said.

'Did she have a heart attack?'

'No. It's erratic and doesn't pump the blood hard enough. They think she needs a pacemaker.'

'Is that a dangerous operation?'

'Any operation is dangerous to a degree. Pacemakers are quite common nowadays but people are usually older than she is. It regulates the heartbeat.'

'That's a relief then, isn't it?'

'Very much so. It's ironic that my father is a heart specialist.'

'And he didn't notice anything wrong?'

'Just as Julian and I said. He expects her to be there for him.'

'How's he taking this news?'

'No idea but I hope it's shaken him up and made him realise what a shit of a man he is.'

'Will you go to Sydney?'

'I'm leaving on Monday. The operation is on Wednesday. I'm not sure how long I'll be a way. A week maybe.'

***

Oliver stayed with Julian and together they visited their mother before and after her operation. His father wasn't operating, a colleague was, but he observed the surgery and came to the waiting room to give them the news. Oliver hadn't set eyes on him since his departure for Taylor's Bend years before. His greying hair had thinned but he still had the upright stance and arrogant stride of a man who expected his opinions and words to be respected and obeyed.

He shook Oliver's hand and clapped Julian on the shoulder.

'It went very well. Quite routine.' He might have been relaying the results to strangers about one of his patients. 'We're not anticipating any problems.'

'Can we see her?' asked Oliver.

'She still in recovery but when she's back in her room you can.' The steely gaze swept over him. 'You're looking well, Oliver. Country life must agree with you.'

'It does.'

He nodded and when he spoke again his voice was less sure. 'I know what you're both thinking. The same as everyone else is. How come I didn't notice Em's condition? I have no excuse, I admit it. I took her for granted and I doubt I'll ever forget that. It worked out this time but it could have been something worse and I might have lost her.'

'*We* might have lost her,' said Oliver.

'Yes. I'm sorry. We.'

His father turned and went back through the surgery doors.

'Wonder how long his overwhelming remorse will last.' Oliver flopped back onto the couch he and Julian had been sitting on.

'I've never heard him say anything remotely like that before,' said Julian.

'It's still about him though, isn't it?'

'Oh of course. But he tried, and that's a first.'

***

Krista missed Oliver's calls. She knew he'd be preoccupied with his mother and his family and wouldn't give her a second thought while he was away. That was natural and she understood completely. But she still missed their chats and the sound of his voice. Her pre-falling asleep mental wanderings became more and more complicated. She could call him but was reluctant to take that step while she was unsure how he would interpret it. If he was phoning her out of a sense of duty he'd be annoyed and feel stalked. She couldn't call him because she'd never been in such a situation before. She'd never been unsure how to approach a man she was attracted to—in love with—never had any doubt of his attraction to her. Or cared so much.

Since when had a phone call become so important?

Her scar was improving and she had to admit that what originally Doc, and now Amy and Abbie, told her was true. Three weeks after the event the raw redness had faded to pink and the lumpiness where the stiches had been had almost evened out. Because she hadn't been to a hairdresser since before the anniversary party her hair had grown and the style was in dire need of a trim, but the benefit of that was the longer side was on her bad cheek and obscured the upper half of the wound. If she let it grow right out evenly on both sides the scar would almost be hidden.

She'd worked steadily on the painting and was two-thirds of the way through the pile Abbie had left. When she'd finished those, Abbie said, her friend Maureen. who was in charge of wardrobe had claimed Krista's assistance with sewing costumes.

'But I can't sew,'

'You said you couldn't paint.'

Krista smiled. 'I do know a bit about clothes.'

She spent hours with Rod and Amy discussing the way their partnership would work. Rod contacted a lawyer friend in Melbourne who would deal with the sale contract. Krista contacted her financial advisor for advice on setting up the partnership as a legal entity. He agreed to come to The Grange and talk to them in two weeks' time. Amy was impressed that he would do that rather than insist they go to his Sydney office.

'He's one of Hugh's advisors and he always goes to Hugh,' Krista said. 'I told him we all had to be there and that you can't leave The Grange unattended. He can stay here so he won't charge us for accommodation. Can you collect him from the airport?'

'Sure.'

The thought of a relative stranger seeing her face was daunting but it had to be endured. Rod and Amy were relying on her to see this through and as they said, she was part of the team. The whole process had become a juggernaut rolling on its way but their excitement was contagious. She'd never been important to anyone before, never had anything of worth to contribute.

Oliver had been away three long days when the doorbell rang midmorning. She wasn't expecting anyone but Lola yapped and gave her away so she held the door open a crack and peered out.

A familiar face smiled back at her, lined and weather-beaten under a battered hat. By his side stood an elderly, plump woman in a pastel pink dress, holding a wicker basket.

'Hello there, love. It's Les and Sal. We've just come to see how you're getting on.'

Krista pulled the door wide, suddenly aware of their scrutiny, dipping her face so her hair dropped over the scar. Lola stopped barking and wagged her tail.

'Hello, Les. Nice to meet you, Sal.' A pang of guilt hit. They'd invited her to visit after she'd come home from hospital, weeks ago, and she'd refused. Doc's words ran through her head. 'People judge others by their actions, not what they look like.' She couldn't possibly turn them away. 'What a surprise. Come in.'

'I hope you don't mind us dropping in like this.' Sal smiled confidently as though she'd be astonished if Krista said she did mind. 'I've brought you some scones. Fresh baked.'

'You haven't eaten a scone until you've tasted Sal's. She wins champion scone maker every year at the show.' Les grinned.

Krista knew a hint when she heard one. 'How about tea or coffee to go with them?'

'We can always do with a cuppa, thanks.'

'I'm sorry I haven't come to visit you,' she said as she led them to the kitchen. 'I haven't been up to going out.'

'Don't you worry about it, love. You've had more than enough on your plate lately.' Sal gave her a kindly pat on the arm. She peered into the lounge room as they passed. 'Oh my goodness, just look at this beautiful house, Les. You should have taken your filthy boots off at the door. Go and do it right now.'

Krista glanced down at his feet clad in old but clean elastic-sided boots. 'Sal, he's fine. Don't worry.'

'I cleaned them special,' he said indignantly. 'I was coming to visit the prettiest girl in town.' He winked at Krista.

She smiled and Sal snorted. 'Silly old goat.'

In the kitchen, Krista started the tea. Sal placed her basket on the table and produced a floral cake plate, large container, a jar of jam and a plastic-covered bowl of whipped cream.

'I'll put this together while you do the tea, love,' she said. 'Where do you hide the knives and spoons?'

Krista opened the cutlery drawer. Sal took out what she wanted and set to work.

Instead of the mugs she usually used, Krista took her mother's elegant and expensive cups and saucers from the cupboard. If anyone deserved the best, Les and Sal did. She set them on a tray with the matching milk jug and sugar bowl, plates and the teapot.

'Let's go out to the terrace,' she said when everything was assembled and ready.

Her guests trailed after her through the house to the outdoor table setting, exclaiming over the furniture, the size and design as they went.

'You must be rattling around in here all by yourself,' said Les as he settled himself at the table under the shade umbrella.

'I am a bit but I haven't decided what I'm going to do yet.'

'Word is you and the manager have bought the place from Littlejohn,' he said.

'That's right. How did you know?'

'Hard to keep secrets around here.' Sal put two jam and cream scone halves on each plate and handed them around.

'It's not really a secret,' said Krista.

She poured the tea. Les put two spoonfuls of sugar in his cup and stirred vigorously.

'This is the life, eh Sal?' he said, sitting back, scone in hand. 'Lord of the manor suits me, I reckon.'

'How are you in yourself?' asked Sal. 'Your face is healing but it's hard to get over something like you've been through. Goodness, it's warm sitting here.'

She slipped her cardigan off, revealing, to Krista's shock, a right arm with skin that looked melted and burned from elbow to fingers. How had she not noticed the scarring on Sal's hand before? Why had no-one mentioned it?

Krista breathed in and exhaled slowly before replying. 'Yes, I ... I think I'm getting better. At first I couldn't bear anyone to see me. Now...' She managed a smile. 'I have my first visitors.'

'I know exactly.' Sal nodded. 'I was never a beauty like you, but this happened when I was fourteen and when I came out of hospital I wanted to hide away.'

'What happened?'

'Hot oil. I was cooking dinner and the chip pan spilled on me.'

'It must have been incredibly painful.' Her own cut paled into insignificance beside the horror Sal had endured. And she'd been a child.

'It was, but now I don't even think about it.'

'No-one does,' said Les. 'She's known for her scones, not her arm.'

'And they're delicious,' said Krista.

'We ran a property out near Coonamble,' said Sal. 'My parents needed me and my brother to help out, so I couldn't hide, and I had to go to school. After the first few week, no-one commented and it was only strangers who stared. But in a country town, strangers aren't all that common and the locals knew about it. But even so,

I was a teenager, I was ugly, and I was sure no-one would ever want to marry me.'

'I did,' said Les. 'Love at first sight it was. That beautiful smile hooked me.'

'Where did you meet?'

'I was a shearer. Came to work on her dad's place and there she was bringing the tea and those you beaut scones for us at smoko.'

'Sixty years ago next year that was. I was eighteen,' said Sal. 'He was a string bean of a bloke but there was something about him. He could charm the legs off a lizard.'

'How could she resist me?' said Les, and took another scone.

Chapter 20

Oliver returned home tired and glad to be out of the city. Going back had been unavoidable and he was happy to have reforged a bond with Julian. The years had made a difference and he sensed a respect from his big brother he hadn't felt before. His mum, of course, had been delighted to have both her boys to herself. Saying goodbye to her had been harder this time than when he stormed off after graduating university, an angry young man defying his father.

His father hadn't changed much, not deep down. He might mouth remorse and pledge to take better care of his wife in the future, but Oliver and Julian had doubts. His mother, however, had taken a look at her life and found it wanting.

'I've had enough of being your father's hanger-on,' she announced. Not that she was thinking of leaving him.

'Goodness no, I'd never do that,' she said when Oliver made a tentative, rather shocked enquiry. 'I love your father and he does love me, despite what you boys might think.'

'What do you mean then?' he asked.

'I'm going to start saying no,' she said.

Oliver almost cheered. 'About time.'

'I'm going to do the things *I* want to do. I'm going to take a season ticket to the opera, go on a cruise with some girlfriends and I'm going to come to your show,' she said. 'Whether your father wants to go with me or not is up to him.'

'Our show won't be anything like what you'll see at the Opera House, Ma,' he said.

She stretched out a pale hand and patted his. 'Do you think that matters to me or, I imagine, anyone else who'll be in your audience?'

'No, fortunately. I'd love you to come and stay.' He hesitated a beat then said. 'There's someone I want you to meet.'

'What's her name?'

'Krista.'

'What a pretty name.'

'So is she.'

'Is it serious?'

'I hope so. I am.'

'I'd love to meet her,' she said.

***

His first thought on waking the following morning was to phone Krista. Then he realised it was five-thirty and got out of bed instead, to prepare for the day. A week off would have its price. At seven, in the middle of the morning chores, he answered his phone with a leap of the heart before he saw it wasn't her.

'Veterinary Practice.'

'Oliver Johnson? It's Barnaby Locke. Our cat was fighting last night and I think she's injured, although I can't see anything wrong. She's really sick and unresponsive. Won't eat and so on. Can I bring her over?'

'Yep. It's probably an abscess from a bite wound. It can cause blood poisoning.'

'I'll be there in fifteen minutes? Sorry to call so early but we're a bit worried and the kids are very upset.'

And so it began.

By the time he'd finished with the cat and Barnaby had gone home to report to the family that Peach was to stay overnight at Oliver's, Margie arrived to prepare for morning surgery and fill him in on the week's events.

She finished the professional aspect and said casually, 'Krista is doing well. Receiving visitors now.'

'What visitors and how do you know?' Stupid question, he knew that. So did she because she ignored it.

'Les and Sal went to see her and said she was lovely. Very welcoming.'

'That's good.' Would he be as welcome?

'She's been working on those sets too, nearly finished them apparently. Abbie's really happy. Those two get on well. Nice for Krista to have made a friend.' Margie eyed Oliver as though she expected a comment but he grunted and turned away. What could he say?

When he surfaced next it was lunchtime, and he escaped to the house for a bowl of tinned soup with the emergency bread from the freezer. A trip to the supermarket was crucial. He could go late this afternoon after he'd been to the Daley's dairy farm. He wouldn't be able to fit in any other calls.

Calling Krista was tempting but he'd leave it till this evening. If she was recovering as well as Margie said, she might be ready for a visit, but he had to be careful in his approach. How he went about wooing her would affect the rest of their lives and it couldn't be rushed. She was like an injured animal, wary and afraid but wanting to trust, wanting to be healed and in her case, loved. A wrong move and she might close right down and negate the steps she'd taken, go on the attack or bolt.

Not phoning while he was away had been deliberate even though he wanted to hear her voice, tell her the little details of his days and hear all about hers. The more time slipped by, the more he missed her with an almost physical pain. He was used to dealing with wounded, fearful animals and trust was the basic building block. He'd only been away a week and she knew and understood why. With any luck she'd be eagerly awaiting his return.

What haunted him was the danger that she would move on without him, forge a new life for herself at The Grange, with new interests and new friends that didn't include him. Margie's comments were bittersweet. He wanted with all his heart that Krista regain her life, but he wanted to be in it.

The trip to the dairy farm took much longer than he expected and he put off going to the supermarket and dropped in to Laurie and Dot's store for bread, eggs and milk instead. As usual they were full of gossip, most of which he let wash over his head, but when Krista's name was mentioned he focused.

'She's coming good according to Abbie. Helping out with the sets and costumes and all that sort of thing for the show. Some bloke from the city is coming to stay with her. Must be a friend of hers.'

'When's he coming?'

'Don't know exactly. Abbie mentioned it but she had the baby with her so she couldn't chat for long. Sweet little thing, that Charlotte.'

Who would that bloke be? A friend, of course, she'd have plenty, but what sort of friend and why would he be coming alone? How long would he be staying?

As he drove, Oliver planned to cook up a big frittata and salad with vegetables from the garden, but when he got home he'd lost his appetite. Krista was obviously not concerned about her scar anymore but she didn't want to see him. Suddenly the phone call he'd been looking forward to making didn't seem such a good idea. He went to the bathroom for a shower and a change of clothes, but the warm water calmed his mind and as he dried himself he came to a decision.

How would he know what she was thinking if he didn't talk to her? Dressed and refreshed, he dialled without hesitation.

'Hi Krista, how are you?'

'Oliver. You're back. How's your mother?' The happy tone lifted his heart.

'She's fine. The operation went smoothly and she went home quite quickly.'

'That's a relief.'

'Yes, it is.'

'What about your father?'

'Much the same.' He didn't want to talk about his father. 'What have you been up to?'

'I finished the sets, so I'm helping Maureen with the costumes.'

'They've got you working.'

'I'm enjoying it.'

'That's good.'

'Thank you, Oliver. It's because of you I got involved in the first place.'

'You're welcome. I'm really glad it worked out. What about The Grange? How's that working out?'

'Really well. My financial advisor is coming next week to give us advice on how to set up the partnership.'

'Coming here?'

'Yes, to The Grange.'

'That's good.'

So that's who the visitor was. He should have known better than get himself in a tangle over local gossip.

Silence. He thought it might signal the end. That they had nothing more to say to each other, even though his head was bursting with questions he didn't dare ask and his heart with love he didn't dare express.

'Les and Sal came to see me last week,' she said. 'I had no idea she had a burned arm. Why didn't anyone tell me?'

'No-one thought of it, I suppose. People stop noticing after a while.'

'I'm glad they came. Sal was ... she helped. A lot.'

The relief nearly choked him.

'Oliver? Are you still there?'

'Yes, Krista, I'd really like to see you. Can I visit? This evening maybe?' He held his breath.

'No...' His heart stopped. 'I mean no, I'll visit you. Is that all right?' She sounded almost afraid of his response.

His heart restarted, beating twice as fast as before.

'If you want, but I don't mind driving out there.'

'I'm not at home, I'm in town, at Maureen's. We've been sorting out costumes.'

'Have you eaten?' Said as casually as he could manage.

'No.'

'Neither have I. Is vegetable frittata and salad okay?'

'Anything is fine. I'll be about twenty minutes.'

Oliver walked up and unlocked the gate, then waited in a fever of impatience for the sound of her car. She was coming to visit, which was a massive step for her to take, but was it as a friend? Was she testing herself by going out but restricting herself to people she knew and who knew her story? People who wouldn't stare and be shocked. Abbie had laid the groundwork but Sal must have given her the boost of confidence, support and perspective she needed to get her out of the house.

Where did he fit in Krista's new world?

A car door slammed then she knocked. He flung the door open.

She was beautiful, more perfect than he remembered. The gold of the setting sun gave her hair and skin a soft glow. He leaned forward and kissed her cheek, carefully casually, the way friends do.

'Come in.'

She had a shopping bag in her hand. 'I brought wine,' she said.

Strands of blonde hair dropped down, partially obscuring her scarred cheek, but she wasn't trying so hard to hide her face. The scar had faded in the weeks since he'd seen her.

'Good idea.'

He turned and led the way to the kitchen. She wore jeans that looked new, and a white blouse. Her plain black sandals had flat soles. She still looked as though she'd stepped out of a fashion magazine but that original arrogance had long gone, and with it the useless trendy clothes.

She placed the shopping bag on the table and removed the bottle. Oliver took two glasses from the shelf and poured.

'To you,' he said and raised his glass.

'To you,' she said and raised hers.

Her eyes met his and held for a long moment, then she looked away.

'Do you need some help with the vegetables? For dinner?' She went across to the bench where he'd put zucchini, tomatoes, garlic and onions on a chopping board.

'Why didn't you want to see me?' he blurted. 'After you went home from the hospital.' He put his glass on the table. He couldn't get through the evening ahead without knowing, couldn't pretend it hadn't hurt.

'I'm sorry. I ... I couldn't face you.'

'But why? Why me of all people? I found you and I took you to hospital. I thought we were in this together.' The weeks of anguish broke through, making his voice waver. He rubbed his hands over his face. 'I'm sorry,' he muttered.

'I was ugly,' she whispered. 'I didn't want anyone to see me like that. Especially you.'

Her words stunned him. 'You were never ugly. You were injured and you're healing now.'

'I understand that now but then, when it happened I ... I'll never be how I was before.' Unshed tears made her eyes luminous, the blue deeper. Fear lurked in her expression, fear of rejection. Fear *he* would reject her. He knew now, knew she loved him.

'No, you won't. You've changed, you're stronger, better and more beautiful than ever.' He stepped forward and cupped her chin in his hand. 'Why did you think a scar would matter to me?' he asked softly.

'How I looked was what attracted you and without that ... what did I have left?'

Was it really that simple and yet for her so cripplingly complicated?

'You. You were still you. Wonderful, amazing, unique you.' He shook his head. 'Did you really think I fell in love with you because of your looks alone?'

'Fell in love?' Her eyes widened and a smile crept across her face.

'I fell in love with you ages ago but what could I offer a beautiful city girl?'

'You. Wonderful, amazing, unique you. I've loved you ... forever.'

Then she was in his arms, body pressed against his, arms around his neck, her lips on his.

***

Krista sat with Oliver's parents for the opening night of *Patience,* along with most of Taylor's Bend. The rest of the population was turning up for the second show the following night. She and Maureen were taking a night each checking costumes backstage so they could both see the performance. Abbie and Rupe sat in the row behind with Georgia, chatting and laughing.

'Oliver's a nervous wreck,' said Krista to his mother, her eyes fixed on him, sitting in the small orchestra in front of the stage, as they waited for the show to begin. The cello solo had given him many a sleepless night lately but she'd heard it at rehearsals, a very funny scene with one of the singers, and it was perfect.

'He could have been a professional cellist,' said his father. 'He has the talent.'

'He didn't want to be,' said Emily. 'He wanted to be a vet, but I'm glad he kept his cello.'

'He's been enjoying playing again—apart from the nerves,' said Krista.

Dr Francis Johnson reminded her of the people Hugh mixed with, the movers and shakers and the people with power. Sitting in an old Arts Centre building in a small country town watching an amateur performance of Gilbert and Sullivan would be his worst nightmare come true according to Oliver, just as it would be for her own mother and Hugh. They hadn't bothered to come. Francis had, she'd pointed out.

The people she'd met in Taylor's Bend worked hard and gave newcomers a chance to prove themselves, regardless of who they were or where they were from. News had broken recently that Stefan Moran was under investigation by the tax department for tax evasion and money laundering with further corruption and murder charges expected to be laid by the federal police in a much wider criminal network. One of the names mentioned had been on Hugh's party guest list.

It was a world she didn't miss in the slightest.

'Oliver's the happiest I've ever seen him,' Emily said, giving Krista's arm a squeeze. 'And it's all your fault.'

'He's really happy you came to visit.'

'We'll be back for the wedding in October.'

'Can't imagine why you two would want to be married here and not in Sydney,' said Francis.

Emily raised her eyebrows at Krista and sighed.

Oliver looked across and caught her eye. He smiled and mouthed a kiss.

'It's our home,' said Krista. 'It's where we belong.'

Thanks for reading *Where There is Smoke*. I hope you enjoyed it. This book is Book 2 in the Taylor's Bend series—Book 1 is *The Secrets That Lie Within*.

Reviews can help readers find books, and I am grateful for all honest reviews. Thank you for taking the time to let others know what you've read, and what you thought.

If you liked this book, here are my other books: *The House At Flynn's Crossing*, *Find Her*, *Empty Heart*, *Evidence of Love*, *Mango Kisses*, *E for England* and *The Ripple Effect*.

Sign up to our newsletter romance.com.au/newsletter/and find out about new releases, must-read series and ebook deals at romance.com.au.

Share your reading experience on:

Facebook
Instagram
romance.com.au

Bestselling Titles by Escape Publishing...

Discover another great read from Escape Publishing...

The Secrets That Lie Within
Elisabeth Rose

A move to a small town might provide her the solace she seeks – until the once peaceful isolation turns deadly.

After her husband is controversially acquitted of multiple crimes, now-divorced Abbie Forrest escapes to the peaceful rural town of Taylor's Bend intent on focusing on her career as a landscape artist. Estranged from her sister and daughter, Abbie tries hard to forge new relationships in the small community without revealing her own secrets.

Town policeman Rupert Perry is attracted to the quiet woman who lives alone on a large block fifteen minutes from town. But Rupe is happy with what he has – part-time hours, a friendly inclusive community, and freedom to grieve for his late wife away from the well-meaning but overwhelming concern of his old friends.

When a series of peculiar and increasingly frightening events threaten Abbie, she is forced to turn to Rupe for help. But will he be able to prevent the escalation of terror as past wrongs demand revenge?

The House At Flynn's Crossing
Elisabeth Rose

She's been through hell, so risking her heart should be easy...

Anxious to rid herself and her twins of the dark memories from their past, twenty–three–year old Antonia moves to the small rural town of Flynn's Crossing. Antonia is frightened but determined to be independent for the first time in her life, so she rents Mango House and settles in to the community to begin the process of healing.

Town councillor and local real estate agent Flynn has secrets. Guilt–ridden over a tragic childhood event, he fled the city and devotes his life to assisting others. He has big plans for Flynn's Crossing. Without change, the town will shrivel and die. But the townspeople are resistant to his ideas, and his discussions with a luxury resort developer.

When Flynn first meets Antonia, he doesn't know her sensationalised past, and Antonia feels normal for the first time. Slowly, as they get to know each other, to trust each other, Antonia begins to consider the possibility of something more. But when tensions over the resort development reach breaking point, she discovers that Flynn hasn't been entirely honest, and her new beginning is at risk of ending. When Flynn has to choose between the town he's devoted his life to and the woman he barely knows, can she trust that the man who healed her heart will treat it with care?

Find Her
Elisabeth Rose

A chance sighting leads to second chances – for hope, for family, and for love.

Five years ago, teenager Antonia disappeared. With no compelling evidence, the police eventually called her a runaway, and dropped the case. Her teacher, Jax, has always regretted not speaking up about the rumours she heard circling the school that day, but a random sighting at a train station raises the possibility that Antonia is still alive – and not too far away.

Antonia's father, Connor has never given up hope that his daughter will be found and returned to her family. When her old teacher, Jax, calls him with a small spark of a lead, he seizes it with both hands, determined to chase it down.

But there's more at play than simple teenage rebellion and the path Jax and Connor travel rapidly becomes more dangerous than either could have imagined, and opens up new possibilities that neither could have expected.

Empty Heart
Elisabeth Rose

One honeymoon, one vanished husband, one desperate wife – and the cop who is tasked to help her, but can't seem to keep his thoughts on the job.

Honeymooner Nikki Spenser emerges from the surf at Surfers Paradise and can't find her husband, her towel, or her clothes on the beach. Carlos has disappeared from her life as suddenly as he entered it.

In despair, Nikki returns to Sydney where she is contacted by Detective Luke Emerson, a reminder from her past she thought never to see again. Luke informs her that the man she married so recklessly in Las Vegas three weeks prior doesn't exist. Everything she knew about Carlos is a lie, and Nikki realises she knows nothing about her husband—not where he is, not even who he is.

As Nikki and Luke chase down tenuous leads, they soon find themselves plunged into an ever–widening sea of international crime and violence, and Nikki is faced with the hard questions–how much of her love is based on lies, and how much is true?

Evidence of Love
Elisabeth Rose

She survived years as a gangland wife, sacrificing everything to the family. But now they're threatening the one thing that she will never, ever give up – her child.

When Maja's abusive gang boss husband Tony is murdered, she takes the opportunity to flee, change her name, and leave her criminal family and her past behind. As Lara Moore, she and her toddler son Petey live quietly in suburban Sydney. Then, one act of kindness threatens to reveal her secrets and unravel the threads of her new life. But Detective Nick is dedicated and determined, the antithesis of everything she was brought up to believe about the police. Slowly, Maja finds herself drawn out of her shell and into his protective embrace.

Investigating Detective Nick Lawson doesn't know what it is about the prickly, reclusive young mother that attracts and intrigues him, but as the facts about her crime-steeped family emerge, Nick doubts whether his career would survive this relationship, even if she were interested.

Then, to Lara's horror, her past meets her present, and thoughts of love and a future are lost as the fight for her child begins.

Mango Kisses
Elisabeth Rose

A sweet, summery, beachside romance from the author of E for England *and* The Ripple Effect.

Sent to assess a deceased estate in a small coastal town, ambitious city girl Tiffany Holland is initially annoyed by the out-of-the-way assignment. But she soon discovers sleepy Birrigai hides a wealth of surprises: a cross-dressing motel manager, a Kissing College and her client Miles Frobisher, the laid back, surf-shop owning, real life sex fantasy.

Tiffany's ambition is to become a junior partner in her financial firm, but small town life and the proximity of Miles gradually seduce her. But a shocking discovery in the estate papers leads to a dramatic change in Miles's circumstances. Emotionally inept, Tiffany is unable to help Miles through the transition, and drives him away. With misunderstandings and secrets creating frost between them, it seems that their summer romance is destined to go cold. Can they overcome their differences and learn to accept their feelings?

www.ingramcontent.com/pod-product-compliance
Lightning Source LLC
Chambersburg PA
CBHW052345020726
47503CB00001B/112